Welcome to my hometown!
Wendy Rich St...

Shooting
Sunshine

by

Wendy Rich Stetson

Hearts of the Ridge Series, Book 3

Cover Art by *Diana Carlile*

The Wild Rose Press, Inc.
PO Box 708
Adams Basin, NY 14410-0708
Visit us at www.thewildrosepress.com

Publishing History
First Edition, 2024
Trade Paperback ISBN 978-1-5092-5777-5
Digital ISBN 978-1-5092-5778-2

Hearts of the Ridge Series, Book 3
Published in the United States of America

Dedication

For Mom and Dad, who always encouraged me to
follow my dreams.

Chapter One

New York, New York
"I used to be Amish." The extra-hot, double shot, oat milk latte burbled in Darcy King's stomach. She clutched the to-go cup in an over-caffeinated death grip, knowing any moment it could crumple and cascade coffee down her white cashmere sweater. "At least my family was...back in the day."

Everyone—every editor and staff writer and freelance photographer like herself—and, oh yes, the terrifying editor in chief of *Hudson Magazine*, Margo Ricconi-Gladstone, stared. Darcy shifted on the conference room windowsill where she perched with other freelancers lucky enough to gain access to editorial meetings and desperate to maintain that status. She swallowed hard, tasting coffee and fear. She'd been advised to fly under the radar. Drawing attention to herself and, in so doing, the ire of every senior staff member was unwise. Some staffers rolled their eyes. Others licked their lips and salivated like sharks set loose in a guppy tank. Assuming sharks had lips...and salivary glands.

Margo slid purple-rimmed glasses the size of luncheon plates into a mane of silver hair. "Amish? Your mother never mentioned that."

A stream of perspiration, hot and sticky, snaked between Darcy's shoulder blades. She knew eventually

Margo would mention her mother, but did she have to do it in front of everyone? If the other staffers didn't hate her already, they did now. Being a newbie photographer angling for a full-time position was bad enough. Even worse was the impression she was only in the room because of family connections. Which might be true to some degree, but she had an MFA in photography, a solid portfolio, and banging new shoes. She absolutely deserved a seat at the table. Or on the teeny-weeny windowsill overlooking Tenth Avenue.

Then again, she could have kept her mouth shut.

Every month the editorial staff gathered to hear the upcoming issue's theme and pitch stories. Glacial-blue eyes glittering, Margo had taken her seat at the head of the room and pronounced the single word, "modernity," like it was the eleventh commandment.

Writers fell over themselves pitching ideas from cell-phone addiction to urban sprawl. They grilled one another mercilessly. "What are your sources?" "Has anyone covered it recently?" "Does this topic really resonate with our readers?"

Margo clapped for attention, interrupting a vigorous debate on the merits of space tourism. "But what about those who take the opposite path like natives in remote island communities? Or those farmers with the quilts and the hideous beards…who are they? The Amish? Anyone have a beat on them?"

The room went uncharacteristically silent. Darcy King had more than a beat. Her grandmother fled the Amish and was shunned like in a cable television movie. She had an in that might finally make a blip on the radar, landing her a permanent position in one of the most prestigious journals of news, literature, and opinion. How could she have kept quiet?

Still in the hot seat, she sipped her latte, noting most of her lipstick smudged onto the cup. Did she have any on her teeth? She made a quick swipe with her tongue. "I'm Amish on my father's side, actually—*was* Amish, I should say. My grandmother left the community."

Margo narrowed her gaze. "Why?"

She bobbled the latte, and the lid popped off. Was this a test? She knew nothing more about her paternal grandparents than what she recalled from the single summer she spent with them after quitting sleepaway camp. She remembered fresh bread, a tire swing, and the intoxicating feeling she could do exactly as she liked every single day once her chores were finished. The summer was, in point of fact, the best of her life. At the time, she was aware *Mammi* Leora used to be Amish, but she never dreamed of asking why.

As to intel from her parents, they barely even texted between work, charitable functions, and nights on the town that made her Brooklyn social scene look like a knitting circle. Deep family convos were not a King thing. Compared to her mother's Park Avenue dynasty, her Pennsylvania grandparents were something of an embarrassment. If her mother knew she'd even mentioned *Mammi* Leora to Margo Ricconi-Gladstone, Isabelle King would blow her well-coiffed top. Darcy nudged the plastic cap carefully onto her drink. "I don't know why she left, but I can find out. We still have family in Pennsylvania."

"Wonderful. You'll go."

Every cubic centimeter of HEPA-filtered air was gasped from the room.

"I'll *go*?" Darcy prided herself in a deep speaking voice that turned the stereotype of the ditzy blonde on its head. In that moment, however, she squeaked.

"Everyone's covering tech. No one's got Amish." Margo donned her glasses and gave Darcy an appraising look. "Take three weeks. You'll need time to establish rapport, and I want a full photo essay. If memory serves, they're fairly camera shy."

Fairly camera shy? That was one expression for a people forbidden by religious law to be photographed. Was her boss joking?

Margo flapped a jangly, braceleted hand toward her slender, stylish assistant. "See Rolff later for details."

Rolff-with-two-*f*s lifted his cell phone in acknowledgement.

She scribbled nonsense into a notebook to avoid the glares, but they sliced through her tastefully layered look. Glancing up, she caught the gaze of a well-groomed photographer. He appeared ready to cut off his man bun and choke her with it. Lengthy out-of-town assignments were unheard-of in the current media climate. Staffers groused they couldn't even attend conferences. A three-week stint was a unicorn that clearly did not belong in the lap of a freelance photographer.

Granted, being a freelancer wasn't exactly enviable. She had no steady salary, job security, or health insurance. She didn't even have a cubicle—she shared a group workspace on days she was in the office. In many ways she was expendable. She wouldn't be missed.

Story of her life.

After the meeting, she slinked upstairs to Margo's corner suite. Though she'd been at the magazine since the New Year, four months of occasional office time and equally as many assignments had not produced a workplace bestie. On this particular flight, she had no wing woman.

Rolff stood sentry at the door. Actually, he treaded sentry at a standing desk anchored above a treadmill. His simultaneous typing and striding seemed as acrobatic as tightrope walkers who skywalked between towers. He tapped a button on a sleek wireless headset and beckoned. "Look at you, Fancy-Pants. Your first photo essay."

Darcy clutched the leather-bound notebook to her chest. "No one is more surprised than I am. Except every single person who's worked here for more than four months. I'm pretty sure they hate me."

Rolff swept a silky scarf over one shoulder. "Honey, they hate everyone."

So, she hadn't imagined the not-so-thinly-veiled animosity. She lowered her voice. "But don't you think it's weird? Why me? Why not someone like..." She struggled to recall a single colleague's name.

"Man Bun? Animal Prints? Overalls Girl?" Rolff nabbed a broccoli floret with reusable chopsticks. "Who can say? Margo's a genius. She's got mad instincts for knowing what's hot, and not every girl from Brooklyn has connections with the Amish." He pointed the chopsticks at Darcy's feet. "What are you gonna wear? Those heels won't last a day in a barnyard."

She flushed. She was Brooklyn by choice. If Rolff scratched with his barely concealed claws, she'd bleed Upper East Side all over his bento box. The shoes were killer, but they were designer discount from her favorite online retailer. She was determined not to dip into her trust fund. "You don't think…" She swallowed, but she couldn't stop herself. She had to ask. "You don't think it's because Margo knows my mother, do you?"

Rolff made a face. He grabbed both sides of the desk and leaned in. "Please. Half the people in this building are here because someone knew somebody who owed something to someone else." He flashed a perfect, white-toothed grin. "Except me. That I'm walking at this fine desk is all Washington Heights hustle. We get the job done. Know what I mean?"

Lithe and fine-boned with coffee-colored skin and an impeccable haircut, Rolff was beautiful. He'd be perfectly at home in the pages of a fashion magazine. Her nose for a story said Rolff was more than pleased the eye. Once this crazy assignment was finished, she'd get to know him better. "I do. And thanks."

"I've seen your work, girl. You deserve this assignment." He grabbed a wireless mouse and pulled up an online calendar. "Margo wants you there May first. Do you have somewhere to crash?"

A twinge tightened her chest. Her grandmother died suddenly soon after their summer together. Her grandfather passed shortly thereafter. Most said of a broken heart. She could stay in a hotel, of course, but to get the real story, she needed to live among the people. How did one wrangle an invitation to an Amish farm? Having publicly claimed a connection, she didn't possess a single name or number. Did they have numbers? Even an address would be a start. She lifted her chin. "I'll figure something out."

Rolff wasn't the only one with hustle. She

belonged at *Hudson Magazine*, and she'd do whatever it took to leverage this story into a full-time position, starting with... Her stomach turned.

Starting with dinner on Park Avenue.

****

Sitting at her parents' ten-foot dining table the following Saturday night, Darcy picked at pan-seared sirloin and roasted Brussels sprouts. Her mother and father presided on opposite ends of the table like the Duke and Duchess of Posh. A bounty of spring flowers couldn't conceal the gaps where her older siblings and their families should have been. She nudged a vase from her line of vision and broke yet another awkward silence. "Where is everyone?"

Isabelle King nibbled one quarter of a sprout. "Max and Zoe are in New Haven at a very prestigious robotics competition."

A sip of cabernet went down the wrong tube, and she coughed. "Aren't they nine?"

"And Garrett's whole brood has the flu," Isabelle continued as if Darcy hadn't spoken. "Poor babies."

For both her siblings to be absent was unusual. Madeleine and Garrett made the pilgrimage from Westport and Tribeca religiously. They knew who buttered their bread—or paid their kids' private school tuitions, as the case most certainly was. Not that they needed the support. Madeleine was a successful real estate lawyer, and Garrett recently made partner at their father's firm. Still, why look a gift horse in the mouth? She'd hoped to talk privately with her father while her mother's attention was diverted by her five charming grandchildren. Now, Darcy was in the tastefully upholstered hot seat. How long before one of them brought up her decision to drop out of law school? Or grilled her on who she was dating?

A bracing sip of ice water cleared her head. Might as well jump into the deep end. "So, this is funny…" She couldn't imagine a subject her mother would find less amusing, but no matter. "I need to ask about *Mammi* Leora."

Isabelle's steak knife squeaked against china. "Must you?"

Fueled by red meat, Darcy soldiered on. Remarkable what half a steak will do after weeks of eating vegan. "It's for work. I've been assigned to photograph the Amish in central Pennsylvania."

Isabelle Turner King lowered her silverware and folded her hands. "I trust you didn't tell Margo Ricconi-Gladstone the family secret."

She swallowed ten thousand snarky retorts and settled for sarcasm. "No one did time, Mother. Being Amish is hardly a family—"

"Oh, my word." Beneath a perfect swipe of youth-enhancing blusher, Isabelle blanched. "You told her."

Lloyd King shrugged as if his blazer was suddenly too tight. "Darcy, you know your mother dislikes airing our family history."

She glanced toward the kitchen. Now would be a wonderful time for dessert. "I was very discreet. The next issue's theme is modernity. Margo asked point blank if anybody had a connection to the Amish. I was the only one."

Isabelle closed her eyes and bowed her head. "How surprising."

Clearly, no other member of the Daughters of the American Revolution suffered such indignity. So,

Darcy wasn't perfect. She wasn't supermom Madeleine or bonny Prince Garrett. Nothing—not Phi Beta Kappa nor prestigious art awards nor an astronomical score on the LSAT she didn't want to take in the first place—nothing impressed them. She might as well trade her pearls for a neck tattoo. "Our family connection scored me my first important assignment, a full photo essay for *Hudson Magazine*. This could lead to a permanent staff position."

Mother's arched brows tried to meet in the middle of her pharmaceutically paralyzed forehead. They failed. "Margo assigned the Amish for your first substantial piece? I imagined you traveling to Myanmar or Ukraine."

"Nope. I'm going to Green Ridge." She handed it to herself for maintaining a civil tone since no one else was present to do so. Curse Maddy and Gar and their hideous spawn. She turned a winning smile on her father. "I need somewhere to stay. Do you know anyone I could contact?"

Dad's gaze bounced from her to her mother before sliding with longing toward his den where awaited a glass of port and the baseball game. "I haven't spoken to my family in years. Not since your grandfather died."

Heirloom pearls slid with cool smoothness between her fingertips. Infiltrating the Amish might be harder than she anticipated. "What was my cousin's name? The dark-haired girl I played with that summer?" A faraway twinkle lit her father's eye. Did he have bittersweet memories of his youth before the mysterious rift he never discussed caused him to leave home for good?

He cleared his throat. "My cousin Daniel's

9

daughter, Sarah. Sarah Yoder. She's likely married now. Her mother ran a fabric shop on Old Cowan Road."

Isabelle made a face like the Brussels sprouts were off. "Are you sure you wouldn't rather go to Appalachia, Darcy? Or Flint? I hear the Great Salt Lake is drying up. You could photograph it before it's gone. I'll discuss it with Margo at the next board meeting."

Her mother served on the board of directors for a children's charity Margo founded. A tête-à-tête over canapés was the last thing Darcy wanted. "Please don't."

"You didn't mind my help arranging an introduction."

Refusing to be sucked into a confrontation her mother so clearly craved, she gritted her teeth. "I was very grateful to meet Margo, Mother. I'm equally grateful for this assignment. I'll try to track down Sarah and make a quick trip to figure out accommodations."

Isabelle downed a teaspoon of mashed potatoes.

Her mother never ate carbs. Clearly, the situation was dire. Darcy summoned the Zen of a two-hour yoga class. "I'd like to stay at an Amish farm. Some appear to rent rooms to visitors craving an authentic experience."

Mother groped for her wine glass. "Now you've completely lost your mind. Lloyd, tell her she's lost her mind."

Dad mumbled through a dinner roll.

Isabelle nodded as though he offered emphatic support. "Darling, they have no electricity."

Ommm. "I'm aware."

"How will you charge your phone?"

The mahogany paneling was closing in. Had her childhood bedroom not been converted into an exercise studio, she might have fled to her room and slammed the door. She swallowed a volcanic sigh. "I'll go to a café."

Dad chuckled. "Green Ridge does not have cafés. At best, they have coffee shops."

"Then I'll go there."

Snorting daintily, Isabelle tossed her napkin onto the table. "I'll call Margo in the morning. This assignment—"

"You will not." She shoved back her chair and stood. At five feet six, she was far from imposing, but thanks to years of dance class, her posture was impeccable. When necessary, she commanded a room. "I've rented a car..." Never mind she rarely drove. "I've got a room booked for the weekend..." Two stars. She prayed it wouldn't have fleas. "And I can find Old Cowan Road on my phone." Which she absolutely could. "I'll be fine."

What she'd do when she got there, however, was another question entirely.

Chapter Two

Green Ridge, PA

Darcy blinked through the spattered windshield. Friday morning in central Pennsylvania bore zero resemblance to Friday morning in Manhattan. Nothing but mud, mud, and more mud between barns, barns, and more barns. Surely soon, she'd spot a sign for Sarah's quilt shop.

"Your destination is on the left," said the soothing voice of the phone's navigation system.

She named the automated map lady Taylor Shift. From the moment she crossed the George Washington Bridge, she'd been chatting with Taylor like they were travel besties, thanking her for lane changes, traffic updates, and advice on achieving the perfect red lip. Now, three hours later, she was certain Tay had lost her marbles. Where the shop was meant to be, Darcy saw only a narrow gravel lane and—too late, a sign. *Sarah Stoltzfus Quilt Shop* was hand-painted on a placard stuck in a wheelbarrow full of spring flowers. Another lane opened on the far side of a metal bridge, and grateful for empty rural roads, she swung around the compact hybrid vehicle and approached from the opposite direction.

Unlike most of her city friends, Darcy drove. Her father insisted all three children obtain their licenses. Her road hours, however, were negligible. She was far more skilled at hailing a cab. Fortunately, traffic was minimal, and by the time she left the interstate, she'd loosened her grip on the steering wheel and her right calf uncramped. Baby steps.

April sunshine broke through clouds, splashing the countryside in pale yellow light. After endless gray days in a concrete landscape, apple-green leaves clashed with darker grass in cheerful disharmony. Distant purple ridges spanned the horizon, providing a pleasing backdrop for picturesque brick and clapboard farmhouses. She itched for her camera. Could she catch the exact moment winter melted into spring? What would it look like? A drop of rain on a fencepost? The wet nose of a lamb? A ladybug crawling up a screen door? Chuckling, she made the turn into Sarah's drive. Half an hour in the country and she was already a poet. Next stop, landscape photography. She shuddered. Not in this lifetime.

Feeling like she arrived not at a place of business but at someone's home, she came around a big white barn into a parking lot between a farmhouse and a single-story, metal-clad structure that appeared to be under construction. Fifty feet from the quiet blacktop, the lot bustled with activity. Wielding tools that looked more modern than antiquarian, men in straw hats climbed ladders and scaled the shop roof. Below, a woman in full Amish garb exited the store with six similarly dressed children trailing like ducklings. She carried a baby in one arm and a bag in the other. The older kids toted bags, too, and middle-size ones towed the youngest by their hands.

Darcy tapped the brakes. If only she could capture that image. A whole family together with no phones and no video games. Just how did one approach someone who rejected photography and ask to take their picture?

Giving wide berth to two gray-topped Amish buggies, she pulled in beside a construction trailer and checked herself in the visor mirror. Her makeup was still flawless and her hair in a tidy pony. She wouldn't be mistaken for Amish, but she was modestly dressed in a skirt, tights, and boots. Twenty years had passed since she and Sarah played together in the creek behind *Mammi* Leora's house. Would her cousin recognize her?

An Internet search combining *Amish quilt shop*, *Old Cowan Rd*, and *Green Ridge, PA*, had been almost too easy. Sarah's place popped up immediately. Darcy scrolled through images of colorful quilts and bolts of vibrant fabrics. Not only did the shop have a telephone number, it had a social media presence. Maybe the relationship between the Amish and modernity was more complicated than she imagined. Five minutes later, her second cousin answered the phone. Sarah not only remembered her, but she had seemed genuinely interested in the scanty details Darcy offered about her visit. Gazing at the shop now, she ran her fingers over the worn leather of her camera strap, unsure how to broach the whole graven images topic.

Opting to leave the camera in the passenger's seat, she grabbed her bag, unfolded from behind the wheel, and stopped cold. She blinked, momentarily unable to process what she saw. Backlit in stark sunshine, an Amish man towered atop the roof like a mythical sun god, balancing what appeared to be an enormous solar panel on one shoulder.

"Samuel!" someone called.

She turned to see another Amish man fling something…a wrapped sandwich maybe…toward the guy on the roof.

Biceps rippling, Mr. Sunshine shot out his free hand, and a short-sleeved shirt the color of a September sky pulled tight across his chest.

He caught the thing like a wide receiver and, laughing, shouted down to the other guy in a language she recognized as Pennsylvania Dutch without knowing how. He was tall and broad-shouldered, and though she'd photographed countless men, she was hard-pressed to recall any who'd been more pleasingly proportioned. She propped a hip against the car door and stared.

He twitched an arm, threatening to chuck the sandwich at the slender guy on the ground. Shaking his head, he snagged it between his teeth and carefully deposited the solar panel and foil-wrapped package onto the roof.

Darcy was not a blusher in the traditional sense. Her face could be reliably counted upon to remain the natural, dewy tone she painstakingly created while staring in the bathroom mirror. However, sometime around seventh grade, she developed an unnerving tendency to neck blush in what, given the constant mortification of middle school, soon became a daily occurrence. The heat started on her breastbone and fanned upward with a resulting rash so violent her mother demanded the pediatrician prescribe a sedative. Free of pharmaceutical intervention, she had long since tamed the irksome phenomenon, assisted by an array of filmy French scarves and the odd cowl neck sweater.

However, when the Amish demigod squatted, black pants straining across a backside she had no business admiring from below and yet no capacity to ignore, Darcy King blushed the mother of all neck blushes.

Almost simultaneously, the sun dipped behind a cloud, and he stood.

As her vision adjusted, she made out his face— high cheekbones, laughing eyes, sculpted lips, and a jaw as square as a city block. The man simply couldn't be Amish. He must be an actor or a model on an Amish photo shoot. Did another magazine scoop her? She scanned the parking lot, but hers was the only motorized vehicle. Apparently, this guy was legit.

He caught her gaze and gave a long, slow smile.

The look pierced her city armor and shredded her insides in the best possible way. She parted her lips and caught herself just shy of drooling. What was wrong with her? Like she'd never seen a hot guy? She was a New York City photographer. Shooting beautiful people was her stock and trade. So, what about this one had her as weak-kneed as a teenager?

She dove into the car and grabbed the dregs of an iced latte. Darcy King did not get flustered. Darcy King maintained her composure. She sipped watered-down coffee, straightened her skirt, and refusing to glance in his direction, strode inside.

Sarah Stolzfus's Quilt shop sold much more than quilts. Fabric, sewing notions, toys, books, canning supplies, bonnets, petticoats, and, of course, stunning quilts overflowed from shelves beneath fluorescent ceiling lights. The distant hum of a generator explained the artificial illumination. Solar panels and battery-powered lights? Already, she questioned everything she thought she knew about these people.

Behind a long counter, ladies in white caps and jewel-toned dresses assisted customers.

A dark-haired woman looked up from cutting a bolt of fabric. Tossing aside a yardstick, she squealed and dashed around the corner to wrap Darcy in a hug.

Unprepared, Darcy stiffened. Unlike her parents, she enjoyed affection, but not so much from perfect strangers. As the hug extended far beyond Park Avenue convention, she relaxed a degree. Sarah's arms were warm, and her cheek was soft. She wasn't a stranger. She smelled familiarly of vanilla and sunshine, and Darcy melted into a warmer embrace than any she could remember since…well, maybe since her grandmother died.

Sarah stepped back and held her at arm's length. "I'd know you anywhere, Darcy King. You haven't changed one bit." Flushed cheeks rose in a bittersweet smile. "I never thought to see you again. When you didn't answer my letters, I figured you forgot about me."

"Letters?" Darcy met her cousin's gaze. "What letters?" Almond-shaped brown eyes, so like her own, narrowed.

"I wrote dozens. Didn't you get them? Maybe I had the wrong address. I could never wrap my head around avenues and apartments." She slipped an arm around Darcy's waist and led her behind the counter to where a table and folding chairs stood beside a mini kitchen. "No matter. You're here now, and I couldn't be happier. Can I fetch you pie?"

Dozens of letters? When the summer ended, the girls promised to write. Darcy had written to her cousin multiple times, but she never received anything in return. Was it possible Isabelle intercepted their entire correspondence? Darcy's stomach churned, and pressing a hand to her middle, she sat. "I'd love some pie. Thanks."

Chattering about shared relatives Darcy surely met but didn't recall, Sarah sliced a huge hunk. "Coffee?"

The scent of apples and cinnamon eased the tension in her shoulders. Who needed yoga when she could have midmorning coffee and pie? "Yes, please."

Darcy didn't follow a strict diet, but she was a thoughtful eater. The odd Park Avenue steak dinner aside, she guarded her health and figure carefully. This assignment would likely provide more than its fair share of temptation. An image of the man on the roof flashed in her mind's eye. She banished it with a sip of sweet coffee.

Sarah sat beside her, cradling a steaming mug. "Tell me more about your project. You said something about an essay?"

She savored a bite of gooey, sweet apples, letting filling and pastry dissolve on her tongue. Despite a week to prepare, she still didn't know how to discuss her assignment. Sarah's community was clearly progressive. She ran a thriving business with a website and electric lights. Maybe a direct approach would be best. "I'm a photographer. I work for a magazine."

Sarah's lips pursed, and she stilled. "I see."

Darcy felt her shoulders creep back toward her ears. She had to tread carefully. "Our next edition explores the theme of modernity. While some reporters will cover new technologies and cutting-edge science, I'm exploring a simpler approach to modern life. That's why I'm here."

Sarah lowered her cup and ran her knuckles over her bottom lip.

Only now that Darcy sat among the Amish did the significance of her assignment truly land. These people were real. They weren't characters in a television show. They maintained a unique and fragile lifestyle in the face of relentless modern society. In their company again after so many years, she knew she had much to learn.

She quieted her mind and spoke from the heart. "Where I come from, modern life is a mixed bag, to put it mildly." She twitched her wrist, displaying the smartwatch that did everything from paying for the subway to tracking her jogs. "We're constantly connected to friends and family through the Internet, and yet…" She thought back to the half-empty dining table on Park Avenue. "The connection isn't always meaningful. To be honest, my most important relationships often feel empty."

She regarded Sarah's plain garb. Her deep-purple dress and black apron were vibrant yet simple. No jewelry. No watch. She couldn't remember the last conversation in which she and her companion weren't also checking their phones, but she had Sarah's full attention. "I know it was a long time ago, but when I think back on the summer I spent with you, even though my grandparents weren't part of the Amish community, I felt welcome. I know *Mammi* Leora was shunned, but I didn't sense it. I'm sure their situation was complicated, and I don't begin to understand how you and I were even able to be friends, but I felt like a part of something."

Eyes shining, Sarah nodded. "You were."

She let her gaze drift to an Amish mother and child quietly paging through picture books. "I think you have something to teach us—the outside world. I'm not sure what exactly. Probably a lot. But if I could spend time with you"—she took a deep breath—"and eventually photograph you in whatever way your community allows, I know I would benefit. I think our readers would, too." Why did her throat feel thick? Eyes stinging, she sipped coffee. This was supposed to be a routine assignment. Get in, make stellar work, and get back to the city where she belonged. So, why was she weepy?

Sarah took her hand. "I want to help. I truly do…"

Uh oh.

"But we're not perfect. Our struggles might be different from yours, but we struggle nonetheless." Sarah motioned toward a rack of Amish fiction. "*Englischers* think because our dress is simple our lives are, too. They aren't. Even getting permission for my Internet site and telephone was a challenge. Our community is opening, but folks value the old ways. Most won't take kindly to posing for pictures."

Darcy felt opportunity slipping away. Not ready to surrender, she tightened her fingers around Sarah's. "I'll be so respectful. I'll ask permission and photograph from a distance to conceal faces. I'm as interested in the places and objects that make up your lives as I am in you. I can tell your stories through those things, too."

Sarah released her hand and tucked a strand of silky dark hair into her heart-shaped, white cap. "How long will you be here? People might remember your grandmother, but they'll want to know you."

"Three weeks for starters." Could she wrangle more? "I just need somewhere to stay."

"You can stay with us." The sweet voice came from a willowy Amish teenager behind the counter. "My *Grossmammi* is renovating our attic to rent to city people who want to experience our ways. The rooms will be well-appointed and offer just enough conveniences. *Mammi* Verna is very enterprising."

Sarah chuckled. "Darcy, this is Rebecca Beiler, and she's every bit as enterprising as her grandmother. Rebecca, meet my second cousin, Darcy King."

Rebecca stopped unloading packets of hooks and eyes from a shipping box and stared. "You have *Englischer* relations, too, Sarah?"

"Our grandmothers were sisters." Darcy extended a hand. "I'd love to speak with your grandmother about renting a room."

Rebecca gave a firm handshake. "We live right over the creek. Come by the farm tomorrow around one. *Mammi* will tell you all the particulars then." She scooped up the supplies and vanished into the aisles.

With an uneasy frown, Sarah watched her go. "Verna Rishel's ideas are more progressive than most. She'd be a good host."

"She sounds perfect. I'm so grateful for the introduction." Accommodations…check! Now to get her cousin on board. She took a final bite and laid down the fork. "What do you think? Could you help me, too?"

Sarah balled her napkin and dropped it onto the empty plate. "I'll do my best, but I need to speak with my husband first. You understand."

Darcy most definitely did not understand. Sarah was a smart, successful businesswoman. The idea she needed to consult her husband about anything was lunacy. She swallowed a protest with a sip of coffee. When in Rome. "I look forward to meeting him."

With hugs and promises to chat when she returned in a week, Darcy gave Sarah her business card and headed out with Verna Rishel's address in exchange. She had a belly full of pie, a conditional offer of help, and a prospective Amish farm stay. Not bad for day one. Satisfied, she strode into the parking lot, ready to check into her hotel and take a long, hot shower.

Several Amish men clustered around the construction trailer, talking and clapping each other on the back. Was Mr. Sunshine among them? She shot a glance at the roof where a shiny black solar panel now fit snugly against the tin. Websites, telephones, and solar were surprisingly modern elements of Amish life. If only photography made the list.

Dumping her bag next to her camera on the seat, she slid behind the wheel. She dropped the key fob into a cup holder and pressed the start button. Dash lights flickered, and the radio kicked on. The motor, however, remained silent. Hybrid motors were notoriously quiet. The guy at the rental place warned her to watch for pedestrians who frequently didn't hear the vehicle approach. She jutted her chin and listened. No hint of a rumble. Not a single vibration came up through the floor.

She studied the key fob and pressed the lock button. The locks clicked. The key seemed to work. Did she not hold the start button long enough? Maybe it was like rebooting a phone. She pressed it again and held.

And again. She maybe even kind of punched it. Just once or twice.

Darcy King might have been driven more often than she drove, but she was no dummy. The button clearly read *start*. She clenched her fists and dropped her head against the headrest. So, why didn't it work?

Regular yoga practice taught her the calming power of deep breathing. Rental-car smell went in through her nose. Coffee breath whooshed from her mouth. Fine. She'd search up how to start a hybrid on the Internet. She scrabbled in her bag for her phone. Not like anyone here could help. Then again, maybe not having a dude mansplain how to start a car wasn't so awful.

She tapped the screen and nearly threw the phone out the window. No service. Off the grid was, in this case, truly off the grid.

Had she left the headlights on? Maybe she drained the battery or the warp core or whatever this thing ran on. Darcy was no slouch. She could assemble a bookcase like a boss, but she had no clue how motors worked. Maybe a user's manual?

She opened the glove box. A slip of paper offered a QR code for an online resource. "Oh, come on!" she shouted to the empty car.

Another cleansing breath did nothing to quiet the buzzing in her head. What now? Borrow the quilt shop phone? Ask Sarah for a ride in her buggy? Walk? Her stomach sank. Darcy needed her cousin's confidence and trust. Unlikely when she couldn't start her own car.

She gazed out the windshield. Maybe reception improved elsewhere on the property. Grabbing her phone, she exited and crossed away from the hulking barn. From the corner of her eye, she spotted the slender Amish man hoisting another panel onto the roof.

Someone held the ladder.

Mr. Sunshine? Or had he ridden his chariot into the sun? She lifted her arm and waggled the phone. No bars. Feeling the heels of her stylish, yet sensible, boots sink into mud, she tried ten feet to the right. Nothing. A grassy hill stood in a field across the street. Would she have to summit it? She waved her arm like an airport ground crew woman and tapped the screen again.

Zero bars.

In place of more colorful language, a frustrated grunt tore from her throat. And then she heard footsteps. The sound of boots on gravel approached from behind. Her pulse tripped. What would he smell like? Like leather? Like wood smoke? Like freshly mown grass on the first day of spring?

Please, oh, please don't be him, and why the heck do you even care what he smells like?

She peeked over one shoulder.

Mr. Sunshine drew near.

And he smelled like the sky.

Chapter Three

Darcy must have misheard.

Mr. Sunshine—who was, annoyingly, even better looking on the ground than on a roof—couldn't have possibly sauntered up and said what she thought he just said. "Um…I'm sorry?"

He dropped his hands to his waist and lifted tawny brows. "I said, I'm good with cars. Can I give you a hand?"

Did he not know he was Amish?

She glanced at the sky…still blue. And at her boots…muddy. The universe didn't appear to have turned upside down. She met his gaze…what color even were his eyes? Green? Blue? Some exclusively Amish shade? Like when phones came out in special colors only available for one season?

He started toward the hybrid.

She hurried behind, refusing to ogle his backside a second time. The slender guy—who, not for nothing, was also smoking hot—called out in Pennsylvania Dutch. Did Mr. Sunshine's cheeks go red? She drew up beside him. Positively ruddy. She tipped her head toward the other guy. "What did he say?"

Her self-appointed rescuer ran a thick palm over his cheek. "Nothing worth repeating." He took hold of the door handle and caught her gaze. "May I?"

May you? Sir, you may do anything you like.

"Knock yourself out. It won't start. I tried like six times."

He swung open the door and, with some effort, scrunched into the compact seat.

She peered in. Knees to chin, he was like a jack-in-the-box before it sprung. "You can move the—oh, you got it."

The seat careened backward, and he gave the dashboard a once-over. "Is the key in the car?"

And there it was. Proof Amish men, too, could be condescending jerks. She balled her hands on her hips. "Of course, it is. I'm not an idiot."

He jabbed a finger toward the start button.

"Don't bother. I tried, but the engine won't—"

Vroom.

The hybrid purred to life like it had been waiting a hundred years for Prince Charming to come along and tickle its button. The buzzing in her head turned up to eleven. She gaped. "How did you do that?"

He grinned from beneath the brim of a cockeyed straw hat.

Were she not irritated to the point of speechlessness, she might have swooned the tiniest bit. Mostly, she was too irked for swooning. "I pressed that button a thousand times. Why didn't it work?"

"Did you step on the brake?"

The rental guy delivered the car already running. He didn't say anything about stepping on the brake to turn it on. "Why would I do that? I want to drive."

Mr. Sunshine gripped the wheel and gazed out the windshield.

Like an eager teenager in his dad's sports car, he could hardly sit still. Did he know how to drive? Just how progressive was this place?

"To start most cars made in the last decade, you need to step on the brake. The owner's manual should say." He reached toward the glove box and paused. His gaze riveted on her stuff. "What's that?"

She was too exhausted for an interrogation. The whole fish-out-of-water scenario made her body scream for a nap. "What's what? My bag? My camera?"

He recoiled like she answered *my python* and sprang from the car.

She stumbled backward, but he landed close enough that she discovered he smelled like soap, too. And just a hint of sweat. Soapy sweaty sky. The combination was nicer than it sounded.

The corners of his lips tucked under. "Why do you have a camera?" he demanded.

So, Amish men could be even bigger jerks than regular guys. Noted. She hoped Sarah's husband wasn't cut from the same plain cloth. "Not that it's any of your business, but I'm a professional photographer." Her words set off a chain reaction she couldn't quite parse. His gorgeous blue-green eyes widened like a spooked animal, and something like anger hardened a jaw she didn't think could get any harder. He took a huge step away like she was a disease he might catch.

"Not taking pictures here, are you?"

"I'm not shooting you, if that's what you mean." She bit her tongue. These people needed to like her. More, she had to earn their trust. One rumor about the nasty New Yorker in the parking lot, and she'd be exiled from Amish country for good. More yogic breathing was required to execute a massive backpedal. "I'm sorry. I don't mean to be rude. I've had a really long day." She slid into the driver's seat. "Thanks for starting my car."

He crossed his arms over his chest. "It's a hybrid."

She ignored the biceps. "Yup."

He hooked a thumb toward the hood. "What do you know about hybrid engines?"

Albeit condescending, he was still talking. Maybe he accepted her apology? "Ah, not much? I know they're good for the environment and get great gas mileage."

He tightened his arms, bunching the biceps. "I wouldn't drive a vehicle I can't repair."

Ok, those were fighting words. So much for eating crow. "It's not my car," she said through a clenched jaw, undoing last Tuesday's acupuncture.

"I definitely wouldn't drive a vehicle I don't own. Where'd you say you were from?" He leaned to one side and checked the license plate. "New York?"

She clenched the steering wheel with one hand and hovered the other over the gear shifter. What stopped her from jerking into Reverse and peeling out like a cab driver on the way to LaGuardia? She knew this guy. He might be dressed differently, but she'd met his type a thousand times. "I'm from here actually. Sarah's my second cousin." That revelation genuinely seemed to shock him. His slack jaw was extremely satisfying.

"You live here?"

"No. Brooklyn." He nodded like everything about her suddenly made sense. Fury licked at her collarbones. She was done. *Sayonara*. Party over. Good-bye. She slammed into Reverse and grabbed the door handle. "Thanks for the help. I really don't drive very often."

"Funny, neither do I." He tucked his thumbs into his waistband and kicked the front tire. "See you around, Brooklyn."

Not if I see you first.

****

Did Pennsylvanians have daily pie? Sitting at Verna Rishel's kitchen table the next afternoon, Darcy sliced the side of a fork into a hunk of molassesy shoofly. The sugary top crumbled, and the filling cut like a dream. If she kept eating like this, she'd have to up the mileage on her daily runs.

A tall, stout woman with rosy cheeks and round, gold-rimmed glasses, Verna settled beside her, nursing a cup of coffee.

The sunny kitchen was remarkably up-to-date with a stove, refrigerator, and running water. When she knocked at the pretty white farmhouse at the end of the lane, Darcy hadn't known what to expect. She clocked the buggy by the barn and a lack of electric power lines, but inside, the home was quite modern, albeit completely lacking any interior design. Weirdly enormous rooms sported painted trim and coordinating curtains in a tragic shade of colonial blue. Mismatched furniture lined the walls like middle schoolers at a Friday night dance. Still, the house smelled of baking and beeswax and felt far homier than the designer showroom where she grew up. The place was also crawling with people. She heard more than saw them. Footsteps bounded up the stairs and tromped overhead while doors opened and closed. Hasty greetings were shouted in Pennsylvania Dutch with answering calls echoing around the house. The day was unseasonably mild for April, and spring seemed ready to burst. Every window was open, welcoming a refreshing breeze and the bustling sounds of a working farm.

Darcy had been greeted with a friendly smile and emphatic orders to address Verna by her first name. In her mid-to-late fifties, Verna was close to her mother's age, yet the women hardly seemed the same species. Two liposuctioned Isabelle Kings would have fit in Verna's dress. Without a dollop of makeup, Verna wore her age openly. Yet, her full cheeks had the vigor of youth, and laugh lines crinkled pleasingly from the corners of her eyes. She was, in fact, quite beautiful. Darcy touched her own cheek, strangely self-conscious of her made-up face.

Verna set down her coffee cup. "We'd be happy to have you as our guest. You're welcome at all family meals and devotionals and free to lend a hand in cooking and washing up. Some nights, our table's fuller than others. My daughter, Nora, and her family live in a house beyond the east pasture. She's got three *kinner* and another on the way. You met her oldest, Rebecca. My son's here with me, and the neighbor boys who lease the fields share a meal as often as not. Here they come now."

The door flew open, and two big-boned and bigger-bearded Amish men burst inside, bringing fresh air on their coats and mud on their boots.

Verna pointed at their feet and chastised them in Pennsylvania Dutch.

Scurrying back to the door, they stomped on the mat and greeted Darcy before trooping into the house.

"Now, where was I?" Verna freshened their coffees. "Not too much to do in the garden yet, but you're welcome there, too. The peas and spinach will need weeding before long."

Darcy didn't know the first thing about plants, and she knew less about cooking. Her chopped salad for one was a richly textured, healthy yet delicious concoction, and her go-to bring-him-home-and-cook-for-him date meal, vegan lasagna, wasn't half bad. However, cooking for a crowd lay squarely outside her wheelhouse. "Sounds wonderful."

Verna sniffed, tightening her arms over her chest. "As for this other business—this photography and whatnot—I can't help you. To be frank, I can't condone it, either. If taking pictures is your sole purpose, our home's likely not the best place."

A corner of pie crust dug into Darcy's gum. Maybe the jerk in the parking lot wasn't out of step with the rest of the community. Convincing Sarah was only the first hurdle. She'd have to earn the trust of every single person she met. "I see."

A deep furrow cut across Verna's brow. "Rebecca tells me you work for a magazine in New York City?"

Back to square one. She sipped coffee and nodded. "I have nothing but respect for your community. As I explained to my cousin—"

"Cousin?" Verna held up a meaty finger. "What cousin?"

"Sarah Stoltzfus is my second cousin on my father's side. Our grandmothers were sisters."

Verna relaxed her hands into her lap. "Leora Mast was your grandmother?"

Her tone was quiet and wondering. A spark of hope lit in Darcy's chest. "I spent the summer here with her when I was nine."

"She was my schoolteacher." Verna's round cheeks

softened into a smile. "The best teacher I ever had. It broke my heart when she jumped the fence, but I understood why."

Darcy rested her fork on the plate. Apparently, Verna held the answer to the mystery of *Mammi* Leora's departure. To the best of Darcy's knowledge, her grandfather wasn't Amish and never had been. Darcy's best guess was *Mammi* left for love. "If I may ask, why did my grandmother leave?"

Behind her glasses, Verna's eyes rounded. "Don't you know?"

Suddenly breathless, she shook her head. Maybe the family secret was deeper and darker than she suspected.

"She left over schooling. After years of teaching, she came to believe that while some folks did fine with an eighth-grade education, others, herself included, would benefit from more. She went to college and taught in the English school. Several years later, she married your grandfather, Homer King."

Verna's tone was matter-of-fact. She didn't seem to judge *Mammi* at all. Far from scandalous, the story was much more satisfying than a love affair. "I had no idea."

Verna peered at Darcy. "You resemble her some in the shape of your face. Like a heart. And the blonde hair, of course."

Darcy coughed. Though blonde as a child, she'd dyed her hair for years. Who knew what her natural color was anymore? No photos of her grandmother hung in the Park Avenue apartment. She had only a single snapshot taken that summer on the farm. In it, she and *Mammi* Leora sat on a tree stump, wearing daisy chains around their necks and in their hair. When she went home, she'd dig out that picture. "I miss her. I felt like I just got to know her and then…"

"The cancer took her quick." Verna shifted her gaze out the window. "Isn't that the way?"

The door squealed, and Rebecca ran inside with a can of paint and a fistful of brushes.

"*Nicht so schnell,*" Verna scolded.

Rebecca skidded to a halt and made a show of walking slowly. "*Yah, Mammi.* Hello, Darcy." She vanished into the living room, and footsteps tripped up the stairs.

Verna frowned. "This family's seen our share of troubles, as well."

Noisy, chaotic, and bursting with joy, the Rishel's home was the farthest place she could imagine from a house of troubles. Her heart squeezed. She'd love to spend three weeks somewhere like this.

A cow mooed, long and low. Men called to one another across the barnyard.

A moment passed while Verna gazed after her granddaughter, then she turned to Darcy decisively. "You may stay. But take care. Folks are slow to come around, and some never will. Make time to know the difference."

Darcy's spark of hope fanned into a flame. "I will."

"And leave us a good review on the Internet. Reviews mean everything to a new business."

She couldn't suppress a laugh. "Five stars all around."

"Well, wait until you've seen the place. It's not quite finished, but you'll get the idea." Verna pushed herself to standing. "Mind you, we've no electric outlets or television. You'll have to go elsewhere to power your gadgets."

"I understand." She trailed Verna across the living room and up the stairs to a landing from which several bedrooms opened, then on through a door at the far end and up another flight. From above, she heard a shriek and a giggle followed by a deep voice that kindled a second fire in her belly at the same time it set her teeth on edge. With a tight grip on the banister, she stepped up into the attic.

Rebecca lunged with a wet paintbrush at a tall, smiling man. Her brown work apron sported a fresh stripe of white paint.

He dodged the attack and whirled, coming face-to-face with Darcy. Jerking back, he pressed a fist to his mouth and muffled a laugh. "Well, look who got her car started."

His light-brown hair stuck out in every direction. His blue-green eyes were the color of the Caribbean Sea. And for some inexplicable reason, Mr. Sunshine was painting her bedroom.

Chapter Four

Why in the name of everything holy was that man renovating *her* Amish vacation rental?

Mr. Sunshine's lips twisted in a grin. "*Guder daag,* Brooklyn."

Panting from the climb, Verna looked from the dude to Darcy and back again. "Darcy King, I'd introduce my son, Samuel, but I'd say you two are acquainted."

Her son? Rumpled and paint-splattered, he was maddeningly hot. She forced a tight smile. "We met at my cousin's store yesterday. I had trouble with my car, and Samuel was kind enough—"

"To keep Darcy company while she solved the problem." He raked a hand through his hair and scratched his head. "Something to do with the brake pedal, wasn't it?"

Mr. Know-it-all Amish mechanic ducked credit for starting her car. Why? Their community seemed progressive, but was his knowledge of automobiles a step too far? Could she get him in trouble with Mom? "Not at all. I'm certain it was you who—"

"Encouraged you to experiment until the motor started. You're welcome." He knelt and dipped a thick brush into a can of paint.

Verna sniffed and wrinkled her nose. "I see."

Darcy guessed Verna did indeed see, hear, and

know exactly who her son was. How satisfying. Keeping anything from this particular mother was likely difficult, especially if, as she said, her son lived under the same roof. Again…why? She toggled her gaze to Samuel. The guy must be in his thirties. Why wasn't he leading his own flock of bonneted ducklings? The two male specimens she'd seen aside, the Amish weren't exactly known for good looks. Why wasn't this guy married at twenty?

Verna smoothed the drop cloth with one foot. "The room is still rough, but we'll *redd* it up by next week. Will it do?"

On the contrary, the attic was lovely, spacious and airy with a slanting ceiling framing expansive views of farm country. Samuel and Rebecca appeared to be putting a second coat of whitewash on shiplap walls, unknowingly—or perhaps knowingly?—creating a modern country vibe. The room felt like a hug by a white linen sheet, cool and warm all at once. It would more than do. Living upstairs from a mansplaining oaf, however, was less desirable.

"I made a special quilt for the bed," Rebecca said from a wooden stool in one corner. Her wet paintbrush dangled, dripping white globs. In her other hand was a dog-eared book.

"You made a quilt? How old are you?"

"Fourteen. I can teach you if you'd like."

At that age, Darcy could no sooner have sewed a quilt than she could have hotwired a car. She was hard-pressed to think what she accomplished at fourteen, other than surviving freshman year at her swanky girl's school. A sudden memory of *Mammi* Leora teaching her to sew resurfaced in a rush. What had she made? An apron, maybe? She could almost feel the needle between her fingers and *Mammi* sitting by her side, patiently watching.

Samuel spun to his mother and spoke something quick and sharp in Pennsylvania Dutch. He cut Darcy a frosty look.

The words rolled off his tongue in a deep, breathy voice that would have tickled her insides pleasingly were the content not clearly negative and directed at her. The smile, teasing as it had been, vanished. Whatever he said, he meant it.

Rebecca jerked up her head and shot a glance toward Darcy.

Verna waved him off and pointed to a board high on the wall. "You missed a spot." Then she beckoned Darcy downstairs.

"Good-bye, Rebecca." Without a word, she brushed past Samuel so closely he nearly painted her sweater.

"*Mach's gut,*" Rebecca chirped.

She almost escaped without a backward glance, but stepping onto the top stair, she couldn't resist. From the corner of her eye, she caught him staring out the window like he was watching an oncoming storm. She steeled her spine. If he had a problem, too bad. In this family, Verna clearly called the shots.

With arrangements finalized, Darcy had just hopped in the hybrid when she spotted movement coming from the house.

Rebecca streaked out the door and down the porch steps, carrying a brown paper bag.

Wisps of white-blonde hair danced around her face, making her look like a creature not quite of this earth. She was all arms and legs, graceful as a ballerina and as lanky as a foal. Darcy pressed the button and lowered the window.

Rebecca thrust the bag inside. "I almost forgot. My mother made whoopie pies this morning."

The rich smell of cocoa supplanted rental car funk. She peeped into the bag. Three wrapped, chocolate sandwich cakes with thick layers of cream filling nestled like sleeping kittens. After two consecutive days of pie, she thought her sweets quota had been filled. Her mouth watered. Maybe not. "Thank you."

"*Mamm* has a baked goods stand at the farmers' market every Wednesday. She's an exceptional baker." Rebecca hooked her elbows on the open window and brought her face to Darcy's eye level. "I believe you sampled her shoofly pie. Perhaps some of your city farmers' markets would be interested."

If the pie was any indication, the kid might be right. She'd rarely tasted better pastry. "I'll keep her in mind." She thought the Amish were farmers, tied to the land and the land alone. Clearly, she thought wrong. They seemed in many ways as business-minded as New Yorkers. So what did they have to teach about modernity? Did bonnets and buggies mask a society as ambitious as her own? And what in the world had Samuel said to his mother? She folded closed the bag and set it carefully beside her camera. "Is Samuel your uncle?"

Rebecca nodded. "One of several."

"He didn't seem happy about me staying in the attic."

"Oh, he's not." Rebecca blinked icecap-blue eyes. "He doesn't trust photographers on account of some story about a picture of him taken in Ohio a long time ago. I don't know details. No one tells me anything." Shoulders slumping, she stood. "Photography is wicked, of course, but Amish people have their pictures taken all the time, from behind or far away." A mischievous smile flitted across her lips. "I think secretly they like it. I know I would."

Moments later, the silky voice of Taylor Shift navigated toward the interstate, and the farm disappeared in the rearview mirror. In Rebecca, Darcy might have one photography subject. Maybe an ally, too? She had three weeks to find a whole bunch more.

****

Spicy tuna dissolved on Darcy's tongue. Wasabi quickened her pulse. Pickled ginger curled her toes. Who needed a man when she had sushi?

She licked soy sauce from her fingers and scanned the neatly packed bags, queued up along her bedroom wall like Madeline's twelve little girls in two straight lines. Having put in a full week at *Hudson Magazine* tying up loose ends, she needed only to finish packing. She pulled sleek, slate-blue rain boots from her closet and tucked them in a tote. She'd pick up the rental car at eight on Monday morning, a cute mini machine that did not need to be plugged in. With any luck, she'd be in Green Ridge by lunchtime. A swig of seltzer sparkled down like liquid sunshine. Her stomach tingled.

Yup. She was nervous.

Running shoes snugged next to her boots, and she snatched another bite of sushi. Long runs in the country would ease her nerves. She threw in a second pair of leggings and her cashmere pj's. The heating in the attic was a big question mark, and May nights could be chilly. For good measure, she tossed in her college sweatshirt. Her mother might have been controlling, but she instilled in Darcy the ability to dress in layers. For that, anyway, she was grateful.

She zipped the rolling suitcase and collapsed onto her bed. Her roommate, Fern, was at an artists' retreat upstate, and Zibby was out with her boyfriend after another long week teaching at PS 72 in Park Slope. Art school classmates Zibby and Fern were her best friends, and they absolutely, positively had busy lives of which she was only a part. Sure, if she dipped into her savings account, she could rent a sleek modern flat in a doorman building, but she was determined to pay her own way. A fourth-floor walkup with roomies it was.

She gazed around her cozy bedroom. Her velvety comforter hugged the bed, the brick wall showed off her photographs in gorgeous relief, and the fairy lights around the bay window winked cheerfully. A desk and a loveseat rounded out carefully curated, largely thrifted furnishings. It wasn't fancy, but it was home.

The snapshot of herself and *Mammi* Leora leaned against the dresser mirror. Faded and discolored, the image was still clear. She gazed at her reflection. Verna was right. She and *Mammi* shared a close resemblance. How strange her father never mentioned. Collapsing onto the loveseat, she grabbed her phone and scrolled through her social media accounts.

Boom.

A photo of Jaxson, the bass player she'd been dating off and on since Halloween, landed at the top of her feed. A knot of air caught in her chest. Time-stamped an hour ago, the pic showed him bleary-eyed, propped on a bar.

A leather-clad redhead clung to him like cellophane.

Nauseated but unsurprised, she gulped seltzer. Jaxson was the latest in a long line of artist and musician boyfriends whose primary assets were that her mother loathed them. They were largely self-employed, always tattooed, and never husband material. She paged through a mental photo album of all the "right" guys she'd dated over the years—boys whose fathers owned companies and mothers went to Mount Holyoke. They were, on the whole, largely dull, always self-centered, and never good kissers. She wrapped a chunky knitted afghan around her shoulders. The artists and musicians bested the trust fund kids on two out of the three areas of weakness. They were, however, even more self-centered.

Incriminating photo notwithstanding, she should at least let Jax know she was taking off. She swiped to her messages.

—*Hey. Going out of town on assignment for three weeks. Queen Margo gave me my first photo essay. Yippee!*—

—*Noooo. What about my gig on Weds?*—

She stared at the screen.

—*Um, did u catch the part about my photo essay?*—

—*Potential manager coming. Need a packed house. Can ur roommates still show? Cld be my big break.*—

Her stomach sank. Well aware he was a textbook narcissist, she was still flabbergasted. She scrolled back to the pic of Jaxson and the girl. His hands wandered in a manner not at all innocent. Back to messages.

—*Speaking of breaks, I need one. Won't have cell service in PA. CU when I CU.* —

Block caller.

Unfollow.

Delete contact.

Removing someone from your life was remarkably easy in the twenty-first century. With three taps, Jaxson was gone. Feeling zero regret, she looked out the window. Streetlight filtered through trees, casting lacy patterns on the sidewalk. In the brownstone opposite, a family of five sat down to dinner. Perfectly framed by the window, they might have been characters on a television show. To them, of course, she must look the same. Except their show was a heartwarming family sitcom, and she was in a pathetic soap opera.

She ripped a ticket stub from Jaxson's last concert off her bulletin board and crumpled it. Surely, all men weren't so clueless. Surely, somewhere, someday— maybe a long time from now, she was only twenty-nine after all—she'd meet a guy with a clue. He existed, right? He'd been born?

She soaked in the soothing smell of lavender laundry detergent and let her thoughts unwind. Somewhere, this very moment, a man who could be fully present in her life was out there, eating a sandwich or walking a dog. Someone in whom she could place complete trust. Someone who would trust her in return. He wouldn't choose his band or his bros or his two more traditionally successful children over her. For him, she'd be enough. For him, she'd be everything.

Would she know her person when she met him? Would a spark of recognition glint in his sea-green eyes? Scoffing, she downed a final bite of sushi. Not those eyes. For her, life was New York or nowhere. For Samuel, life was clearly nowhere. Classic chic city mouse meets mansplaining country mouse. Her person, if he truly existed, was not in the middle of cow country. Right?

Chapter Five

In the quilt shop kitchenette, Darcy sipped weak, but creamy, coffee poured from a stand-up, metal percolator like the ones at church functions. Had only four hours passed since the cute barista by the car rental place handed her an overpriced cardamom latte? From a practical standpoint, how easy it was to leave New York. Monday morning traffic was busy but moving; she simply got in the express lane and drove. Untangling from the city emotionally, however, was a feat of escape artistry. The five boroughs had her heart and soul chained tight.

Strange, when she was home, New York was all the world, and all the world aspired to New York. She flicked her gaze from Sarah to the other round-faced young mother, Amity Yoder, who joined them at the table. Admiring their naturally pink cheeks and smooth skin, Darcy knew these women no more wished to be in New York City than in outer space. Feeling her shoulders loosen and her jaw unclench, she understood why. Outside, the blustery May afternoon felt more like March. Inside, the shop was as warm and cinnamon-scented as Mrs. Claus's lap. Scissors snipped gaily, and women chattered in Pennsylvania Dutch. Darcy watched a giggling girl spin a rotating rack of zippers. The colorful fasteners flew like a whirligig, splaying in a blurred rainbow. She'd never been anywhere that felt more fully and completely female, in the absolute best sense of the word.

Clomping boots and a chorus of male voices forecast an atmospheric change, as two men blew through the door.

Darcy glanced up from her coffee and into the eyes of Samuel Rishel. He was dressed in a black wool coat and stocking cap like a cross between a hipster and a superstar quarterback. Both looks were irritatingly pleasing.

His gaze heated, but sliding to the camera bag on the table, it froze.

Okay, photography was forbidden! Understood. She twined the leather strap around her hand in a possessive coil. What was this guy's hang-up? What happened in Ohio?

Sarah pushed back from the table. "Are you finished? Are we running entirely on sunlight?"

Keeping a safe distance, Samuel came around the counter trailed by the tall, slender man Darcy remembered from her first visit. Both wore heavy tool belts and toted power drills.

Samuel snatched two cookies from a plate and tossed one to his friend. "Almost. We need to finish the battery installation."

Sarah bounced her gaze from Darcy to Samuel and back again. "You've met, right? Of course, you have. You'll be living...well, close by, I suppose." Sarah's lips curled into a grin just this side of rascally. She fluttered her fingertips against her cheek. "Samuel and Tucker's solar business would be fascinating for your magazine—"

"Oh, I don't know—" Darcy began.

"Absolutely not," Samuel declared at the exact same moment.

Darcy slanted a raised-brow, pursed-lip, was-that-tone-really-necessary look that would have made her mother proud. She hated herself a little bit, but Isabelle had certain skills.

"Well, all right then." With a humph, Sarah deliberately moved the plate of cookies away from the men.

Samuel scowled. "We'll let you know when we finish." Hitching up his tool belt, he loped through a door in the back wall.

The slender man brushed a shock of dark hair from his eyes. "Don't mind him. It's hard being so handsome. Women want to take his picture all the time." He met Darcy's gaze. "He needs to keep the paparazzi at arm's length, know what I mean?" With a wink, he stretched a long arm across the table, grabbed a cookie, and left, whistling a song that very much sounded like, "Mamas Don't Let Your Babies Grow Up to be Cowboys."

Slack-jawed, Darcy stared after him. "Paparazzi? How does he…? Wait, what?"

Sarah flapped a hand. She scooped up Amity's coffee cup and refilled it. "Don't mind Tucker. Or Samuel, for that matter."

Amity adjusted a straight pin at her waist, loosening her apron. "Tucker McClure is not your usual Amish."

Sarah tucked a knee and sat, sliding Amity her cup. "He married Nora, Samuel's older sister four years ago now, was it?"

"*Yah*." Amity spooned sugar into her coffee and

stirred. "Such a blessing to that family. Seems like he's been here forever."

Sarah scooted close. "Tucker's *Englischer* comes out sometimes. Especially when he wants to give someone a shock."

Darcy was pretty sure *Englischer* was the word for someone outside the Amish community. "He wasn't always Amish?"

"Oh no. He was a country western singer. Very famous, apparently. Have you heard of him?"

"Not really a country fan." She hadn't been able to put a finger on what made Tucker different. Something in his gaze was cannier. Did he really give up performing to become Amish? Would the rules against photography apply to him, as well? Another story she'd have to tease out. "Do many outsiders join?"

"We lose more than join." Sighing, Sarah passed the cookies. "Which brings me back to your project. Amity, tell Darcy your idea."

Amity settled a basket in her lap and fished out knitting needles and yarn. "My husband, Mose, gave up farming for making campers. It's good-paying work and regular hours. I think folks might be surprised to see our men working side by side with *Englischers* in an Amish-owned factory."

Darcy's photographer's intuition tingled. When she came to rural Pennsylvania, she never dreamed of shooting a factory. "I think so, too."

Rebecca scurried behind the counter, laden with bolts of jewel-toned fabrics. "She'll need a man."

Darcy bit back a laugh. She needed a man, all right, but not in the way Rebecca suggested. Did a whiff of soapy sky linger?

Coming to her feet, Sarah lightened Rebecca's burden and passed the shears. "Nonsense."

"Rebecca might be right." Amity eyeballed the sleeve of a blue baby sweater. "Mose figures the fellas will be open to picture taking, but you'll have to sweet-talk the boss. For my part, he said to keep clear. He wants me nowhere near those worldly English men."

A bolt of amethyst cotton unspooled across the counter, landing with a *thunk* at each turn. Rebecca lined up the yardage carefully and cut with a smooth swipe. "Men don't need to sweet-talk. They just ask. I'm not saying it's right, but it's a fact."

Darcy followed the girl's every move. Rebecca was like no teenager she ever met. How sure of herself she was. How confident in the correctness of her views. And though Darcy hated to admit it, she had a point.

"I fed Elam two kinds of stromboli last night, and by dessert, he agreed to my helping Darcy. I was never much for sweet talk, but I'll ride along." Sarah plonked a sensible black sneaker onto a chair and tied the lace. She smiled at Darcy from beneath thick dark brows. "With you doing the asking, I think we'll get in."

Darcy eyed a blush-colored lip stain on her coffee cup. Just what shade of lipstick was best for crashing an RV factory? She was about to find out.

****

Later that afternoon, Darcy hoisted her suitcase onto the luggage rack in her attic bedroom and dropped her shoe tote. "Thank you. The room is perfect."

Verna ran a finger over the oak dresser top and checked for dust. Apparently satisfied, she centered a small vase filled with fragrant white flowers. "Let me know if you need anything. If you're hungry, supper's in an hour. I'd best see to the potatoes."

A Shaker-style pegboard spanned the entire wall. Darcy slung her bag over a hook, kicked off her sneakers, and flopped onto what certainly felt like a featherbed. Day one: zero photos. She swiveled her head to one side, easing a crick in her neck. For all his roof scaling and solar panel hefting, Samuel did not show up to carry her luggage. Probably best. Would she have had to tip him? Awkward. She ran a hand over rows of cotton quilt squares in a bewitching color combination. Rebecca's quilt was exquisite. Lavender, teal, garnet, black, and salmon patches formed a giant diamond, framed by a thick border of solid plum. The queen-size bed was a luxurious oasis in the whitewashed room, which, unlike the downstairs, was as gorgeous as any on a modern farmhouse design site.

She still had on her puffer, but the room was snug, and she unzipped it. Not a whisper whistled through the dormer windows. Verna had offered a kerosene heater. With her cozy cashmere pj's, Darcy wouldn't need it. She blinked slowly, her eyelids drooping.

Sometime later, she awoke to the sound of distant voices with no idea how long she'd slept. The slanted white ceiling glowed purple in the twilight. Muzzy-headed and unable to remember her last daytime nap, she inhaled the smell of fresh paint, stretched like a cat, and rolled off the bed, groping for her shoes in semi-darkness. Finding her phone in a coat pocket, she tapped the flashlight app. Three bars lit at the top of the screen, but her battery was dangerously low. Thank goodness, in the attic, unlike the quilt shop, she had service. The beam caught a floor lamp next to a glider. It appeared to be attached to a huge battery encased in a wooden cabinet. When she returned, she'd figure out the contraption. Planning to scrounge dinner and charge up in the car, she grabbed her bag and keys.

Cheerful conversation accompanied her down to the living room. Drawn like a moth to a streetlamp, she tiptoed to the kitchen archway, where she lingered unnoticed. A family supper more unlike the one she endured at her parents' apartment was hard to imagine. But for the traditional Amish clothing, the scene was like something from a feel-good holiday movie.

Verna placed a heaping bowl of mashed potatoes on the table and took her seat at the head, directly across from a gentleman sporting a traditional long, white Amish beard.

Moony-eyed, the older fellow followed Verna's every move.

Engaged in an intricate dance of passing food, eating, and assisting young ones, grown-ups and children filled out the table, Samuel among them.

Ruddy-cheeked and intent, he tilted his head toward Rebecca, chewing slowly and nodding.

Ignoring a plate heaped high with food, Rebecca chattered, bright-eyed, and bounced as if she could barely sit still.

The room echoed with conversation, and though Darcy couldn't understand a single word, she knew the gathering was harmonious. She witnessed no strained silence or forced laughter. No eye rolls or checking of phones. Love, pure and simple, shimmered in the glare from the gaslight and pinged off the wooden cabinets like bouncy balls. Watching it, she felt her throat thicken. Again, brought to tears by total strangers? She pressed a palm to her chest, willing her emotions to stay inside her body where they belonged.

Glancing up from her meatloaf, Verna spotted her. "There you are!" She stood and beckoned. "Darcy, you know Rebecca and Samuel, of course, and I believe Christian and Mattias Lapp came through last week—they help out on the farm. Meet my daughter, Nora, her husband, Tucker, and their twins, Lavelle and Faith."

Sitting between the toddlers, Tucker smirked knowingly.

But knowing of what?

Fair-haired and lovely, his wife nodded hello and returned to wiping one girl's nose.

Verna gestured to the gentleman across the table. "And this is Deacon Elmer Zook." She snatched an empty plate and restocked it from a pan of dinner rolls. "Pull up a chair. We've plenty to eat."

She swallowed past a lump that refused to quit her throat. Her insides tugged, pulling her toward the space between Samuel and Verna. She could imagine, for a night, these people were her family. She could talk and laugh and pretend she belonged. Her gaze shifted from Rebecca's smiling face to Samuel's suddenly stoic one.

The little muscle in his jaw fluttered. His brow turned to stone.

Unsteady and unmoored, she didn't have energy to spar. She made a delicate effort to clear the weepies from her throat. "I'd love to, but not tonight. I have a few errands to run. Thank you, though. Next time." With a wave, she faded into shadows and sprinted for the door.

Safely behind the wheel, she rolled down the car window and gulped chilly night air. Seriously, what was wrong? The sight of a happy family might render anyone misty-eyed, especially if their own situation was less than ideal, but she nearly broke down in the pan of buttered rolls.

The night was inky beneath a starless sky. Her headlights cut a path down the winding lane and onto country roads. She focused on breathing deeply, in through the nose and out through the mouth. Nothing was amiss. She was simply tired and hungry and more than a teensy bit nervous about this assignment. After dinner and a shower, she'd feel like herself.

Fields and farmhouses gave way to neighborhoods. At a stoplight, she plugged in her phone and turned down Main Street. Whimsical globed streetlamps stood sentry before stately Victorian homes. She remembered those funny lights from the summer she spent, but she'd forgotten how charming downtown Green Ridge was. Or maybe she never noticed? She was only nine, after all. She peered down a side street. Which way to *Mammi* Leora's house?

An imposing, brick high school rolled by followed by quaint shops and restaurants. On the first floor of a building adorned with curlicued gingerbread trim, a neon-pink cupcake shone through a picture window. The matching sign read *Pammy's Place*. She made a note to return for a cupcake and Wi-Fi. A niggling feeling said she'd need the reality check of a twenty-first-century café.

A hole-in-the-wall joint called House of Pizza was one of few places open after business hours. A sprightly elderly gentleman delivered her hot tuna sub with a friendly invitation to come again, and she ate in the parking lot. Maybe almost crying in front of a room of strangers rendered her particularly impressionable, but the sandwich was, without question, the best she ever tasted. A crispy toasted bun gave way to peppery tuna salad with exactly the right amount of searing onion bite. Melted provolone blanketed the tuna, and tomato slices added zing. She licked her fingers and pondered a second sandwich before coming to her senses and heading toward the farm. With any luck, she'd shower and make it to her room without encountering the Rishels.

The farmhouse was dark and quiet. Treading lightly, she slipped upstairs for pj's and toiletries and then down to the second-floor bathroom. By the sallow light of an overhead fixture, the room was Spartan but spotless. A lukewarm spray issued from a small showerhead, but she hadn't counted on any warm water when she signed up for an immersive Amish experience. The chunky bar of oatmeal soap gave off a clean scent and left her skin surprisingly smooth. In a child-sized, oak-framed mirror, she took in her appearance. Thick hair dangled heavily around her face and dribbled onto her buttery pajama top. With no hairdryer, she'd resort to braids and buns in the coming weeks. Scrubbed clean of makeup, her cheeks were flushed, and her brown eyes were smudged with gray. Oddly, she looked tired. She didn't feel tired. Could a person operate on a baseline level of exhaustion for so long, she no longer knew what truly rested felt like?

Pressing an ear to the door, she listened for movement and, hearing none, eased it open. In the glow of a flickering kerosene lamp, the landing was exactly as she'd imagined an Amish home interior. As a photographer, she was keenly attuned to light. Sometimes, she fancied she could touch it. The challenge of capturing this beautiful shadowy space made her fingers itch for the shutter button. She was mentally adjusting camera settings when she heard a door unlatch.

His shirt was open at the collar. His suspenders hung loose around his hips. His feet were bare, and his chin was dusted with tawny stubble.

If she looked tired, then he looked exhausted. Though her pajamas provided full coverage, she hugged her clothes and toiletry bag to her chest. Still, his eyes rounded as if she appeared in her skimpiest lingerie. She gestured toward the attic stairs and shuffled to her right. "I was just…"

"Are you finished in the…" He stepped in the exact same direction.

She skittered to the left. "Sorry."

He leapt aside the same way.

A thousand times she'd done this dance with strangers on the street. Never did her accidental partner get so close or smell so good. With a giggle, she looked up into his face. He was very tall.

His hand scrubbed over his chin, and he inched back, trailing his gaze down her body.

She clutched the bundle tighter, but she could hardly be outraged. In the rare moments she wasn't thoroughly annoyed, she'd ogled aplenty. Not that he was ogling. He was too polite. The attention was more admiring and not unpleasant at that. She took a giant step back and gestured grandly toward the bathroom. A chuckle rumbled low in the chest she refused to ogle yet again.

He nodded toward the open bathroom door. "Work okay for you?"

"Uh…I think so. Like a regular bathroom."

Pleasure cracked the angular planes of his face. "*Gut.* I only finished building it last week. Before I installed the shower, we bathed in a tub in the kitchen."

As golden lamplight kissed his cheeks, the real question was how she, or anyone with a pulse, could *not* imagine him bathing in a metal washtub like a cowboy. She set aside the image for later review when she could divorce it from his irritating personality. "Might be awkward for your guests."

"You tell me. I thought you English went in for that sort of thing."

A neck blush threatened. Now he was flirting? *Good luck, dude.* She was queen of teasing banter. She flipped her hair over one shoulder, displaying her satiny smooth, clean-scented, unblushing neck. "To be frank, the shower was lukewarm."

"Oh?" His spine stiffened.

Oo. That revelation might have stung a bit. "And the light is dim, and the mirror's too small."

He anchored his hands on his hips and stared. "You understand the constraints I'm working under?"

"Perfectly. You asked." Watching him fumble for a comeback, she took the opportunity to smell him again. What was his scent? Not knowing would bug her until she identified it. Not cologne or hair product, of course. Was sky smell a medley of oatmeal soap and something else? She lifted two perfectly shaped brows that by the end of this adventure in rustic living were sure to resemble caterpillars. "Anything else? I can start on the bedroom, if you like." The bedroom was flawless, but sparring with him gave her a jolt in the best way.

With a bitter-edged chuckle, he shook his head.

Was he used to women standing up to him? She couldn't imagine Verna kowtowing to any man. Or Rebecca for that matter. But Sarah and Amity? Did Amish women typically cross him?

She caught a flash of amusement, and a lightbulb lit above her head. Metaphorically, of course. He might hate her for being a photographer, but he liked her sass. The realization kindled a desire she assumed would lay dormant in the land of dairy cows and unkempt beards. She let her gaze linger over the notch at the base of his throat and the knifelike collarbones on either side. Her heart skittered. Expecting a dearth of romance, she'd downloaded several steamy novels. Maybe she didn't need them. Then again, maybe she'd need them all the more.

He retreated to the bedroom doorway and propped an arm on the frame in a classic book-boyfriend pose.

What was his private space like? Was it neat as a pin? Were contraband movie posters plastered to the ceiling? Was it as pleasing as the room he created upstairs?

"Something wrong with the attic?" he drawled.

With two steps and a peek over his shoulder, she'd have an answer. But no. She was in this man's home for work and not a forbidden love fling. Invading his privacy was one step too far. Softening, she sighed. "Honestly, the attic is perfect. I love it."

He let his head rest against his forearm, and his eyelids went heavy. He yawned. "*Gut.*"

What was it about sleepy men that thoroughly undid her? She took a sharp breath and zipped up her insides. "Goodnight, Samuel."

"Why didn't you eat supper with us?"

The question stapled her feet to the floor. *Um...because you were staring daggers, and everyone was so happy, I started to cry?* She swallowed toothpasty spit. "I had errands."

He narrowed his gaze. "You're a terrible liar."

"Well, you're a terrible host." Soft candlelight and an empty house compelled brutal honesty. She couldn't hold her tongue. "You glared like you wanted me to leave."

"I did?" He heaved a deep breath, and his shoulders pressed into the doorway. "I didn't mean to."

Might as well lay her cards on the table. Did the Amish even play cards? Probably not. "Look, I know you don't like photographers because of something that happened a long time ago in Ohio or whatever, but I'm not that person. I don't take pictures of people who don't want me to. I'm a professional, okay?" His intent gaze was as searingly refreshing as a hot towel on a transatlantic flight. After a minute, though, the undivided focus was too much, and she shied away. "Well, goodnight."

"So, why didn't you stay for supper?"

His voice was so low she could barely make out the words. But she did, and the question hit her with the shockingly solid heft of a feather pillow. She stared at the flickering lamp, and a yellow splotch coalesced in her vision. Though painful, it was better than looking at him. "Your family was so..." She cuddled her clothing tighter. "I've never had..." Trying to express herself with words was impossible. She was a visual person. Images were her currency. Talking just got her in trouble. Her throat constricted, and something dense welled up. Under no circumstances would she weep in a hallway in front of a stranger. Tightening her jaw, she stared at her feet, feeling the corner of her right eye burn. Brushing away the tear would mean acknowledging its presence. Running would mark her a coward.

She froze.

The floorboards creaked. The smell of sky strengthened. She could feel the heat from his body and his breath on the side of her face.

"*Ach*, Brooklyn…"

His hand on her cheek was tender. His thumb dragged across her skin with exquisite slowness, wiping away the single tear.

She hadn't been touched like that in…possibly ever? She could run ten miles on a lark, but she suddenly had no faith in her legs to support her. Every ounce of street-smart, city crustiness threatened to crumble with the rising need to collapse into the arms of this…this…farmer! Seriously, something must be wrong.

Sniffing, she stumbled aside, bumping into the table holding the lamp. She flattened a palm on the surface, feeling the smooth wood like a living thing. Fire averted, she jerked away. "I'm fine. Goodnight." Then she whirled and mounted the stairs two at a time, back straight and head held high.

She'd go to her grave denying she cried.

Just one problem.

As she fled, she caught a glimpse of his thumb and one single tear, glistening in the golden lamplight.

Chapter Six

Still shaky from last night's encounter with
Samuel, Darcy gripped the camera bag and clung to her
confidence for dear life. The modest reception area of
Schmucker's Camper Factory had enough space for a
desk, two folding chairs, a gas fireplace in a faux-brick
wall, and the factory door, which Dale Fischer blocked
entirely with his denim-and-flannel-draped frame.
She'd faced many gatekeepers in her time but none as
imposing as this guy. She was used to bouncers and
maître d's but not plant managers the size of
refrigerators with temperaments to match.

Morning sunshine streamed through Venetian
blinds, trying as hard as she was to warm the room.
Flirting her way into a camper factory wasn't exactly
how she imagined gaining access, but at this point,
she'd try anything. She tucked a loose hair behind one
ear and wrinkled her nose. "If I could just sit down with
you and Mr. Schmucker and discuss the project—"

"No discussions." Fischer crossed thick arms atop
a round belly. "We've got RVs to build, and them fellas
don't like their pictures taken."

With a swish of skirts, Sarah came to her side.
"Darcy understands our customs. She's agreed to
conceal the men's faces. Her magazine in New York
City is seen by thousands. The publicity would be

wonderful *gut* for business."

He scowled. "Can't imagine city folks want our campers."

Sarah was a smart businesswoman. When charm failed, appeal to the bottom line. Darcy followed her lead. "You'd be surprised. New Yorkers have money to spend and a yen for travel. Mose Yoder assured us—"

"Mose put you up to this?" Scoffing, he slumped against the doorframe, exposing a slanted view of a busy factory floor.

On tiptoes, Darcy glimpsed the unfinished shell of a teardrop-shaped camper and heard the whine of mechanized tools. "Not exactly. Mr. Yoder's wife, Amity—"

"Figured as much." Fischer snorted. "Stick to quilting, ladies, and take your pictures somewhere else. We've got a quota to meet."

Abandoning reason, Darcy resorted to the old standby of going over the man's head. "Perhaps Mr. Schmucker would feel differently. If I could simply talk—"

"Girlie wants pictures of the Amish." He yanked up his tool belt and, chuckling, lumbered into the factory, closing the door soundly behind him.

"Girlie?" Darcy choked a sound like a cat coughing up a hairball. "What a spectacularly rude man!"

Sarah collapsed into a folding chair. "I'll admit, that went worse than I imagined."

"Who even says girlie?" Darcy paced from fireplace to desk and back.

A mousy, young receptionist glanced up from her computer. "He does. All the time. You'd be better off with Mr. Schmucker."

Darcy stalked to the door, barely refraining from hurling it open and charging onto the floor, flashbulb blazing.

Sarah fanned herself with a camper brochure. "I hate to admit…"

Darcy shot out a hand. "Don't you even think it, Sarah Stoltzfus."

Sarah shrugged. "Maybe Rebecca was right. Maybe you do need a man."

Surrendering to the current mission's futility, Darcy made the forty-five-minute drive back from the camper factory in less than thirty. No one called Darcy King *girlie*, and she absolutely did not need a man. She floored the gas pedal and took the turn onto Old Cowan Road like she was fleeing the cops.

Sarah's gentle hand landed atop her shoulder in a gesture of comfort and caution. "The factory was only one idea. We'll think of others."

She hung a hard left into the quilt shop parking lot. "Did you hear the way he interrupted me?"

The passenger's door flung open, and Sarah planted both feet on the ground. "Speak to Verna Rishel. She'll likely have ideas. We'll have better luck tomorrow." With a cheerful wave, she hurried away and was immediately intercepted by two skipping girls who wrapped themselves in her apron, almost knocking her over.

No wonder her cousin was unruffled. Sarah had a home and a family. She had a life. All Darcy had was this photo essay, and so far, it was a bust. Ire sizzled in her chest like Korean barbecue but far less delicious, and she peeled out of the parking lot. She hadn't expected the keys to the kingdom, but she thought she'd get a sit-down with the owner. Instead, she was laughed out of the lobby by a flannel-clad baboon.

Her quads twitched. She desperately needed a run. A run would clear her head and help her regroup. Today was a fluke. Darcy King did not storm around waiting rooms and drive like a crazy person. Darcy King was an accomplished photographer who knew how to talk to people in delicate circumstances. She listened, and she put her subjects at ease. The farmhouse appeared, and the sickening memory of weeping by lamplight closed her throat. Darcy King did not cry in front of strangers!

Seriously, what was the matter? Since she arrived, she'd been an emotional wreck. The tears must be connected to her grandmother. After all, she'd only just gotten to know *Mammi* Leora…to love her…when she lost her. Maybe she never truly mourned. But did she have to start now? The timing was rather inconvenient.

She tucked the car beside the barn and sprinted to her room. In a heartbeat, she was dressed in leggings and out the back door. Slinging a foot onto a stump, she bent over one knee, considering her route. Old Cowan Road was more heavily traveled than she liked. Accustomed to New York City parks, she didn't enjoy dodging traffic. She caught her foot for a quad stretch and settled on the other direction. She'd head past the barn and down the farm lane between fields. Maybe she'd eventually have to veer onto paved roads, but maybe not. She wasn't used to trail running, but her shoes were sturdy, and more than anything, she needed to thoroughly exhaust herself.

She started out fast, darting between fruit trees and along the vegetable garden, where Verna sliced a hoe between rows. Leaping a puddle, she hit the dirt road, setting a quick but comfortable pace. She passed the barn and an open shed housing buggies of varying styles. The scene would make a pretty photo for a calendar or jigsaw puzzle, but she was after more than picturesque. She needed story, and for story, she required access. But how?

Beyond more outbuildings, the scent in the air changed from manure to mud and moss, and she came to a bridge over a rushing creek. She dashed across the slatted surface and down the lane a quarter mile or so until she came to a pleasing, single-story structure at the edge of the woods. It was a modern rustic cabin with natural wood siding and floor-to-ceiling windows. The roof angled up in front, creating a protected overhang beneath which Adirondack chairs and a firepit invited lounging. Once past, she swiveled to check out the side elevation…

And smacked solidly into someone emerging from the woods.

Her ankle turned, and she shrieked, grabbing onto the first thing that presented itself—a muscly arm sheathed in blue. Her shins tangled with long legs, her sneakers bumped boots, and for the briefest second, a hand threaded around her waist, and her feet left the earth. Something hard and plastic dug into her side. Whipping around her head, she smushed her nose into a massive shoulder and sucked in the scent of cotton and…

Please, oh, please don't let that smell be sky.

"Whoa. Easy. Are you all right?"

Did Samuel think she was a horse or a human? She touched down in a rocky rut and stumbled sideways, breathing hard. Her heart whammed against her rib cage with considerably more force than the short jog merited. She planted her hands on her knees and bent over, testing her tweaked ankle. "Why did you burst from the forest like a crazed animal?"

"Why are you in my yard?"

"I'm running, obviously. Or I *was* running." She straightened and, dividing her thick ponytail in two, tugged it tight. Her skin tingled beneath the jogging tank and leggings she knew hugged every curve. Again, she was fully clothed. And again, she felt completely exposed...though a tiny part of her didn't hate it. "And what do you mean *your yard*?"

He opened a hand toward the house. "My workshop. And sometimes my home. I split my time between here and the big house, depending."

So, wait. Where did he actually sleep? "Depending on what?"

"Whether the person staying with my mother is trustworthy. You passed." He shifted focus to the object in his hands, a scuffed and battered transistor radio.

What was an Amish guy doing with a radio? "Are you supposed to have that?"

He settled onto the low, cement porch and fiddled with the antenna which was held together with duct tape. "It's battery operated."

She followed, crunching through river stones surrounding the chairs and firepit. "It plays music."

"I'm a grown man, and this is my house." Plopping his elbows onto his knees, he gazed up with a crooked smile. "What do you plan to do? Tell my mother?"

"I might. She's been very welcoming." She picked up a smooth white rock and tossed it from hand to hand.

"Why didn't you tell her you fixed my car?"

"Why aren't you married?"

She fumbled the rock, and it hit the ground with a crack. "That's intrusive and irrelevant and doesn't make any sense, anyway."

He set the radio to one side and tipped back on his hands, stretching long legs. "Likewise."

His navy work pants were threadbare and dusty at the knees. The heavy, steel-toed boots were weathered, too. Soon, those pants would tear, and his knee would poke through. She swallowed hard. Next, she'd imagine him in a kilt. She shook her head and rotated her foot at the ankle. Still intact, even if her pride wasn't. The disastrous factory visit gnawed at her. She needed the run. "Sorry for crashing into you." She turned to go.

"Why were you running so fast?"

Dropping back her head, she let out a lung-cleansing sigh. He hated her project. If she told him about the morning, then he'd just laugh.

"Visit to Schmucker's go badly?" he asked.

She interlaced her fingers behind her back and dipped down, masking her irritation with a hamstring stretch. "What do you care? And how do you know where I went?"

"Amish grapevine. Nathaniel Schmucker not keen on the idea?"

"I wouldn't know!" A breeze gusted, and with sweat cooling, she shivered, peeking at him from between her knees. "His patronizing, bully of a gatekeeper didn't let me inside."

He snapped to sitting. "Dale Fischer treated you poorly?"

"He called me *girlie* and slammed the door in my

65

face." Coming upright, she rubbed her goose-pimpled arms. She was angry, yes, but more, she was afraid. Sure, this was only her first attempt, but what if she fared no better on her second or third. Good-bye, coveted staff position.

"I see."

Bracing herself, she got a jolt of surprise when he didn't appear smug or mocking. Head bowed and elbows on knees, he almost looked…prayerful.

His lips tucked under at the corners, and he glanced up from clasped hands. "Did you happen to notice solar paneling on Schmucker's roof?"

"I don't think so." She was so anxious upon arrival and so furious when she left, she barely noticed anything. Not good for a photographer whose primary job was observation. "Honestly, I'm not sure."

A bird tweeted in a sound as insistent as a police siren, but instead of a headache, it sparked a glimmer of hope. Searching, she spotted a red-breasted robin hopping through the field. *Cheerily, cheer up, cheer up,* it seemed to say.

Samuel stood and stared off toward the ridge. "Why don't you and I go back tomorrow? I've been meaning to talk to Nat about solar installation. You give me a ride, and in exchange, maybe I can convince him to sit down with you."

Mouth agape, she stared while the robin doubled down on springtime singing. "Why would you do that?"

Shrugging, he bent over and retrieved the radio. "That's not how you treat a woman. Dale Fischer should know better. Besides, just because I don't like what you're doing doesn't mean it shouldn't be done."

She choked back a bitter retort. Sniping at the guy

offering help was about as productive as punching holes in a parachute. Besides, she was mighty curious to know how he thought a woman *should* be treated. "Thank you, Samuel." Her collarbones heated. Speaking his name for the first time felt…familiar. Intimate, even. Had he noticed? Or was he too busy making mental lists of the many ways she and her photography were immoral?

He turned a knob on the radio, and static hissed like a whisper. Startled, he jerked up his head, and a slow grin crept across his face. "You're welcome. Darcy."

With her own name echoing in her ears, she sprinted away, eager to leave him before he left her. A flock of birds took off from the field, wings flapping like the applause of children. In a single moving mass, they shifted in shape—first a cloud, then a heart, and then a sinuous stream like a winding river. She pounded her feet against dirt, and her whirling mind focused. Which did she dread more: the conversation with Nathaniel Schmucker or forty-five minutes in a car with Samuel? Blood rushed to her skin, prickling across her chest and down her spine. She pumped her arms and dashed toward the ridge. The sound of the creek melded with the rush of blood in her ears. Maybe a better question was…which was she more excited about?

Chapter Seven

Less than twenty-four hours later, Darcy slapped on a socialite's smile while inwardly cursing Dale Fischer and the hideous, fake-brick wall.

Samuel shook the manager's beefy hand and said a few words in Pennsylvania Dutch.

Thereupon, Fischer whisked them off to meet the factory owner without once calling her *girlie*. Or *sugar*. Or *babe*.

"How did you do that?" she muttered from her seat at the conference room table.

Interlacing his fingers, Samuel extended his arms until the knuckles cracked. "Dale grew up Amish. I reminded him of certain events from our running around days. He owes me."

Of course, she knew about *Rumspringa* when Amish young people experimented with the world outside their community. She always thought the rebellion was exaggerated for reality TV, but Samuel's gaze held secrets. Maybe she was wrong.

When he'd met her at the car earlier, he made a critical appraisal through the window and frowned.

She bristled. Her appearance was perfectly respectable. Modest, even.

He yanked open the passenger's side door. "Did you bring pie?"

Was every day pie day around here? "No."

"Cookies?"

The morning sun was bright, and the day promised to be mild. She dug in her bag for sunglasses. "I have to bribe them with baked goods?'

He slid into the seat and closed the door soundly. "It's not a bribe. It's a gift. Don't you know the difference?"

At his insistence, they jostled down the farm lane past his studio to the sweet little cottage where his sister Nora and her family lived. He ran inside and returned with a container of Nora's legendary sugar cookies.

The long drive was blessedly normal. Comfortable, even.

Clear of the farm, he reached for the stereo knob. "Mind if I switch on the radio?"

Swallowing more nosy questions about the rules, she shook her head. A country western station wasn't her first choice, but she tuned out the music and silently rehearsed what she'd say if she finagled an audience with Nathaniel Schmucker.

Finally, the moment arrived. Beneath buzzing fluorescent lights in a conference room that might as easily have been in Long Island as in Amish country, Darcy explained her project in deepening detail, reflecting her growing commitment to an endeavor that seemed like it might never get off the ground.

Nathaniel Schmucker was a short, squat man about her father's age, with keen eyes and a contagious laugh. He offered coffee and enjoyed several cookies before politely declaring that while he appreciated Darcy's enthusiasm, his men had a quota.

Samuel nudged the container Nathaniel's way. "Have another. Nora made them."

"Don't mind if I do." The gentleman took a hearty bite, raining delicate golden crumbs.

Leaning back in his chair, Samuel caught his hands behind his head. "I might be wrong, but wasn't Leora Mast your schoolteacher?"

Stubby fingers raked through a salt-and-pepper beard, dislodging cookie bits. "She certainly was. Why?"

In New York society, family connection was everything. Who would have guessed farm country would be the same? Then again, why was she surprised? Doesn't everyone crave connection? Darcy leaned forward, smiling. "She was my grandmother."

"Well, why didn't you say so?" Nathaniel's whole demeanor shifted. Twinkly eyed, he helped himself to another cookie. "Do you know, Teacher Leora taught me arithmetic using nightcrawlers?"

Samuel chuckled. "Sounds about right from what I hear."

"I couldn't figure out subtraction for the life of me. That pesky minus sign was a splinter in my backside. Finally, Teacher Leora sent me down to the creek to dig up twenty worms." He planted both hands on the table and bounced in the squeaky office chair. "I came back with a handful and found her drawing a chalk circle on the big slate stone by the outhouse. 'Put the worms in the circle,' she said, 'and when three wiggle out, you come inside and tell me how many are left.' On she went like that, and in no time, I was multiplying and dividing, too. Eventually ran out of worms and had to use roly-poly bugs. They were less cooperative." Chortling, he slapped a hand on his thigh and gazed through a window at the bustling factory floor. "Where would I be without mathematics?"

Nathaniel had been cordial from the start, but now, he was positively jolly. Sensing an opening, Darcy inhaled deeply. "I have tremendous respect for you and your workers. I won't photograph faces, and I'll stay well out of the way. Our readers will see the quality of your products, and I think they'll learn something. I certainly have."

The lines around Nathaniel's eyes deepened. "I suppose a few pictures won't hurt none." He pushed back his chair. "Come along. I'll tell the men."

Darcy scurried to follow. At the door, she paused and caught Samuel's gaze. *Thank you*, she mouthed.

He dipped his head and smiled.

She managed not to faint. With every passing day, he was more of a puzzle. He escorted her, wrangled access, and even thought to bring up *Mammi* Leora, but he was working an angle, too, right? Childhood memories definitely buttered up the boss. Steeling mushy insides, she whipped around and entered the factory floor.

"Wait there, Samuel," Nathaniel called over one shoulder. "I'll be back in two shakes to hear about this solar business."

Beneath a mile-high ceiling, the skeletons of five campers stood in a row like dinosaurs at the Museum of Natural History. Men swarmed each one, moving in and around one another in a swift, smooth ballet. Colorful tubes coiled from above, connecting heavy-duty tools to a power source. Pneumatic nail guns whiz-popped, and drills whined. The contrast between the men's plain dress and the high-tech machinery was arresting. Fortunately, light filled the room, and she could easily shoot without a flash. She couldn't risk distracting the workers.

At a tidy desk, Nathaniel took up a microphone and cleared his throat. "Don't mean to interrupt, fellas— lunch is in half an hour, after all—but we have a guest. Miss Darcy King will be taking photos for a New York City magazine. She's Leora Mast's granddaughter, for those of you who knew her. Don't you worry—she'll keep her distance and leave your ugly mugs out of the pictures. You won't even know she's here."

Darcy checked her watch. "They eat lunch at ten?"

"Shift starts at five. These fellas are home by two or three in the afternoon to do their farm chores."

"So, they effectively pull double shifts."

Nathaniel puffed out his chest. "Helps to have a stake in the company. We operate on a profit-share model. Our men have more than a daily wage motivating good work. They got ownership." He replaced the microphone and ran a handkerchief over the dusty desk. "Out in those huge factories in Indiana where I learned the trade, boys don't got nothing like that. They run all day, rushing to make their quota so they can get home. Ain't nobody running on my floor. They work fast, but they take pride in what they build. Watch your step now. Parts come flying in from overhead."

Darcy drew a lungful of air, scented with machine oil and sawdust. She pulled out her camera, peered through the viewfinder, and disappeared. Details she hadn't seen with the naked eye came into focus. A bicycle parking area beyond an open garage door with straw hats and orange safety vests looped over handlebars. A stack of unfinished cabinet doors waiting to be stained. A wide metal slide extending from the second level, and a man at the top pushing down tubs of purple and pink electrical wire like they were children on a playground. So many hands. Calloused, work-worn hands running computer-aided design software and operating power saws.

Opaque skylights offered no clear view of the sky, despite the fact the vehicles the men built transported *Englischers* to the great outdoors. Though the workers didn't seem stressed, the energy was different here than at the Rishel's farm where the Lapp boys loped from barn to field and back. These men were focused with no time spared for idle chatter.

From a storage bay to one side, a single man carried the entire side of a camper. The huge piece of fiberglass rested on one shoulder, and the man's arm thrust through what would become a window. Lightweight and backed with foam, the piece was made of no natural material, though plenty of hand-crafted wooden components would comprise the interior. With the man's face concealed, she tracked the walking wall, triggering the shutter in bursts, and jumping when someone brushed past her. She twisted the lens, pulling out for a wide shot.

A second man took hold of the camper wall and flashed a cheeky grin. "Cheese!"

He was young, with chestnut hair in a bowl cut and a gap between his two front teeth. The photo cried out to be taken. Rebecca's words rang in her ears. *I think secretly, they like it.*

The first man mounted a step ladder and popped up above the wall. "Quit messing around and hold her steady."

Her would-be model pulled an "oopsie" face and secured the piece. He nodded toward his partner. "Don't mind Mr. Grumpy over there. He's jealous he ain't as handsome as me."

She couldn't keep in a giggle. "May I ask, do you enjoy the work? Is it satisfying?"

The wall safely anchored, the man came to her, his gaze sliding toward the open garage door. "On a day like today, I'd rather keep bees like my father." He tugged off his work gloves. "But honey don't pay the mortgage. Campers do."

"*Denki*." She shot a hand to her mouth. The Pennsylvania Dutch word just slipped out. How did she know it? Did *Mammi* Leora teach her? Or had she heard Sarah say it? Either way, it felt nice.

"*Gern gschehne*," the man answered.

As if responding to a bell only they could hear, suddenly the workers removed safety glasses and secured power tools. Coolers of all shapes and sizes appeared, and chatting amiably, the crew relaxed around tables by the door.

Darcy dashed up to the mezzanine level and with one hip propped against a railing, she trained her lens on the men. They weren't all Amish. She noted the English guys handled the electrical and heating components while their Amish coworkers focused on assembly and finish carpentry. Now, they sat together, munching on sandwiches, and drinking from tall thermoses.

Frame. Shoot. Frame. Shoot.

She tracked one *Englischer* as he ambled to the open door and lit a cigarette. When young Amish men mingled with the English, what temptations arose?

Away from watchful gazes, they could get in all kinds of trouble. For as good as these factory jobs were, they presented problems, too. Still, farmland was expensive. And "honey don't pay the mortgage."

Deep in conversation, Samuel and Nathaniel emerged onto the floor. The older man clapped Samuel on the shoulder, and the two shook hands.

She shifted the lens and framed the shot, hovering a finger over the shutter button. She wanted to—oh, how she wanted to. But knowing how Samuel felt, she couldn't. He and Nathaniel parted in the manner of men having settled on a deal. With any luck, the visit was as productive for Samuel as for her.

He scanned the room, stopping when he met her gaze.

From high on the mezzanine, she brought the back of one hand to her forehead. " 'Oh Romeo, Romeo, wherefore art thou Romeo?' "

"What?" He darted a look behind and cupped his hands around his mouth. "Who's Romeo?"

With a chuckle, she relaxed the dramatic pose. Did he honestly not know? Or was he teasing her again? "Nobody important." She checked her viewfinder and scrolled through the photos. They were gritty, kinetic, and raw…and strangely, unexpectedly beautiful. She might impress Margo, after all. Satisfied, she jogged downstairs. After an appreciative farewell to Nathaniel, she practically skipped out the door into the May sunshine. Slivers of pink and white peeked between leaves of crabapple trees, ready to explode into flower. The sky was powder-blue, dappled with fluffy white clouds like kids made in drawings. Country music poured from the rental car speakers and rather than scoffing, she felt a madcap urge to sing along. She hated country music. Didn't she? Shifting into Reverse she caught Samuel's gaze.

A smile teased at the edges of his lips.

She nosed onto the two-lane road. "What?"

"You look happy."

Straightening her arms, she hooked her thumbs under the wheel and stretched, flexing her fingers. Given her tendency to weep in his presence, she must appear ecstatic in comparison. But she was happy. Today's work told a fragment of a larger story—a story she was only beginning to understand. "I made some beautiful photos."

He tilted his head to one side and sucked a cheek. "Not everyone would find beauty in a factory floor."

"Maybe not." She waved a hand toward the lush valley dotted with farms. "But when I say beautiful, I don't mean just pretty like these fields or a sunset. The beauty I'm chasing is deeper." She bunched her lips, struggling to express how she approached the work. "Beauty lies in function. What story do ordinary objects tell in context? A bundle of wires or a piece of fiberglass can be transcendent when its purpose is revealed." Catching a breath, she snuck a look. Why even try to explain? But his expression was open and his gaze attentive. She lifted one shoulder. "I'm better with images than words."

"And you can do all that without showing peoples' faces?"

"A face is often the least interesting part of a person." She dropped her gaze to his hands, long-fingered and tanned with neat square nails and thickly calloused palms. They were capable hands. The hands of a builder. "Hands tell a more compelling story."

He shifted, crossing his arms, and tucking his hands beneath them.

Did his hands tell a tale he'd rather hide? Surely, he had secrets. Could she read them in his palms? "Anyway, I can't do anything if I'm not in the room. So, thank you. I was beginning to fear I'd never get my project off the ground."

"Now that Nat's given his blessing, you'll find others more welcoming."

"Let's hope so." She crested a rise, and out of nowhere, an Amish buggy appeared dead ahead. With a start, she slammed the brake pedal, and the seatbelt tightened. Giving the carriage plenty of room, she shifted into the oncoming lane. Fortunately, the road was straight and wide...and she didn't speed over that hill.

Samuel stuck his head out the window and peered into the buggy. "It's Luke Troyer." He waved and settled into the seat, shaking his head. "Luke and I had some wild times in our youth days. Now, he's got forty acres and six *kinner* with another on the way."

"Wild, huh?" In the rearview mirror, Luke Troyer was indistinguishable from every other bearded, straw-hatted man she'd seen. "Like parties and stuff?"

He chuckled. "And stuff."

Scandalized and tantalized, she goosed the gas. "And that's allowed?"

The radio volume dipped, and releasing the knob, he leveled a look. "You're awfully concerned with the rules, Brooklyn."

"I want to learn. Was all this craziness during your Rumspringy thingy? Or was that invented for television shows?"

He barked a laugh. "*Rumspringa. Yah*, it's real. The simple translation is 'running around,' and usually, it's not as crazy as *Englischers* make it out. In my case, however…" He winked.

"Intriguing." Here was a thirty-something dude with a solar panel business, reveling in his glory days like the frat boys who made Williamsburg, Brooklyn, intolerable on Saturday nights. Then again, when Samuel chose to settle down, all revelry would end. No tailgates at the alma mater or drunken poker nights with friends. Maybe the occasional jaunt down memory lane was understandable. Which yet again begged the question, why hadn't he settled down? "What comes after the wild nights of *Rumspringa*?"

"Baptism. Joining church. Marriage." He rubbed a hand over the back of his neck. "In time, most people choose marriage over beer."

The reason for that choice shimmered unspoken, sparking mini glittery rainbows from head to toe. Apparently, the Amish did not…um…fool around. "So now that you're a church member, you don't hit the bars with Luke and your old buddy Dale Fischer?"

The road dipped into a rural village, smaller even than Green Ridge. A post office. A church. A gas station. Beginning to think he wouldn't respond, she peeked his direction.

A tendon in his neck twitched. "I'm not a church member."

His voice was brittle, and the conversation took a hard left. Feeling suddenly on shaky ground, she licked dry lips. What wouldn't she give for an iced latte? "Why not?"

"That, Brooklyn, is a story for another day."

Whoa. Of all the tales she'd sniffed out lately, none was more enticing. Her stomach grumbled. She should have grabbed a cookie at Schmucker's. If she offered to take Samuel for a treat, would today be the day he spilled? Or would he be weirded out by the invitation? Gripping the wheel, she decided to try. "Can I buy you a cupcake? I know your sister has piles of baked goods, but I'd like to thank you. Do you have time?"

"Let me check my schedule." He mimed picking up a cell phone and tapping an invisible screen. He scrolled up. He scrolled down. "I have a two-thirty appointment, but I'm free until then."

Any trace of awkwardness evaporated. In her passenger seat sat a drop-dead gorgeous, total goofball of an Amish man, and she was about to take him on a cupcake date.

Chapter Eight

Darcy ran a hungry gaze over a mouthwatering array of cupcakes, each more exquisitely decorated than the last. As a New Yorker, she'd patronized her share of cupcake joints. Pammy's cupcakes, however, were one of a kind. They were decorated with icing flowers so realistic she almost hated the thought of eating them. Roses, tulips, and daisies splayed atop cupcakes twice the size of typical city ones. She crossed both arms over her belly and muffled a growl.

The woman behind the counter was forty-something, with short blonde curls and the kind of generous figure that made Darcy want a hug. Darcy fluttered her fingers over the display. "I've never seen such gorgeous cupcakes."

"Thank you. I make them myself." Sporting a pink apron with a logo matching the pretty neon sign, the woman yawned and covered her mouth. "Excuse me. My goodness. My day started at four-thirty, and it's catching up. I'm Pammy." She extended a hand bejeweled with turquoise rings. "I don't think I've seen you before." Her gaze shifted to Samuel, and her cheeks went as rosy as her apron. "Or you either, come to mention it. You, I'd remember."

Darcy took her hand. "Darcy King. I'm in town a few weeks for work." She gestured toward Samuel. "I'm actually staying at a new short-term rental my friend Samuel's family runs."

Samuel lifted one cheek, and laugh lines shot from the corners of his eyes. "Nice to meet you."

Good Lord, his voice was smooth as buttercream. Pammy's brows arched a hair as if to ask, *Is he with you?* Darcy barely waggled her head in response. *Yes and no.* The secret language of women really was universal.

With a sage nod, Pammy piled napkins and forks on the tray. "Enjoy!"

Suffused with the buttery scents of baking, Pammy's Place had a homey vibe. Darcy clocked plenty of electrical outlets beneath garlands of cheerful vintage aprons. The quest for power was complete. She could easily imagine plopping at a table, plugging in her devices, and spending a whole afternoon editing photos. Not knowing how Samuel felt patronizing an English establishment, she homed in on a secluded spot in a back corner.

Grabbing the tray, he made for a café table right in the front window. He lowered onto the delicate, curlicued chair, plunked his elbows on the table, and surveyed the joint. "Nice place. I wonder if she's ever considered solar." In a single bite, he dispatched half a sunflower cupcake.

He licked his lips in obvious delight, and an admonition to slow down died on hers. This was a thank-you treat. He could eat as quickly or slowly as he liked. She took a fork to hers, lingering over the first nibble. Cloudlike icing gave way to homemade cake in a delectable combination of sweet and crumbly. She chased it with a slurp of milky iced coffee. The coffee was garden variety. The cupcakes were Garden of

Eden.

"I've been thinking over your project," Samuel began without preamble. "I have some thoughts."

Funny, she didn't remember asking him to think over her project. *Return of the Mansplaining Jerk*, now showing at a cupcake café near you. "Okay…?"

"I believe I'm starting to understand."

Her fork bounced off the table and landed on the tray. "I'm sorry, what?"

Another quarter of cupcake disappeared, and he rubbed together his hands. "You're not the sort of photographer I imagined. I still have concerns, but I want to help. Besides, I'd like you to stay. *Mamm* needs your positive room review on the Internet."

Wow did this family grasp the concept of online customer feedback.

He pushed from the table and crossed one leg over the other in the expansive way of guys taking up two subway seats.

"I'm planning several visits around the community to tell folks about solar power. You're welcome to come and share your project. Many will remember your *Grossmammi* fondly, and they might be willing to help. And if they're glad to see you, they might be even gladder to see me."

Not a critique—an invitation! Her heart soared. "Thank you—"

"But I want to be very clear," he interrupted, lowering his voice. He leaned forward, fixing her with a glacial gaze. "No pictures of peoples' faces. Not a one."

A huff of exasperation puffed her cheeks. "I told you already, Samuel, I won't—"

"I mean it." The muscle in his jaw bunched. "I

heard what you said about how you work. I'm interested. And I trust you."

"I trust you, too." The words popped out, and a fragment of her soul died of embarrassment. She scrabbled for her coffee and tried to drown the mortifying admission with a slurp. Still, she spoke true. He might not have asked for her trust, but he had it.

"Deal?" He thrust out a hand.

With a deep, coffee-infused breath, she shook. His hand was warm but not sweaty. His grip was strong but didn't crush. A Goldilocks handshake—just right. Only raw core strength kept her from oozing under the table like a jellyfish. She gave a quick nod and let go. All business. No oozing. "Deal."

"*Gut.*" He popped in the rest of the cupcake. In an instant, his expression lightened, and he cast a longing look on the display case.

"Can I get you another?"

He ducked his chin. "One with a rose?"

As they finished their treats, chatting more like old friends than new business partners, Darcy relaxed like she hadn't with a man for years. With no need to pretend she'd read the latest article in *The New Yorker* or dined at Brooklyn's hippest eatery, with no text messages buzzing or work calls demanding "just one second," with Samuel's focus squarely on her, she bloomed like a buttercream flower on a cupcake.

The bell above the door jingled, and a mustachioed mailman in shorts and a vest bebopped inside.

"Hidey-ho, Pammy." He plunked a fistful of mail atop the counter and leaned on one jaunty elbow. "How's my favorite cupcake...baker?"

"Oh my gosh," Darcy whispered. "The mailman

has the hots for Pammy." She eyeballed the fourth finger of Pammy's left hand. No ring.

Samuel blinked, doe-eyed. "Who?"

"Shh!" She scooted her chair partway around the table for a better view. "The mailman likes the cupcake lady. Look."

Pammy casually flipped through the letters, tossing aside junk. "About dead on my feet, Al. I need an assistant."

Darcy gawked. Pammy was oblivious, too.

Al planted a palm on the counter. "My niece Bailey's looking for a job. She's a real hard worker— got the old Raffensburger stick-to-itiveness like her uncle."

"I remember Bailey. I taught her in Sunday School years ago." Glancing up from the mail, Pammy gave Al's hand a quick squeeze. "You tell her to stop by. Thank you."

The bald spot atop Al's head pinkened. "I most certainly will." He knocked on the counter and headed out the door. "Tomorrow, I'm taking a cupcake break!"

Pammy tore open an envelope and fished out the contents. "I'll believe it when I see it."

"What did I tell you?" Darcy hissed. "Totally in love."

Samuel swiveled, following Al's retreat. "You're awfully confident, Brooklyn."

Nibbling her bottom lip, Darcy watched Al dance a jig across the street. "I know a man in love when I see him."

Samuel came back around. "And have you seen the face of love so often?"

Darcy felt her brows take the slow elevator to her

hairline. A neck blush threatened, and she sipped a long drag of icy coffee. He might have dropped a smooth come-on, but he'd never cruised a midtown bar at cocktail hour. She was a professional at fielding passes. "Some." She balled her napkin and tossed it onto the tray. "Have you?"

"Some." Holding her gaze, he ran a thumb through a glob of icing and licked it clean. "I guess time will tell if you're seeing it now."

A ribbon of longing unspooled deep inside, but she concealed it behind an uptown veneer. Park Avenue doesn't crack. "I suppose it will." Gazing from beneath her lashes, she speared the last bite of cupcake and savored it even more slowly.

His Adam's apple bobbed. He finished his water in one gulp.

Tossing her ponytail, she rose and gathered the trash. Was he joking, flirting, or simply naïve? Whatever the game, she was ready. She'd uncover his past well before she breathed a word about her own.

****

Darcy laced up her sneakers and took off down the farm lane, bathed in golden-hour sunlight. The first mile was always a slog, especially with Pammy's cupcake bouncing around her belly. This sugar binge had to stop. Still wary, she'd skipped family dinner again, opting for a grocery store salad in her room before heading out on a run. After pie and cupcakes, the greens had gone down like a detoxifying tonic.

Despite the recent collision with Samuel, her ankle was fine, and she sprinted the half mile to his studio. With casual disinterest, in case he happened to see, she checked out the façade. It was as perfectly proportioned as the man who inhabited it. What was it like inside? Cluttered and dated like the farmhouse or as spare and lovely as the attic suite? Picking up her pace, she focused on the path. Last night, she cobbled together decent mileage by staying on dirt roads, but she needed to watch her step. An injury would end her photo essay in a snap.

Blood sang in her ears, drowning the sounds of twilight. When she ran, she rarely listened to music. In the city, she liked to be aware of everyone and everything. Here, in the country, taking in the landscape was more than enough to occupy her mind while her body worked. The clouds had dissipated, and the sky was a clear, blue vault like the ceiling of Grand Central Station, soon to be studded with stars. Her heart pounded, and she felt her shoulders ease.

After a day with Samuel, she was coiled like a giant spring. Quick and funny, he kept her on her toes, offering opinions on all manner of topics while freely admitting what he didn't know. When was the last time she met a guy like that? Squinting into the dusk, she turned a corner, entering a section over-canopied by trees. Lest she forget, though he made her insides sizzle, he was also Amish, and while not hitched to a proper Plain woman yet, he would be in time. Making out by the firepit was so not happening. Thank goodness for running.

The lane dead-ended in a hidden pasture that appeared unplowed. Breathing hard, she gazed over spiky weeds and knee-high grasses. Even as she pushed her body to numb exhaustion, squishy, zingy feelings she'd rather not examine flooded her chest before blasting out her fingers like laser guns. *Pew-pew-pew!*

She shook herself, and her ponytail lashed her cheeks. No complicated gloopy stuff allowed. She was here on a mission, and, flirty or no, Samuel disapproved of her life's work. Full stop. Besides, she had no time for romance. Her role as a staff photographer waited. She only had to sprint up and grab it. Kicking up dust, she spun and raced toward the farm and her peaceful attic oasis.

Directly above the room where he sometimes slept.

After a mile, she approached Nora and Tucker's house. Equally as pleasing as Samuel's, the single-story home might have been built for a house-flipping show instead of an Amish farm. It had a rustic ranch vibe, with a chunky wood railing spanning a generous front porch. Cheerful flower baskets hung beneath a red tin roof, and a vinelike plant coiled up a trellis on one end. The place was quiet when she first passed, but as she approached now, she spotted a figure on the steps.

Garbed in an amethyst dress, Rebecca bowed her black-capped head and scribbled with intent.

Darcy slowed to a stop. "Hi."

With a quick breath, Rebecca jerked up, and upon seeing her, gave a friendly wave. "Oh, hello. Pumpkin and I came outside for some peace. Didn't we, kitty?"

Curled atop Rebecca's feet, a big orange tabby lifted its chin.

Rebecca obliged with a vigorous scratch.

The breeze kicked up, wafting the tang of fertilized fields, and drawing goose bumps on sweaty skin. Darcy rubbed her bare arms. The eastern sky had deepened to azure, giving way to yellow, orange, and coral over the western ridge. She gazed out over the fields. "I'm not used to such quiet nights."

"I expect not." Rebecca scrunched her nose and stared at the sky. "I'd like to visit New York City someday."

Dewy grass tickling her ankles, she ambled toward the porch. "It's very different from here."

"I long for different from here."

Darcy swallowed a gasp. Though she was a wee bit obsessed with their rules, as someone so annoyingly observed, she wasn't sure the comment was, well, kosher.

"I'd settle for Colorado." Rebecca waggled her wrist, tapping the lap desk with her pen.

Darcy opened her mouth to ask why Colorado, when from inside came the screech of an unhappy child or maybe two, and a male voice singing "Ain't Nothing but a Hound Dog." She felt her mouth fall open and snapped it closed. Nothing she experienced that day remotely resembled her expectations of Amish life.

A dark silhouette passed in front of the window, swaying and bouncing. The crying only intensified.

"Children are a blessing. They're also quite loud." Rebecca dropped her pen and folded her hands. "I suppose life could be worse. If *Mamm* married Mervin Zook as he wanted, then I'd be caring for dozens of horrid Zooks instead of sitting outside writing a letter to Uncle Jonas. I'd have no time to even dream of going to Colorado."

This family kept getting more and more intriguing. She mounted the steps and waved a questioning hand.

Rebecca scootched to one side, dislodging the cat.

"Colorado?" Darcy sat and leaned against a post. The cat snaked around her ankles with velvety stealth. "Why?"

Rebecca danced her fingertips over the stationery. "Uncle Jonas lives there. You haven't heard about our family tragedies, have you?"

Was Rebecca being overdramatic? Neither Samuel nor Verna gave the slightest hint of secret family woes. Was the tragedy to do with Samuel's church status or the mysterious Ohio photographer? Darcy pulled her knees to her chest. "No."

With a quick glance over one shoulder, Rebecca leaned in. "They are multitudinous. My father and Uncle Jonas's first wife were killed by a logging truck when I was three. *Mamm* was in the buggy, too, and was gravely injured. It's terribly tragic, of course, but I don't remember any of it." Her rosy lips sloped into a frown. "I don't even remember what *Daed* looked like."

Darcy's stomach knotted tighter than her sneaker laces. In a culture with no photographs, how would a child remember a parent who died years ago? "I'm sorry. That must be hard."

"Very. But *Mammi* Verna says difficulty is a miracle in its first stage. If *Mamm* didn't have a hip replacement a few years back, she never would have signed up for tap dance classes with the English old people and met Tucker." She shuddered. "I might have become a Zook."

A fussy squawk raised hairs on the back of Darcy's neck, but the crying abated. Scrambling to make sense of the story, she extended both legs and gave her hamstrings a good squeeze. "Your mother dances?"

A smile flickered across Rebecca's elfin face. "Not officially," she whispered, beckoning Darcy closer. "But, sometimes I hear singing, and I catch her and Tucker acting suspicious, and I know they've been dancing like they used to. My mother laughs a lot more since she learned to dance."

Privacy in a bustling Amish household must be at a premium. How could one keep anything secret? "I heard Tucker joined the Amish. Is that common?"

The cat leaned against Rebecca's hip and flopped, curling into a tight ball.

Rebecca shook her head. "Tucker is exceptional. He was a famous singer, but that life left him empty, so he came to *Gott* and to us. He also loves my mother very much. Isn't it strange how something awful can lead to something *gut*?" She set aside the letter and dragged the cat into her lap. "I should be thankful *Mamm* didn't leave the Amish like Uncle Jonas, but I can't help but wonder what life would be like. For starters, I'd still be in school." She sighed. "Uncle Samuel says if *Mammi* Verna had another child jump the fence, she might have a heart attack like *Dawdi* Wayne. He was my grandfather."

In the fading light, Rebecca's skin was luminous. Though possessed of childlike innocence, she was a teenager and utterly unlike any Darcy knew. Her thoughts tumbled out with no trace of self-consciousness. She was an open book but given how readily she spoke, perhaps a book seldom read. A question Darcy had no business entertaining burned on her tongue, and given the odds Rebecca would answer, she couldn't hold back. "Does your Uncle Samuel ever talk of leaving?"

Rebecca dropped a kiss between furry ears. "He doesn't have to. He's like Uncle Jonas. The wanting to go shines in his eyes." She met Darcy's gaze. "Don't you see it?" Her fingers stroked over the cat's head and down its back. "But he has to take care of *Mammi* Verna now that Jonas married an *Englischer* and has his own family."

Verna Rishel seemed quite capable of taking care of herself. Darcy bit back a comment on women's independence. Rebecca was a child of her culture, and Darcy came to observe, not to correct.

The girl released a handful of cat hair into the breeze. "But you and I both know how enterprising *Mammi* Verna is."

Darcy stood down. No lesson required. "We surely do."

So, Samuel's brother flew the coop and married an outsider no less. She knew little about Amish culture, but she was pretty sure quitting was only slightly easier than getting out of organized crime. What would happen if Samuel ever chose to go? Or did his brother truly score the only ticket out of town? "Do you ever see your Uncle Jonas?"

Rebecca gazed at the letter with downcast eyes. "Less than I'd like. *Mammi* Verna writes every week. I know she wishes he'd move home. He's shunned, but he and Tessa visit more often than at first. Tessa grew up in Green Ridge, and they stay at her family's house, which appeases the bishop, even though *Mammi* looks sad when they drive away at night. You should hear what *Mammi* says about the bishop when she thinks I'm not listening."

Her eyes shone with impish glee, and Darcy fought the urge to giggle. Rebecca's spirit was infectious.

"Anyway, last Christmas, Jonas stayed three whole weeks, and I played with my cousins every day. For English *kinner*, they are surprisingly clever and well-behaved, even though they all have red hair."

Darcy thought her family was complicated. The Rishels were practically a soap opera. Still, a bustling family holiday at the farm with brothers and sisters and cousins galore must be…magical. "I bet your family Christmases are nice."

"The food is delicious. My mother's pies are legendary." Rebecca scratched the cat's ears. "You should eat dinner with us tomorrow."

Knees cracking, she grabbed the railing and pulled to standing. The top of her left foot snugged in one hand and her quad lengthened in a stretch. "I might."

"After all, it's included in the price of the room."

Excellent point. She planted her left foot and grabbed hold of the right. If yoga had taught her anything, it was the need for balance. "I better run back before dark."

Rebecca peered down the road in the direction Darcy came. "Who's chasing you?"

She let out a breathy chuckle. The girl was joking, right? "No one."

Rebecca's smooth brow crinkled. "If no one chases you, why do you run?"

Her heel thunked onto the step, and she bent over her knee. "Running clears my head. It quiets my thoughts and helps me feel less anxious."

Rebecca nodded. "Like prayer."

Darcy straightened and drank in dewy nighttime air. How was the girl so wise? "I suppose. Goodnight, Rebecca."

"*Guder owed.*"

Darkness closed in, and Darcy ran, leaving behind the singular girl who seemed to see through her skin to her soul. Blood cycled from heart to fingertips and back, while crickets played an endless song of spring. Settling her mind, she focused inside. What if she ran toward and not away? Toward peace, not away from stress. Toward goodness. Toward wholeness.

What if running really was more like prayer?

Chapter Nine

The next morning, Darcy slid into a chair at the kitchen table and buried her hands in the fleecy kangaroo pocket of her college sweatshirt. Rain pelted the windows, and wind rattled the glass. The night had been chilly, and she emerged reluctantly from a cocoon of quilts, lured by the smell of bacon. By nature, Darcy was an early riser, but she had yet to arrive downstairs before the others. At seven-thirty, she had the sense she was well past family breakfast and at risk of being labeled a layabout.

Verna dropped homemade biscuits onto a cooling rack beside a basket of fresh brown eggs. "*Guder mariye*. Can I fix you bacon and eggs?"

Every day on the farm, Darcy was served a hot cooked breakfast. Accustomed to light morning fare and fonder of savory than sweet, she skimped on pancakes, muffins, and coffee cake, but bacon was her kryptonite. "Yes, please. *Denki*."

Verna smiled over one shoulder. "Were you cold last night?"

She stirred thick cream into a mug of steaming coffee. "I piled on extra quilts. It was cozy."

"I prefer sleeping cold, too." Verna grabbed a mixing bowl from the rack and wiped it dry. "How's your stay? Is the room *gut*?"

The crack of eggs and the swish of a wire whisk

made the kitchen even homier on a gloomy spring morning. Though weak, the coffee traced a steamy path to Darcy's belly, and she wrapped both hands around the mug. "It's lovely—clean and quiet and so well appointed. How will you get word to prospective guests?"

"I believe the bishop will permit Internet advertisements, but I'll need help." Verna dumped the eggs into a frying pan and leaned a hip against the counter. "Until then, I'll hand out flyers at Sarah's shop and the Farmers' Market."

Darcy perked up. A design challenge combined with an opportunity to help someone who had already given her so much? Perfection. "I'd be happy to take photos and mock up a simple brochure. The pictures can be used for an online listing, too."

Verna dropped perfectly browned bacon onto a plate. "I couldn't possibly trouble you."

"It's no trouble at all."

Scrambled eggs mounded next to the bacon followed by a biscuit, and Verna set the wide, shallow bowl at Darcy's place. "Can I take it off the cost of the room?"

She waved away the offer. "You've been so welcoming. Consider the flyer my gift."

Verna's round cheeks lifted. "*Denki* kindly."

Darcy could picture her as a younger woman. Though no warmer and fuzzier than Isabelle King, she must have been a force to be reckoned with and a comfort to her husband and children. She was still a force today.

"If she could see you now, your *Mammi* Leora would be proud." Verna piled the remaining biscuits into a container and snapped on the lid. "I don't abide silly notions of spirits walking among us, but I'd like to believe she does see."

Darcy's throat tightened. Blinking back tears, she forked up pillowy eggs and let them dissolve on her tongue.

Samuel burst in from outside. Rain spattered his heavy work coat and dripped from his hat brim. He stopped short, grinning. "*Mamm*, did you make the *Englischer* cry again?"

Darcy sniffed and wiped her nose on her sleeve. "I'm not crying."

"Good. Because I need a ride to the hospital."

The cast iron skillet clanged into the sink. Verna blanched. "Are you hurt?"

Snatching a piece of bacon, Samuel yanked out a chair next to Darcy, spun, and straddled it. "*Nee*. I'm meeting Doctor Richard about solar installation at his medical clinic. He's visiting a patient this morning and said we could talk afterward. I'd thought to drive myself, but…" He glanced toward the window and back at Darcy. "Maybe you could take some pictures?"

Verna grabbed a dishrag and set about scrubbing. "Who's in the hospital?"

"Esther King. Dr. Richard talked her into surgery for her gall bladder." He caught Darcy's gaze. "She runs a farmstand and won't take kindly to missing the spring season."

Darcy perked up. "King? I wonder if we're related?"

"Now I think on it, I believe she's Leora's husband's cousin. Your *Grossdaddi's* family went Mennonite well before Leora left." Verna dunked the skillet into the rinse pan. "We didn't have so many surgeries and whatnot in my day." Her lips pinched tight, and she hefted the skillet into the drying rack. "But, if Doctor Richard says so, who am I to argue?"

Buzzing, Darcy popped in a final bite of biscuit. "Give me a minute to get ready." Moments later, hair tidied and teeth brushed, she was rushing across the second-floor landing when the hiss of a male voice from downstairs brought her skidding to a stop.

"She's a photographer."

He said it like she was an arsonist. In her mouth, the fresh minty taste soured.

Verna responded in quick, decisive Pennsylvania Dutch.

The language was a curious blend of soft and hard, but coming from Verna now, it was granite. Torn between dashing to the attic and staying put, Darcy wrapped her arms around her middle. She was raised better than to eavesdrop. She was also raised not to talk about people behind their backs. Certainly not when they were in the same house.

"She is *not* one of us," Samuel shot back.

Darcy hugged herself tighter. Their day yesterday had been flirty and fun. She even dared to think he might like her. Had she misjudged completely?

"Her grandmother was my schoolteacher," Verna said.

Samuel's snort was a punch in the gut. Darcy knew she should stop listening. She knew, but she couldn't make herself go.

"Do you know how to make a website?" Verna went on. "Tucker showed me some at the library. They are very smart."

Darcy edged toward the staircase and peered down through the narrow opening.

The sofa groaned, and Samuel's legs sprawled over the armrest. "Tucker could figure it out."

Verna plunked her hands on her hips and loomed over her offspring. "She's a professional from New York City, and we need all the help we can get. The cost of keeping up the farm has stretched us to the limit."

His legs jerked. "She gets under my skin."

"A blind man could see that, *Soh*."

All elbows and knees, Samuel clamored to standing. "She thinks she knows everything."

Darcy drew back and inched toward the attic stairs.

"Well." Verna sniffed. "That makes two of you."

Outrage fueled Darcy's flight upstairs, and steely determination filled her rainboots as she stomped back down. Samuel casually met her at the door as if he hadn't just bad-mouthed her to his mom. What were they? Middle schoolers? She breezed past and opened the best umbrella money could buy. After trashing two dozen drugstore models, any New Yorker worth her salt got a quality umbrella. Striking off toward the car, Darcy did not share hers. Samuel was thoroughly drenched by the time she *remembered* to unlock the passenger side door.

He opened his mouth but then closed it and said nothing.

Didn't have to be a genius to surmise he'd been overheard. Clearly, he only proposed their arrangement in hopes memories of *Mammi* Leora would butter up reluctant solar customers. No more cupcakes. No more banter. This relationship was strictly business, and she'd suck as much or more from it than he.

The radio blared country music. She switched it off and sped down the two-lane road. Fog shrouded the ridges, and water puddled in ruts from buggy wheels.

Rounding a bend next to Sarah's quilt shop, she felt the eerie slow-motion lift of hydroplaning. Rain jackhammered the windshield, and she pumped the brake, steering into the skid like a pro. Who said city girls couldn't drive?

He pressed one hand to the ceiling and gripped the center console with the other. "What happened to the first car? The hybrid?"

She shrugged. In point of fact, it was fidgety and over-engineered, and she couldn't rely on finding somewhere to plug it in. Or someone to help her start it, for that matter.

"I liked it," he said.

"Feel free to rent one the next time you take a trip." She clamped down on her bottom lip. Excessive snark was unbecoming. Grimacing, she jammed the turn signal and swung onto the main road.

St. Luke's Hospital was surprisingly modern. A glassy atrium led to a waiting area with sleek couches and chairs.

At the front desk, a chatty volunteer directed them to Esther King's room on the third floor.

The last time she'd been inside a hospital was to visit her mother after a "minor surgical procedure" upon which Isabelle refused to elaborate. Filled with flowers from her many friends and associates, the otherwise sterile room was profoundly uncomfortable. An air of sickness made Darcy uneasy, and she stayed the minimum time required to satisfy her filial duty.

Esther's room couldn't have been more different. At the head of the bed, a handsome dark-haired doctor swiped the screen of a digital tablet. His patient sat erect, her watery, gray eyes bright and her cheeks touched with pink. An IV bag hung at her side next to a monitor that beeped with reassuring regularity. About a dozen other Amish, from bundled babies to gray-bearded gents, occupied every available surface, from the foot of the bed to several folding chairs, to the windowsill. No phones buzzed. No television droned. All eyes focused on the doctor. Darcy yearned to take out her camera but held back. She had to tread carefully.

The doctor gave his patient's shoulder a gentle squeeze. "You're recovering beautifully, Esther. We'll have you home the day after tomorrow."

Relief lit every face. The baby cooed, and white-capped heads bobbed as several conversations broke out at once.

Catching sight of her and Samuel, the doctor held up a finger. He jotted a note with a stylus and tucked the device into a pocket. With a quick word to his patient, he met them at the door.

Samuel extended a hand. "Dr. Richard, this is Darcy King, the New York photographer I told you about. She's staying in *Mamm's* new guest room for a few weeks."

The doctor sanitized his hands and shook, his gaze toggling from Samuel to her and back, before landing squarely and lingeringly on Darcy.

The look was loaded. In fact, it was just shy of a winky face emoji. What was that about?

"I'm Richard Bruce. Welcome to Green Ridge.

King?" He waved the stylus toward his patient. "Any relation?"

She nodded. "Mrs. King is a distant cousin. Would you mind introducing us? I'll happily explain my project, and if everyone is agreeable, I'd love to get a few shots of you with the family. I'll conceal faces, of course. I'm committed to depicting the Amish without violating their principles."

He handed her a card. "You can email me the photo release."

The charming doctor made introductions with grace. Not that she cared, but her mother would adore this guy. She checked his ring finger. Married...figured. The guy oozed *Eau de Catch* along with antiseptic and aftershave.

Amid hushed conversations in Pennsylvania Dutch, Esther beckoned. "Come closer. I want to see you."

Sidling through the crowd, Darcy moved to the head of the bed. The rain had stopped, and diffuse light from the window cast a glow over the woman's papery skin. "I'm so pleased to meet you, Mrs. King."

"Call me Esther. Oh, but you look like Leora. Doesn't she, Mary?"

A plump woman paused in her mending and studied Darcy's face. "*Yah*. The hair."

Esther patted the bed. "Now, sit and tell me why anyone would want a picture of an old woman."

Minding the IV, Darcy perched and once again explained her photo essay. Bolstered by her success at Schmucker's, she laid out her request in thoughtful detail. "This project is special to me," she said in conclusion. "The idea that I might include my family makes it even more so."

Esther's eyelids fluttered closed, and her cheeks went slack.

Had she fallen asleep? Or worse? Darcy darted a look to the doctor who'd shifted attention to his phone. Right. Phones were still a thing.

Esther opened her eyes and turned to a lanky, bearded man sitting on the windowsill. "Jacob?"

The man gave a gentle nod.

Esther lifted her chin and flapped a hand in the doctor's direction. "Put that gizmo away, Doctor Richard, and come have your picture taken."

"*Denki.*" Alight with fizzy excitement, Darcy prepped her camera. "Everyone, please continue as you were. You'll hardly notice I'm here." She raised the viewfinder, nestled the camera against her cheek, and disappeared.

At some point, the doctor and Samuel withdrew into the hallway.

She was distantly aware of hushed male voices below the chorus of Pennsylvania Dutch. Soon, even those sounds disappeared, and all she heard was her own breathing and the camera's mechanical clicks and whirrs. Compared to the factory, the scene was intimate. Despite the institutional setting, it was homey.

Young hands settled atop stooped shoulders, and a straw met dry, cracked lips. A plump pillow nestled behind a white prayer cap. A mop-haired boy bent over a picture book.

Emerald skirts and hospital linens. The flash of knitting needles and metal bedrail.

What's the story?

Slatted shadows crept across a straw hat beside a half-eaten tray of hospital food. Modern medical equipment blinked unendingly in the background. No one fidgeted. No one left.

Frame. Shoot. Frame. Shoot. Frame. Shoot.

Gentle patience. Quiet faith.

What's the story?

Crouching in the doorway, she felt a presence at her back. It was steady…alert…waiting.

The story is love.

****

An hour later, in the hospital parking lot, Darcy eased the car behind a buggy hitched to a lamppost. Thick clouds tickled the ridges with wispy fingers. The rain picked up again. Her heart and memory chip were full, but her brain spiraled. Just who was the man in the passenger seat? Was he adversary or advocate, friend or opportunist? "You knew I was related to Esther King when you invited me, didn't you?"

"I figured as much."

Safely beyond the horse, she accelerated. "I heard you earlier. I know you disapprove of everything I am. Why help at all?" She shot him a look. If he was surprised, he didn't show it.

"I don't disapprove of you—"

"You disapprove of my work," she bit out.

"That's different."

"No, it's not. I am my work." She thumped a hand against her chest. "Work is the most important thing in my life."

"Well." He shifted and gazed out the window. "That's sad."

Spluttering, she ratcheted the wipers to high. "I don't need your pity."

"But you do need my help."

"Right back at you, buddy." Spraying water like a cab driver, she yanked the wheel and rounded onto the highway, heading for open road.

He glanced toward the farm in the opposite direction but said nothing.

If he didn't like where she was going, he could find his own way home. The wiper blades squeaked, and Green Ridge's pathetic commercial strip appeared. A dollar store. A carpet shop. A fast-food joint. Blink and she'd miss it. She stopped at a traffic light next to a sprawling Pennsylvania Dutch restaurant with two tour buses and scads of cars in the parking lot. Decorated with blood-red hearts and canary-yellow birds, a giant hex sign on the roof was the only slash of color in a sidewalk-gray world. The tourist trap was as authentic as the replica New York City on the Las Vegas strip. On a whim, she veered off the road and drove the length of the building.

Beneath an overhang, a family posed for a picture, their faces shoved through openings in a wooden cutout of a cartoon Amish family. #padutch #amishcountry #beards.

Gross.

Regardless of how she felt about Samuel, the exploitation of his culture was icky. Did that restaurant reflect anything authentic about the Amish? Were the Amish-made products it sold truly made by Amish hands? She pulled into the parking lot, grabbed her camera, and shot. Through the rain-streaked window, the people were blurry. She played with focus and light, sharpening the painted Amish figures and obscuring faces in raindrops. Even catching the reflection of her camera in the glass.

Finally, the family dashed to their minivan.

She quickly scrolled through the images, flagging the most interesting shots.

"May I see?"

So now he was the photography police? She jerked up her head. "Don't worry. I hid their faces."

He gazed, unblinking. "I'm not."

His expression was as open as his niece's the previous night. Still, unwilling to surrender the camera, she rested her forearm on the center console and tipped toward him, angling the digital display. His arm snugged against hers, warm and solid. His shoulder grazed her jacket. She whiffed oatmeal soap and rain-dampened wool, and her irritation ebbed as affection lapped at her belly. Traitorous insides! Could they not stay strong for forty-five seconds?

Click. Click. Click. One after another, photos flashed on screen.

She heard his breath, slow and deep, and the occasional soft sound when an image was particularly good. And he did clock the good ones. Even an untrained eye instinctively recognized quality. Or perhaps just this very perceptive untrained eye.

The restaurant photos ended, giving way to the final shot in the hospital. She hesitated. "Would you like to see more?"

He nodded.

A strand of unruly hair grazed her temple. Her breath snagged. He was so attentive. So single-minded on nothing but her work. Her heart seemed to push against her ribs, straining toward him—a man who, despite his misgivings, focused solely on her.

The windows clouded, and she swallowed a giggle.

Not exactly the glass-steaming scenario passersby might imagine. When she came to the final shot, she inched back into her seat. Now that he'd seen her work, what would he say?

With his coat sleeve, he swiped a clean arc on the window and stared out.

Maybe he'd say nothing. He'd likely never seen photos like hers. Or maybe he had to think a bit. Nothing was wrong with thinking before speaking. More people could stand to adopt the habit, especially after viewing art. She inhaled patience and waited.

The camera's power switch toggled smoothly off. The display went dark.

"A woman took my picture once. At the Ohio County Fair." He shrugged out of his coat and reached a long arm to toss it into the back seat. "I was nineteen or twenty at the time."

The Ohio photographer? Maybe she should drive. Conversation in motion often flowed more freely. She shifted into gear and dodged gaping potholes filled with rainwater. In minutes, the strip mall gave way to countryside, fields replacing parking lots as the streetlights faded.

"My friends and I were messing around. We'd spent all afternoon trying to convince a group of Amish girls to come party with us at the lake. We bought everything you could imagine on a stick—corn dogs, candy bars, chicken. We took them on rides and threw balls at milk jugs for prizes. But when we were ready to go, they laughed and ran off. Seconds later, the photographer appeared."

Fixing her gaze on the road, she didn't dare twitch for fear he'd clam up, and she'd never hear the story.

Curiosity crackled in her chest, and for no good reason, she turned right at a quiet crossroads. She didn't know why, but the road felt familiar, like she'd ridden on it in a dream.

Samuel tilted his head to one side, and his neck cracked. "She was young and pretty like you, with a big smile and a bigger camera. Yeah, I was impressed by that camera. I wanted to take it apart and see how worked."

Note to self: don't leave Samuel alone with a camera. Side note to self: he thinks I'm pretty. She dragged her teeth over her bottom lip and let the compliment sparkle across her collarbones.

He opened the glove box and closed it again, then rooted in the door compartment before pulling out a stray packet of ketchup. "'I'm new in town,' she said. 'Just visiting my aunt. Can I take your picture?' The fellas hooted, and after being jilted by those Amish girls, I felt like a pretty big man. She knew pictures weren't allowed. She said, 'None of my friends in California believe you guys are real. I'll show them the photo, and then I'll tear it up. I promise.'"

Another crossroads. A bridge over a narrow stream. A jig into the woods and up a hill. She drove in silence, giving him space.

He tossed the ketchup from hand to hand. "I leaned against my buggy like I'd seen guys on car magazines do. Six months later, that photo was on the cover of a romance book at the big box store in town."

She felt her jaw unhinge. No wonder the guy hated photographers. He'd fallen prey to the worst possible kind. She pulled into an overgrown country lane and slammed on the brakes. "But that's illegal. You could have sued."

"Amish don't believe in suing." He gave a bitter laugh and dropped the ketchup into a cup holder. "But they do believe in public shaming. I had to make a confession before the whole church congregation." He dug his fingers into his thighs until his knuckles went white. "Not my finest hour, Brooklyn."

She tipped toward him, yearning to wrap him in her arms. She wanted to apologize for every intrusive idiot who ever pointed a lens at the Amish, and yet she cringed with borrowed shame. Was she any different from that woman? She stared through the windshield at the burnt-out shell of a farmhouse. The ruined building sparked a blurry childhood memory, but she pushed it aside. "I'm so sorry. That photographer should never have done that."

"I was an idiot. I got what I deserved." He raked a hand through his hair and squeezed the back of his neck. "I tell you this because the difference between the picture that woman took and what's on your camera is so vast, I don't understand how both can be called photographs. What you do is…something else."

Relief whooshed from her body, and she released the steering wheel. She *was* different. He looked, truly looked, and he saw. With one simple sentence, he acknowledged her and her work in a way no one, not her parents nor her peers nor even her mentors, ever had. She met his gaze, hoping her expression spoke the gratitude she couldn't find voice to say.

Ever so slowly, he tucked one finger beneath her chin and lifted it level with his. "Fifteen years ago, a photographer took something I can never get back. But you take nothing from people. Your pictures make them seem bigger, and that's a gift."

Her lungs seized, and she swallowed against thick emotion that welled every single time she was alone with this guy. Now, though, the thickness wasn't sour. It tasted like joy. "Thank you," she whispered.

As if caught in a sudden wind, he swayed. His lips came perilously close, and she felt the gentle puff of his breath on her cheek. She ran her gaze over his mouth, already tasting his kiss.

But then he stilled. And he lowered his hand and sat back in the seat. "Where are we?"

She turned a fuzzy gaze on the collapsed roof and soot-blackened siding of a home she once knew so well. Bitter replaced sweet on the back of her tongue. "*Mammi* Leora's house. It burned down, and I never even knew."

Chapter Ten

Who says a cupcake can't be breakfast? Spread out
on a table at Pammy's the next morning, Darcy plugged
in her laptop and connected to the Wi-Fi. The previous
day's storm had blown through, and the morning was
sunny and brisk. Several other parties apparently found
cupcakes a suitable breakfast, too, and the cheery café
was bustling. She deserved an indulgence. Yesterday
had been way more than she expected. Between the
hospital shoot, Samuel's confession, and the discovery
of *Mammi* Leora's house, she'd tossed and turned for
much of the night before finally falling into a restless
sleep, interrupted by unsettling dreams she forgot
immediately upon wakening.

She nibbled moist chocolate cake and watched as
images uploaded to the computer. Satisfaction as sweet
as her morning coffee lifted her cheeks. Samuel was
right. The photos were good. His comment about
making her subjects seem bigger touched her deeply.
Wasn't that every artist's goal? Use something small to
tell a larger story? See the universe in a blade of grass?
Reveal the divine inside every being? She thought back
to parables and Sunday School lessons. Weren't they
exactly the same?

So, what was her perspective on the Amish in
modern life? Slowly, she scrolled through the images.
Every day, the project felt more and more personal.

After all, it was her family's story, too. She wanted to get it right. On impulse, she grabbed her phone and pulled up her father's contact. He'd be in the office, but maybe he'd pick up.

The call instantly went to voicemail. "You've reached Lloyd King. I'm unavailable at the moment. Please leave a message at the tone."

Her father recently replaced his phone, and the recording was recent. Deep and assertive, his voice was the same she'd heard all her life—a voice you'd trust with your most sensitive legal issues. But she clocked a new breathiness and the slightest wobble in tone. Her father was getting older. She sighed. They all were.

"Hey, Daddy. Just checking in from Green Ridge. I don't know what you and Mom were talking about— they not only have cafés, but they have cupcake cafés. Anyway, I'm fine. Settling in." Through the window, she spotted Al, the mailman, dashing across the sidewalk, his mustache neatly groomed. Would Pammy notice? "So, I found my way to *Mammi* Leora's house yesterday. Were you aware it burned down? Did Aunt Mary or Uncle Mark ever mention? Okay, well, say hi to Mom." She ended the call right as the bell jingled.

Al trotted inside.

Pammy had her back to him, pouring coffees for two customers in tennis skirts.

Al's eyes went moony, and his shoulders sagged, as if helpless in the presence of such a creature.

He was undeniably smitten. Darcy scrunched her face, silently rooting him on.

Snapping himself to reality, he ran an index finger and thumb over his mustache and strode to the counter. "Good morning, cupcake…"

"Baker," Pammy finished in chorus, depositing colorful mugs beside two daisy-topped cupcakes. She slid them toward the tennis players and wiped the counter with a rag. "Got anything other than bills?"

Al riffled through his bag. "The flyers for the Spring Arts Festival came in. The chamber of commerce gave 'em to me, and boy, are they beauties. Almost as pretty as…" Al stopped, mouth open, gazing at Pammy.

Pammy brushed crumbs into the sink and rinsed the cloth. "Pretty as what?"

Al cleared his throat. "As these here cupcakes." Returning to his bag, he pulled out a glossy brochure and presented it with a bow. "For you, my lady."

Pammy whapped his shoulder with the rag, leaving a wet streak on the crisp cotton uniform. "What's gotten into you?"

"Spring fever, I suppose. Makes a fella giddy." He hitched the bag over one shoulder and gave a two-fingered salute. "See ya tomorrow, Pammy."

Darcy chuckled. She knew exactly what had gotten into Al, and she wished Samuel was here to see it, too. She sipped coffee and caught herself. She wished Samuel was here? She swallowed. Yes. Yes, she did.

Still holding the leaflet, Pammy watched him go. She laid a bejeweled hand at the base of her throat and, with the other, fluffed her silky curls.

Maybe tomorrow Al would make his move.

With the latest episode of Love at the Cupcake Café complete, Darcy lost herself in editing. Her cupcake sat half eaten, and her coffee cooled. Sifting through photos, she cropped, sharpened, and boosted the saturation until the story of each shined clear.

Editing was a precision job, and Darcy was a master.

The bulbous bottom of Pammy's coffeepot swooped in. "You're the New York City photographer, aren't you?"

She checked her phone. Almost two hours had passed. "How did you know?"

"My aunt plays pickleball with Dale Fischer's mother-in-law. Can I freshen your coffee?"

"Yes, please." The café was empty of everyone but the tennis players who were long since finished eating. A person could stay at Pammy's for hours, simply because it felt like home. "It's all delicious. I just got wrapped up, and your place is so cozy."

With blue-lidded eyes slitted, Pammy studied her. "Don't go anywhere. I have something for you."

"For me?" Darcy called to her back.

Pammy waggled a hand. "One sec." Minutes later, she emerged with an old leather camera case and a tote bag. She plopped next to Darcy and set the case onto the table.

Darcy closed her laptop. "What's this?"

"That camera was my Dave's." Pammy laid a gentle hand atop the case. "He was something of an amateur photographer. Oh, he was all kinds of things: a volunteer fireman and a karate black belt and a big brother to some kids up in Williamsport. I could go on. But it was photography that made him happiest at the end." She nudged the camera in Darcy's direction. "Take a look."

The black leather was brittle, but the snap popped open easily. Inside, she found a vintage thirty-five-millimeter camera. She eased it from the case and turned it in her hands, enjoying the graceful design, the tactile texture, and the curved lens. "It's beautiful."

"Now, is that something you could use?"

Darcy hadn't shot on film in years—not since her first photography class in high school. She'd learned how to develop photos in a darkroom, loving the glow of the red light, the smell of the chemicals, and the sound of paper swishing in the solution. For years now, all her work had been digital.

Pammy's chest lifted in a sigh. "It's not doing any good sitting on a shelf. I've got extra lenses and a flash in the bag. I thought with you being a professional and all, maybe you could put it to use." She tucked a curl behind one ear. "Besides, after she left the Amish, your grandmother was Dave's teacher. He'd be tickled to think you had it."

Mammi Leora strikes again. Darcy fitted the camera into the case and snapped it. "I'd be honored. But call it a loan. You might want it someday."

Pammy shoved back from the table. "I'm too old to pick up a hobby, and this place keeps me busy morning to night. Lately, I can't keep my eyes open to watch those British bakers on TV." She stood and swiped her hands down her apron.

"What about that helper you talked about hiring?"

Pammy quirked a brow.

Darcy held up a hand. "I don't mean to pry, but I when I stopped in the other day, I heard the mailman mention his niece."

Green eyes glittered teasingly. "I remember. You and that tall drink of water were sitting in the window. I'd like to roll in that man's hayloft, if you get my meaning." She gave a hearty laugh and let it fade with a long, musical sigh. "Funny, Al hasn't mentioned Bailey since. Maybe he forgot. He's acting so odd lately."

Darcy King was raised not to poke her nose into other peoples' business. Matchmaking was unseemly. It was also her mother's favorite guilty pleasure. On that issue anyway, Darcy and Isabelle agreed. "Why don't you call him?"

Pammy extended a hand and straightened her colorful, stacked rings. "Call Al?"

"You really don't want to miss the baking show. It's so good this season."

"Oh, I love those fancy Victoria sponges," Pammy said, imitating the British judges.

Darcy bit into her cupcake and moaned. "Good thing they don't allow Americans. You'd run away with the competition."

"You know who does the funniest English accent?" Pammy asked.

"Al?"

"Al." Pammy poured herself a coffee and settled on a stool behind the counter. "Maybe I will give him a ring."

Darcy's heart felt as light and bright as the buzzing, pink sign in the window. Matchmaking was a breeze…for other people, anyway. If only the affairs of her heart could be so easily wrangled. She matched the neon sign with a brilliant smile. "I think you should."

****

With the day's editing done, Darcy ambled down Main Street, perusing springtime shop windows. Hanging flowers spilled from every lamppost, and doors were propped open, inviting idle browsing. Her boots clicked, and her skirt swished around her ankles. Like a girl in her Sunday church dress, she wanted to spin and watch the flowy fabric billow. She ducked into an old-school camera shop, making note of their printing services, and picking up a few rolls of black-and-white film. To think Pammy simply gave her Dave's camera, asking nothing in return. She was definitely not in New York anymore. With a quick prayer of thanks to *Mammi* Leora, she vowed to put the camera to good use. She could bring in the film for development, but she'd much rather do it herself. Where could she find a darkroom?

A colorful flyer taped to the back of the register caught her eye. It was the same one Al gave Pammy, advertising the Spring Arts Festival. Promising artisanal food and over one hundred juried artists, the event was far more upscale than she imagined. She snapped the QR code and scrolled through vendor displays from previous years. More than a few photographers were represented, and she had a pang for a collection of her own. She loved being part of a magazine, but striking out independently held a different appeal. In the past, she turned up her nose at commercial landscapes and family portraiture. Had she judged too quickly?

She tucked the film into her bag and headed out. Photography was everywhere, beautifying offices, hospitals, and private homes. The idea of her work displayed where people would enjoy it daily gave her a bubbly thrill. What kind of collection would she create? Samuel thought her point of view was special. Cue second bubbly thrill. What stories would her pictures tell?

The phone vibrated in her pocket. Expecting a response from her father, she was surprised when an unfamiliar number popped up.

—Quilting frolic at my house. 3 pm. Bring your camera.—

She stopped beneath the marquis of an Art Deco movie theater. The scent of buttered popcorn wafted on the wind. A quilting frolic? Was that like a bee? And who issued the mysterious invitation?

—This is Sarah's work phone. Bring snacks if you like.—

Mystery solved! Back in the day, *Mammi* Leora taught her sewing basics, but Darcy hadn't picked up a needle in years. If she wanted photos, she'd better pitch in. A quick web search defined a frolic as any Amish work party from raising a barn to making noodles. The primary components appeared to be bounteous food, hard work, and good fun.

She navigated to her message app and typed.

—See you there!—

Darcy's customary hostess gift was a box of macarons from her favorite Cobble Hill bakery and a bottle of Rosé. As she knocked on the farmhouse door, she surveyed the grocery store, cheese-and-veggie plate. Less fancy and, hopefully, more appropriate. These people surprised her every minute, but she was fairly confident they didn't tipple at quilting bees.

A hubbub met her at the door, and her tummy tripped. She'd attended swanky galas and elegant opening nights, but crashing a quilting bee, even as an invited guest, was a first. She remembered *Mammi* Leora's twinkly eyes and welcoming lap. These women were cut from the same cloth. Still, maybe she'd keep her camera in its case. For starters, anyway.

The door swung open. In a mudroom-like entryway, Rebecca held a chubby-cheeked toddler on one hip. "*Guder daag*." Spotting the cheese tray, she widened her eyes. "Oo. Fancy." She swung the squirming girl high into the air and deposited her, giggling, on well-worn linoleum.

Barefoot, the sticky-faced cherub tottered away, bouncing from wall to wall like a pinball.

Darcy surveyed the cheese, noting a garnish of parsley and curlicued cocktail toothpicks. "Too fancy?"

"Not for me." Rebecca gestured toward a pegboard. "You can hang your coat and bag. Everyone is in the sitting room."

Women's voices sailed in a sound between a hum and a song. A baby's cry burst over the top, followed by the whistle of a tea kettle.

Nerves fluttered canary-like in her ribcage. "How many are here?"

"Not many. Sarah and her *Grossmammi*, Sarah's daughter Arleta, Annie Amos and her mother, Lydia, Lovina Lapp, and Amity Yoder. Plus all the *kinner* who aren't in school. My mother wanted to come, but the twins are teething." She shivered. "Enough said."

At the end of the hallway, a spacious living room opened, sun-flooded and cheerful. Simple blue curtains draped tall windows, thrown open to the spring day. A jingle of harnesses came through the screens, adding to the chorus of women and children. Occupying much of the room, a colorful quilt stretched over a rustic wood frame anchored with clamps at the corners. Darcy idled in the entry, clutching her ostentatious cheese like the only guest who didn't realize the Halloween party wasn't a costume party.

"Darcy!" Sarah bustled from the kitchen, drying her hands on a towel. "I'm so glad you came. Everyone, this is my cousin Darcy. She's Leora Mast's *kinnskind* and the photographer you've heard about." She took the proffered tray. "This looks *wunderbaar*."

Seated in folding chairs, the ladies glanced up from their work, offering smiles and nods.

"The spitting image of Leora," a woman said, dimples welling beneath merry brown eyes. She nudged her younger companion. "Do you remember Leora, Annie?"

Nearly identical dimples puckered rosy cheeks. "I wish. I know she was a wonderful *gut* teacher." She met Darcy's gaze. "I'm Annie Amos, and this is my mother, Lydia. As you can guess, your *Grossmammi* was her teacher, too."

Introductions followed in rapid succession, but years of social engagements trained Darcy in the art of quickly learning names and making connections. "I'm delighted to meet you all. This quilt is exquisite."

Sarah's grandmother, Orpha, sat at one corner, clutching the rack with gnarled fingers. Slack-cheeked and dull-eyed, she listed to one side, as if at any moment she might topple.

Sarah dropped a kiss on the woman's wrinkled forehead. "Tell Darcy what the pattern is."

A light kindled behind Orpha's eyes. She fluttered a hand over the quilt top. "In my day, they were all Log Cabin, Wedding Ring, and Trip Around the World. This one's new. It's called Love Within." She took careful hold of a needle and made a row of delicate stitches.

"Love Within," Sarah repeated, gently patting her grandmother's shoulders. She murmured in Dutch and hurried back to the kitchen.

The name suited the pattern perfectly. Squares and rectangles of varying sizes created a central heart surrounded by diagonal, colored stripes that shot to the borders like sunbeams of love. The pattern was modern—almost an optical illusion requiring focus to spot the heart in the mass of purple, gray, and lavender patches.

Annie offered a folding chair. "Needles, thimbles, and thread are in Sarah's basket. Do you sew?"

The moment of truth. Darcy inhaled deeply. "I used to."

Lovina Lapp, a round-faced blonde in her twenties, tittered.

Annie brushed it off with an eye roll and a friendly laugh. "Join us."

A basket overflowing with supplies sat beside a modern sewing machine. The machine was retrofitted with an old-fashioned treadle like a relic from the Garment District, and the power cord dangled uselessly. Almost without thinking, Darcy snugged a silver thimble over the middle finger of her right hand and withdrew a needle from a tomato-shaped pin cushion whose twin sat on *Mammi's* sewing table twenty years ago. She settled next to Annie and threaded the needle in one try.

As she ran her gaze over swooping lines faintly sketched on the quilt top, she was flooded with memories. Her grandmother bent over a quilt in the church social hall surrounded by chattering women. A smaller quilt frame in the farmhouse kitchen, and *Mammi* patiently demonstrating the tiny stitches that make a quilt strong enough to last a century. She recalled quilting was different from piecing the fabric squares to make the colorful designs. Quilting was the meticulous process of stitching together the decorative top, a layer of soft batting, and the fabric backing into a kind of sandwich, later to be bound and finished.

She slid her left hand under the quilt and held the needle between her right thumb and ring finger in the awkward grip that had seemed so strange at first, but as the summer wore on, it became almost second nature. Easing the point into the cloth until it barely pricked the finger of her left hand, she rocked the needle back and forth, watching for the shiny tip to emerge before poking it down again, until four stitches appeared. Carefully grasping the tip, she pulled the needle through, delighted when the stitches almost disappeared into the fabric, perfectly spaced and delicate as a butterfly's footprints. "Not bad," she breathed.

Annie leaned close. "Leora taught you well."

That something in her bones remembered or perhaps always knew how to sew sparked a thrill deep inside. For hundreds of years, her ancestors had woven cloth and bound it with thread. Did that knowledge reside in the DNA? Was it waiting, dormant, for an opportunity to emerge? If never used, would it still be passed to Darcy's children and grandchildren? Typically, she gave scanty thought to her as yet unimaginable offspring. Just then, she saw them so clearly, tawny-haired and blue-eyed, carried piggyback down a country lane by a man who smelled like sky. The image was ridiculous yet so intoxicating that she indulged it, almost hearing their chatter over the sound of a babbling brook. How adorable those kids would be.

Children of women younger than she ran wooden trains in circles around her ankles, disappearing and reappearing from beneath the quilt. The ladies conversed in a seamless mixture of English and Pennsylvania Dutch. Though her fingers stiffened, she moved them like she'd quilted every day since she was nine, and something inside her let go. She felt the release like an unclenching, as if her spirit was held by one of the clamps binding the quilt and someone came along and loosened it. She had one task and one task only: to sew. If she took pictures, she took pictures. If not...not.

Sarah emerged from the kitchen with a sleeping baby in her arms. "Just how much do we have to raise if we want to buy those solar panels?" Snugging the infant in her lap, she sat across from Darcy and took up a needle. "I'd like to see installation at the schoolhouse by next fall, if Samuel and Tucker can accomplish it."

As if conjured, Samuel leapt from Darcy's thoughts and into the conversation. She jerked and jammed the needle into her fingertip. Flinching, she wrapped the finger tightly in her skirt. The last thing she wanted was to bleed on the quilt.

"Maybe Darcy could ask," Lovina said. "You're practically part of the family, aren't you?"

Since when were Amish girls catty? Darcy tilted her head in perfect imitation of Isabelle King's what-could-you-possibly-mean face.

Flushing, Lovina took up her needle.

"Nora quoted twenty-five thousand dollars," Annie answered.

Frown lines creased the corners of Sarah's mouth. Glancing up from her work, she met Darcy's gaze. "The schoolhouse needs improvement. The lights are too dim for the children to read, and the coal stove isn't sufficient to keep them warm."

"Not only that, but the soot makes them cough." Annie tied a quick knot and snipped the thread. "Dr. Richard has been encouraging us for years to replace it."

Rebecca, who until now had stitched silently in the corner, jabbed the needle into the quilt. "Why won't the menfolk make a special collection?"

"Men have short memories." Annie's mother, Lydia, arched her back and rolled her shoulders. "They think because something's always been a certain way, it ought to stay the same."

Rebecca scowled. "If that were the case, we'd all be British citizens who believed if we sailed far enough, we'd fall off the face of the Earth. It's malarky!"

"It's what?" Annie asked with a chuckle.

Rebecca punched the air with a fist. "Malarky. It's an *Englischer* word Pappy Hank uses, and it's a good one."

Sarah shifted the baby in her lap. "Twenty-five thousand is quite a sum."

"Thirty-five quilts, give or take." Annie rethreaded her needle. "If we work hard, we could hold an auction late summer, maybe?"

"Does that leave enough time for Samuel?" Lovina dipped her chin and flushed.

She lingered over his name like she enjoyed the saying of it. Darcy took note. No doubt, a bevy of women were interested in Samuel's time. Had any of them caught his eye? She laid down the needle and shook out her hand. More importantly, she'd stumbled upon yet another amazing story. These women took it upon themselves to finance solar installation at their children's school. What better example of modern Amish life could she find? Not only did she want to photograph the effort, she wanted to help.

Though tempting, simply writing a check was out of the question. The mere offer would be insulting. But a community auction in August seemed both too late for the school year and possibly not the best source of income. The quilts were masterpieces. They told their own stories, and the stories were deep. Put them in front of the right buyers and they could sell for twice what the Amish would pay. "Have you thought about the Spring Arts Festival?" she volunteered.

Every face turned toward Darcy.

She cleared her throat, feeling like she was back at the editorial meeting having once again opened her big mouth. However, if she'd learned anything from her mother, and this trip revealed she learned quite a lot, it was how to organize a benefit. "High-quality artists from all over bring their work right here to Green Ridge. I imagine buyers come from Harrisburg and Scranton...maybe even Philadelphia."

Rebecca leapt to her feet. "I love this idea. We could also sell pillows and table runners like we have in the shop."

"If you marked up prices a bit, you wouldn't need so many items." Darcy scanned faces, gauging how her suggestions landed. "And we could take orders to fill at a later date."

"We?" Lovina peered over her snub nose.

"I don't mean to overstep." She shot Sarah a deferential look. "I think your work is astonishing. If all the quilts are this beautiful, I know you'll do very well."

From the corner, Orpha sniffed. "This one's average. The piecing is uneven."

Sarah laughed. "Only *Gott* is perfect, right, *Mammi*?"

Annie bounced a preschool-age girl on one knee. "If we work hard the next few weeks, we could have a good inventory. I wonder how to sign up for a booth. Do you suppose we need a computer?"

A plastic cow landed atop Darcy's foot and galloped up her shin, propelled by the giggling toddler she met at the door. Grinning, Darcy extended her leg like a ramp. "I'd be happy to handle the logistics." Even as she volunteered, she knew the task entailed more work than any of them likely realized. After filling out and submitting an application, she'd need to procure a tent and display tables and figure out how to accept credit cards on the fly. Still, the challenge was exciting. The image of these sweet children needlessly shivering through arithmetic galvanized her spirit.

Shifting the sleeping babe onto one shoulder, Sarah stood. "Just because we do the town sale doesn't mean we can't have an auction later. What do you think?"

Orpha folded her hands atop the quilt. "Don't ask *Gott* to guide your footsteps if you aren't willing to move your feet."

Annie's mother patted the older woman's hand. "I'd say that's a yes. Now, let's eat. I'm *hungerich*, and the sloppy joes smell wonderful *gut*."

Darcy gazed at the quilt she now had a minor hand in creating before following the tantalizing scents of beef and barbecue sauce into the kitchen. No longer simply documenting the community, she was becoming involved. The negotiation might be delicate, but she was a professional. She could remain an unbiased observer and still help her cousin. After all, earning enough trust to be accepted was what she'd been working toward from the start.

But trust was a fragile thing. Now that she had it, she had to make certain not to break it.

Chapter Eleven

With red and raw fingers from an afternoon of quilting, Darcy snuggled on the bed in her cozy attic room and opened her email. After almost a week among the Amish, her phone didn't exactly feel like a relic, but it wasn't an extra limb, either. The shift was slight but freeing. At the top of her inbox, a rare message from her father beckoned. Curiosity piqued, she tapped with a tender fingertip and read.

Dear Darcy,

I suppose your discovery of Mammi *Leora's house was inevitable; yet somehow, I hoped you wouldn't. These many years later, its deplorable condition is rather a beacon of shame. When* Mammi *and Pop passed, the execution of their estate fell to me as eldest child and an attorney to boot. I distributed their few liquid assets, but regarding the house, I was neither conscientious nor timely. Uncle Mark and Aunt Mary wanted it sold but, not to put too fine a point on it, I dragged my feet. I can't say why other than perhaps misplaced feelings toward my childhood home. The result, of course, is as you observed. To the best of my recollection, the fire was attributed to old wiring and animal infestation, but ultimately, the cause was neglect. My neglect, to be precise. Fortunately, before they moved away, Mary and Mark emptied the house. They took what they liked and left the remainder at*

Keystone Storage on Route 45. I would consider it a favor if you stopped by the facility to determine if anything of value remains. The combination lock code is 8-9-34: Mammi's *birthday. When you come home, we'll discuss the best way in which to dispose of the property. While far overdue, a quick sale would likely benefit all.*

Warmly,
Dad

The phone dropped from her fingers, and she stared out the window, letting the message sink in. She'd assumed that drafty, old, wonderful house was sold years ago. Closing her eyes, she walked through the rooms in her mind, amazed how much she remembered: *Mammi's* wedding china in the hutch and Pop's tins of chalky, pink peppermint candies; the lidded bowl of instant coffee and the colorful globe banks packed with pennies; cartoon juice glasses and hundreds of family photos. Her father neglected them all, until finally, the house lit itself on fire.

Disgusted, she groped in her laundry bag for dirty running clothes, stripped, and jogged downstairs. How could he have been so irresponsible? She loved that house, and he never even mentioned they still owned it!

Outside, the sun sank toward the horizon, and the farm was quiet. Dinner was long finished, and the Rishels were no doubt home, winding down after a long day of work. She should be doing the same on *Mammi* Leora's breezy front porch. Although she was still a girl when her grandparents died, no one asked her what she wanted. She'd loved the house more than anyone had. She had a trust fund. She could have bought it.

Her lungs tightened, and she pounded over the

bridge so hard she thought she'd punch right through. The racing creek echoed the blood in her ears, and as she passed, she barely even noticed Samuel's studio. She was a quarter of a mile beyond when the sound of quick footsteps made her whirl, fists clenched to fend off a threat. She'd taken self-defense at Vassar. She had moves.

Dressed in navy work pants, a white undershirt, and suspenders, Samuel jogged up beside her. His cheeks were flushed, and his hair tossed crazily around his face.

Keeping her pace, she stared. He was just a lot to take in. "What are you doing?"

He shook the hair from his eyes. "Running."

She waited. He declined to elaborate. "Why?"

He shrugged. "The same reason you are, I guess."

"I run to exorcise my demons."

"Sounds good."

Was he mocking her? She was inclined to think so, but his expression was earnest. She scowled. For Darcy, running was a solo pursuit. Plenty of people had invited her to train, but she always declined. She ran where she wanted, when she wanted, and at the pace she wanted. No chitchat. No distractions. She was a selfish runner, and she liked it. The sooner Samuel learned, the better. With a quick breath, she shifted gears, speeding past Nora's cottage in what she knew was a seven-minute-mile pace. If this guy wanted to show her up, he'd pay.

But he didn't try to pull ahead. He simply matched her, stride for stride.

Long shadows crept over freshly plowed fields. She breathed the loamy scent of earth. Five minutes passed and then ten. Their footfalls struck an even cadence. Their breaths rose and fell in sync.

He didn't race, and he didn't talk.

His steady presence almost made running together pleasant. Annoyance ebbing, she tossed him a sidelong look. "Your niece thinks my running should be more like prayer."

He gasped a chuckle. "Sounds like Rebecca."

"She might be right."

"Wouldn't be the first time. She's irritating that way."

His cheeks were scarlet, and his breath came hard, but he didn't flag. Surprised how well he kept up, she cut her pace. "So, do the Amish jog…recreationally?"

"Ah, no." He dragged the back of a hand across his glistening forehead. "Manual labor pretty much covers our exercise needs."

"Not for nothing, some of you could stand to hit the gym." His laugh surprised her, and she clapped a hand over her mouth. "Did I say that out loud? I'm sorry. It's just, you guys eat a lot of pie."

"The food almost makes up for the lack of creature comforts." He stumbled over a root and lurched to keep his balance, coughing raggedly. "Can we…?"

With a bouncy twirl, she pirouetted and jogged backward. "Slow down?"

"Or stop." Halting, he dropped his hands to his knees and leaned over, back heaving. "Yeah," he gasped. "Stopping would be okay."

A giggle slipped past her lips. "Lightweight."

He raised a hand. "Get back to me when you've plowed ten acres with a team of draft horses."

The image was like something out of a movie with sweeping backdrops and a dramatic soundtrack…plus biceps, pecs, and sweat. She swallowed. "You've done that?"

"Of course." He leaned back, anchoring his hands on his hips and gulping air. "It's hard, but in a different way. Running like this is madness."

She trotted to his side. "Want to walk instead?"

Breath slowing, he nodded. "How far do you usually run?"

"Five or six miles—"

"Six miles?" His jaw plummeted. "Why?"

He was so incredulous she had to laugh. "The aforementioned demons. Now, the prayer, too, I guess. We'll see how that goes."

"I know what I'd pray for. An end to the running."

They shared a chuckle, and as the sound died, the crickets crescendoed their evening song.

"Do you have many demons?" he asked.

The question was personal, but in running with her, he'd earned the right to ask. More, she actually wanted to share. She slung an arm across her chest and hooked it with the opposite elbow, stretching tight muscles behind her shoulder blade. "My demons are my own creation, I suppose. My family has strong opinions about how I live my life, and my older siblings are wildly successful. I grew up under a lot of expectations." She switched arms, stretching out the other shoulder. "Expectations I decimated when I dropped out of law school. I chose my own path. That's why this photo essay has to succeed."

He stopped and studied her a long moment. Then he cut a hard right into the woods. "Come with me."

"Samuel!" She hesitated and then scurried after, discovering he didn't bushwhack into the brush but entered a narrow path. "Where are we going?"

"I want to show you something." He glanced at the sky. "But we have to hurry."

Beneath the forest canopy, the light was dim. Brambles scratched her bare legs, and she was glad for the thin hoodie covering her arms. Along the path, dainty white flowers clustered among roots and rocks. She crouched, cradling a blossom between two fingers. Every plant in Central Park was curated, but these were true wildflowers. Delicate petals splayed boldly from spindly stems and arched over leaves shaped like mini lily pads. The closer she looked, the more she saw. Finely ribbed, the petals were so white, they were almost lavender, and dewdrops clung to them like diamonds. She cast her gaze over a forest floor carpeted with flowers. Some were snowy, and others leaned toward pink. Though no nature photographer, she longed for her camera and a telephoto lens.

"Starflowers, *Mamm* calls those." He pointed. "And yellow violets beneath that oak. They're unusual."

The cheerful yellow flowers were like tiny laughing faces. "Yellow violet. Kind of an oxymoron, huh?"

He extended a hand. "Come on. We don't want to miss it."

She stared at his hand, long fingered and large, and her breath hitched. Springing to her feet, she took it. Her smooth palm met his rough one, and a tingle raced up the delicate skin on the underside of her arm. Her gaze met his, and the moment felt like a century and a millisecond at once.

One corner of his mouth twitched. His fingers

tightened around hers, and he headed up the path.

The air was a sap, moss, and dew-laced cocktail. She sipped a sweet woodsy lungful and followed. Farther on, the path veered up a short, steep hill at the base of the ridge. It jagged in a series of switchbacks, and she released him to take hold of saplings offering themselves as handholds. She clambered atop a rock, and her pulse thudded in her throat. Where was he leading?

After a short climb, the path leveled, snaking through a grove of white birches. Ahead, the forest parted, and twilight beckoned. Fringy ferns stroked her calves, and she approached an opening where a steep, rocky cliff dropped off. She tiptoed to the edge, and her heart expanded with the fields and sky. Below, the valley splayed like a patchwork quilt of meadows and woods, dotted with barns. If only she had her camera.

He settled on a boulder that might have been placed for the sole purpose of sunset watching. She joined him. The stone was cool and rough against her thighs, and a breeze rustled the leaves. She tucked her fingers into her sleeves, dizzily wondering what holding Samuel's hand meant. Maybe out here, no rules applied. Nothing meant anything, and everything meant something, but who knew or cared what.

With an eerie cry, a huge bird swooped from a tree and launched into nothingness.

Samuel scootched forward, gazing over the ledge. "Red-tailed hawk. See how the tailfeathers are russet in the sun?"

She craned her neck, but the bird was already too distant to make out colors. Wings outstretched, it soared in seemingly effortless circles. "We have those in the city."

He settled back beside her. "Really?"

"They nest in tall buildings and make a huge mess, actually. The most famous one was called Pale Male. When residents tried to evict him from their fancy Fifth Avenue building, the city went bananas. They almost arrested the poor maintenance guy. But Pale Male wasn't the only one. My friend who grew up on the Upper West Side said hawks live high atop statues on the Cathedral of Saint John the Divine." He gazed upward, as if imagining spires among the clouds.

"New York has a cathedral?"

She nodded. "The inside feels like somewhere in Europe. It's spectacular."

He crossed his arms over his chest and squinted into the sun. "I'd like to see that."

Golden-hour glow lighted his face, making the planes of his cheeks and the angle of his jaw as sculptural as any statue anywhere. "The cathedral or Europe?"

One cheek bunched in a half smile. "Both." He tilted his head and slanted a look. "You ever been to Europe?"

At eighteen months, she made her first trip to Paris. Her aunt had a house in Provence, and every summer they took surfing lessons in Biarritz. She'd spent Christmas in London, a semester in Madrid, and backpacked Italy with Zibby and Fern. But was anything she saw more beautiful than this quiet Pennsylvania sunset? She gazed at the sky. The sun was molten beneath a layer of wispy salmon clouds topped with periwinkle. Different, but no more beautiful. "Yeah, I've been to Europe."

"I'd travel anywhere really—Europe, South America, New York." He shifted, uncrossing his arms and pinning his hands beneath his thighs. "You're not the only one bucking expectations, Brooklyn. My guess is European travel was required for you. For me, it's…" He lifted his shoulders and let them fall. "Impossible."

Her stomach tightened. She couldn't imagine feeling chained to one spot. She rocked sideways until their shoulders bumped. "No travel? At all?"

He dragged a heel, scraping a divot in hard-packed ground. "We hire buses to Niagara Falls or Florida. Some go farther west." He took a deep breath, and his shoulder pressed against hers. "There's a difference between sightseeing and exploring. I want to explore."

Restless energy seemed to pulse over his skin. He let out a laugh that wasn't quite bitter but wasn't quite genuine either.

"No one would be surprised if I built a car and drove away, least of all *Mamm*. But she might dig her own grave and lie down in it once I left." He jutted his chin, and the muscle in his jaw flexed. "My brother's leaving tested her faith. Mine might break it."

Darcy couldn't imagine anything breaking Verna Rishel, but Samuel knew his mother better than she. She looked to the horizon—his only horizon—where the sun dipped halfway behind the far ridge. The wind shifted, and rays shot through the clouds like a calendar photo of a sunset.

Sipping an arm behind her, he tipped back and gazed at the sky.

An urge to nestle into the hollow of his shoulder tugged at her belly. To feather kisses along the razor-sharp line of his jaw. To run a hand through his thick, tawny hair. Awash in wooziness, she clung to solid rock. What about him had her weeping one minute and swooning the next? She ran a slow gaze over his profile, backlit by the setting sun. His allure went beyond good looks. She'd dated plenty of hot guys. This particular man was utterly unexpected, and she was a sucker for a dark horse.

Above his forehead, the evening star winked into view like a tiny miracle. Straightening, she scanned the sky for more. "I don't often see stars."

"You don't?"

The half-voiced question caressed over her skin. She shook her head. "The city lights are too bright. Seeing apartment windows at night and knowing a whole life exists behind each one—that's kind of like stargazing in that I feel like one small part of a massive universe. But it's not the same. Sometimes, I forget the stars exist."

He was quiet for a moment. Then he sat up and brushed together his hands. "We could stay and watch them, but we'd have a tough walk back."

Would that be so terrible? Darcy was in no way a camper, as witnessed by the fact she dropped out of summer camp at age nine. But the idea of cuddling on the edge of a cliff and watching the stars…? That kind of outdoorsiness she could get behind.

With loose-limbed ease, he stood and extended a hand. "We should go."

Without a second thought, she took it, relishing the current that zinged from her fingers to her soft and gooey core. She trailed him through a forest completely transformed by darkness. The starflowers glowed like their namesakes. Nighttime sounds of whiny, chitterychattery things she could neither identify nor see enveloped her. Off in the woods, a branch snapped, and she tightened her grip. His answering squeeze was reassuring.

Down the steep slope, he kept hold of her hand, pivoting to check she maintained footing.

She was fine. She saw well in the dark, and, having not exhausted her legs with a long run, her descent was strong and steady. Still, having him watch over her was unfamiliar and not entirely unwelcome.

Once through the woods, they emerged onto the farm lane and were greeted by a sound like a million distant car alarms but way more pleasant. "What's that noise?"

"Spring peepers. Guess they don't live in New York City, either?"

She chuckled. "They do not." Still hand in hand, she walked beside him in comfortable silence. Rocks crunched beneath her step, and she realized she had no idea what he wore on his feet. Did he run two-and-a-half miles in work boots? Amish women often wore black sneakers. Maybe he had a pair, also.

Light shone dimly from Nora and Tucker's cottage. Tonight, the house was quiet. In these times, how rare and yet how lovely to have multiple generations on the same land. Lovely for them, anyway. Living with her parents and siblings would be a nightmare. The memory of her father's email crept back, dulling the night's enchantment. To think he kept such a secret. She sighed. Did she know her family at all?

"Penny for your thoughts, Brooklyn."

The moon and stars seemed like old friends she hadn't seen lately, but with whom she picked up as if they'd never been apart. Funny, she felt safer here in the open, holding this man's hand, than she did in the city where she'd lived her whole life. Maybe safer wasn't the right word. More available? More willing to share? "My father emailed. He told me what happened to *Mammi* Leora's house." Like she was a bubbly champagne bottle, shaken and popped, she spilled— from quitting camp, to her summer in Green Ridge, and finally, the sting of her father's betrayal. She talked until, in near darkness, they arrived at his studio.

He pulled her down gently beneath the eave. Only then did he release her hand.

She settled at a careful distance. Was handholding over for good? Was it just a twilight, forest kinda thing? Even more…did it mean anything? She flexed her fingers and gave her quads a deep rub. "I have no clue what's in the storage unit, but I'm going tomorrow morning. Part of me is afraid. I'm not sure why." A gazillion miles away, the full moon was bright as a streetlamp. She let her shoulders sag. "Who am I kidding? I'm scared I'll start crying again."

"Would you like me to go?"

His face was in shadow, but she felt him looking. Even in the dark, the gaze was kind. Gratitude shuddered through her. "You'd do that?"

"On one condition."

Bracing herself, she tightened her shoulders. "What?"

"You come to family dinner on Sunday."

She hung her head. Was she more likely to weep alone in the storage unit or at dinner? Why choose? She'd probably sob snottily at both, and after hearing her pathetic saga, he should know. Did he want to shove their family unity in her face? She stared at her hands, just able to see their outlines in the dark. No. He might be a recreational mansplainer, but he wasn't cruel.

Of course, she could face the storage unit alone. Stuff was just stuff. But she knew her tears weren't idle. Her city armor was thick, but for one reason or another, it was cracking. How nice to have someone beside her if it crumbled. Maybe even to pick up the pieces. She took a deep breath, unsure if the scent of sky came from the air or the quiet man beside her. The smell was expansive. It opened a drawer inside her heart. It made room. "Thank you, Samuel. I'll take that deal."

Chapter Twelve

"Eight…nine…thirty-four." With shaky fingers, Darcy dialed in the combination and tugged the lock on the bright-blue garage door at Keystone Storage. It didn't budge. She groaned and huffed warm air into her cupped hands.

After the hike last night, the temperature had dropped, and the morning was clear and cold. Though her phone forecasted an unusually hot weekend, the storage facility seemed refrigerated from the outside in. The place was cheerful enough, a crisp, white, cement block structure with squat, blue planters flanking the office door. Nothing seemed likely to make her cry except the darned lock. Regrouping, she gave the combination a second go, and still, it held. "Come on!"

Beside her, Samuel shifted and buried his hands in the pockets of his work coat. "Would you like me to try?"

With a flourish, she stepped aside. "Be my guest. The dial is probably rusted. I should ask the guy for cutters like they use on those storage reality shows—"

Snick! The lock fell open in his hands.

She gaped. "Stop doing that!"

"It's simple." He handed her the lock. "You turn past the second number and keep turning—"

"I know! Don't you think I know?" She stuffed the stubborn clasp into her coat pocket where it lay like a stone against her thigh.

He knelt and grabbed the door handle, then looked over one shoulder. "Do you want me to open it?"

"Yes, please." Her voice sounded small. She took a yogic breath, in through the nose and out through the mouth. "Sorry I snapped. This whole thing just…"

He nodded. "I know."

The garage door screeched an objection to having been disturbed for the first time in years. Dust motes whirled, carrying the smell of musty cardboard. She stepped closer and peered inside. The unit was the size of some NYC studio apartments and neatly stacked with labeled boxes. Uncle Mark and Aunt Mary did a good job. She switched on her phone and swept the flashlight from a battered push mower to a metal garbage can holding shovels, rakes, and brooms. The acorn finials of her grandparents' bed peeked out behind a laundry basket of plastic kitchen containers. The maple china cabinet towered against one wall. Coming up on tiptoes, she spied the matching dining set and *Mammi's* favorite rocking chair, covered in a thick coat of dust. No *Mammi*. No Pop. Only stuff.

Samuel stepped inside. "Where do you want to start?"

How about by slamming the door and running? She caught one foot in a quad stretch and scanned the row of locked doors. Better to reseal the time capsule and let the items live forever in the *Mammi's* house of her memories than face them like this. Her opposite foot snugged into her hands, and she leaned into the stretch. But a still, quiet voice whispered to stay. *Mammi* had more to teach, and her possessions were all that remained. Steeling herself, Darcy entered the unit, trusting she'd find what she needed.

A medium-sized carton labeled *kitchen* snagged her interest, and she peeled away dried tape. Coughing, she yanked out a pile of mildewed dish towels. On her next trip, she'd bring trash bags. Underneath lay pots and pans, baking sheets, cooling racks, an eggbeater, and a metal cookie tin that rattled when she pulled it out. She pried the lid from the tin, and her heart squeezed. Nestled inside were dozens of miniature cookie cutters in the shapes of animals—a cow, a duck, a rabbit... Suddenly, she could almost taste *Mammi's* Christmas cookies, so thin they were translucent, with tiny nonpareil balls for eyes.

Cradling the tin, she sat on a dusty stool. She visited in the summer. Why did she remember celebrating Christmas? She could hear Bing Crosby on Pop's old hi-fi and *Mammi* singing along. She recalled plugging in a little ceramic tree and the lightbulb inside setting tiny glass ornaments aglow.

Samuel nudged aside a plastic tub and came beside her. "What did you find?"

She pulled out a mini horse and ran a finger over the metal edge. "*Mammi* made me Christmas cookies. I remember decorations, too, but I know I never spent the holidays here."

"I saw a box labeled *Christmas*." He squeezed between cardboard towers and pointed toward a carton.

"Can you put this on top?" She snapped on the lid and extended the tin.

He took it. "I think the dining set is Amish-made."

"I'm not surprised." She closed the kitchen box and, spinning, opened one labeled *bedroom*. The scent of rose talcum powder flooded her senses, and she was back in *Mammi's* room, nestled into the cozily saggy mattress while *Mammi* dressed for church. At the top of the box was a pink, plastic powder puff embossed with pretty flowers. If she shut her eyes, she could see it on *Mammi's* dresser next to her hairbrush, mirror, and comb. *Mammi* was not a lipstick and ruffles person. She liked rainslickers and sensible shoes. The dresser set had been uniquely feminine among the possessions of a dungarees-wearing schoolteacher and wife of a tire salesman. Setting aside the powder puff, she uncovered *Mammi's* blue jewelry box with the gold trim where she kept all her necklaces and… The memory Darcy sought clicked into place. "Pins," she breathed. "*Mammi* loved pins."

The box was empty. Surely, Aunt Mary had taken anything of value, and rightly so. Darcy removed it, revealing what she sought: dozens of tiny boxes stamped with department store labels. *Mammi* had so many pins and brooches that she kept them individually in her top dresser drawer. Darcy remembered browsing through them, marveling at egg-shaped Easter pins, lacy Valentine's hearts, and St. Patrick's Day four-leaf clovers. But most of all, *Mammi* loved Christmas pins.

As Darcy opened boxes and examined the contents, she met again the woman she only vaguely remembered. As a girl, seeing adults as their own people was nearly impossible. They existed only in relation to her—her grandmother, her mother, her dad. By all accounts, *Mammi* lived a rich life, full of love, joy, and, yes, sorrow, too. Leaving the Amish couldn't have been easy, nor likely was the estrangement from Darcy's father and her final battle with cancer. She swallowed past a lump in her throat. If only she remembered more.

The jewelry box triggered one key memory, however: a very special brooch that unlocked the secret of a summertime Noel. She lifted cover upon cover, searching. Rhinestone flowers sparkled, and silver bells shone. Where was the Christmas tree pin? She couldn't quite picture it, but she'd know it when she found it.

Samuel squatted beside her, brushed together his hands, and held them out. "What do you have there?"

"I remember…" Her voice caught. "*Mammi's* birthday was August ninth. Pop took me to the mall and gave me ten dollars to pick out a present." She handed him a turkey pin and opened another box. "In the back of the jewelry section at Biscoff's were the sale items. I'd never picked out a present on my own. Pop must have waited half an hour while I considered every pin." A jack-o-lantern grinned from her palm, and she set it next to the turkey. "Finally, I found the perfect one. It was gold with red and green—oh!"

Yellowed cellophane tape held together the box. Inside, nestled on a pad of cotton, was the birthday pin. Seeing it again after all these years, she felt the corners of her eyes prickle. Glittery "gemstone" ornaments covered the gold-tone tree, topped with what she'd been certain was a genuine diamond star. "*Mammi* said it was the prettiest pin she'd ever seen. She wore it to church every Sunday for the rest of the summer."

With careful fingers, she removed it. The gold was discolored. One of the stones was missing, and another appeared to have been glued back in. A tear slid down one cheek, and she brushed it away. "*Mammi* loved nature, so it seemed perfect. I didn't think about it being a Christmas pin until she opened it, and then I was so embarrassed. But *Mammi* said, 'Shouldn't we live every day as if it's Christmas?' And since I'd be back home in December, we should have our own Christmas in August." Her chest tightened, and she hiccupped a shaky sob. "And she made Pop get out all the decorations, even though it was ninety degrees, and we baked cookies and sang carols." She sniffed and dragged a sleeve across her face. "It was the best Christmas ever, and we didn't have a single present. We didn't even have a tree. We hung ornaments from the banister and curtain rods."

Setting aside the boxes, he laid a gentle hand on her knee. "It sounds wonderful."

She ran a finger over the bumpy, green-gold surface. The rhinestones caught the sunlight and glinted. "Nobody else ever loved me like that." She gazed from beneath a heavy brow. "Maybe no one ever will."

"*Ach*, Brooklyn…" In a heartbeat, he dropped to his knees and took her in his arms.

She pressed her cheek into his coat and let herself weep for the grandmother she was never allowed to mourn and the woman she was forbidden to remember. Shoulders shaking, she sank into an embrace so tender it only made her cry harder. Clutched close to her heart, the pin dug into her palm. It was gaudy and garish, and *Mammi* wore it again and again and clearly kept wearing it after Darcy left, simply because Darcy gifted it.

When she went home that fall, she'd expected her family to be different. She waited for the cuddles and attention she'd grown used to. When they didn't come, she locked the summer's memories deep inside her heart. Then, her grandparents died, and she buried the key. That kind of love couldn't have been real. Growing up in the shadow of siblings who seemed much more beloved, she convinced herself she must have imagined it.

A hand came to rest on the back of her head.

She squeezed closed her eyes, and grief juddered in her chest.

He tightened his hold on her waist and nestled his cheek against her hair, speaking quietly in the language of his ancestors.

She needed no translation. The sounds landed softly in the heart of the girl she'd been. He unlocked the door without a key.

"You deserve that kind of love," he whispered. "Every single day."

A breath made more of light than air zoomed into her lungs, sparking her insides like a million twinkly Christmas bulbs. Her heartbeat skittered, unable to decide if it wanted to slow or race. Part of her melted. Part of her burst into flame.

He inhaled deeply, his belly pressing against hers, and the hand drifted down to her shoulder blades.

A car pulled into the parking lot, and in the distance, an ambulance sounded. The siren was the first she heard in a week. Her jacket crinkled, and she traced the cool, smooth circle of his coat button like a worry stone. She was in a musty storage unit, surrounded by mountains of her grandparents' junk, and yet, in the arms of an Amish man, she felt cherished in a way she hadn't since she was nine. She did feel loved, and the sensation turned her to jelly, even as it scared the stuffing out of her. It made her want to teleport back to her real life, and at the same time, she wondered if the storage unit could be zoned for residential occupancy. How sturdy was that acorn bed…?

The pin gouged her hand, and she shifted, releasing the pressure.

He swallowed and eased away, trailing a hand down her spine. "Are you all right?"

Mustering every scrap of courage and lashing it together like a life raft, she met his gaze. Gone was the cocky jerk who snarked about rental cars and sneered at photography. Gone was the arrogance and mistrust. Instead, the most intriguing man she'd ever met looked at her like she was a thing to be treasured. He didn't fidget and squirm. He didn't split his focus between her and a shinier object across the room. Concern, compassion, and maybe a teensy-weensy bit of desire simmered in his sea-green eyes.

And in that moment, Darcy fell.

She fell hard.

The earth shifted on its axis a scintilla of a fraction of an nth of a degree, and her life shifted with it. Everything and nothing changed. Her heart exploded, but it still pumped blood to her tingling hands. Her mind was blown, but reality appeared much the same. So she shook herself and stood, halfheartedly elbowing the universe back into alignment. Her legs were trembly, and she stumbled a step, bumping into an oversized box. The lock thudded against her thigh, and she half saw a label written upside down. Realizing what it said, she craned her neck and read it again. Neatly printed in all caps was one word: *QUILTS*.

She tucked the pin into her other pocket and tore away the tape. The cardboard flaps flopped open, revealing a layer of yellowed tissue. She lifted it. Surely the entire box didn't contain… "Oh, my gosh." She beckoned to Samuel who stood staring outside with an inscrutable expression. "Look."

He ran a hand through his hair and tugged the ends, then swiveled.

She pointed to a quilt top, pieced in what she recently learned was a log cabin pattern. The colors were classically Amish: vibrant garnets, teals, and blues. Fearing the quilt would disintegrate at her touch, she extended trembling fingers, but the piece was made to last. Tissue slid from the folds and floated to the floor like autumn leaves. Beneath the quilt was another, stitched in a stunning star pattern. She handed Samuel the first and pulled back the second to reveal another. And another. All told, the box contained more than a dozen quilt tops.

Quilt tops she could give to Sarah and her friends to complete for the Spring Arts Festival. Feeling like she'd guzzled a quadruple-shot latte, she bounced on her toes and spun to Samuel. "Will you help me carry this box to the car? We need to go to Sarah's right away."

****

"She had fifteen unfinished quilts. Can you believe it?" Darcy bit into a yeasty, homemade roll at Sunday dinner the next evening and let out a sigh. Why would anyone eliminate carbs when bread could taste so good?

"My word." Verna passed the roll plate. "Have another, Darcy. If you don't mind my saying, you could use some meat on the bones."

Imagining her mother's horror, Darcy grabbed seconds. "I don't mind a bit."

The big oak table was full. Verna had added a leaf to accommodate Darcy and Deacon Elmer Zook, who praised each dish as if Verna ran a Michelin-starred restaurant. He wasn't wrong. Though heavy and rich, the food was excellent.

Samuel grinned over a bowl of creamed celery.

Her stomach did an equestrian show jump, leaping over a fence and a hedge and several koi ponds all at once. Having fallen for Samuel, she now had no clue what to do. She was no babe in the woods. She knew he liked her. He held her hand in the dark and patted her hair, for Pete's sake. But notwithstanding the transcendent delight of bringing an Amish man home to mother, the affair would doubtless end in heartbreak more painful than any dalliance with a drummer. Outside of vampire and romance novels, forbidden love was a nonstarter. Not for nothing, Romeo and Juliet bit it in Act Five. She beamed like a dopey schoolgirl and scarfed chicken pot pie that closely resembled soup. Homemade noodles never tasted so good.

Surprisingly, Amish church was held biweekly. This week was an "off Sunday," and folks visited friends or family and attended worship in other districts. That morning, Verna had gone to see Nora and the children, and Samuel was presumably in his workshop. After an early run, Darcy devoted several hours to the festival application and arrangements. The house was quiet, but she didn't mind. She stationed herself on a sunny porch rocker and started at every shadow, thinking Samuel had come. But he didn't appear until supper, tousled and unsettlingly gorgeous. During the silent prayer, she'd studied him from beneath lowered lashes. He needed a proper haircut.

They all did. Apparently, grooming wasn't an Amish thing.

At Samuel's side, Rebecca listened, bright-eyed. "With Leora's quilts, does Sarah think we'll have enough for the arts festival?"

Nodding, Darcy forked a bite of orange gelatin salad. Something tangy lingered on her tongue. Shredded cheddar cheese? Strangely delicious. "I filled out all the registration forms and uploaded sample photos. We're all set."

"Speaking of photographs…" Deacon Elmer pushed aside the shallow bowl that served as a dinner plate and turned his attention to Darcy. "I hear you're photographing our community for a big-city magazine."

Darcy sipped water, gathered herself, and once again explained her project. Nora and Tucker had also yet to hear the details, and her ideas frothed with exuberance. She described the photos she'd made in the camper factory, the hospital, and the quilting frolic.

Deacon Zook folded his hands and held her in a steady gaze.

In this room, listening trumped speaking. Nora's toddlers babbled and fussed, and food was fetched and passed, but focus always returned to whoever spoke. Darcy felt heard.

In the ensuing silence, Deacon Zook sat back, stroking his long, white beard.

Her stomach wrenched. After all she'd done to earn peoples' trust, would the church put the kibosh on her work? She dug her teeth into her bottom lip and slid Samuel a look.

He dipped his chin in a gentle nod.

Reassured, she let out a breath. To have this man as

an ally after a photographer upended his life was nothing short of miraculous.

"Your project sounds thoughtful," Deacon Elmer said in a kindly voice. "Respectfully, the bishop and I would like to see your photographs before they appear in the magazine. Would that be possible?"

The bishop wanted photo approval. Though the request was perfectly reasonable, Darcy fought an urge to laugh. "Absolutely. I'll have prints made at the camera shop and share them before I leave. Will that do?"

Deacon Elmer clapped together his hands. "*Denki*, Darcy." He mopped up a final bite of pot pie with half a roll. "Wonderful *gut* dinner as always, Verna. Dare I hope for a slice of Nora's shoofly pie?"

Nora finished wiping the round cheeks of one of her twins. "Of course. However…" She shot Rebecca a stern look. "I meant to send home a second pie for Mervin, Joanna, and the children, but I'm afraid we'll have to wait."

Bristling, Rebecca pursed her lips. "How was I to know Pumpkin liked shoofly pie?"

Her expression was as defiant as any Darcy ever dared give Isabelle King. Everyone at the table seemed to hold their breaths.

Nora's fine, feathery brows rose almost to the edge of her head covering. "A barn cat belongs one place and one place only. A barn."

Pink splotches erupted on Rebecca's cheeks. "Pumpkin is part of the family. She's like a *schweschder* to me. Besides, the barn is cold at night."

Scoffing, Nora pushed back from the table. She thrust her hands into mitts and yanked a pie from the oven.

Imagining that naughty orange cat crouched on the counter, eating Nora's legendary pie, Darcy once again struggled to keep a straight face.

Samuel tilted toward his niece and spoke quickly and quietly in Pennsylvania Dutch.

Rebecca clasped her hands beneath her chin. "You will?"

"There's no need, Samuel." Nora dished out pie with brisk efficiency.

"I don't mind. I like the cat." Samuel shrugged. "She's good company."

The deacon lifted a stubby finger. "A wife would be better."

The tips of Samuel's ears went red.

Darcy watched the action like a tennis match. With each passing minute, the evening was increasingly entertaining. *Bring on the Amish family dysfunction.* She knew it shouldn't delight her so much, but it did.

One of the twins threw a messy spoon onto the floor at the same moment the other planted one into her dark curls.

A passive observer until now, Tucker extended an arm and snatched the fallen utensil. He extracted the other from his daughter's hair, stood, and met Nora at the sink. Leaning in, he murmured something in her ear. With a playful squeeze around the waist, he began serving pie.

Nora's jaw relaxed, and a giggle slipped past the delicate fingers covering her mouth. She reached for a plate. "Sit, Tucker."

He laid a protective hand on her round belly. "You sit, Twinkletoes."

The sweetly funny nickname sent a pang through Darcy's chest. The moment was public yet private, casual, and yet incredibly intimate. Darcy longed for that kind of tenderness. Embarrassed to watch, she shifted her gaze...and met Samuel's. It was steady, smoldering, and incandescent as the propane light hissing on the ceiling.

A trace of mischief twisted his lips. "That settles it. Pumpkin will sleep with me."

For half a second, she thought he said Brooklyn not Pumpkin, and a neck blush exploded. The comment was so overt. It dripped with double entendre and yet was thoroughly innocent. His deep voice liquified her bones, and she struggled to sit upright with her innards turned to shoofly pie, gloopy and sweet as molasses.

Dessert fixes most everything. Within minutes, family equilibrium was restored. The deacon chuckled like a jolly, skinny Santa, and Verna glowed. The twins twittered, and Tucker pulled out his guitar. Nora gazed at him with naked affection, and Rebecca snuck secret glances at a hidden book in her lap. In the midst, Samuel sat silently, gazing at Darcy with a face like the Cheshire Cat.

Families were families. Not one was perfect. But this meal bore as little resemblance to Park Avenue suppers as it did to dinner with the King of England for the simple reason that every single person at the table was in the room. They weren't listening to headphones or texting colleagues or checking the score of the baseball game. An unspoken agreement to remain present assured a basic level of trust Darcy never felt in her own family. No matter what, the Rishels weren't going anywhere.

Well, she supposed the oldest brother had.

Samuel made a show of peeking at Rebecca's book.

He wasn't going anywhere.

A kernel of sadness hardened in her throat. She washed it down with sweet, iced tea.

The wanting to go shines in his eyes. Don't you see it?

Maybe. But for tonight, anyway, she wasn't leaving, either.

Chapter Thirteen

Darcy grabbed the handlebars and swung a leg over the cherry-red bike frame. As the family dinner ended last night, Rebecca had mentioned a tour bus would visit the quilt shop first thing Monday morning, and Darcy was welcome to take photos. Rebecca typically bicycled to work, and if Darcy wanted to borrow Nora's bike, they could ride together. So, bright and early, Darcy had packed her camera into her backpack and donned leggings, sneakers, and a tunic dress, suitable for cycling and work. She hadn't biked since her last high-school summer in Nantucket, but she remembered how. Right?

Gritting her teeth, she spun the pedals into alignment. "It's just like riding a bike," she muttered, "because it *is* riding a bike."

Samuel tucked a wrench into his pocket and squeezed the back tire. "I don't think Nora's ridden since the twins were born, but the bicycle is in fine shape. I greased the chain and put air in the tires. Just watch out for chipmunks and cars."

Annoyance flared in her chest, matching the temperature of what was already an unseasonably steamy morning. *There's the know-it-all dude she knew...and loved. Kinda. Sorta. Totally. Not.* "I know how to ride a bike," she snapped. She adjusted her headband and snugged her ponytail tight. "How was your first night with Pumpkin?"

"She snores." He dragged a hand over his chin and squeezed the muscles at the back of his neck. "She walked on my head for about an hour and then fell asleep on my pillow." He sneezed and wiped his nose with a handkerchief. "I'm not sure if I'm allergic to her or the pollen." He sniffed and sneezed again three times in quick succession.

After a balmy weekend, the yard had exploded in color. Fruit trees in neat rows behind the house were frosted with white and pink flowers, and powdery pollen coated her rental car.

With a whoosh of tires, Rebecca flew down the farm lane, ducking beneath crab apple branches seemingly wrapped in cotton candy.

Samuel blew his nose and tucked the handkerchief into a pocket with the wrench. "Tomorrow, I'm seeing possible clients over on Shade Mountain. Want to come along? I'm driving."

"In the buggy?" Her heart skipped. She'd been longing for a carriage ride but didn't dare ask.

"No. On a motorcycle." Rolling his eyes, he swung the tire pump over one shoulder. "I leave at dawn. It's a good distance, but folks in that district are traditional. If I come in your fancy car selling solar power, I might not make it in the door. I doubt you'll get permission to photograph them, but maybe you'll find some interesting subjects on the trip."

Sparkling water replaced every ounce of her blood, and she fizzed with excitement. Did this pass as a date in Amish culture? Then again, why would he bring an *Englischer* to visit a conservative family? Unless... "Former students of my grandmother?"

He lowered his chin. "Come to think of it…"

Cheeks flushed, Rebecca skidded to a stop. "*Guder mariye*." She pulled a bundle from her bike basket and tossed it at Samuel. "*Mamm*'s trying a new cookie recipe for market. Let her know what you think."

One-handed, Samuel snagged the cookies and clutched them to his chest. He swiveled to Darcy. "Will you join me? I'll make it worth your time."

A fresh pump of CO_2 whooshed in her veins. So what if he only wanted her for her family connections? What else was new? "Count me in." His answering smile belied the invitation as purely mercenary. He was glad she said *yes*. And she was triply glad he was glad.

"We'd best get going." Rebecca leapt onto the saddle and took off, spewing pebbles in her wake.

"Good luck keeping up with that one." Lifting the pump in farewell, he loped toward the barn.

"Thanks for the tune-up," she called. Then, without thinking, she planted her feet on the pedals and rode.

A blossom-scented breeze tossed her hair, and she shifted into a higher gear. Though she wasn't a cyclist, her legs were strong, and she caught Rebecca by the time they hit Old Cowan Road. Traffic was sparse, but Darcy was glad to veer onto the town bike path. Sarah's shop was only a few miles from the farm, but she far preferred the wide gravel lane, overcanopied with trees. She pulled up alongside Rebecca, matching her stroke for stroke. "I forgot how much I love biking."

Rebecca pressed her lips, but a wicked gleam glinted in her eyes. "Technically…?"

She drew out every syllable as though savoring a piece of chocolate fudge. Darcy motioned for her to continue.

"Bicycles are forbidden in our church district." She covered her mouth and giggled. "*Mamm* learned to ride in Ohio where they are permitted. After her hip surgery here, she got the bishop's permission to continue for medical reasons. Then, I convinced Tucker to get me a bike so *Mamm* wouldn't have to ride alone when she was expecting the twins."

"Clever girl." Sunlight dappled the path. A branch snapped beneath her tires, and Darcy gripped the handlebars. "But I don't understand. Do the Amish allow biking or not?"

"Depends on what the leaders in your church district decide."

"There's not one set policy?"

Rebecca spluttered. "Goodness, no! Every *Gmay* has a different *Ordnung*. That's the set of rules we live by. We have some things in common like plain dress and horse and buggy use, but beyond that, we're as different as can be. *Mammi* Verna says Shade Mountain district was quite strict when she was a girl, but attitudes are changing. For the better, if you ask me."

Forest gave way to farms, and the tang of fertilizer supplanted the dewy scent of fresh green grass. In a nearby field, a teenage boy stood atop a farming implement pulled by a team of four horses, exactly as Samuel described. He held the rains with the steady assurance of someone absolutely at ease wrangling massive animals.

Rebecca watched him, veering toward the edge of the path. She righted just in time to avoid a bush.

A boy who made Rebecca ride off the road? Darcy wanted details. "Do you know him?"

Rebecca gave a quick nod. "Eli Weaver. He was in

my grade at school." Though she kept her expression even, a hidden crush tugged at the corners of her lips.

Even at a distance, Darcy noted thick chestnut curls and tanned skin. The boy was cute. Did Amish teens date? Rebecca was transparent, but Darcy imagined such a question would be, for lack of a better word, cringey. What teenage girls liked talking about boys with adults? She waded in carefully. "Now that you're working, do you still hang out with friends?"

"Not as much. We see each other at church and on visits. In two years, I'll join the *Youngie*, and then I'll go to youth singings and Sunday gatherings. Of course, everyone will immediately pester me to get married, but..." Her voice trailed off, and her gaze drifted to the boy. "I have a lot to accomplish first."

"As well you should."

"If you and Uncle Samuel got married, would you join the Amish like Tucker?"

Darcy's foot slipped, and she swerved, losing control of the bike. Dodging a ditch, she yanked the handlebars and wobbled back to the middle of the path.

Rebecca skidded to a stop. "I'm sorry. Did my question startle you? *Mamm* says I should think before I speak, but I thought that question about a hundred times. At no point did I stop wanting to know the answer."

"I'm good." Heart pounding, she dismounted and walked the bike toward Rebecca. What made her ask such a question? Rebecca was incredibly mature for fourteen, but her lack of a filter sometimes made her seem far younger. "Nothing's going on between your uncle and me."

"That's what you think." Rebecca didn't try to hide

her glee. "I know a little something about love."

Darcy choked a laugh.

Dismounting her bike, Rebecca scurried to Darcy's side. "I do! I've been witness to several love affairs. I knew Uncle Jonas was in love with Tessa long before he did, and when my mother started smiling for no reason, I guessed it wasn't because of her hip replacement, even before I met Tucker." She surveyed Darcy head to foot. "You're not like Tucker, though. He had a deep yearning in his soul, in addition to great love for my mother, of course. You have your photography and your life in New York. You always seem so certain of yourself. I admire that."

Darcy stopped short. She tried to project self-confidence, but having Rebecca reflect it back was surprisingly heartening. "Thank you." A conversation with Tucker was in order. She could as scarcely imagine becoming Amish as she could living on the moon, but the last week had changed her. She felt herself slow down in a way not at all unpleasant. She seemed to be seeing and feeling more deeply. With a cleansing breath, she resumed walking. "I keep bursting into tears, though."

Rebecca matched her stride. "Well, that's understandable. Your *Grossmammi* died, and you never had a chance to say good-bye."

She thought of the charred shell of *Mammi's* house, the storage unit, and the pin. How was this kid so smart? "Maybe you're right."

Up ahead, a path branched to one side, and a sign with an arrow read *Sarah's Quilt Shop*.

At the fork, Rebecca stopped. "Before we go, I have a question." Catching her bottom lip between her teeth, she peered toward the shop and back in the direction they came. "Not really a question, I suppose, but a request and a rather unconventional one."

How could this conversation possibly be more unconventional? Her curiosity was piqued. "Sure."

"I've pondered this for several days. I suppose I've been thinking about it for years, but I never had the right person to ask." Rebecca lowered the kickstand and bunched her apron in tight fists. "I might as well just say it." She blew out a quick, sharp breath and met Darcy's gaze. "Will you photograph my family?"

All the air evacuated Darcy's body at once, and she anchored a hand on the bicycle seat.

"I know my request breaks every rule imaginable, but the truth is…" Rebecca's sweet voice faltered, and she swallowed hard. "I can't remember my *Daed's* face. I've tried. I've thought over every memory, and even though I was young when he died, I have several. But where his face should be, I only see a smudge." She wiped a tear with the heel of one hand and shook her wrist. "I've asked *Mamm* to describe him, and she does in her way, but it's no use. I can't remember. I know we'll be reunited in Heaven, but that seems an awfully long time from now. At least, I hope so." She sniffed and stared at the sky. "But nothing in life is certain. And if *Mamm* dies or *Mammi* Verna or Uncle Samuel, I don't want to forget them, too."

In the distance, a motor rumbled followed by the hissing sigh of brakes. The tour bus had arrived. Darcy's promise to Samuel lodged in her throat like a fishbone. *No pictures of peoples' faces. Not a single one.*

Rebecca swung her gaze to Darcy. "You aren't

saying anything."

A heartbreaking mix of hope and fear shone in her ice-blue eyes, and as hard as Darcy had fallen for Samuel, she fell equally as hard for his niece. She respected the Amish. She admired them. After a week, she even desired to emulate them to some extent. But she could not understand a culture that refused to give a child a single photograph so she could remember her parents' faces if ever they passed away. That was a mistake—a mistake she was uniquely positioned to fix. "Yes."

Rebecca jerked like she'd stepped on a live wire. "Yes?"

Projecting certainty she didn't quite feel, Darcy straightened her spine. "Yes." Slender arms flung around her shoulders, and a flushed, wet cheek pressed against hers. Rebecca smelled of vanilla and soap and teenager and was the dearest, oddest, most wondrous girl Darcy had ever met. How could she possibly say no?

"*Gott segen eich.*" Rebecca tightened her arms and squeezed. "That means God bless you."

"*Mammi* used to say that, but I forgot until now." She brought her lips to the dainty whorl of Rebecca's ear. "But this is our secret, all right? I'll take the photos, and I'll give them to you, but you must swear to keep them hidden." Grasping Rebecca's shoulders, she stepped back and held her at arm's length. "No one can ever find out. Promise?"

With tears streaming, Rebecca nodded. "I knew you wouldn't tell my mother. I knew it."

Though as a girl, she sat in the family pew at church every Sunday, Darcy hadn't prayed from the heart since her grandmother died. Now, though, she sent up a doozy of a prayer. She asked God for strength and reassurance. And for Samuel Rishel to never ever find out she broke her word.

****

Half an hour later, Darcy stood on a chair in the back of the quilt shop and peered through the viewfinder. The display bed was piled so high it looked like a toddler bundled in winter clothing.

Rebecca and Amity pulled back quilt after quilt, revealing ever more beautiful ones below.

The tourists from North Carolina "oohed" and "aahed."

The quilts were sold on consignment and ineligible for the Spring Arts Festival. Given the enthusiastic response, a number of women would make a tidy profit today. And rightly so. The pieces were breathtaking.

"Are they machine washable?" a woman asked in a breathy Southern drawl.

"*Yah.*" Sarah straightened the pile at the head of the bed. "Years ago, my grandmother made them with wool, and those you couldn't wash. These are cotton and flannel. They wash up wonderful *gut* on delicate."

Darcy zoomed in, framing a cell phone camera focused on a quilt. Blue jeans and black aprons. Permed gray hair and white prayer coverings. Phones, phones, and more phones. Work steadied her, but inside, she was a jumbled mess. While photographing the Rishels was unquestionably the right course of action, it was also a breach of a solemn promise.

Frame. Shoot. Frame. Shoot. Frame. Shoot.

Four photos. Maybe five—Tucker, Nora, Verna, Samuel, and the twins. Rebecca could be trusted. She'd

163

keep her word.

Sarah gestured toward a two-toned quilt with overlapping rings of teal fabric on a white background. "Now, that's a Pickle Dish Double Wedding Ring. It's a traditional pattern with more modern coloring, wouldn't you say? It's six hundred."

"And worth every penny," a shopper murmured.

Next appeared pieced colorful leaves in greens, blues, purples, and rusts. "That's your Autumn Splendor," Sarah said. "Our young ladies aren't watching television at night. They're designing and making items like this. Very creative."

Amity and Rebecca took hold of the bottom hem and pulled it up to reveal a snowy white quilt with intricate stitching creating an embossed feathery border and a grand star around a central medallion.

Everyone in the room took a breath.

Sarah smoothed the all-white bed covering. "Do you know what this pattern is?"

"Heirloom?" said an older woman from her perch on a rolling walker.

Sarah smiled. "You must be a quilter."

Eyes shining, the woman nodded. "Since I was a girl."

"This is the highest priced quilt in the bunch for *gut* reason." Sarah flipped up the bottom to reveal the back. "It has no wrong side."

Darcy lowered the camera. The quilt had no hidden, messy underside. It was perfect. The guests dispersed to browse potholders, pillows, and more, and Darcy sidled between them to the quilt display. Flipping gently through, she admired up close the hundreds of fabrics and shapes, so precisely cut and assembled. Women's work, yes, but artwork, too. This art lived among people, was snuggled, and used, not hung on gallery walls.

She studied the patterns, repeating the names in her head: Wedding Ring, Autumn Splendor, Mariner's Compass, Heirloom. Most quilts were given as gifts, carrying wishes for happiness and good health. Maybe the quilt blocks were talismans, ancient designs blessing all who slept beneath. What if every thread was a strand of a spell? The more she thought, the more the names seemed emblematic less of the designs and more of the magic sewn into each square. As if by sleeping beneath them, people would be granted marriages as intertwined as double wedding rings, autumns of splendor, compasses to guide by, and the legacy of love. She adored her velvety duvet, but did it have power to protect her in her sleep? Probably not. She felt a slim arm twine around her waist and whiffed vanilla.

"I'm glad you came, Darcy King," Rebecca said.

"Me, too." She settled a hand atop Rebecca's. "What's the name of the quilt pattern you made for the guest room?"

"Sunshine and Shadow."

She squeezed Rebecca's fingers. "Perfect." Today, the sun shone. Her ride back to the farm would be bright and bonny. Tomorrow? A tiny shiver danced up her spine. Let the quilt keep shadows at bay...at least until she returned to New York.

Chapter Fourteen

Before dawn the next day, Darcy left Verna yawning in the kitchen and stole out the back door with two biscuit sandwiches wrapped in foil. She'd dressed in layers with a down vest over a sweater and tee, guessing temperatures were bound to rise. Her phone had completely died, and she didn't have a chance to charge it after shooting the quilt shop. She was flying blind, weatherwise. The sky had paled from charcoal to smoke, though all signs suggested the sun didn't plan an appearance anytime soon.

She scurried around the barn and headed for the buggy shed, her promise to Rebecca weighing heavily on her heart. Breathing the savory smell of bacon, she clutched the warm packets to her chest and felt the backpack bump against her spine. It contained only Dave's film camera, her water bottle, and a few granola bars for the road. After what Samuel said, she doubted this family would allow photography, and she opted not even to try. She wanted to experience the day not as an invisible woman peering through a lens, but fully present as herself. Her story of the Amish and modernity was still jumbled in her mind like the jigsaw pieces Verna had strewn across a table in the living room. The edges were coming together, but the whole picture was still unclear.

Just outside the shed, the horse was tied to a fence.

Samuel emerged from darkness, dragging the boxy gray buggy like a cowboy and swinging it into position.

She lingered unseen. Cowboys were never her type. Honestly, she didn't really believe they existed. They seemed fabrications of Hollywood, not living, breathing people. Samuel wasn't a cowboy, of course, but something in his quiet confidence hitching up the buggy made her belly trip.

In soft German, he spoke to the horse. The gentle words easily carried across the windless barnyard.

The animal stood with preternatural stillness. She noted his shiny coat and tangle-free mane. He was well cared for, and Samuel handled the creature with respect.

Lawyers, bankers, and businessmen comprised her parents' social set. What did they make besides money? At least the drummers and artists had skills. They could do *something*.

Samuel reached into the buggy, flipped up the right side of the windshield, and fed through the reins.

If the zombie apocalypse came, Samuel would survive. This man had cowboy skills. He could take care of himself and his family. He could take care of her, who had no skills to speak of. Check that—she could sew a little. She could stitch up clothes. Maybe even a wound.

Shivering, she started toward him. May she never have the need to sew a gash with a needle and thread. But any kid who grew up in the ghostly shadow of the World Trade Center knew disaster sometimes struck. She would spend today with a man who mastered the basic skills needed to survive in a crisis. He was capable. The notion was reassuring. More, it was intoxicating.

Also, he knew how to start a hybrid. The memory of their first meeting tugged at her lips, and she met his gaze. "*Guder mariye.*"

"Morning, Brooklyn," he drawled.

Total cowboy. "I brought you grub." She offered a sandwich. "I don't suppose your ride has heat."

"Won't you be surprised if it does?" He grabbed a handle and swung inside. "Hop in. We have a long road ahead."

Cautiously, she planted a sneaker on a round metal step embossed with a pretty star. Such a charming detail on a vehicle designed to be plain. As the passenger, she hopped inside on the left like they were in England and was met by a blast of warm air from a dashboard grate. "What the…?" She held chilly fingers to the heat. "You weren't kidding."

"Too hot?" With a turn of a knob, the flow lessened. He took up the reins. "*Yah*, I tricked her out."

"Tricked her out? You sound like a teenager."

"What can I say? I listen." He clicked his teeth.

The horse shook his mane and pulled.

She sank into a springy seat covered with purple velvet brocade like an antique sofa and slid closed the door. Though starving, she clutched breakfast in her lap and surveyed the interior, too excited to eat. She hadn't known what to expect from the inside of a buggy, but what she discovered was most definitely not it. The dashboard was a rich chestnut, shellacked to a shine. Far from simple, the console curved like a Victorian dresser and was inset with gadgets and gizmos. At her knees was a small, hinged door with an ornate handle, set alongside a row of three silver knobs. A glove compartment maybe? On a lower shelf, a clock the size of a pocket watch was mounted beside a wooden cup holder. Mauve carpeting covered the floor, topped by floormats. Spinning, she peered into the back at a second bench, upholstered in the same purple fabric.

"You like it?" He tugged the reins, stopping to check for traffic, and with another flick, the buggy trundled onto asphalt. "It's old, but it's got charm."

"It's beautiful." Headlights reflected in puddles, and she was glad for the lack of early-morning traffic. She gestured to the knobs. "What do those do?"

"Turn signal, headlights, and interior lights." He pointed to each as he named it. "The battery's in a compartment under your feet, and that's the knob for the windshield wiper." He craned his neck and peered at the lowering clouds. "We might need it this morning. Supposed to clear up by afternoon."

"Ingenious." She swung a knee onto the seat and sat sideways, running her gaze over his profile. "And super cozy."

"It's no hybrid SUV, but it gets the job done."

A proud grin belied his humble words. He might be one of very few Amish who knew the ins and outs of solar technology, but he loved a well-appointed carriage, too. What a curious combination. "Want your sandwich?"

"*Yah.*" He popped open the door in the dash. "Napkins are in the glove compartment, and a thermos of coffee is behind the seat. We've got twenty miles to cover—about two hours or so. There's a quilt in the back, if you're cold. Make yourself comfortable."

Watching barn after barn roll by, she munched buttery biscuit with fluffy eggs. The buggy's gentle rocking was strangely like the subway. It jostled side to side, but springs prevented her from feeling every bump. The horse's hooves *clopped* a regular rhythm, and belly full, she felt her eyelids grow heavy. She rested her cheek against the seat, closed her eyes, and drank in the smell of soap and sky.

Sometime later, she woke to the patter of rain. The windshield wipers squeaked, and to her left, a car crept past. She swiped a circle of condensation from the window and, bleary-eyed, watched the car's occupants take her in. Could they see her ponytail and vest? Did they wonder who she was? Were they maybe a skosh jealous? She felt Samuel shift, and her nap-heavy bones stirred. Coming sleepily to her knees, she fished out the quilt and pulled it into her lap, just to have something to cuddle.

"You're awake." He held the reins in one hand and worked the wiper with the other. "Are you cold? I can turn on the heat."

"Not really." Her words slurred. Notoriously slow to wake, she pressed her lips, knowing she couldn't be relied upon to guard her speech. The moody weather and the scent of coffee and the simple nearness of him made sleepiness something soft and vulnerable. She wrapped the quilt around herself, and as she spun toward the window, she felt her shoulder graze his. His quick inhalation was almost imperceptible, but she caught it. Did Amish kids make out in buggies? What a tantalizing thought. If the rain picked up, and they had to pull over, would she find out?

No longer in the valley, they climbed a winding, forested road. Here and there, a dirt lane branched, offering plenty of private places to park.

But the rain let up, and Samuel released the wiper.

He settled back, allowing not only his shoulder but his whole side to nestle against hers.

The buggy traveled at a pace any self-respecting New Yorker would find excruciating—a crosstown cab at rush-hour pace. A Long-Island-Expressway-on-Memorial-Day-weekend pace. A pace that should make her sigh and wriggle and stare at whoever was driving, but today, she wanted to sigh and wriggle and stare for entirely different reasons. Taking a long pull from her water bottle, she let her thoughts slow to buggy speed and reinvested in her pledge to be present. At eight miles an hour, she spotted all kinds of things in the woods. The white tail of a deer flashed like a warning and bobbed into brush. Some variety of pink bush bespeckled the green-and-gray landscape. A wooden door peeked between branches, betraying an old stone structure built into the hillside. A basement filled with smugglers' gold?

An SUV flew over the mountain, coming toward them at what felt like light speed. She clutched the quilt and leaned the opposite direction, pressing even more firmly into Samuel's side.

He tightened the reins, and the horse held steady.

The car slowed suddenly, and she remembered the sensation of tromping on the brake when they came upon Samuel's friend. She could almost feel the seatbelt tighten. Clammy fear crept up her spine. Rebecca's father was killed in a place like this. Buggies and automobiles did not belong in the same world, and yet, they shared the roads. How was that not a terrible idea?

Yet again, she took in Samuel's shaggy hair and plain attire. He wasn't playing dress-up, and this was no cosplay. How did the Amish possibly think they could maintain their customs in an era of drones and bullet trains? At times, her photo investigation seemed to have only one conclusion: the relationship between the Amish and modernity was folly. It was madness. It was suicide.

The ropy muscles in his forearms flexed, rippling beneath tanned skin. The sun broke through the clouds and lit the fine dusting of hair on his wrists like gold.

His existence was also audacious. Oozing integrity and anchored upon faith, his culture was bolder than almost anything she could imagine—radical even. Now, that was a thought. The radical anachronism of the Amish.

Or were they simply stubborn? She trailed her gaze over his flinty jaw, imagining dropping a kiss beneath that rugged chin...feeling the warmth of his skin, the scratch of tawny stubble, and the flutter of a racing pulse. Breathing the ozone tang of sky, she let her lips part. Was the idea enticing simply because it was forbidden? No. She'd exhausted her yen for rebellion with a grungy parade of artists and activists. Samuel was...someone else entirely. She swallowed and refocused on the road. Though fully awake now, she distrusted her treacherous thoughts. What was a safe topic of conversation? She uncapped her bottle and swigged sweet well water. "Do you like waffles?"

He leaned into the seat, arching his back. "Waffles? Sure."

Metal wheels on asphalt made a racket, but she was close enough to hear joints pop. "How do you cook them? My waffle iron plugs in."

He scratched behind one ear, and his hair stuck out

at crazy angles. "*Mamm's* is cast iron and goes right on the stovetop."

How she longed to smooth that ill-behaved mop. "Old school."

He cut a sidelong look. "Old school?"

"Companion term to tricked out. O.G. Old-fashioned. Back-in-timey." She gave his shoulder a gentle punch. "Dude, it's not just your waffle iron. You kind of eat, sleep, and breathe old school." Except, of course, he didn't. He was so much more interesting.

His sudden laughter was a plunge in the Atlantic on the first day of June—surprising, refreshing, heart-stopping.

The sound faded with a sigh. "Oh, you're funny, Brooklyn. And for a skinny person, you talk about eating an awful lot."

"Why do you think I run?"

"I thought it was for prayer."

Rebecca…so wise and so much trouble. Darcy had decided that when she took the portraits, they'd be on black-and-white film—one negative, one image, one print. She had Dave's camera loaded and ready. Just where and when she'd make the photos, she had yet to determine, but make them she would.

The road pitched upward, and Samuel flicked the reins. "Come on, Hunter."

The forest opened, and she glimpsed blue sky. *Enough to make a sailor's pants*, *Mammi* used to say. Darcy could easily imagine shooting Nora, Tucker, and the girls. Her fingertips tingled with anticipation. To capture Nora's quiet beauty, Tucker's lanky ease, and the girls' ruddy good health would be a joy. Even Verna's special brand of fortitude was a delicious challenge. But Samuel...? How could she shoot Samuel? And yet, how could she not? Setting aside his physical beauty—which, while not insignificant, wasn't exceptional—what about him demanded immortality in the one-and-only photo of a lifetime? Could she capture his curiosity or the special brand of wryness in his humor? The generous, yet laser-sharp, quality of his attention? How about the gentleness of his touch?

Cresting the ridge, the buggy cleared the woods, threading sunlit meadows the color of green apples.

He yawned and tilted his head from side to side. "Troyer's farm is just ahead."

As a photographer, she couldn't capture the sound of his voice, but she'd never forget it. A pang of anticipatory missing him pierced her heart.

With a shake, she pulled up straight, tossing the quilt into the back and shrugging off her vest. With no tint to the windows, the buggy heated like a greenhouse. Squinting, she spied a stark farmhouse and barn atop a gentle rise. Even before she saw the buggy, she noted the telltale lack of power lines, marking the farm as Amish. Situated atop Shade Mountain with views to the south and west, the location was a stunning echo of an Alpine meadow. She half expected Julie Andrews to twirl across the field followed by children in matching overalls. "What a lovely farm."

"Thought you'd like it." He tugged the reins and trundled into the drive. "Winter's rough up here, but I haven't seen a prettier piece of property."

A stoop-shouldered man strode from the barn, his straw hat flaxen in the sun. Like puppies, two boys snapped at his heels. Shielding his eyes with one hand, he tracked their approach. After a moment, he waved and entered the house with a sprightly gait.

Samuel stepped on a floor pedal, and the buggy came to a stop. "That's Abel Troyer. The *kinner* are great-grandchildren, I believe. He and his family have made chicken coops up here for as long as I can remember. They've got a lucrative business." He waved at the vast expanse of sky. "So much sunshine. They're perfect candidates for solar."

The Spartan surroundings were plainer by far than the Rishel farm. Was that an outhouse? "Will they be open to it?"

He leapt from the buggy, spreading his arms wide. "It's God-given energy right out of thin air. What's not to like?"

She bounded out the other side, eager to stretch her legs. The buggy was comfortable but not exactly spacious. "You're a good salesman, Mr. Rishel. And you're no dummy." His arm slid across her shoulders in a touch affectionate but brotherly. Snugging against his solidly muscled side, however, sparked thoughts that were anything but fraternal.

"That I am not," he said into her hair before releasing her.

The morning passed in a strange, but pleasant, blur, populated by people who welcomed her with crooked-toothed smiles and sweet, lukewarm coffee, while making no particular effort to speak English. Any wariness at Darcy's presence evaporated when Samuel shared her family ties. Apparently, *Mammi* Leora taught in this district as a young woman before moving down to Green Ridge. Abel's son, Jethro, and his wife, Patience, were both *Mammi's* students, as were several others.

Settled under a tree amid women and children, Darcy watched as Samuel, straight-backed and confident, accompanied the men to the chicken coop factory. An earthenware bowl of freshly picked pea pods landed in her lap. She pieced together their plan to can soup for a local Amish grocery, and many were on hand to help. Babies and toddlers played under watchful eyes of children hardly old enough to tie their own shoes. Yet, they wiped noses and proffered toys like attentive little mothers. School was out for the summer, and girls and teens clustered in tight circles, bent toward one another until their black *kapps* kissed, giggling without a care in the world.

The yard smelled of cut grass and wood smoke, and the only sounds were the exuberant songs of springtime birds and the occasional distant whoosh of a car. Amidst the rippling stream of women and work, Darcy sat as if on a raft, letting Pennsylvania Dutch eddy with the familiar sounds of a summer long gone, while the swirling motion of work carried her downstream. Though she loved fresh peas sautéed in pasta dishes or in salads, never in her life had she shelled them. Mimicking the women who rained peas from their fingertips by the dozens, she set about her task. Sometimes, the stems snapped cleanly, unzipping the pods at the seams to reveal waxy green pearls side by side. Sometimes, the shell crushed, or the string broke, and she had to crack the pod like a peanut and scoop out her treasure.

The moment her stomach grumbled, plates of sandwiches and bowls of mayonnaise-drenched pasta salad appeared. Quietly, she ate and listened, perfectly comfortable not to be on the inside as she'd been at the quilting, but not on the outside, either. For a period of time she could in no way reckon, she was content, soaking in sunshine as her fingers cramped and peas piled impossibly high in the bowls.

Sometime later, a chorus of men's voices arrived on a rain-scented breeze. The sound turned heads and propelled women from their seats. The girls swiveled like a synchronous flock of birds, clearly wondering if younger fellows came, too. They did. Lunch break was called at the factory, and more sandwiches and tea arrived. Voices swelled, and the men came in a uniform mass of dark pants, jewel-toned shirts, and work boots.

She easily spotted Samuel towering above the others, his long stride and full-bellied laugh unmissable. Even among his people, he was an outlier. The other men his age were married. The women, too, yet she noticed them notice him. What must they think? Believing him a church member, did they wonder at his solitary life? Did they talk? Surely, they did. And no doubt, more than one matron schemed on behalf of a long-single daughter or widow.

He's mine.

Completely irrational, the thought burned behind her eyes like a Broadway marquis.

He's mine, and I'll take him away.

The instant he met her gaze and his jolly smile softened into an expression far more tender, the fire of jealousy abated. She lifted her brows. Had the meeting gone well?

One corner of his mouth quirked, and he gave a quick nod.

Good. *Mammi* Leora might have granted access, but the deal, if done, was all Samuel. She cocked her

177

head in what she hoped was a universal wanna-get-out-of-here gesture.

He lifted his chin, and his eyes darkened. Grabbing a sandwich or two, he clapped Abel on one shoulder and Jethro on the other and strode in her direction.

She stood and let him come. *Wanna get out of here?* had meant a lot of things in her lifetime, but in every case, the desired outcome was to be alone. No matter what came next, and what came next was usually a whole lot of fun, no one else was invited. However, she'd never had *wanna get out of here?* be followed by a ride in an Amish buggy. Let alone a toasty Amish buggy that took a deliciously long time going from here to there. Her heartbeat might have slowed, but the force of her pulse quadrupled.

"Ready to go?" he said.

She brightened her expression, dispelling any traces of expectation like the morning's clouds. After years of practice, she knew how to be breezy. "Yeah. You?"

Ducking his chin, he reached for her hand. "I have somewhere I want to take you."

A tidal wave of anticipation hit in a skin-tingling rush. "I can't wait."

Chapter Fifteen

The flowering bushes were mountain laurel, and they lined the meandering path like snow-covered hedgerows dipped in pink. Darcy cupped a delicate blossom. The buds were like peaks of piped meringue atop a key lime tart. In bloom, they were fairy teacups ribbed with rose and stained on the bottoms with leavings of raspberry tea. The more she looked, the deeper she fell, yearning to shrink to the size of her pinky fingernail and curl up inside a flower like a forest sprite. She chuckled. Even as a girl, she wasn't a fan of fantasy. For an artist, she was quite concrete. But something about the man and the woods made reality's edges soften in a world gone slightly sideways.

After leaving Troyers', he'd driven a mile or two down the mountain before veering onto a side road and tying Hunter to a shady tree. They were on state forest land, crisscrossed by trout streams, deer paths, and hiking trails. He took her hand and led her to a path marked *Susque Run Trail*.

Her palm met his with tantalizing familiarity. *I know you. I've held you before.* Work-hardened calluses rasped supple skin. His hands wielded tools. He shouldered massive panels to harvest sunshine. How easily he might carry her, if ever he desired.

Steps from the parking lot, she'd entered a tunnel of flowering brush, passing beneath blossom-heavy arches like the ceiling of a gothic cathedral. The beauty sparked metaphor upon metaphor. Maybe she was more of a romantic than she thought. Still holding his hand, she twisted in all directions before whipping off her pack and dropping onto her back to gaze into lacy vaults of emerald and blush.

Eyes dancing, he stood over her. "What are you doing?"

She beckoned. "Lie down and see."

The path was rocky and narrow. He wedged his shoulders between roots and lay head-to-head with her...or rather head-to-shoulder, bringing their ears side by side.

Finally settled, he made a deep-chested sound of approval. "Would you look at that."

His ruddy cheek was close enough to kiss. Clutching her backpack and Dave's camera, she breathed the soapy smell of his skin and nosed a hint of grape. Did mountain laurel have a scent? She ran her gaze over his profile from the faint creases in his forehead, down the straight line of his nose, over lips like a marble sculpture, to that rock hard jaw. He let his head fall to one side, and the upside-down view of his face made her giggle.

"Do you do this sort of thing often?"

"I don't typically flatten myself on Broadway, but I do what's required to see." A fluttering snagged her attention, and she caught a flash of wings. "Seeing from every angle is my job."

Rising, he shook, brushing off his pants and extending a hand.

With his help, she'd almost floated to standing. Two miles later, she still walked on air, scampering across a simple plank bridge over a creek. The wind had picked up, tossing her ponytail into her eyes, and rustling the laurel that grew even thicker over mossy rocks on the banks. Who knew this assignment would involve so much hiking? She liked it and thought she'd keep it up once she went home. Her roommates, Zibby and Fern, had long talked of renting a house in the Catskills. Maybe this summer they should.

"Here it is!" he called from around a bend.

Snugging the backpack to her shoulders, she hopped a lichen-covered rock and rounded into a clearing.

Hands on hips, he stood with his back to her, gazing at a massive stone staircase climbing thirty feet into the air…to nothing.

She stared at the strangely magical structure that seemed to spring directly from a story book. It was grand and graceful, supported by three stacked-stone arches curving into the side of the hill. It was almost Adirondack in design, as if it came from one of the great camps in the far northern reaches of New York. Lush ferns carpeted the base, and mountain laurel climbed the stairs, rooting into cracks between stones. Fronds tickled her ankles as she waded to his side. "What is this place?"

He shielded his eyes and arched back, surveying the treetops. "Not sure. Most say it's all that's left of a castle. Others claim it's haunted."

The day was so cheerful she struggled to see the macabre in the mysterious stairway, but she imagined that shrouded in snow or beneath stormy skies the place would assume an eerie vibe. She nudged an elbow into his side. "Have you ever spotted a spirit?"

He chuckled. "As *Youngie*, my friends and I came often and stayed late into the night. But no. No ghosts. The only mischief was our doing."

The wind gusted, bending spindly trees until leaves swept the top stair.

With two long strides, he was beneath the lowest arch which towered over his head by several feet. He laid a hand on the stone support and pushed.

Did she imagine, or did the whole structure tremble?

"We used to leap from the top step to the hillside. Wouldn't do that now." He emerged and sprawled on a low stair. "I thought maybe someone should take its picture before it crumbles into the mountain."

"I see." Her lungs tightened. Rebecca's impulse exactly, but where she wanted to capture flesh, Samuel thought only of stone. Still, he'd surely understand his niece's request, wouldn't he? Swinging off her pack, she took out Dave's camera and framed the shot with Samuel front and center, resting on his elbows and staring at the sky. If she blurred the focus and widened the aperture, he'd look like a ghost himself. She traced her index finger over the hair-trigger circle of the shutter button. And she lowered the camera. "Hey!" she called, shooing him aside.

He jumped up and trotted out of the picture.

Frame. Shoot. Frame. Shoot. Frame. Shoot.

"That's a different camera." Coming closer, he extended a hand.

She ducked out of the strap and looped it over his palm. "It's a film camera. The cupcake lady gave it to me. My other camera is—"

"Digital, *yah*." He resumed his spot on the stairs

and turned the device in his hands.

She perched just below. "I haven't shot on film for years, but somehow, it seems right." Amish life was analog. Images of it should be, too.

At her hip, a tenacious little mountain laurel clung to the stone with its roots splayed like fingers. Mesmerized, she stared into a cluster of flowers. The blossoms were geometrical. Nature and math met in tiny angles and planes. If only she had a macro lens. Even in black and white—maybe especially in black and white—every facet of the flower would tell a story. The white petals made exposure tricky, and she'd have to compose the proper background, but she could do it. "If I had a darkroom, I'd develop these myself," she murmured.

"I can build one."

Lost in the laurel, she'd almost forgotten he was there. Tiny pebbles dug into her forearms, and she brushed them, sending a shower *pitter-pattering* onto bluestone. "Where?"

"In my shop. Rebecca's taken up half the place with those crazy quilt hangings she makes, and of course, there's the cat to contend with. What size would it need to be?"

Was he offering access to his private space? The space where he slept more often than not? The way he leaned back onto his elbows and tilted his head felt like an invitation, and her pulse, which had slowed to Amish time, rocketed to Manhattan pace. Mouth suddenly dry, she groped in the backpack for her water bottle. "Not large. Five by five, maybe?"

"What would you need inside?"

She bobbled the cap and caught it between her

knees. "Just the basics. Counters on either side and shelving for supplies and chemistry. A stainless-steel sink, if possible. Vents for air flow and an outlet to plug in a safelight. Running water is ideal, but not essential." She held the bottle to her lips and paused, flicking a glance his way. "It could be quite rudimentary."

A lazy grin inched across his face. "I got all that and more, Brooklyn."

Oh yes. Yes, he did. Licking her lips, she drank. Was this the guy who only a few weeks ago recoiled from her camera like it was poison? Who lectured his mother on the evils of photography? And did he now offer to build a darkroom in the inner sanctum of his Amish workshop? A gulp went down the wrong tube. Coughing, she pounded her chest with a fist. "But why? Why would you do that?"

He tilted toward her, elbows on knees. "Because I like you, Darcy King. If you don't know by now, you're not as clever as you look."

Tucking one leg, she whirled, her cough instantly suppressed. "What do you mean, you like me?"

Lowering his gaze, he muttered in Pennsylvania Dutch.

Blood rushed to her neck. "I'm sorry, what?"

He sighed and shook his head. "Don't make me put words to this."

"I'm not making you do anything. You volunteered." She jammed on the bottle top and screwed it tight. So tight she might, in fact, need help opening it again. "I'm no Amish *maedel*, crocheting doilies for my hope chest. I'm going back to New York in two weeks where I have a job and a life."

"I know it well. I only wish I was going with you."

184

He spoke so quietly she almost didn't hear. She slid the bottle into her backpack and zipped it closed, just to occupy her hands while her mind went bananas. Forget the fact she casually dropped *maedel* into conversation. Did he mean *with her*-with her? Or just with her?

He opened the top button of his shirt and tugged at the collar. "For once in my life, I want to stand on a street corner with thousands of people and have nobody know my name. I want to bite into something like nothing I've ever tasted. I want to see the world from the fiftieth floor of a skyscraper."

Yearning to grant every wish coursed through her. Twenty-four hours was all she needed. She ran a finger over a clump of velvety moss the color of Ireland. "Those things are all possible, Samuel."

"Not without breaking my mother's heart." He worried a smooth gray stone between his fingers with an expression heavier than all the rocks in the stairway to nowhere.

The picture was so needlessly tragic she had to push back. "Have you met your mother? I've rarely known a more capable woman. Besides, Deacon Elmer is crazy about her. Do you think she might remarry?"

He tossed the stone deep into the woods. It landed without a sound. "I'd like to think so."

"And the deacon has children?"

"Many."

"Either way, she'll be fine." She straightened, bumping her back into his knee. Her first impulse was to jerk away, but instead, she eased into him, feeling her belly flip when he tensed and rooted his foot. "You owe your family nothing but love. You can climb a

185

staircase to nowhere, or you can get on a bus to Port Authority. It's your choice."

He let out a low chuckle. "And that right there is why you'll never become Amish."

"Oh gosh no!" she exclaimed. "I mean, I admire you tremendously, and I respect your brother-in-law's choice, but…no. No way. Nope."

Gently, he drew her ponytail from between them and laid it over his thigh. "Where does all this advice come from?"

"Years of therapy and a highly dysfunctional family." She caught her heels on the step and hugged her knees. "Who would have thought the Upper East Side princess and the Amish farmer would have so much in common?"

He tugged her hair lightly. "I'm no farmer, Brooklyn."

"And I'm no princess." She sighed and rested her head against his knee. "Who knows where either of us belongs, really?" And then she felt his hand on her head, strong fingers rubbing deep circles over sensitive spots she didn't even know existed. A barely voiced sigh escaped like wind before an oncoming train.

A tremor shook him, and his muscles hardened again. "I've screwed up my life to the point I don't belong here, but I don't picture myself out there, either. Sometimes, I'm so paralyzed I can't see past the end of the week. So, with you…" He withdrew his fingers and stroked her hair with a warm, wide palm. "With this, I don't want to put on any kind of name. Because to call it something is to acknowledge it's happening. And if I do that, I have to face the fact it can't. I want a day…a week…two weeks, even where I leave open the chance

I could have something with a woman unlike anyone I've ever known. The only *Englischer* I trust farther than I can throw her. I don't want to leap to the end. Because the end isn't good."

The words were harsh, but his touch and tone were so gentle. Her breath juddered. "It's not?" She turned to him. She couldn't not.

His hand slid over her hair to her cheek. "The end is impossible."

Surrendering, she let him cradle her face, relishing for just a moment the sensation of being held. His smile was so beautifully heartbreaking, she thought she'd cry. Again. "Nothing's impossible."

His thumb traced her cheekbone. "Maybe for you, Brooklyn. For me, the two of us together is a world gone upside down and backward."

An upside-down, backward world sounded marvelous. Like looking in the wrong end of a kaleidoscope and seeing every tiny sliver as a massive rainbow shard. "That's it!" She jerked to her knees, flinching when her kneecaps rolled over stone. "Where's the camera?"

"That's what?" Cocking his head, he gestured to the stair above him.

She planted both hands on his knees and met his gaze. He opened his heart, and she changed the subject like flinging aside one dress to throw on another. "I'm sorry. I heard everything you said, and it made my head go swimmy. But in the spirit of living in the now—together—no labels—I just remembered something. I promise we'll get back to the other stuff, because I really, really want to, but first, I have to show you something. It's called reverse lens macro photography,

187

and it's going to blow your mind."

Very tenderly, he returned his hand to her cheek and leaned in close.

The scent of sky was intoxicating. It was fresh and lineny like laundry right out of the dryer or beach towels on a line. She took hold of his forearm to keep from tumbling into the bed of ferns.

His lips were a whisper away. His gaze searched hers. And then he very gently kissed her.

She hadn't expected his lips to be so warm. Like his touch on her cheek, they were the perfect blend of soft and firm. As she let her eyelids flutter, she went boneless, save for the fingers grasping his wrist to stay afloat. The breeze was insistent. It cooled the perspiration on the back of her neck and seemed to carry the sound of laughter, as if the former occupants of the castle were gathered on a long-gone verandah, and she and Samuel had stolen away in secret. She sensed something inside him stir and caught a barely voiced exhalation thick with longing, but he didn't draw her close. He savored her like a fine wine. How often she'd been guzzled by a kiss. But not now. Samuel's kiss seemed to say, *Let later be later. Let now be now. Oh yes, I can be very…very…slow*.

Her heart swelled, drumming against her ribcage and pushing aside thoughts of later. Later was a quagmire. She was no more prepared to give this thing a name than he. The two of them together was as unreal in her world as in his. But his miraculous lips and his tender, yet insistent, touch and the way he made her feel like kissing was something she'd never done properly even once her entire life was very real. Despite vowing not to, she wracked her brain for a label to describe what, in fact, they could be, hoping beyond hope the only option wasn't star-crossed lovers.

****

The irony of losing the electrical connection between the camera body and the lens was not lost on Darcy. With tingling lips, she'd finally parted from him. Ever so carefully, she reached above him on the stairs, feeling the glancing touch of his chest against her shoulder blades. Inching past to snag the camera had felt flirty and teasing, but also, she desperately wanted to shoot the mountain laurel before she lost the light. Now, propped on the stairs, she anchored the inverted lens to the camera body with one hand and with the other readied to trip the shutter.

He crouched behind, peering over her shoulder.

His curiosity was intoxicating. She'd take a few shots of an intrepid wee shrub holding fast to an enchanted staircase and then give him a turn. Through the viewfinder, she saw spindly stamens tipped with fuzzy pollen. Or were they pistils? She remembered nothing about biology. An elbow brushed against her hip.

"What are you doing now?"

Her pulse skipped, and her body executed a thousand natural processes. Well, she'd forgotten plant biology, anyway. "I flipped the lens backward, jury-rigging it into a macro lens. That cut the electrical connection to the camera, so I have to do everything manually." She shifted forward and back, observing different planes of the flower moving in and out of focus. "I've set the shutter speed at one two-hundred-fiftieth of a second. Fortunately, the lens is old, so I can adjust the aperture for a good depth of field and sharpness." Smelling of moss and time, the gray stone provided an amorphous textured background, and the afternoon sun set the blossoms aglow. She had only a few rolls of film, so she had to be choosy. She framed the shot, wedged her elbows on the stairs like a tripod, inhaled, and tripped the shutter. The satisfying *click* triggered all kinds of endorphins in her brain.

Frame. Shoot. Frame. Shoot. Frame. Shoot.

Other than one class in school, she'd never shot in macro. Typically, her close-ups contained context in which small elements told their stories. Now, the minute was a landscape all its own. Feeling like Alice falling down the rabbit hole, she became smaller and smaller while everything around her grew. What if, instead of focusing on tiny details within a big world, she explored the universe inside the microscopic? What secrets might magnification reveal? Finished, she sat up, rolling her shoulders and stretching her neck.

"Did it work?"

"Mm hm." He'd been so patient, but now, he hummed with barely contained excitement. She popped open a new canister and reloaded the film. "Your turn."

His eyes saucered. "Really?"

She unlooped the strap, pulled off his hat, and slung the camera around his neck. "I'll pick up a reverse mounting ring at the camera shop. Until then, you have to hold the lens super snug." Had he ever looked through a microscope? She didn't know much about Amish schooling besides the disturbing fact it stopped at eighth grade. She doubted one-room schoolhouses were outfitted with science labs. Then again, *Mammi* Leora seemed exactly the kind of woman to bring in a microscope so her students could experience the wonder in snowflakes and grains of salt. She handed him the lens. "What do you want to see up close?"

He surveyed the site. Then, without a word, he crossed to the base of one of the stone arches and laid down on his belly, disappearing into ferns.

What had he found? She came up beside him and crouched on the spongy soil. Propped on his elbows, he held the camera like a pro and focused on a trio of mushrooms. Poking up from the ground like perky sisters, they were exactly like a fairytale drawing of mushrooms, lacking only white dots on their red, waxy caps.

Peering through the viewfinder, he shifted back and forth as she had. "Oh, my word," he whispered. He hovered a finger over the shutter button but didn't shoot.

"Move until the background blurs, and the mushrooms are crisp. Then keep as still as you can and trip the shutter. Sometimes, I hold my breath."

"May I?" he asked.

Again, with the *may I*? She swallowed, surfing a swell of longing that surged with his request for consent to take a simple photograph. When he asked like that, he *may* do whatever he pleased. She ran her gaze from his narrow waist, up the black suspenders, and over his shoulders to the mop of light-brown hair. "Mm hm," was all she could manage.

His stillness was something to behold. Yet, watching the muscles of his back ripple through cotton, she had no doubt he could spring like a cat if something fierce crept from the woods. A bug buzzed in her ear, and she swatted at it. Did snakes live in trees? Or bears?

Bears lived in caves, right? At least they did in the Central Park Zoo. Sitting up on her knees, she skootched until her shins nudged his calves.

Never in a million years could Darcy have imagined this moment, crouched in the woods beside her Amish crush, grass-stained and dirty, having spent the morning shelling peas and the afternoon photographing flowers. Flowers! Surely next, she'd make calendars and greeting cards.

"Oh hello, ant," he said. "Climb the mushroom like a good little fellow." He rocked back onto his knees, sticking his bum in the air like a yogi.

The camera clicked with a sound like permanence. *These things existed on one May afternoon in the lives of a woman and a man. These mushrooms and rocks and ferns. This wee ant. A staircase to nowhere.*

They might contain multitudes, but the objects were tiny in an existence that was, by his account, equally small. She'd spoken truth. She could never live a life proscribed by the distance a buggy traveled in one day. Even so, she didn't shy from his kiss. She kissed him back with her whole self. Theirs was an expansive kiss…a kiss like the ocean he'd never seen.

He sweet-talked the ant in Pennsylvania Dutch.

Models could be so uncooperative.

Giggling, she tipped back on her hands, feeling dampness seep between her fingers. She lifted her cheeks and squinted, blurring the treetops. The day demanded nothing, offering only the breeze and the delicate fragrance of laurel…and certain assurance her time in Pennsylvania would end. Whether she wanted it to or not.

Chapter Sixteen

The next morning at Pammy's, Darcy glanced up from her laptop and right into Samuel's face. She almost spat out her coffee.

At eleven on a cloudy spring morning, Pammy's was quiet. Darcy had been spread out on a roomy table long enough to see the breakfast rush ebb and flow. Fully charged, her devices glowed cheerfully. Although email, paperwork, and arts festival plans were on the task list, she'd spent several hours trolling online ads for darkroom equipment and, finding nothing, editing photos from Sarah's quilting frolic.

And daydreaming...reliving the day before while savoring her scone until she could have sworn Samuel's lips tasted not only of coffee, but strawberries. So, when she looked up from a particularly compelling photo of arthritic fingers tipped by silver thimbles and saw him there...and yet not...she was stunned.

In the lull, Pammy had apparently poured a coffee and lost herself in a book. An Amish romance novel to be precise.

The Samuel on the cover was younger, with smooth skin and a guileless gaze, leaving no doubt this photo was the one taken at an Ohio county fair many years ago. She saw why the photographer couldn't resist. He'd opened to the lens as fully as a mountain laurel in bloom. Plus, he was smoking hot—always an asset in a cover model. She collected her dishes and carried them to the counter, depositing the plate into the pan.

Pammy turned the final page with a melodious sigh. "I love a happy ending." She dropped the paperback onto the counter. "Can I get you a refill?"

"Please." She extended a finger and slyly spun the book until Samuel beamed right-side-up from the cover of *The Amish Bachelor's English Wife*. How apropos. Even in print, his sea-green eyes curled her toes.

"It's a swoony one. Want to borrow it?" Pammy slid the hot coffee onto the counter. "I'm starting this one next." As if by magic, she produced another novel. It featured a young Amish woman, eyes downcast, in front of a red barn. "Sometimes, I like a simple, sweet story, happily ever after guaranteed. You know?"

"I do." She felt compelled to hide her affection for romance from her ultra-savvy New York friends. Not so in Green Ridge. With oddly trembling fingers, she took the book and coffee. If Pammy recognized the cover model, she didn't reveal it. "Thank you."

Pammy settled onto a high stool and adjusted the floral bandana keeping her pretty blonde curls off her forehead. She gestured toward Darcy's messy workstation. "What have you been up to all morning? You hardly looked away from your laptop. Hope you tasted the scone."

"The scone was delish. I edited photos, and I spent forever trying to track down darkroom equipment. Yesterday, I took a bunch of pictures with Dave's camera, and I'd love to develop them myself. You wouldn't know anyone with equipment to spare? I'm building…well, my friend, Samuel, offered to build a darkroom."

"Samuel, huh?" Purple-polka-dotted nails tapped on the counter. "That dishy Amish guy I saw you with last week?"

And five seconds ago, on your book cover. "The same."

"Lucky girl. Believe it or not, I might have what you need. I didn't mention because I figured you'd be here such a short time, but Dave installed a darkroom in our garage. I have all the stuff out back. It's yours, if you want."

"Really?" Tears erupted like lava spurting from a volcano. If it wasn't so pathetic, her uncontrolled sobbing might be funny. "Thank you."

"Oh, sweetheart, you don't have to cry. It's the least I can do." She handed Darcy a pretty paper napkin. "After we spoke, I thought to myself, why that gal's right. I should give Al a call. So, I did. Now, he's helping me clean out the shed, and Bailey starts work on Thursday."

Daintily, Darcy wiped her nose. "I'm glad." She folded the napkin and tucked it into her jeans pocket. Half-and-half swirled into her coffee like no plant-based alternative could. "Sorry to break down. Lately, I seem to cry at everything."

Pammy plonked an elbow on the counter and smushed one round, rosy cheek into her hand. "I cried for two years after Dave died. Happy, sad—didn't matter. I just cried. Television commercials were the worst. Hit me right in the feels." She straightened the pile of napkins until the scalloped edges lined up neatly. "He's been gone eight years now. It's time I emptied the shed. Swing by this weekend, and I'll have the equipment ready."

The coffee was hot and impossibly creamy. Darcy drank coffee at nearly any temperature, but a steaming cup was uniquely delightful. "I went into my grandmother's storage unit the other day. She died when I was a girl. I'm not sure I can ever empty it."

Pammy scrunched her snub nose and stared at the pressed-tin ceiling. "I suppose if you never clean out, you have no room for anything new. Course I don't pay rent on the shed like you must. But all that stuff's been paying rent in my heart, I think. I'll keep the important things and give the rest away." She lowered her gaze and winked. "To someone, maybe, who has a cute Amish carpenter to help her use it."

"For a week and a half, anyway." Darcy let her gaze wander out the window to where the trees lining Main Street hung heavy with pink blossoms so close in color to Pammy's walls, they might have been planned.

Pammy's palm smacked the counter. "A gal can have a lot of fun in a week and a half." She unleashed a hoot. "And I hear you entered the Amish quilt ladies in the Spring Arts Festival. I suppose how long you stay is up to you."

Along with coffee, Pammy served up the exact sentiment she, herself, expressed to Samuel. His life was his to do with as he pleased. So, why did Darcy feel trapped in her own?

She slid back into her chair and toggled to her email. Having let her phone and laptop die, she'd neglected all messages since Friday. A rare lapse for someone who took pride in quick responses. Then again, she was profoundly off the grid. Allowances could be made. Scrolling, she noted nothing vital on the work front. She missed this month's editorial meeting, but she was fairly certain no one missed her.

A message signed, *Get it, girl*, from Rolff linked to an online expense form. She got it all right. In the Amish way, anyway. A giggle leaked out, topped with a quick, coffee-scented snort. What would Rolff advise about her liaison with Samuel? Was liaison the right word? Fling? Affair? Did smooching on a magic staircase a dalliance make? Samuel gave her a nickname. All good romance heroes nicknamed the heroines, and Samuel's was swoon-worthy. The way Brooklyn rumbled from his chest turned her brain to pot pie. If she had to lay money on Rolff's pick, she'd go with Team "Have Fun" Pammy.

But what kind of fun? She had to admit, once Samuel got over the ridiculous fear she'd photograph every Amish man, woman, and child in the county, he'd been pretty great. Time spent with him was fun. Sometimes fraught, sometimes unnerving, but always surprising and beautiful and, yes, fun.

In return, she planned to violate his trust on a deeply personal level. The lovely coffee taste in her mouth soured. For his sake, not to mention her own, perhaps she'd best hit the brakes on the fun train. Maybe give him space. Her spirits sank at the prospect, but she wasn't wrong. Should she even let him build a darkroom? She could easily order prints from the camera shop. She planned to swing by this afternoon for the reverse mounting ring and more film. Imagining locals handling photos of the Rishel family, she shuddered. These pictures were top secret. No one should see them but herself and Rebecca.

Her thoughts spiraled and her stomach with them.

Could she have him build a darkroom and then, while he was out, develop shots of his family? Of course not. Better to take the film to New York for processing and deliver the photos at a later date. But when? And how?

An email from her mother popped up onscreen, bursting the balloon of her whirling anxiety. Bolstered by coffee and wishing for something a wee bit stronger, she opened the message.

No subject line. Of course. Isabelle King needed no prelude.

Darcy,

Saw Margo at the Art4KidzNYC Board Meeting last night. We had only seconds to chat, but she is genuinely enthusiastic about your assignment and feels it could lead to a staff position. You could have toppled me with a feather, especially as I'm down five pounds since last week's stomach bug. Your father's family is completely irrational. For your sake, I hope a few agree to pose. I still think you'd fare better in Appalachia, but what do I know?

Many thanks for the Mother's Day arrangement. For future reference, the florist on Madison has fresher flowers.

Ta-ta,

Mom

She could spend hours parsing messages from her mother. Was "genuinely enthusiastic" sincere or sarcastic? Written with surprise or disbelief? Maybe both. Suddenly, another email notification from Rolff pinged. Curious, she toggled to her inbox and clicked a message with the subject line *Meeting with MRG.*

D,

You have a meeting scheduled this afternoon at

4:40 pm with Margo Ricconi-Gladstone. She requests status update and samples of work. Video conference link attached below.

Rolff

P.S. You got this. Slay.

Completely absorbed in her project, in a way, she'd forgotten Margo would ever see it. Since when was she more concerned with the bishop's photo approval than with her boss's. She fetched a glass of ice water from the pitcher Pammy kept on the counter. Did Margo always check in with photographers in the field, or was this honor reserved for the daughters of friends? Or for newbies whose work couldn't be relied upon to pass muster?

The water cut a cold, sharp path to her jittery belly. She checked the time. A fraction over four hours to prepare. Preliminary editing had separated exceptional shots from merely good. Her desktop favorites folder contained two dozen or so. Perhaps she should winnow down to six? The track pad clicked, and the folder opened, revealing vivid thumbnails. Ultimately, the photos chose themselves. They leapt from the screen, demanding their stories be told. Her work was good. Coffee-enhanced jitters didn't snuff her excitement at the opportunity to share it.

Tucking the romance novel deep into her bag, she began the process of unplugging devices and stashing cords in appropriate pockets. Four hours was more than enough time. All she needed was a change of clothes, a tuna sub, and a place to set up for the meeting. Her laptop slid into its padded pocket, and she rested a knee on the chair. The first two were easy enough, but the last was a doozy. The right location had high-speed

Internet, good lighting, and sufficient privacy. Pammy's was perfect in some ways, but she couldn't count on a mothers' group not to arrive with screeching toddlers or a bunch of old fellows with bad hearing and lots to say, entertaining as they might be.

With one final sweep to make sure she hadn't forgotten anything, she shouldered her bag and waved to Pammy. Somewhere was the ideal spot for a career-making video conference. She just had to find it.

****

A short time later, Darcy texted Sarah from the town parking lot.

—I feel funny asking, but do you happen to know of a quiet place with good Wi-Fi for a video call?—

Sarah answered almost instantly.

—My office behind the quilt shop. It's yours, whenever you need.—

After a week and a half among the Amish, Darcy was unsurprised to discover tucked behind the quilt shop, a comfortable workspace wired for speed. Sarah was nothing if not resourceful. Wood-paneled and tidy, the room was outfitted with a desk and filing cabinets, a bulky, yellowed desktop computer, and a printer. Curtains normally covered the windows, keeping electronics concealed from a community that tolerated but did not enjoy their presence, even for business. Open, they admitted a remarkably flattering afternoon glow.

Her presentation to Margo nearly completed, Darcy advanced to the final photo. The image of gnarled fingers and a threaded needle was so kinetic she could swear it was video and not a still photo. She made a point to look at the web camera and not Margo's face onscreen. "This last image is from a quilting frolic my cousin, Sarah, hosted in her home. Sarah's grandmother has significant memory loss, but she was hands-down the best seamstress in a room with women a quarter her age. The Amish don't hide the elderly behind closed doors. They have no nursing homes. Even the very old contribute to their families and community."

"No nursing homes? No retirement?" Margo leaned back in her chair, grimacing. "Admirable but unpalatable. I can imagine my daughter-in-law's face when she hears I'm moving in." She gave an explosive cackle.

Darcy chuckled and cleared her throat. "The women are making quilts to fund solar panels for their children's school, because the men don't see fit to finance the improvements through the church. The tension between cutting-edge solar technology and the age-old tradition of quilting is compelling. Not to mention the way this endeavor turns the idea of the submissive Amish woman on its head."

She ended the slideshow, and Margo's bright-red lipstick and leopard-print glasses dominated the screen. After pulling on a sleek black top and pinning back her hair, Darcy herself had applied makeup for the first time in days. Peering into the bathroom mirror, she'd felt something like a clown, even though the look was fresh and natural. Having gotten used to nothing but tinted sunscreen and clear lip gloss, any color seemed conspicuous. She checked her appearance in the tiny box on the upper right corner of her screen. Still flawless. She relaxed her forehead, clutched her hands in her lap, and waited for her boss's verdict.

Margo came forward, bracelets clattering against

her desk. "Don't fall in love with these people."

Darcy's stomach lurched. Were photos of her and Samuel floating around the lunchroom at *Hudson Magazine*? Did Rolff say *Get it, girl* because he knew? "Excuse me?"

Margo swept a snowy bang from her forehead. "The work is good, but it teeters on an edge. You cannot get sentimental. Even a hint—a drop—a *soupçon*—will kill it." She balled her fist and shook it at the screen, rings glittering in the brilliant sunlight of a tenth-floor corner office. "Give me tension. Is the modern world tearing the Amish to pieces? How can it not? Will they survive?" She thrust open palms toward the ceiling, and the stacked bracelets jangled to her elbows. "Who knows? Find those teenagers who put on dungarees and smoke cigarettes, the ones trying out the world before they decide to stay. Your work is too beautiful. Show me ugly."

Rumspringa was not the story of modernity Darcy wanted to tell, although she suspected Samuel could enlighten her tremendously in that regard. Still, Amish gone wild was surprisingly obvious. Especially for Margo. Squaring her shoulders, she gazed levelly at the camera. "I hear what you're saying, and I'll cast a wider net—"

"A grittier net. Give me barnacles and shrimps and the bottom feeders with whiskers and bulging eyes."

"A gritty net. Yes." Darcy set her jaw and dug her fingers into her quads. The next nugget of news might not go over well. "One caveat—I did grant the Amish bishop photo approval."

Margo froze.

Her eyes bulged like one of the aforementioned

fish. For an instant, Darcy wondered if the connection cut out.

One arched eyebrow, black as coal, twitched. "You did what?"

"I wasn't permitted to photograph otherwise."

"Have I taught you nothing?" Margo said through a wolfish smile.

Did her boss suddenly fancy herself a mentor? Genius or not, when had the woman modeled anything beyond blind ambition?

"Solve the problem, Darcy. Knowing your mother, I have no doubt you will. *Au revoir!*"

In the middle of blowing a kiss, Margo froze again, and the meeting ended.

Darcy collapsed into the desk chair.

Gritty, huh?

Great.

Chapter Seventeen

Knuckles rapped on the car window, and Darcy jumped, fumbling the last bite of tuna sub. Since finishing with Margo, she'd been sitting behind the wheel in Sarah's parking lot, barely tasting the delicious sandwich while conflicting thoughts fought a cage match in her head. The story Margo insisted upon was not Darcy's preference. But if Amish rebellion wasn't the hook, what was? She couldn't deny the draw. Grit sold magazines. If she made the pictures Margo wanted but with the integrity she, herself, required, she'd have a compelling piece. But would she get the photos past the bishop? If not, could she bring herself to publish anyway?

At the sound of a second gentle tap, she roused and opened the passenger's side door.

A lanky body clambered inside, garbed in rain-speckled violet. "*Denki.* I'm too pooped to ride, and this weather is *baremlich.*" Just off work, Rebecca dropped her head against the headrest, closing her eyes. "That means terrible," she said through a yawn.

Baremlich, she repeated to herself. By the time this project was finished, she hoped her Amish friends didn't apply the term to her. She jammed the Start button and swung out of the parking lot. Wasn't Margo's opinion the only one that mattered? She was in Green Ridge for one reason alone: a staff position at

Hudson Magazine. In the heated confusion of her…whatever…with Samuel, she'd lost sight of the mission. Her future was in New York, not, as Samuel so aptly observed, among the Amish. If Margo wanted grit, grit she would have. All that remained was to find it. She slid Rebecca a glance and switched on the radio.

The girl held a small plastic cooler on her lap. Her head lolled to one side, but at the sound of country music, she perked up and tapped her toes.

While outwardly obedient, Rebecca clearly had her own mind. Perhaps their agreement could be extended into a little *quid pro quo* very discreetly. "About your request from the other day…"

Suddenly pale, Rebecca tightened her grasp on the cooler.

"I haven't begun yet, but I will. I didn't forget."

Slender shoulders eased. "*Denki.*"

"I've been crazy busy with the photo essay. I was just on a video call with my boss to review my work." She swept a hand across her forehead. "Whew, she's tough. In a boxing match between your *Mammi* and Margo, I wouldn't know who to bet on."

A silvery giggle escaped around the slender hand clapped to Rebecca's mouth.

"*Mammi* Verna could probably take her." Rebecca let out an uncharacteristic snort, and Darcy joined her. The image of Verna and Margo slugging it out with massive foam clubs like ninjas on a television show was too good.

"Was your boss pleased?" Rebecca asked.

The door opened. She'd be a fool not to enter. "In some ways, yes. In others, not so much."

"She didn't like the pictures?"

Disappointment shimmered in Rebecca's sweet voice, and Darcy's heart swelled. "She liked them a lot, but she urged me to go in a different direction." Considering how to phrase her request, she eased onto Old Cowan Road. "I want to ask you a question in some ways as delicate as the one you asked me, but if you don't feel comfortable answering, you don't have to. All right?"

Rebecca hugged the cooler tightly. "*Yah*. Of course."

She pressed her lips and gripped the wheel. "If I wanted to find Amish kids behaving in ways adults wouldn't approve of, where would I go?"

Rebecca's iceberg eyes slitted. "You want to photograph *youngie* breaking the rules?"

She waggled her head. "Ish?"

"I'm only just out of school and not part of the youth. I haven't joined a gang—"

"You have gangs?" Switchblades and drive-bys flashed in Darcy's brain.

"*Yah*. The Rockys, The Pinecones and The Drifters, for some. I don't expect I'll join one, but I can't say for sure. That boy we saw on our bike ride— Eli?" Her pale cheeks pinkened. "He's in The Hummingbirds. They run somewhat wild."

Rebecca's crush was a bad boy. Darcy understood the appeal. "Okay, well, if I wanted to find The Hummingbirds on a Saturday night, where would I go?" Vacant lots? Abandoned houses? A set of stairs to nowhere?

"Oh, that's easy." Rebecca relaxed her tight grip. "Baseball games. They watch The Lumberjacks play in the stadium up near Williamsport. You don't have to wait until the weekend. They go most nights the team is in town."

Out of habit, Darcy flipped her blinker before swinging into the farm lane, though no other vehicle was in sight. "I'll check it out. Thanks."

Rebecca bounced in the seat, turning. "If my mother says yes, may I come? Professional baseball, even if it's only minor league, isn't permitted for church members, but I'm not one yet. Normally, she'd forbid it, but if Tucker overhears, I might have a chance."

She was in no way surprised to hear Tucker bent the rules, and Rebecca used it to her advantage. The Kings were diehard baseball fans. She'd watched scads of games from the luxury box in the Bronx her father's law firm provided. A baseball game might not be the rough environment Margo had in mind, but the photo possibilities were intriguing.

"Would you be wanting to take their pictures?" Rebecca asked. "Eli and the boys at the game?"

"I might. Yes."

Rebecca picked at a masking tape label on the cooler lid. "Samuel won't like that."

"Probably not." She pulled up next to the barn and cut the motor. The barnyard and garden were quiet in the rainy, pre-supper lull. Did Rebecca know Samuel wasn't a church member? Having him at the game might present problems, but it might solve some, too. And she couldn't deny how intoxicating taking him to his first baseball game would be. "Do you think he would enjoy watching a game?"

Mischief glinted in Rebecca's eyes. "I think he'd love it."

Oh yes, Rebecca was as aware of her uncle's church status as she was of the many love affairs that kindled in her orbit. Maybe with popcorn and peanuts and a charming niece as distractions, Samuel wouldn't notice Darcy disappear with her camera. Maybe, in turn, he'd prevent Rebecca from being spotted by the boys and implicated in Darcy's behavior. And maybe, just maybe, she could pull off grit without anyone getting dirty.

****

When Darcy came to the narrow dirt road two miles beyond the Rishels' lane late the next afternoon, she hardly recognized the man in the shadows. Notably, he was alone. She'd expected Rebecca, as well.

Secondly, he wore jeans.

Actual denim jeans.

And a T-shirt.

And a baseball hat.

Had she been a cartoon character, her eyes would have bugged out to a crazy *bazoinga-wowza* sound effect. He didn't exactly look English, but nobody would mistake him for Amish. The shirt fit tight across his chest, and though not skinny, the jeans hugged what appeared to be rock-hard thighs. She snagged her iced coffee and took a long drag. Unsure if she'd have to sweet-talk rebellious teenagers, she'd dressed up a touch, too. Her cropped peasant top had a low scoop neck and puffed sleeves. The denim skirt skimmed her knees, and cute sneakers completed the look. Would Samuel notice?

Checking over one shoulder, he threw open the door.

She thrust out a hand. "I'm sorry, sir. I don't give

rides to strangers."

He dove in, bumping his knees on the dash.

"Who are you? I've never seen you in my life." She lowered her sunglasses and blinked. Damp hair curled from beneath his cap, and he smelled of soap. She rounded her eyes, teasing. "Samuel Rishel? Is that you?"

"Ha ha." He rubbed a hand over one kneecap. "Rebecca can't come. Nora was iffy to begin with, and then the twins came down with fevers."

"Poor kid. I'm sorry." She was sorry for herself, too. She'd counted on Rebecca to distract Samuel while she trolled the stadium for Amish hoodlums. Giant bags of candy bulged in her bag, in case bribery was required. Now what? Arguably, she should have gone alone. This game was work, not play. Without Rebecca…well, she'd have to figure it out.

She tapped the phone in its holster, and her old friend, Taylor Shift the map lady, issued directions with robotic self-assurance. *Don't worry*, she seemed to say. *Your path is clear.* Presumably, the Amish never suffered the panicky feeling of being lost, peering at unfamiliar landmarks with no idea where to turn. How often she'd emerged from the subway onto a street corner she'd never seen, watching her blue dot gyre on the map app until she got oriented.

"The phone tells you where to go?" He picked up the device and studied the map.

"Yeah. Much easier than navigating while driving. Safer, too."

"Ingenious." His finger hovered over the screen. Then he fisted his hand and replaced the phone. He tugged at his shirt and wrenched around to scratch one shoulder.

His crisp tee would require about fifty washes to soften. The jeans were deep-blue with bright stitching. She could almost hear the new denim crunch. But the hat was sun-faded and frayed, sporting the logo of a company she didn't recognize. Tractors maybe? Or fishing gear? Not that the effect wasn't pleasing, but why was he dressed this way? Did he buy everything this morning, or did he have a secret stash of normal clothes? Dared she ask?

Maybe music would put them both at ease. She switched on the radio, and a country song she'd heard often enough lately to know the chorus played. She could come around to country music. The lyrics were catchy, and the men sang like men. If all went well, she'd break her promise to Samuel seven ways to Sunday tonight and then go back and do it again at the farm. Her life was a country song waiting to be written.

Restless energy coiled in his limbs, and he tapped his hands against his thighs.

The memory of the last time they were alone electrified the air. Having kissed, they couldn't return to the status of innocently flirty. Some lines couldn't be uncrossed. She licked her lips, tasting strawberry lip gloss that reminded her of high school when every interaction with a boy felt as charged as this one. His shoulder was very, very close. "Nice jeans."

He pulled the cap down over his eyes. "Thanks."

"Why are you wearing them?"

"Don't people generally wear pants to baseball games?"

"You don't," she shot back. "Not this kind, anyway."

He interlaced his fingers between his thighs, and his knees dropped open. "Well, Brooklyn, it's like this. Professional sporting events are too worldly for church members. As I'm not a church member, I go with a clear conscience." He flapped his knees together and let them fall. "The others in my district are under the false impression I *am* a member. If word got out I attended a game, my family's standing in the community would suffer. At best, the bishop would have words with me. At worst, I'd have to make a church confession. Though it wouldn't be my first, it might be my last."

His tone was half-joking, and she kept her voice light. "That sounds unpleasant."

All the humor drained from his face. "Unpleasant is far too pleasant a word."

Since when was a baseball game such a minefield? Maybe this evening was a mistake. She turned down the radio. "Samuel. I invited you and Rebecca tonight because I wanted to thank you for being so helpful, but I couldn't live with myself if my actions hurt your family. We don't have to see the game. We can go for ice cream or take another buggy ride." The car idled at a traffic light next to a billboard advertising *Ralph Feely's Reptileland*. She jerked her chin toward the sign. "How about Reptileland? Lizards are cute. I could do without snakes but…"

"You're too pretty to spend the night with a bunch of snakes."

Her blouse was so open at the neck that were she to blush, he'd likely summon a doctor. She inhaled deeply and imagined the biting wind off the Hudson. "Thank you."

He waved a hand. "Besides I'm unrecognizable.

Don't you agree?"

His smile hijacked her breath. She nodded, but the nod was a lie. He was completely recognizable.

He tugged at the tee. "The clothes are a precaution. Our *youngie* rarely go to games, and none are likely to run to the bishop. They know the proverb about slandering a servant to his master."

Darcy was not familiar with that particular saying, but she guessed it did not end well for the slanderer. The notion of church confession was also horrid. She could imagine Samuel, tall and defiant, standing before the congregation with blazing eyes and an iron jaw. Though the scene was straight from a movie, she couldn't let herself romanticize it or allow it to happen. "Are you sure?"

"Absolutely. Besides, I've heard the nachos at the stadium are extremely spicy." His eyebrows waggled a dare. "Wanna try them?"

She'd sampled *habanero* chilis in Austin and Indian curry on the Lower East Side. Both nearly incinerated her face. For him, she'd play along. "Why not?"

The evening was cool with a slight breeze. She'd purchased seats behind the dugout on the third base side, high enough to survey the crowd yet close enough for a good view. Compared to a major-league stadium, the park was intimate. She easily heard the smack of balls hitting leather and players' conversations as the home team finished their warm-up. The sun sank behind the stands, casting their section in shade. Balancing a box of nachos on her lap, she slipped sunglasses into her hair and settled in. "Baseball is played in nine innings." She pointed to an old-fashioned scoreboard over the left field wall. "The teams take turns batting and fielding, with each doing both every inning. If we're lucky, we'll see lots of hits and home runs. Games with no offense are boring."

His eyes narrowed, and he regarded her a moment. "You know your baseball, Brooklyn."

Did he think women didn't understand baseball? "I've gone to games my whole life. My father and brother are huge fans."

He slurped soda from a plastic cup emblazoned with the home team mascot, a bright-blue, goggle-eyed bear with a raccoon cap and a plaid shirt. "You don't talk about your siblings much."

"They're perfect. What more can I say? They have successful jobs and proper spouses with whom they produced profoundly gifted children." She raised her own soda in a toast. "To Princess Maddy and Bonny Prince Garrett. Long may they reign."

He clunked his cup against hers. "They sound boring."

"Painfully." She sipped sugary soda. Fizz sizzled a path to her tummy. "They can't help it. I'm lucky to be so fascinating."

A skinny, bespectacled boy in a scouting uniform trotted to a microphone on the pitcher's mound.

Doffing their hats, both teams lined up in front of the dugouts.

Clutching the world-famous Forest Fire Nachos in one hand and tucking the soda in the cup holder, Darcy rose.

Samuel stood beside her, holding his hat over his heart.

His hair matted and curled at the ends in a serious

case of hat-head. Still, only fear of smushing the nachos kept her from throwing herself at him.

The diminutive scout pushed up his glasses, opened his mouth, and sang the national anthem in a soprano so sweet and pure it could have shattered glass. All around her, kids and old men sang heartily, breaking into applause after "the land of the free," like fans did at every stadium in every corner of the country. The breeze carried whiffs of fried onions and cut grass, and the mowed lines on the field met in perfect ninety-degree angles, as if no matter what happened in the world, baseball remained.

Yet, she was here to immortalize delinquency. She scanned the crowd for suspenders and bowl cuts—anything marking a group of boys as Amish. Dads downed hot dogs. Kids chattered and squirmed, gazes more on the field than on phones. Most of the scrolling was done by Moms who likely saw the evening as a rare moment to relax. Surely, at a baseball game, Dad could be the parent on call. The speakers blared the opening lineup, and she ran her gaze up and down aisles until finally snagging on a group of young men sitting on the first-base side where sun still slanted into the stadium.

Suspenders? Check. Mop tops? Check. Much like Samuel, they didn't look like regular teens, but they surely didn't look Amish, either. They swigged soda from two-liter bottles and moved in the erratic, unpredictable way of teen boys, as if at any moment, one or more might blast into space.

She'd stuffed her camera in a hobo bag with the candy, currently shoved under the seat. When to make her move? Should she excuse herself to the restroom and try for the final rays of daylight? Or wait and shoot the boys beneath the night sky? The first batter came to the plate, and she relaxed into the seat. Later. For now, she needed to teach Samuel everything she knew about baseball. She leaned into him, bumping shoulders. "The beginning of every inning is called the top, and the second half is the bottom. The away team always bats first with a solid player as the lead-off hitter. You want a guy with a high on-base percentage, meaning he's likely to make it to first without getting out."

She'd barely spoken when the Steel City Ironmens' shortstop crushed a line drive for a single.

Noisy and good-natured, the home crowd groaned.

"Shake it off, boys!" she yelled, like she'd rooted for The Lumberjacks since birth. Catching the irresistible ballpark frank scent, she flagged a roving vendor and purchased two.

Samuel propped an elbow next to hers on the armrest and chuckled. "You're quite a fan."

She shrugged. "Baseball's the only sport I enjoy, and at a small stadium like this, you really feel part of the game. I like seeing the players' faces. The drama is all right there." She nestled her dog next to the nachos and clasped her hands beneath her chin. "It's kinda thrilling."

He bit into a hot dog with all the fixings. "It is."

Afternoon fell to evening, and baseball totally showed off. The game surged in short, high-intensity bursts of home runs and double plays. Between innings, enthusiastic spectators pedaled tricycles through an outfield obstacle course, and an epic base run of the pickles, Dill, Sweet, and Bread-and-Butter, took place.

Darcy put her money on the guy in the sweet pickle

costume, and Samuel bet on the dill.

Both went down when Sweet and Dill collided, spiraling in circles while Bread-and-Butter ambled in for the win. When Sweet tumbled into the home team dugout, appearing to genuinely irk the players, he was tossed onto the field by the Lumberjack mascot.

The cartoonish antics were just dumb enough to be funny, and Darcy laughed so hard she nearly choked on her hot dog.

Samuel became an instant baseball fanatic. When the Lumberjacks' spunky left fielder skyed a sacrifice fly into deep right field, bringing the game within one, he leapt to his feet with a whoop.

At the seventh inning stretch, she rose and fished a hoodie from her bag. Her camera lurked at the bottom, strap coiled like one of Ralph Feely's snakes. If she was doing this, the time was now. She darted a glance at the Amish boys, and her spirits sank. Nothing about them was gritty. If anything, with their ill-fitting clothes and black suspenders, they looked kind of dopey. Even the one scrolling a phone just seemed normal—a shaggy-haired kid at a ballgame with friends.

Still on his feet, Samuel cupped his hands around his mouth. "Let's go, Jacks!" he shouted in chorus with the final strains of "Take Me Out to the Ballgame."

She turned to him, his strong profile stark in the stadium light. He'd swiveled his hat backward when she explained the concept of rally caps and listened while she talked small ball and six-four-three double plays. His boundless curiosity made her want to make out in a very public place. He might have mansplained motors on their first meeting, but he allowed her to lay out the rules of baseball like he was from another country—which he was, sort of. After years of being lectured by her father and Garrett, being the baseball expert was a rush. How much did minor league teams cost, anyway?

Chewing her straw, she studied the Amish boys. Even if she was completely transparent, could she approach them, as a pretty woman had once approached Samuel, and ask them to pose? Plastic squeaked between her molars. Her chest tightened. Not with Samuel in a ten-mile radius. She couldn't do it. And she couldn't shoot his family without telling him. When the moment was right, she'd share Rebecca's request. She swiveled in his direction. She had to.

Samuel caught her staring and hoisted the untouched nachos. Dotted with grayish-green jalapenos, the orange topping had congealed, and a wrinkly skin coated enormous chips. "You ready?"

The announcer called the name of the next batter, the Ironmen shortstop who was three-for-three with two RBIs.

She drew a long breath. The smell of fake cheese flooded her sinuses. "Let's make it interesting. One chip, equal in size and cheese volume, and five peppers each. No drinks." She pursed her lips and cocked her head in challenge. "First one with an empty mouth wins."

He squinted one eye. "Wins what?"

How little he knew of her tolerance for spice. "Bragging rights?"

"I need more than that."

She darted her tongue over suddenly dry lips. *You win, I teach you to drive. I win, I take photos of everyone in your family including you. No? I've got other ideas…* Lost in him, she only barely registered the smack of bat meeting ball and the collective gasp of the crowd. His eyes were flirty. His wide mouth curled in a teasing invitation to be kissed. Ready to RSVP *yes*, she swayed closer.

Then, he gasped and shoved in front of her, pushing her into the seat with sudden force.

The air whooshed from her lungs, and her head whipped against the seat back. The stadium whirled, and breathless, she heard nothing…felt nothing for what felt like forever but might have been mere seconds…until hands grabbed from behind. Who was touching her? Cheers rose. The hands clapped Samuel on the back and ruffled his rally cap.

Dazed, she let her head fall to one side, tweaking her neck as she glimpsed the giant instant replay screen. Fifty feet tall and in full color, Samuel clutched a baseball in one bare hand. So much for flying under the radar.

A friend of her brother's was hit by a foul ball, shattering his cheekbone. Two surgeries later, his face still wasn't the same. Had Samuel saved her from the same fate? How?

Almost instantly, the game resumed, and he sat, looping an arm around her shoulder and pulling her close. "I'm sorry I pushed you. I was afraid you'd get hit."

The ball was bright-white and dappled with scuff marks. Against supple skin, it would have been hard as iron. She pressed her head against him and squeezed closed her eyes. "Did you just barehand a foul ball?"

A chuckle vibrated through his shirt. "I did."

Pulling away, she caught his gaze. His eyes were a

touch wild, and his chest heaved. "How?"

The ball dropped into his lap, and he shook his hand, opening and closing the fingers. "Before I went to Ohio, I played third base for a team not far from here. Those boys over there..." He nodded toward the Amish teens. "They play, too. All Amish kids are baseball fans. When you're running around, folks look the other way."

She felt her jaw give way. "But I...but you...you let me explain everything."

He gave a crooked smile. "You seemed to enjoy it. I need to read this *Moneyball* book. Maybe they have it at the library."

A sick feeling welled in her belly. "I feel so stupid. You let me go on and on."

Lightning fast, he touched her cheek. "I wanted you to. I like listening to you."

He spoke slowly, making sure she heard even through her shock. His palm was hot. Likely, it stung. She nuzzled her cheek into it, wishing her skin was icy cool to soothe the hurt. "Thank you." His lips met hers in a kiss like a blessing. As if he needed to ensure she really was whole and intact. He pulled away, and she strained toward him, caring nothing for who saw. "I came to take photos of the Amish kids," she whispered. The words just slipped out, and she winced. Perhaps he'd quite literally knocked the sense out of her.

"I know," he breathed against her lips.

She jerked back, blinking into lights that framed his head like a halo. "How?"

He shrugged. "I know you."

She took his hand and then released it, forgetting and then remembering how it must sting. "I won't do it.

I can't…even with their permission." She scrabbled in the holder for her soda cup. It was still full of ice and might be soothing. "I don't feel right after what happened to—"

He stopped her with a kiss.

He might be Amish, but in his brand-new jeans, he seemed to have zero qualms about public displays of affection. She felt her fingers freeze and heard a kid behind her say, "Ew, gross," but she didn't care. She'd happily kiss him until the stadium went dark. The *crack* of a well-hit ball split the air, and only then did she startle away, cowering against his shoulder.

"Going…going…gone!" the announcer's voice boomed over the speakers. "The Lumberjacks take the lead!"

The crowd erupted. From somewhere above, popcorn rained, and she reached for it like a child catching snowflakes. Then she pressed the soda cup into his palm, now bright-red and swollen.

He exhaled, dropping back his head with a sigh. "Thanks, Brooklyn."

She'd told him the truth. One truth, anyway. Now, to find the right moment to tell the rest.

Chapter Eighteen

Darcy had dated enough musicians to recognize good ones. Returning from her run the next morning, she caught the unmistakable sound of a guitar masterfully played. She'd awakened early with the taste of Samuel on her lips and her promise to Rebecca like a barbell in her gut. She needed a cleansing workout, and she got it. She checked her watch. Seven-minute-ten-second pace. Not bad on rutted, dirt roads. She slowed, enjoying the endorphin high that almost, but not quite, matched the feeling of being in Samuel's arms. She ran hard enough and long enough that her mind cleared, and maybe, just maybe, she had a brief moment of peace that felt like prayer. She breathed in gratitude and exhaled a quiet plea for guidance. Her answer was a melody drifting over meadows on a cool and windless morning.

Bent over his guitar on the front porch steps, Tucker appeared so like the country superstar she'd cyberstalked, that, were her breath not already ragged, he would have taken it away. The guy was legit hot. To think he gave up everything. For what? Love? Family? God? Though he dressed Amish and spoke their language, he was tangibly different. A quality in his manner—a casualness in his movement, maybe, or an awareness in his gaze—kept him separate. The transformation was hard to buy. She was tempted to call his bluff. Was he all in? Really and truly?

The song sounded distinctly like "Welcome to New York." She caught his gaze and gave a canny look. More than canny…challenging. Every inch the Nashville superstar, even in suspenders, would he allow photos? What did Tucker McClure think about the Amish and modernity? What did he know? More…what was he hiding from? She softened her expression with a friendly wave.

He swept shiny, dark hair from his eyes. "*Guder Mariye*, Darcy."

Did he lean on the Dutch a skosh? "*Guder Mariye*." She leaned just as heavily back. "You're playing my song?"

"Bingo." Childish babbling came through the screen door, followed by Nora's calming voice. Dishes clinked. In the distance, a dog barked.

She caught a foot in a quad stretch. "How are the twins? I heard they had fevers."

"Snotty messes. I swear they get sick every two weeks." Resting the guitar on his lap, he tipped back on his elbows. "I can't complain. Today, I'm singing in the pediatric ward at St. Luke's. I know how lucky I am."

According to online sources, several years ago, heavy drinking and a midnight run-in between Tucker's car and a daycare center cut short his career. Soon after, he'd disappeared, leaving rampant speculation as to where he'd gone. Gossip sites intimated he'd joined the Amish and offered blurry photos as proof. The idea was roundly shot down as absurd. Most fans believed he was a fisherman off the Alaskan coast. A supporting photo showed such a convincing likeness, she had to wonder if he leaked the shot himself.

"Wanna come?" he asked. "My grandad Hank was going to drive, but he's got his tap-dancing class later."

"Old people tap dancing is adorable." She shuffled her sneakers in the one step she remembered from a brief foray into tap. "Can I join?"

He strummed a minor chord. "Been there. Done that. Believe me, you don't want to."

A willowy figure appeared at the door. "Tucker, the girls want the song about the yellow submarine. Apparently, I don't sing it right." Rebecca yawned. "Hello, Darcy."

Darcy gave a sympathetic wave.

"You gotta learn more than the chorus, Beanpole. They like the verses. All thirty-seven of them." Chuckling, Tucker unfolded himself from the step and stretched. "Be right there."

Rebecca planted her hands on her narrow waist. "I don't like Beanpole, either. Try a different nickname." A shriek rang from the house, and with a sigh, she trudged away.

"I'd love to go to the hospital," Darcy said. "I'll drive...unless you want to?"

He slung the guitar over one shoulder. "Pretty sure my license expired."

Like Samuel, Tucker didn't take himself seriously. Maybe that's why the men worked so well together. A disconcerting thought slithered its way into her calf stretch. Had Samuel talked about her? He didn't seem like one to kiss and tell, but she couldn't say for sure. Just what did Tucker know? "Would it be all right if I took a few photos?"

"Sure. Just keep my identity on the DL." He winked. "This town is crawling with paparazzi."

"Word." She shot finger guns. "I got you."

She joked, but the convo was weird. Tucker was for real, right? All-in with the dramatic life change from Nashville to an off-the-grid cottage on a farm. Was he content to swap the Ryman Auditorium for the children's lounge at St. Luke's Hospital and transform ten thousand screaming fans into two dozen children and families, singing along to silly songs about the moon and burps and accidentally swallowing bugs? Standing on a plastic kiddie chair a few hours later, she wondered.

As she shot over children's shoulders, blurring profiles and homing in on details, she caught a faint echo of her story. Forget Margo and gritty. Darcy was on the right track. The story of the modern Amish was one of contrast—incongruities that together offered new meaning. She might not publish shots of cigarettes and alcohol. But she'd tell the truth…the truth she cared about…the truth she believed.

She pivoted, and Tucker's lean face filled the viewfinder. If he was faking Amishness, he was an excellent actor. Mossy eyes twinkled above a neatly trimmed beard. Vocal cords that could have gone platinum filled a cheerful room in a rural medical facility. She floated a finger over the shutter button, but her personal vow to shoot the family on film and not digital was one she wouldn't break.

Pajama-clad in wheelchairs and hooked up to IV tubes, children who could dance, danced. A few clapped along from hospital beds.

Toes tapping and heads bobbing, doctors, nurses, and support staff crowded doorways and lined the sunny yellow walls.

Regardless of the venue, Tucker McClure drew a crowd.

She lowered the camera. What did this man's radical choice say about the Amish and modernity? Over ice cream later, she asked. The afternoon felt more like June than May, and the Softee Freez, an old-fashioned ice cream stand, was as busy as a New York bagel shop on Saturday morning. Young families and elderly folks alike enjoyed sweet treats on picnic tables and benches. A handwritten sign advertised the day's special flavors, while an old-school letter board displayed options for shakes, sundaes, cones, and more.

Sprawled on a bench, Tucker gnawed the straw of a strawberry milkshake and gazed at the cloud-streaked sky. "I'm just one guy. I can only talk about my experience."

Streams of vanilla soft serve leaked from her peanut butter dip top. Central Pennsylvanians will dip anything in peanut butter and to very good ends. She licked a glob from her chin. "From what I hear, your experience is pretty singular. People romanticize Amish life, but not many join. Were you welcomed?"

"To begin with, yeah. I spoke some German so that helped, and I grew up on a solar-powered potato farm in Maine. The guys were happy to hand me a hammer at barn raisings once I proved I knew how to use it." He sat up, adjusting his hat. "When I seemed inclined to stick around, though, they made dang sure my feelings for Nora were sincere. Nothing like an interrogation over pot pie. Once they understood I was joining up for more than her, they took me seriously." He crossed one long leg over the other and splayed an arm across the back of the bench. His fingers tightened on the top slat.

"Can't say it was easy. Plenty of times I thought if I could steal Nora and Rebecca away, I would. But I didn't want easy. I wanted right. This life and this faith are a kind of right I've never experienced before." He gestured to people ducking in and out of cars, talking on their phones. "Once I gave all that up, I felt whole."

Unlike much of the clothing she'd seen on Amish men, Tucker's was impeccable. The fabric was crisp, and his boots were mud-free. No patches or threadbare places showed on elbows or knees. For him, simple wasn't sloppy, and it wasn't lean. How did they get by? Verna spoke of money troubles, but between the solar business and Nora's farm stand, the McClure family appeared secure. Tucker hadn't renounced comfort but only convenience. He hadn't forsaken technology. He simply shifted his relationship to it. Technology served him, not the other way around.

"I'm gonna be honest because I see something of myself in you." He lowered his drink and gave her a level look. "Love isn't a good enough reason to do this."

Soft serve plastered to the roof of her mouth, exploding through her head in a brain freeze. She blinked and swallowed hard.

"The last four years, I've spent most of every day with Samuel. You get to know a person in a buggy. He's as solid and thoughtful a guy as I've ever met." He rubbed a hand over his beard and tugged the ends. "He watched his father die and his brother leave, and that scrambled him up some. Sobered him, too, eventually. He's all jokes on the outside, but inside..." His voice trailed off, and he squinted at a plane flying so high it couldn't be heard. "He's soft. Maybe he was born to this life, but he's no more made for it than you. Electricity runs in his veins. The guy understands motors better than the mechanic who kept up our tour bus back in the day. With an education, he'd likely be an engineer, but instead, he's…" He played a chord progression on the bench and drank. "Well, he's not going anywhere."

The cold eased its grip, and she ran her tongue around the cone, heading off a sticky mess. The conversation had veered seriously off course and was barreling like a freight train toward a cliff edge. A piece of peanut butter shell cracked in a chunk. She removed it delicately, nibbling while she considered how to respond to an avalanche of information she hadn't requested but found she craved. And yet, did any of what Tucker said really come as a surprise? Maybe the revelation Samuel watched his father die. She hadn't known that.

Miraculously, she didn't tear up. She'd made some progress.

A bee swooped in, circling her ice cream like a drunken tornado.

She flinched. She hated bugs, and for good reason. Bitten, she inflated like a balloon. More than once, mosquito bites swelled her eyes closed.

Tucker thrust his shake in her direction, and the bee alit on the lid. Leaning way over, he deposited the cup on the far end of the bench and rubbed his hands down his thighs. "I like it melted, anyway."

"Thanks." She savored a sweet and salty lick. What exactly did he want her to do with all this information? "So back to modernity…"

"Right." He crossed his arms and leaned back, legs

Wendy Rich Stetson

spread wide. "The Amish aren't blind. They aren't
pretending it's eighteen fifty or whatever, and they
don't want to rewind the clock. Technology has
benefited them as much as anyone. They just use it their
way." He shifted and bumped shoulders. "Look, no
community is perfect. The Amish have bad seeds like
everyone else. You can no sooner generalize about
them as you could about New Yorkers—bunch of
loudmouthed, standoffish jerks."

"Hey!" She gave him a good-natured thwap.

He winked. "They—*we* live in a modern world.
But we do so by our rules without letting worldly
influences interfere, for the most part. You need
discipline to live intentionally. And that, as the poet
said, makes all the difference." Shooing the bee, he
reclaimed his shake. "You asked one question, and I
went on for ten minutes, but don't think I didn't notice
how you changed the subject." He caught her gaze and
gentle humor lightened his expression. "Be careful with
Samuel, okay? He talks a big game, but he's a teddy
bear. Take care of yourself, too. This isn't New York
City."

"That it isn't." She tilted her head, and her ponytail
slid over one shoulder. "Why are you telling me all
this?"

"Like I say, I maybe walked this road a couple of
years ago. It's not easy." He came forward, propping
elbows on thighs." For a while, I couldn't see a way
forward, but my wife gave a good piece of advice. She
told me to have faith."

"Faith, huh?" A micro snort slipped past her sticky
lips.

He gazed at her steadily over one shoulder. "That's

exactly what *I* said. Then I gave it as a name to our daughter."

Daring to imagine a life with Samuel, she stilled, heart catapulting, but reality stepped on the brakes. Faith was fine for other people—people like her cousin Sarah and *Mammi* Leora. Faith didn't pay the rent on a third-floor walkup in Cobble Hill. And it certainly didn't secure staff positions on *Hudson Magazine*, even if it did weave through her photo essay like a silver filament, catching the light when she turned her head just so.

Faith was scary. Faith meant surrendering control.

She balled her dirty napkin and chucked it into the trash. Who was she kidding? She'd never controlled anything in her life.

Pushing aside thoughts of love, she trudged up to her attic room late that afternoon. Her work was excellent, but fears of disappointing Margo and losing the opportunity of a lifetime wormed into her thoughts. She slung her bag onto the glider and flopped on the unmade bed, arms outstretched.

The quilt puffed like a bellows, and a piece of notepaper took flight, shooting off the nightstand and onto the floor.

Rolling onto her belly, she inched to the side of the bed and, too lazy to rise, stretched as far as she could, pinching the paper between two fingers.

A message was written in the neat, square hand of a draftsman.

Darcy,
Come by the workshop.
I have something to show you.
S.

He'd been in her room while she was gone. And she didn't mind one bit. She closed her eyes. Faith wasn't faith if it was untested. But her life would be so much easier if Samuel was just a tatted-up drummer like the rest.

Chapter Nineteen

Ten minutes later, Darcy stood at the workshop door, summoning the courage to knock. Did Samuel typically have female guests? Somehow, she didn't think so. She flattered herself she might even be the first. Belly fluttering, she licked her lips, tasting the vanilla lip balm she swiped on before tidying her ponytail and speed walking to his place. Ready to rap, she cocked her fist.

The door flew open.

"Oh!" She jumped, pressing a hand to her racing heart. "Jiminy Christmas, you scared me! I don't know why—like, who else would be opening your door?" An explosive giggle surfaced like the air bubble that belched when a new jug went onto the water cooler at work. "Listen to me—Jiminy Christmas. I sound like George Bailey." She clamped down on her bottom lip. Nervous much?

He leaned a muscley forearm on the doorframe. "You found my note?"

"Sure did." She bounced on tiptoes for a glimpse over his shoulder. A long wooden workbench. A pegboard. So many windows. Tools. "Have you had many…friends…come by?" The question was absurdly intrusive, but she couldn't resist. She was bubbly and babbling and dying to know.

He stepped to one side and opened a hand. "You're

the first."

"Lucky me!" Anticipation flooded her chest, and she entered. Inside echoed outside with a spare, airy vibe that instantly quieted her nerves. A generous workspace was divided from the rest of the structure by a sliding barn door on a metal track. Spanned by thick beams, the ceiling slanted downward from front to back, topping shiplap walls painted crisp white. Apparently, Samuel was shiplap before shiplap was cool.

All across the front and back, multi-paned, industrial-looking windows hinged open from the tops, mitigating need for supplemental lighting. A breeze smelling of the creek mingled with grease and something she couldn't identify, tangy and almost sky-like. She took a few giddy steps toward an expansive worktable on casters, crossing a cement floor that was solid beneath her squishy sneakers. She bounced her gaze from a metal tool chest to a long shelf lined with oodles of little objects. Dragging her fingertips over the smooth worktable, she moved closer. Dozens of sculptures fashioned from scrap metal stood in a neat row. "Samuel? What are these?"

He came up beside her, spreading his arms and flattening his palms on the bench. "I guess I'd call them my doodads."

Four screwdrivers with colorful, plastic handles composed the legs of a whimsical giraffe who gazed with eyes made of nuts at a delicate dragonfly with butter-knife wings and tentacles of tiny springs. A mishmash of gears, nails, and bicycle chain links comprised a ferocious steampunk dragon, but the hummingbird sculpted from baby spoons and cocktail forks, bouncing on a thin wire, was seemingly unafraid. "Did you make these?"

His cheeks flushed. "*Yah.* Some of them move." He pointed to a robot between two rabbits. "I rigged that guy to a mini solar motor, and he walks." He gestured to the smaller rabbit. "She hops."

Almost imperceptible soldering attached a tail of springy wire to the rabbit's adorable backside. "They're charming."

With a swipe of his thumb, he dusted a guitar-playing frog. "I've always liked making things from metal—second only to taking stuff apart, I guess. When Faith and Lavelle were born, I made matching butterflies from soup spoons and mounted them on stakes for Nora's garden. She probably thought them too worldly, but Tucker got a kick out of them. They're in the iris patch."

Amish law might forbid "graven images," but the lanky, musical frog bore a remarkable resemblance to Tucker. A book-reading kitty had more than passing similarity to Rebecca, and a chubby bear with glasses like Verna's sat knitting in rocker. Several half-finished projects littered the work surface. Who else was he sculpting?

She propped a hip against the bench and surveyed the other half of the space. A sewing machine sat directly beneath a window on the front wall.

Beside it, Pumpkin was curled up in a square of sunlight, snoring audibly.

Fabric scraps littered the floor, and sewing implements were scattered willy-nilly. Apparently, Rebecca kept a less tidy work area than her uncle. The adjacent wall was covered floor to ceiling with illustrated quilt patterns sketched on oversized paper. At first, they appeared similar to those in Sarah's shop, but closer examination revealed the designs were quite inventive. They were bold and geometric—almost, she dared to think—modern. One was comprised entirely of bird squares. Darcy was no bird nerd, but even she recognized a cardinal, a blue jay, and a robin. Another was woodland themed, with deer, bears, foxes, and squirrels surrounded by leaves. Worthy of framing, the patterns were meticulously drafted and keyed with colored pencils.

"They're remarkable, aren't they?" said a low voice over her shoulder.

She scratched the cat's chin, feeling purrs vibrate her fingertips. "They're Rebecca's original designs?"

"Naturally." Crossing his arms, he stepped back and studied the wall. "She pieces them from scraps she brings home from work." He gestured toward a tall cupboard. "She's got a dozen in there and two more underway."

"Wow." She spun, taking in the entire room. With high ceilings, bright light, and generous workspaces, the environment sparked creativity. She'd love to park at that worktable and edit photos for hours. Even more, she'd love to shoot the space itself…and the craftsman who inhabited it. "Did you build this all on your own?"

He grabbed a broom and swept. "I had help. That's kind of how things work around here. Folks lent a hand with framing and the roof and walls. Tucker and I did the interior and finish work." He unhooked a dustpan from a peg, passed the broom, and knelt at her feet, broad-shouldered and lean.

No cleaning lady here. The workshop was his

space, and pride of ownership radiated from him. Almost Scandinavian in feel, her attic guest room bore no resemblance to the rest of the farmhouse. In relation to this building, however, the design made perfect sense. Carefully, she nudged the pile into the dustpan. "It's lovely. How did you come up with the plan?"

A stray triangle of robin's-egg fabric escaped, and he snagged it. "The library has a good selection of architectural magazines. I built what I like. But I didn't bring you here for this." He stood and headed for the sliding barn door, dumping the pan into a bin. "Come see."

With a squeak, the door trundled to one side, revealing a compact living area. The smells of corn muffins and spicy chili bubbling on a hotplate made her stomach growl. Smoothing a hand across her middle, she followed, checking out the room with what she hoped was a stealthy eye. A modest kitchen lined the back wall, complete with a sink, a mini fridge, a table, and two chairs. To the other side, a log cabin quilt topped a daybed beside shelves crammed higgledy-piggledy with books and magazines. His sleeping space was spare but cozy and definitely designed for one. Was he lonely out here on his own? Why hadn't he married and started a family?

He entered a hall beyond the kitchen and nodded toward a closed door. "It's right through here."

Peeking into a modest bathroom, she scurried to meet him.

His lips twitched like he held back a smile. "Go on."

With trembly fingers, she turned the knob and blinked into blackness like the entrance to a cave.

Unafraid, she stepped inside, feeling him follow, and her senses went on high alert. His arm snaked across her shoulders, and his muscles tensed like he reached for something.

With a solid *click*, the room illuminated with a glow of a Martian sunset. Gasping, she clasped her hands and stared. Beneath open shelving, counters lined both walls, one containing a stainless-steel sink, and the other a broad, empty surface. A cabinet stood at the far end with a chunky wood top, and a ventilation duct accordioned across the ceiling. The space wasn't large—maybe five feet by nine, but it was all she needed. She blinked, disbelieving. Could he really have built a darkroom on the edge of the woods? And in the span of a day or two? "Samuel. How....?"

He nudged past and brushed sawdust from a counter. "I found an excellent book about darkroom construction at the library. The librarians were very helpful."

Crimson shadows painted the planes of his face like he was a comic book hero. "I bet they were."

"So…" He dropped his hands to his hips and gazed up from beneath his brow. "What do you think?"

Think, she did not. She threw her arms around his neck and kissed him.

Startled, he stumbled backward, catching her around the waist. He planted his feet and pulled her close. "You like it, then?" he asked in a low rumble.

Grateful, giddy recklessness fueled her embrace, but now, snug in his arms, her heartbeat slowed, and her insides shimmered like moonshine on the Long Island Sound. She let out a long, luxurious breath and came up on tiptoes. "It'll do," she murmured against his lips. The tang of sky she nosed in the workshop seemed to rise from his skin. Then, his arms tightened around her, and her feet left the floor. The room spun, and she let out a yelp. Her bottom landed on what was, unsurprisingly, a supremely sturdy counter. Leaning back, she drew him over her until her head snugged against the wall. "You made shelves for my chemistry." She arched her back and eyed the one above her. "Wide ones."

"Eighteen inches." He dropped a line of kisses from the tender spot beneath her ear down the valley of her neck. "And two counters, one dry and one wet. Plenty of room for developing trays."

"You did your research." She buried her face in his hair. It was silky and tickled her nose. She giggled and ran a hand across his shoulders to squeeze the thick muscles at the base of his neck.

He groaned, rolling his head. "You'll note the safe light, of course."

She rubbed deep circles into thick muscle, feeling his shoulders ease. "If I turn it off, will any light leak in?"

"Only one way to find out." Keeping an arm around her, he drew her closer and extended an arm for the switch. With another *click*, they were plunged in darkness.

His chest rose and fell against her cheek. The ventilation fan hummed, and she gazed into thick, dark black, searching for a shred of sunshine. She found none, only the warmth of his body and the scent of his skin and the tiniest breeze from the fan. For a time, the world vanished. She couldn't tell up from down or inside from out. There was only him…the thud of his heart…the matching beat of her own.

He shifted, nuzzling over her hair, and his lips found hers.

They were soft and gentle as the night. In the darkness, her senses sharpened. His touch felt like a question, as if through it, he could know her. She relaxed against him, wanting to be known. How long could they stay hidden like this? Alone in a tiny house by the woods, with not a single person on a planet that might or might not still exist knowing where they were…

"Samuel?"

Except Rebecca.

His chin scraped her cheek with a rasp not remotely unpleasant. Busted by a fourteen-year-old, she clutched him and buried her face in his shirt as if, when Rebecca burst in, she would be invisible.

Dropping his forehead gently against hers, he grumbled deep and low in Pennsylvania Dutch.

She had a pretty good idea what he meant.

"Samuel?" Rebecca called again. "Did you remember to feed Pumpkin?"

He pulled away. "I'm in the darkroom. I'll be right out."

With delicious slowness, he untangled from her, leaving his lips for last. A faint pleading sound escaped, and she groped blindly, catching hold of his suspenders.

He wiggled free, taking her cheeks in calloused palms. "Do you want to stay for dinner? I made chili."

As if she could see through the dark, she brought her lips directly to his. "If you cook as well as you kiss, I'd love to." In an Adirondack chair by the firepit, she savored surprisingly spicy chili and sweet, buttery cornbread. Pleasantly full, she deposited the dirty dishes in the kitchen and, returning outside, detoured to the sewing machine.

Having eaten quickly and snuggled the cat, Rebecca settled in at her sewing station. Needle flashing and fingers flying, she appliqued a calico acorn onto a leaf. She hummed while she worked, the sound sweet and girlish.

Though manually operated, the machine was sleek, modern, and apparently capable of all manner of stitches. Darcy leaned in close. "What a cute chipmunk. Are you making another woodland quilt?"

"*Yah.* I tinkered with the design some." Rebecca's foot worked the treadle in a steady rhythm. "I'm hiding tiny bugs and flowers for children to find like a puzzle. I just finished that square." Pausing, she tugged a corner of fabric. "Can you spot the dogwood blossom?"

A bunny peeked out from a stump with a tiny pink flower tucked behind one ear. Darcy ran a gentle finger over the fabric, marveling at the deceptively simple artistry. "Your work is exceptional."

Rebecca snorted. "It's adequate."

Even among the Amish, the tendency for women to undervalue their efforts persisted. "It's extraordinary," she insisted with enough force to make Rebecca stop pedaling. "Samuel says you have many completed quilts. What will you do with them?"

Rebecca glanced at the cabinet and shrugged. "I've given away several. They make nice gifts for *boppli*. They're different from traditional patterns, but I suppose I could sell some at Sarah's."

"You could sell them anywhere. Why don't you contribute a few to the arts festival booth and see how they do? If they generate interest, I'll help you find stores to stock them."

Rebecca slung an elbow over the back of the chair and spun. "Like in New York City?"

She peeped through the window to where Samuel arranged logs for a fire. His niece was industrious, with an ambitious streak she likely kept hidden. More though, Darcy sensed the girl wanted to contribute. With a growing family, how long could Nora keep up her baked goods business? Naturally, Rebecca would want to help. "New York and elsewhere. My sister lives in Connecticut. I'm sure she'd love one for her kids' rooms."

"I will. *Denki.*" Nimble fingers slid a wee green leaf from a pile of fabric, and Rebecca pinned it beside the acorn. "Maybe if someone sells my quilts in New York, I'll have reason to visit."

Given Rebecca's dreamy tone, she might have been discussing a trip to the moon. The city was so close and yet a universe away. Still, once she was on her *Rumspringa*, she might be allowed to visit. Darcy could imagine the slender figure perched on a Brooklyn fire escape, taking in every detail of the streets below. And if Rebecca came, perhaps her uncle would, too. "I can't think of anything nicer."

Back outside, Samuel touched a match to a tidily constructed fire. "What were you two talking about?"

The sun had set, casting the patio in shadow. She settled into a chair and zipped up her hoodie. Flames crawled from twig to twig. What made a fire so mesmerizing? Hours could pass while she watched wood slowly char. "Entrepreneurship. New York City. The usual. Rebecca's going to offer her quilts at the

Spring Arts Festival."

He scrubbed a hand over his chin. "New York? You planning to steal away our girl?"

"She'd make an excellent roommate. Mine are likely to get married any second, and I'll be alone."

"And Rebecca won't?"

"Get married?" She planted her feet and glared. "She's fourteen!"

He jerked his head toward Nora's cottage. "Her mother wed at twenty-one."

A shiver only half for show shook her. "Rebecca takes after you. She'll not be tied down."

Grunting, he tossed a stick onto the fire.

Squirrels clambered noisily between treetops, and twilight fell. The night went from azure to violet to silver, and sparks streaked like fireflies through dusk. Her ponytail smelled of wood smoke. She couldn't remember the last time she had a blowout. If she never had another, she might actually be okay.

Rebecca emerged, munching a corn muffin. Her gaze bounced back and forth between them and settled on Samuel. "The two of you sitting in the dark is rather unconventional." The firelight flickered, illuminating an impish grin. "But I won't tell. Don't forget Pumpkin's bedtime snack. *Gude Nacht*!" Humming, she tripped down the lane into darkness.

The sound of Tucker's guitar drifted on the evening breeze. Every chord was a bittersweet reminder Darcy's days on the farm were dwindling. She gazed over freshly tilled fields, struggling to believe Brooklyn still existed. It did, of course, as did London, Paris, and Rome. At that very second, turtles wandered the Galapagos and lions prowled the savannah, while humans summited Mount Everest and paced the Great Wall of China. She glanced at Samuel. Every single moment contained multitudes, even if he never had chance to see it.

Her chest tightened. The time had come. This was the moment to tell him of his niece's request. And yet, she hesitated.

The peeper chorus started in earnest. She flashed to his cozy living space and imagined it by lamplight. In her real life, a night like this usually ended with a glass of wine and… She shifted in the chair, pulling on her hood and tucking her hands into her sleeves. A chilly gust swept down from the ridge, but her skin felt hot and stretched tight.

He shot to standing. "Are you cold? I'll get my quilt."

"Oh no. It'll smell like smoke."

He sidled behind her, heading for the door. "I don't mind. I like it."

She jumped up, bumping toes. "No, really. I'm fine." Face-to-face in the half-light, she dropped her gaze to her sneakers. *Tell him, you coward. Now!*

A tickle danced over her wrist and down one finger. She let her eyelids fall. A featherlight circle traced on the palm of her hand, and her spine gave way. With delicious slowness, he interlaced his fingers with hers. One…two…three… If she explained what Rebecca wanted and why, surely, he'd understand. Surely, he'd agree. His palm pressed against hers in a touch more intimate than any she could remember. "Samuel?"

"*Yah?*"

She breathed deeply, taking in smoke and chili

powder and…him. "Why do you smell like the sky?"

He laughed and twined an arm around her waist. "Like what?"

Gutlessness withered her soul, but since she'd asked, she really wanted to know. Leaning into the crook of his arm, she gazed up. "You have this sort of tangy scent—"

"Good, I hope."

"Very good. Like the sky after a storm."

He frowned and lifted his cheeks toward the sliver of moon low on the horizon. "I think what you're smelling…besides good old-fashioned manliness, of course…"

She thumped him lightly on one shoulder. "Is what?"

"Metalwork. Welding and soldering give off ozone, I believe, which combined with the sweat and the manliness…"

Ew, but intoxicating…

"Smells like sky." He grinned. "That's one of the nicest things anyone has ever said about me. Thank you."

She hooked a finger under one suspender and dragged it down his body. The gesture was meant to be teasing, but feeling the rise and fall of his chest, her lungs zinged. "What do I smell like?" The question slipped out on a breathless whisper.

He lowered his face to her neck, his lips skimming tender skin, and inhaled.

Her vision blurred, and only the strength of his hold kept her upright.

He righted and gazed at her, his lids heavy and his breath slow and deep. "Cinnamon and cloves. You smell like Christmas, Darcy King."

The tears didn't sting so much as tingle with a pain that was nearly pleasure. Something about this simple observation cut to the heart of who she was, or rather, who she aspired to be. Christmas was a *Mammi* Leora smell, warm, complex, and savory with a touch of sweet. A scent she believed she could photograph. A single tear escaped, but she didn't try to hide it. As she felt his thumb graze her cheek, she knew he thought of that moment on the landing. She'd tried to deny it, but hadn't she known even then she'd fall in love?

His brow creased.

A reassuring smile lifted her cheeks. "Happy tears." Then she reached up and traced the line of that city block jaw with the tip of one finger. "Kiss me?" His body swayed like an oak after the first thwack of a lumberjack's axe. He took her hand and dropped a kiss on her palm so scorching, she thought it would leave a scar.

Breath suddenly ragged, he curled his fingers around hers and pulled her hand to his chest until they stood a heartbeat apart. "I want to kiss you as much as I've wanted anything in my life. But if I start, I won't have the strength to stop. And while that might be a whole lot of fun, I'm not sure I could live with myself tomorrow."

There was that word again. *Fun.* What did he have against fun? Fun was good. She was one-thousand-percent pro-fun.

But though she ached, she couldn't deny the rightness of his words. If she kissed him, and they went inside, the thing between them that stubbornly refused to be named would get messy and maybe even awful.

And right now, being with him was the furthest thing from awful she'd ever experienced, and she didn't want to wreck it. Not until she had to.

So, with a feathery kiss on one impossibly high cheekbone, she backed away, shivering in the night air. He made a sound deep in his chest that shot like an arrow to her gut, but she let it land and didn't go to him. "Goodnight, Samuel."

He stopped in the doorway, bracing himself on the doorframe and letting his head hang. "Goodnight, Brooklyn."

She left before she lost the will to go. On the nightstand in the attic, her phone was dead as stone. So, she dug out Pammy's romance—the one with a face on the cover she'd come to adore—and since she couldn't do one dangerous thing, she chose another.

Chapter Twenty

Stifling a yawn, Darcy slung the camera strap around her neck and shifted the curtain to one side, allowing a misty morning glow to suffuse the kitchen. She'd read the romance novel in one night. More accurately, she devoured it, casting herself as the hapless English heroine and, of course, Samuel as the dreamy Amish hero. Fiction, meet reality.

"You missed breakfast." Verna set a plate of muffins on the table and reached for the coffeepot. "Did you have trouble sleeping?"

"I stayed up too late reading." And even later *thinking…* She pocketed the lens cap and focused on a delicate rosebud platter in the hutch.

Cream, sugar, and two coffee mugs joined the muffins. Verna chuckled. "One of life's great pleasures. Though you suffer in the morning."

"As with so many pleasures." Satisfied with the shot, she spun, scanning for details to entice prospective visitors. Although the idea of someone else sleeping in her attic room rankled, she'd promised photos for a flyer, and she always kept her promises. Most of them, anyway.

Verna settled at the table and pulled a shiny crochet hook from a bag. "Well now, I can't say as I agree. The truest pleasures are like to soothe my soul and send me to sleep satisfied." The hook flashed, and a ball of navy yarn became a granny square. "Though a dose of righteous anger does the same now and again. Either way, if I follow *Gott's* will, I generally wake smiling."

Perhaps only guilty pleasures hampered sleep.

The day was overcast and cool, and chicken soup bubbled on the stove. Served with a hunk of fresh bread, it would make a delicious lunch. She slid the loaf close to the steaming pot, framed, and shot. The shutter clicked high and fast and familiar. The image flashed on the digital screen. *Beautiful*. Beside the stove was a calendar thumbtacked to the wall. It featured the type of generic nature scene she typically pooh-poohed, accompanied by an Amish proverb. *When fear knocks at the door, send faith to answer.* Yet again, faith.

"How do you know God's will?" The question slipped out, nosy and intrusive. For years, Darcy knew precisely what she, herself, wanted in life: to blaze a path in the cutthroat world of photojournalism. She'd do more than climb the ladder. With a seat at the table, she'd tell stories that mattered and create change. Her goal was so close she could taste it. But would that life bring happiness? Would she greet every morning with a smile? She lowered the camera. "How can anyone know?"

Verna set her crocheting in her lap. "To begin, I read the scriptures, and I ask *Gott* for guidance." She scooped a heaping spoonful of sugar into her coffee, poured a dollop of cream, and stirred. "The answer doesn't often come directly. Much as I'd like a letter, *Gott* hasn't seen fit to write. But when I need to make a decision, maybe even a big decision…" She sipped, squinting over the rim of the mug. "I let the prayer dwell in my heart. I don't poke at it like a snake or scratch it like a healing wound. I leave it be for a time and watch it sidelong, like a bird I'd like to hop into my hand and nibble seed. Sooner or later, I wake up knowing what to do."

"And if you don't?" Darcy gripped the camera. Motherly wisdom was something she'd never had. Now, suddenly, she craved it. "What if you never wake up with an answer?"

Verna gave Darcy a gentle smile. "Then I didn't ask the proper question at the start."

She let her gaze drift out the window and pointed the lens slantwise through the glass, framing fruit trees in full blossom and a whimsical garden gate that seemed out of character on an Amish farm. The world teemed with mystery, if only one bothered to look.

"Even so, I can't say I always did right." Verna sighed heavily and resumed her yarn work. "Should I have moved the boys to Ohio, leaving my eldest children here? Now, they're scattered to the winds and like to roam, which is not our way." Fingers flying, she frowned. "But who am I to say it's not theirs?" She cut Darcy a quick, sharp glance. "I see my *kinner* for who they are. They're none of them fools, and they'll do as *Gott* leads. The Lord's sent plenty of folks to this farm uninvited. They changed our lives."

Darcy's shoulders tightened. She was one such intruder. Was motherly wisdom about to become scolding?

Verna's jaw loosened, and crinkles shot from the corners of her eyes. "Nearly always for the better. Give that soup a stir, will you? Shall we do some pictures outside or wait for the weather to turn?"

Relief washed over her, and she joined Verna at the

table. "Let's stay inside where it's cozy. I could use another coffee." Half an hour later, Darcy had a caffeine boost and more than enough photos for a flyer. That afternoon, she mocked up a simple logo and uploaded the best shots. With minimal editing, the design came together easily. The farm and guest suite sold themselves. Satisfied, she set aside her digital camera and removed the completed roll of film from Dave's. She now had two rolls of macro photos, and she couldn't wait to develop them. Tomorrow, she'd gather the darkroom equipment from Pammy and give Samuel his lesson. In school, she'd excelled at developing prints. She reviewed the steps in her mind, confident the procedure would return like riding a bike had. Snugging the film into an empty canister, she flicked her gaze to the flyer.

Were Verna's earlier words a blessing or a warning? She loaded a new roll, clicked closed the back, and chose blessing, knowing with absolute certainty her relationship with every member of this family was about to change.

****

Family dinner that night was a silly, rollicking occasion with the Lapp boys relating a side-splitting tale of a narcoleptic sow and a livestock auction gone awry. After almost two weeks on the farm, pitching in with cleanup felt as natural as bowing for silent prayer. Much to Darcy's relief, neither made her cry. Though she was fairly sure the tears weren't finished yet.

The morning clouds had dissipated, leaving behind a hazy afternoon and an evening that would have benefitted greatly from a thundershower, but none dropped by. As if by unspoken agreement, everyone wandered outdoors once the last dish was dry, seeking relief on the banks of the creek.

Hurling aside caution, Darcy dashed to the attic and grabbed the freshly loaded camera. Pammy's romance shone from the night table like a warning beacon, and she tossed it into her bag. She needed to get outside before the daylight faded. Only a month from the summer solstice, the days were long, and the gloaming was especially lovely. She skipped through the kitchen and burst outside into a dusk so airless she could hardly imagine night would bring respite. Yet, the stillness held a kind of glowing beauty and a welcome lack of expectations. In the city, such nights felt suffocating. Here in the country, the family set up lawn chairs beneath fruit trees and wiggled bare toes in dewy grass. The creek babbled, wafting a mossy dampness that could almost be mistaken for air conditioning. She roamed her gaze over the assembled party. Where was Samuel? How much cooler his workshop on the edge of the woods must be.

Verna motioned her toward an empty chair.

"I'll take a few more shots for the website. Don't mind me." Weeds tickled her toes through sandal straps, and she scampered toward the garden. She rested Dave's camera on a fence post, focused on the whimsical gate, and shot.

With the slightest shift—maybe a half an inch—her viewfinder framed the entire family. She traced a circle over the shutter button with a fingertip. Capturing a person's whole entire life in one image was a daunting task. The responsibility to do it right weighed on her heart. She focused on Rebecca's slim figure, nestled cross-legged in a chair. Forget composition, color, and light. What would Rebecca want?

Right, wrong, or something in between, her intention settled with irrevocable weight upon her. The moment had arrived. Her heartbeat skittered and then slowed. The distant squawks of "Verna's ladies" in the hen house mingled with the buzz of busy bees and the squeak of the screen door. Who would have thought betrayal would be so quiet?

Long-limbed and lanky, Tucker sprawled on the back steps. Framed by apple and peach blossoms, he bent his dark head over the guitar and noodled on a folksy version of "Amazing Grace."

The harmonies were deep and complex, even as the simple melody shone through. The Amish and modernity encapsulated in a single hymn. Tucker had been photographed before, of course, hundreds and hundreds of times. His joking about paparazzi aside, would this one picture really matter?

One of the twins giggled.

He glanced up and chuckled, too.

Click, and his image was hers. With a quick inhale and absolute certainty the sacrifice she made for a fourteen-year-old girl was worth it, she toggled the lens.

Nora reclined in an old, woven lawn chair, her swelling belly pressing against amethyst cotton and her head tipped back in a rare moment of repose. Her cheeks were apple-blossom pink, and tendrils of damp hair, the color of wheat, curled at her temples. Though shooting in black-and-white was right, what depth of color this image could have.

Tucker struck a heartbreaking chord.

Nora glanced in her husband's direction.

The moment was almost too intimate, but Nora's

simple joy cried out to be captured. She was Samuel's sister, and her fine-boned features called to mind so clearly what a daughter of his might look like that Darcy struggled for breath. She steadied herself, focused, and shot.

Click.

At Nora's feet, Lavelle and Faith dunked plastic animals into a dishpan of water. A miniature horse galloped the perimeter of the pan, and with a single sweep of one twin's arm, it launched high into the air. Both girls squealed, reaching for the toy with chubby fingers. Sunlight caught a trail of droplets.

With an instinct she couldn't have described had she tried, Darcy captured a millisecond of magic.

Click.

Where was Samuel? She had no time to wonder. Having committed to photographing the family, she couldn't stop now. Street photography had honed her ability to intuit windows of opportunity when light met subject in a moment of kismet. In minutes, she would have them all. Rolling her shoulders, she steadied her gaze.

Never truly idle, Verna lounged next to her daughter. The crochet hook flashed more slowly in the heat. She stopped to wipe a hand on her apron and looked down upon her granddaughters. Tenderness bathed her face in loveliness.

Click.

The breath eased from Darcy's lungs. *Only two more.*

A few feet away, Rebecca was lost in reading.

As so often happened, the girl appeared different through the lens. If Nora was an echo of Samuel's unborn children, Rebecca was a reflection. Emotions danced across her face like quicksilver. Her lips formed silent words with childlike unselfconsciousness. Darcy shooed a pesky mosquito. Rebecca hadn't requested a picture of herself. The idea might never have occurred to her. And yet again, it might.

Family portraits comprised an artful gallery wall in one long hallway on Park Avenue. Gazing at them, Darcy sometimes felt her childhood with such immediacy she could swear the photos had been taken yesterday. Without a single image, how did an Amish woman remember the girl she was? When adult sorrows came, and in this family, they came in battalions, how did one escape to the carefree landscape of memory? Certainly, they managed as they'd managed for years. But wasn't the opportunity to look in the eyes of one's fourteen-year-old self a gift?

Something Rebecca read seemed to surprise her, and she covered her mouth with one hand. With a sideways glance at her mother, she angled away her body and hunched over the book. Turning a page, she sighed and stared at the sky with wide-eyed wonder.

Darcy crouched low, aimed between fence posts, and shot.

As if she sensed it, Rebecca wheeled and, meeting Darcy's gaze through the lens, gave a secret smile.

"What are you doing?"

Darcy jumped, catching the camera on a rail and nearly wrenching it from her grip. Blinking up into Samuel's face, she grabbed hold of the fence and jerked to standing, scrambling for anything but the truth. "Just shooting pics for the rental flyer." Pulse pounding, she scanned the lens, blowing splinters from the plastic rim.

The glass seemed intact. Thank goodness. "The garden gate is so unique." She focused on the intricate lattice of curlicued branches and shot. "Did you build it?"

He sucked the inside of one cheek. "That's the Prodigal Son's work. My brother Jonas made it for his first wife before she died, and he left."

His voice was edged with bitterness. The tragedy and Jonas's leaving still stung, and yet, some part of Samuel clearly envied his brother. She fiddled with the gate, and the metal latch rattled. Reminders of betrayal often came in pretty packages. Though she just joined the ranks of betrayers, she longed to ease his pain. "He's almost as good a carpenter as you."

His gaze narrowed. "That's your film camera. Wouldn't you use digital for the flyer?"

Invisible hands tightened around her throat. Of course, he noticed. He noticed anything remotely mechanical, and he'd gotten an in-depth photography lesson on their hike. She bonked her forehead with the heel of one hand like a caricature of a ditzy blonde. "Oops."

His expression clouded.

He couldn't possibly know…could he? Neck flaming, she unscrewed the lens. "I'm obsessed with macrophotography. Will I ever shoot full size again? I might need to shrink myself and live inside a buttercup like a bee."

She was covering, grasping for normalcy, and doing a laughable job. Still, she spoke the truth. This foray into photographing minutiae unlocked something in her brain, and she longed for a proper macro lens to use with her digital camera. If she looked deeply enough, could she spot the seven seas in a drop of rain or a sliver of star stuff in a single grain of sand? She'd like to try.

A welcome breeze lofted flower petals like confetti. Squealing, the wee girls extended open palms to catch them.

Was a smaller life a richer one? Was that the secret of the Amish and modernity? Was it the key to happiness?

He took a few steps back, regarding her down his long, straight nose. "You have a lot of bees in Brooklyn?"

The question felt pointed. A prickly reminder that in less than a week, she'd take her prying pictures of people who didn't want to be photographed, publish them in a fancy New York magazine, and never look back. The notion chafed. She screwed on the reverse lens with steady, sure strokes. "More than you might think. I've seen a honeybee on a sixteenth-floor balcony. Universe, grant me the tenacity of a New York City bee."

"*Gott* needn't waste time with that request." He slid her a grin, but his gaze was wary. "I think you have it covered." He pushed off the fencepost and ambled toward his family.

She'd done it. Oh jeez, she'd done it. She'd betrayed him a thousand and one percent. Her mouth tasted unpleasantly of the ham loaf that lay like a brick in the pit of her stomach. What now? How should she behave? What would her mother do? She steeled her spine. Isabelle King would act completely normal—confident the choice she made, however questionable, she made for good reason. And Darcy's reason was undeniably good. She refused to let things get weird.

"Hey, I'm picking up darkroom equipment from Pammy tomorrow," she called to his back. "I'll come by the workshop after."

He kept walking.

She jogged a step or two to catch up. "Guess who will be there cleaning out her shed?"

Not breaking stride, Samuel spun. "Who?"

"The mailman. Al." She pursed her lips in smug satisfaction. "I told you I knew a man in love."

"Guess I should never doubt you." Revealing nothing, he turned away.

Guilt did not rest quietly in her soul. Feeling like the negatives burned brightly enough to sear through metal, she clutched the camera. He had every reason to doubt. She'd broken his trust, and if discovered, she'd never regain it. Reining in a groan, she whirled back toward the garden. Some cool-headed New Yorker she was. She'd acted all kinds of shady, and the vibe between them instantly changed. It turned heavy and sour like milk that was slightly off.

She clamped her jaw and pointed the lens at the garden gate, focusing on delicate splinters springing from the twigs like curling hairs. Only one week remained. As promised, she'd teach him to develop film. She'd brainstorm any final images for her essay, help the Amish women through the arts festival, and then go home to Brooklyn. Fun was fun—or not so fun, as the case might be—but she had a job and an apartment and a life to resume.

And resume them she would…just as soon as she found the courage to take Samuel's picture, too.

Chapter Twenty-One

Over cardboard boxes jammed in the backseat of the rental car the next morning, Darcy gave Al a dubious look. Square and bulky, the vintage photo enlarger teetered on the cushion's edge. "You really think you can fit it in? I don't mind making a second trip."

Al hitched up the denim shorts that had replaced his mailman's uniform for the day. "Compared to packing the mail truck at Christmastime, this here's a piece of cake." He slid out a box of developing chemicals and plunked it on the driveway behind Pammy's Place. Sunlight bounced off the hood, and he shielded his eyes. "Let me have another crack at it."

Darcy stepped back, giving Al free rein, and retreated to the shed. Crates and tubs littered the fenced-in yard behind the bakery, but inside, the shed was empty save for several sets of shelves that appeared brand-new.

Pammy stood in the open door, sipping an iced tea. "Dave would be so glad you're making use of his things. He was such a generous guy."

Al yanked another box from the car. Beneath an old concert tee, the muscles of his back rippled.

"Seems this one might be cut from the same cloth." Darcy took a long draw from her own iced beverage, giving Al a thorough once-over. She tipped toward

Pammy, lowering her voice. "And turns out he's kinda ripped."

"I like a man in uniform." Pammy giggled. "And out of it."

"Pammy!" She teased, splaying a palm on her chest in mock horror.

Pammy jutted a hip and propped an elbow against the doorframe. She was dressed down in a cute lime-green tee and a white visor, but her manicured nails matched the shirt, and her makeup was impeccable. She peered at Darcy over cat's-eye sunglasses. "Uniforms come in all different types, don't they? I'd say a straw hat and suspenders can be as dreamy as dress whites."

Maybe, but context was everything. "Not where I come from."

Pammy straightened and scanned Darcy head to toe. "Upper East Side—maybe Park Avenue is my guess. Fancy, all-girls private school. Summers in Martha's Vineyard where your first kiss was a prep-school boy, then a liberal arts college where you majored in photography instead of premed, just to stick it to your folks. Now, you might say you're a starving artist, but those shoes are designer, and you're as ambitious as any of those New York types. You're just not sure what to do with the inconvenient fact you're in love with an Amish guy." She slid the sunglasses into her hair, grinning. "Am I close?"

Darcy almost spit iced coffee all over Pammy's white capris. Gathering herself, she swallowed hard, managing to minimize the amount of cold brew that went down the wrong tube. "Nantucket, not Martha's Vineyard, and I majored in poly sci. I even took the LSAT. Also, love is a very strong word." She gave a little cough. "But yeah. Close. How did you do that?"

Pammy extended a foot and regarded her matching pedicure in flip-flops. "Being a baker is like being a bartender. You get to know people. Also, I read a lot of romance."

Recalling the happily ever after of *The Amish Bachelor's English Wife*, Darcy huffed a sigh. "Me, too."

Beneath a gnarled crab apple tree, Pammy brushed pollen from an ornate wrought iron chair. She sat and beckoned.

Darcy tiptoed around boxes and joined her in the shade. The yard was overrun with bushes and weeds, but it held the same secret sweetness as hidden gardens behind New York City brownstones. She followed Pammy's gaze to Al who had completely unpacked the car and began anew.

He wiped his forehead with a bandana and stuffed it in his back pocket.

Pammy's pink cheeks rounded. "Yep, he's one of the good ones. Guess I can't blame myself for not seeing it until now." The ice cubes rattled in her cup. She sipped and set it on a wobbly table between them. "Dave and I were a second chance romance. Read a couple of those, huh?"

Darcy traced a fingertip over the scrolled metal tabletop. "Maybe one or two."

Pammy propped an elbow on the back of her chair and fanned herself with one hand. "We dated for a hot second in high school, but then I ran wild, barking up every wrong tree from here to Wilkes-Barre. When we finally found each other again, I didn't care a bit he was in remission. I just thought, well that's it. He's my happily ever after." She stretched and grabbed the nearest crab apple branch. "And for a good long time, he was."

How did anyone go on after such a loss? Yet, even with a broken heart, Pammy delivered joy one cupcake at a time. "I'm sorry."

Pammy sniffed the flowers and promptly sneezed. "Every single time, they make me sneeze, but I smell them again and again. I'd do it all over with Dave, too. No matter how hard it was in the end." Eyes glistening, she released the branch, and it whooshed skyward. "After he died, I thought, 'Well, Pam, guess your life just became a lonely widow story. Better adopt ten or twelve cats!' " Her laugh soared over the sound of boxes dragging across gravel and Al humming eighties rock. "And then a nosy New Yorker set up shop in my bakery and with two words opened my eyes to someone who'd been right in front of me all along. I guess now, I'm a later-in-life romance."

"Not so late," Darcy protested.

"Oh, honey, life takes more twists and turns than anyone could think up in a book. You might believe you know your story, and it might look something like the one I guessed. But remember, your ending's not written yet." Pammy reached across the table and took Darcy's hand. Sunlight caught the sparkly stones in her stacked rings, glinting green like her eyes. "No one writes that romance but you. Give yourself the happily ever after you want—not the one you think you deserve." Sitting back, she cast her gaze toward Al, and bewilderment lit her pretty features. "I love a surprise ending—one that makes me wonder what came next long after I finish the book. Don't you?"

She did. So why, as she drove the expertly packed car to the Rishel farm, did she find the prospect of her own surprise ending utterly terrifying? She'd always fancied herself a rebel, but Pammy's lovingly spot-on description made her sound like a caricature of herself. Was her life such a stereotype? Was she doomed to relive the stories of past generations, clawing to the top since the time of the Vanderbilts? All of them...except *Mammi* Leora.

Lead-footed, she sped past the entrance to Sarah's shop where a group of big-hearted women labored tirelessly for their children. Their desires were simple: family, friends, faith. One teeny-tiny stitch at a time, they toiled for heat and light—admirable priorities for any era, modern or otherwise.

So, what did Darcy King want? Really and truly? And when was the last time she acted on it?

How much easier was it to react to someone else's plans? To stubbornly buck expectations?

How much harder to reckon with her own authentic desires?

Because, of course, if those desires couldn't be met, she'd have to face heartbreak unlike any she'd known. Deeply wanting something or...someone raised the stakes to a nearly unendurable degree.

Acting on a suspicion that the road where she met Samuel for the ballgame led to his workshop, she nosed into the country lane and tapped the brakes, not wanting to jostle equipment on the bumpy surface.

Sunlight through leaves dappled the road. Shadows shifted with unseen breezes so the ground itself seemed to move. She stopped and rolled down the window, drinking in the grassy scent of fields and the woodsy dampness of forest air. The futility of trying to capture the entirety of a moment on film, the sight and the smell and the feel of it, overwhelmed her, and yet, she longed to try.

Photography. She loved photography with the purity of a snowfall and the blaze of a beachside bonfire. The day she stopped seeing the world with an artist's eye would be the day she died. Editorial to commercial and everything in between—she loved it all.

But did she love *Hudson Magazine?*

She loved being part of a respected and renowned periodical. She loved the access it provided. She loved being paid to be exactly where she was, and earning this opportunity through dedication, tenacity, and a heaping dose of hutzpah.

But did she…*love…Hudson Magazine*?

In the distance, hooves clopped down Old Cowan Road.

And did she love Samuel Rishel? Really and truly?

She closed her eyes and let the question settle over her heart as Verna described the other morning.

Do I love Samuel?

A bird flitted from the treetops and alit on her side mirror. She jerked for the button, thinking to close the window before it flew into the car with a kerfuffle of feathers and feet. But this was no dirty street pigeon, and she checked her impulse, managing not to spook the tiny creature.

The bird was gray with white cheeks, a black throat, and a jet-black cap like a little beanie. An image of *Mammi* Leora filling her birdfeeders arose. A chickadee maybe?

The bird twitched its head in the manner of all wild things. She couldn't say it looked at her exactly. The gaze of a bird was something flintier than a horse's or a dog's. A bird's soul didn't live in its black and shiny eyes...but she might have felt her own soul as she sat silently watching.

As suddenly as it came, it was gone.

Fortunately, the lane did lead to Samuel's front door. She could never have carried the equipment from the farmhouse, and she hated the idea of asking for help.

The workshop was quiet. Rebecca didn't appear with skirts and fabric scraps flying, and Samuel seemed to be gone. She'd told him she was coming. Despite their awkward encounter the evening before, she expected he'd be there. She steadfastly refused to think about the cause of that awkwardness. Profound betrayal mingled messily with true love. Best to focus on setting up the darkroom. Maybe he left the door open?

A piece of paper torn from a notebook lay on the front stoop under one of the smooth stones that comprised his patio. Her name was written in pencil in a neat, square hand.

Darcy,

I'm needed to roof Leroy Amos's new furniture showroom. I'll be back before supper. The door is open. You may bring in your equipment.

S

Pocketing the paper, she turned the knob and was nearly knocked flat by the scent of sky. Was it the collected fumes from a morning's work or simply the remnant of this man's existence? He'd said the smell was from welding. Still, she didn't quite believe it wasn't mostly him.

She stood on the threshold, running a hungry gaze over every surface. Once inside, she shouldn't snoop. But from the doorway, nothing was off limits.

The gaping barn door offered a clear view into his living quarters. The quilt was folded neatly on the narrow bed with linen-cased pillows in a tidy pile nearby. A single coffee cup stood on the counter. A sepia stain dribbled down the side. A yellow number two pencil lay atop an open spiral notebook on the table.

The pegboard was empty save for a black brimmed hat. So stark and beautiful against whitewashed shiplap, it was like an image from an Amish calendar. Samuel's winter hat. It wasn't a costume. It was an article of clothing that covered his ridiculous lack of a haircut and kept him warm when he rode in a horse-drawn buggy to three-hour church services on Sunday mornings.

His hat belonged to him, and he belonged to it and to the life it came from.

She could love every part of him—the sea-green eyes that never strayed when she spoke, the ready smile and quick wit, the Peter Pan complex, the one crooked tooth, and the way he held her like he'd been holding her forever. Still, she did not share his life. Her heart clenched, and she stiffened against the ache. She never would.

Shaking herself, she unloaded the car, box by box, and set up the darkroom he built. Even though they both knew they would enjoy it together for less than a week.

He also knew she loved photography, and with this

gift, he returned a part of it she'd lost in the quick-paced digital age. Standing at the counter, she closed her eyes, clutching the cartridge opener in one hand and the film canister in the other. By feel, she aligned them properly and summoned the sensation of removing film, winding the delicate coiled strip onto the reel, dropping it into the tank, and sealing it tight. Developing film into negatives wasn't as much fun as making prints, but the fact it had to be done in absolute darkness was all the more exciting. Practicing on a spare roll would be prudent, but she had none.

With her equipment arranged, she closed the door, switched off the safelight, and checked again for any leaks. Finding not even a sliver, she relaxed into a thick, welcoming blackness so close to the optimal temperature for developing film she couldn't have planned it better. "Thank you, Dave. Thank you, Samuel," she whispered and popped open the first roll of film.

****

The negatives had been drying for hours, and Darcy had run a brisk 5K followed by a shower and a protein bar. With the afternoon sun gradually sinking, she parked herself on Samuel's patio and pondered whether to venture a fire. Fire building was not in her wheelhouse. Nantucket summer bonfires were always commandeered by the boys, with the girls clustering in twos and threes on the periphery, waiting for the moment they might be invited to slip behind a dune.

She hadn't thought about Chet Marshall for years—not until Pammy brought up her first kiss. The event had been clumsy and anticlimactic. Even then, Darcy was a lover of romance, and the burger-scented fumble bore zero resemblance to the sublime smooches of her dreams. If she were honest, the intervening years offered few better examples.

Still, she continued to believe a good kiss was no means to an end. A kiss was not an hors d'oeuvre. Done properly, it was a meal unto itself, complete and satisfying. Who would have thought the only five-star kisser to cross her path would drive a buggy?

She giggled, and a shadow fell across her feet.

"Something funny, Brooklyn?" Samuel's broad shoulders drooped, and dark crescents smudged the tender skin beneath his eyes.

He towered over her like a mountain. As if, even exhausted, he could protect her from any storm. Not that she needed protecting. She rode the subway twenty-four seven. But she liked the feeling. "If you must know, I was thinking about first kisses. Mine, to be more accurate."

He took off his hat and ran a thick hand through his hair, making it jut in a thousand directions. "How was it?"

"Profoundly disappointing. Yours?"

A worn leather toolbelt spooled to the ground with a clank, and he collapsed into the chair beside her. "Wonderful."

She came up on her knees, dropping her chin into her hand. "Really?" She dragged the word out, relishing the extra syllables. "Go on."

His palms splayed over the chair arms, and he leaned back, closing his eyes. "Emma Lapp—Christian and Mattias's sister. She was fair like you, but with blue eyes like robins' eggs and the tiniest hands. I took her home in the rain one Sunday in June, and when we got to her farm, we saw the most spectacular double rainbow. I thought *Gott* sent us a sign."

She knew nothing of Samuel's romantic history, but she struggled to imagine him getting serious at a young age. "Alas, it wasn't meant to be?" She teased, but his chest fell like something heavy sat upon it.

He lifted his chin and stared into the treetops. "First, Nora's accident happened, and then, my father died, and we moved to Ohio. I hoped Emma would wait, but she married and went west to Indiana."

His tone held no bitterness, but she saw sadness in the downward curve of his lips. Wary, she sank back in the chair. "I'm sorry." His shoulders twitched as if his clothes were suddenly two sizes too small.

"*Ach.* We were young. How can anyone know at twenty if a person makes him happy? How at thirty? Sometimes, I think I'm not made for..." He let the words fade.

"I suppose you have to have faith," she said, surprising herself. Something like skepticism furrowed between his brows, and the awkwardness of the evening before slunk in like a skunk, wafting stink.

"Can I trust you, Darcy King?"

Her mouth went suddenly dry, and she forced a laugh. "Probably not."

His eyes rounded, and he laughed, too.

The sound was rich and deep and cut right to the part that hated herself for having betrayed him. But what could she say but the truth? What was done was done, and yet, it wasn't done at all. She still needed to take his picture.

He came forward and snagged a pile of spindly brush. "A roof is a good place to think. From Leroy's, I could see from the mountains to the river. I've passed most of my years in this valley between. I might be the biggest fool who ever lived, but I want to trust you. *Gott* himself only knows why."

Her very bones sang with wanting him to. But oh, how he shouldn't. "You're a gambling man."

Sliding out of his chair, he began laying twigs atop the brush in a teepee shape. "I've never taken life seriously, and I'm not about to start." He put his knee to the middle of a longer stick and grabbed both ends. With a crack, it snapped clean. "So if you're up to something, tell me right now, and we'll go back to being strangers."

She nearly vaulted from the chair, falling to her knees beside him. Stones pierced the stretchy fabric of her joggers, jabbing the tender spot beneath her kneecap, but she didn't care. She took hold of his arm and pulled him around to face her. "I don't want to be strangers. I want to be—"

He cut her off with a kiss.

Yours.

And his kiss was a twelve-course meal.

Like she weighed less than a bag of groceries, he slid one hand around her shoulders and the other beneath her knees, and, standing, lifted her into his arms.

Feeling weightless and dizzy, she clutched his neck and buried her face in the cool cotton of his shirt, as the forest and fields spun.

With a little huff of effort, he settled into a chair, pulling her onto his lap and draping her legs over one arm.

She let a hand slide to his shoulder, tracing the hills

and valleys of muscle and bone like a three-dimensional map. "Thank you. Those stones are pretty, but they're painful."

"Well, I needed to be certain," he murmured into her lips.

"Of what?"

"That I could carry you should I ever have need." He shifted, pulling her against his chest. "A man just likes to know."

Even as her heart expanded, she cringed. He wanted to know so much...so much she could not now share. A lie by omission was still a lie, no matter the reason. Didn't every liar think herself justified? *But I can explain* were words she never hoped to utter to this man who was, right then, muddling her senses with the kind of kiss that, while not a prelude, hinted at a symphony to leave her breathless. Less than a week remained. She told him flat out not to trust her, and he kissed her. Couldn't the truth just...wait? Or better yet, remain hidden forever?

"Hey," she said, when he'd left her lips to drop kisses beneath the angle of her chin. "Don't start the fire."

"I can do two things at once." He hovered his mouth over her neck and sucked in a breath. "I won't let the house burn down."

Cool air against damp skin sent shivers across her collarbones, and she shifted just far enough to catch his gaze. "I'd like to see you try, but first, I have a promise to fulfill."

His tanned brow wrinkled, but his eyes were still half-closed. "What's that?"

"I set up the darkroom. Want to develop some

film?"

His gaze sharpened. "*Yah.* I would."

"Good." She kissed his cheekbone, letting her lips linger over the knife edge of skin and bone, tasting salt. "We'll come back to this later. I promise."

That word again...*promise*. Promises were complicated. Promises got her in trouble. Teaching him how to develop film, though...surely that promise would bring nothing but joy.

Chapter Twenty-Two

"Are you certain you don't need to jot down any of
this?" An hour later, Darcy removed the photo paper
from the enlarger and slipped it into the tray of
developer. She shot Samuel a look. He followed her
every move with the focus one might apply to
disarming a bomb.

He shook his head. "What's next?"

His shirt purpled in the crimson glow, and he was,
somehow, even more handsome. Her knees wobbled,
and she suddenly had an image of dancing together in a
downtown club, the shifting light transforming him,
chameleonlike, until he could be any one of a million
urbanites…a sculptor, a comedian, or an engineer. He
was, in fact, all those things, and though she barely
remembered her own cell number, she had no doubt he
could replicate every step of the printing process she
demonstrated thus far. She set the timer on her phone
for sixty seconds and took hold of the plastic tray. "This
is the best part. Watch." Gently, she sloshed the
developer back and forth over the paper. A tiny ocean
at her fingertips.

He came up behind, settled his hands on her waist,
and peered over one shoulder.

Only intense desire to experience this moment with
him prevented her from shoving aside the trays and
pulling him onto the counter she had no doubt could

support both of them. She held her breath and let the miracle of photography unfold.

He spoke something in soft Pennsylvania Dutch and moved even closer.

Speckled and sweet, the mushroom resolved amid a forest of mosses and twigs.

Seeing an image appear like a ghost in a mirror always made the hairs on her arms stand on end. "Agitate it gently." She released her hold. "You try."

Reaching around, he rocked the tray like the print was a newborn babe.

She spun, snaking her arms around his neck and nuzzling the spot just below one ear.

He squirmed. "I can't see."

"It's only a test print."

"So, it's not important?"

She caught his earlobe between her teeth and tugged. "It's vital."

Ding!

Spinning, she grabbed the tongs and lifted the photo ever so carefully by one corner. "Now, it goes into the stop bath for ten seconds, but don't let the developing tongs touch the bath." She'd barely resumed her exploration of his jawline when the phone dinged again. "And now, into the fixer for thirty seconds— same drill." Her phone buzzed with a text notification, but she swiped it away, keeping a close eye on the clock. "Then we'll rinse it under water and switch on the light to assess the best exposure time by examining each portion of the print. How'd you rig running water, anyway?"

"A tank like I use in the kitchen."

Another message pinged. She pivoted to the sink

and ran the print back and forth under the lukewarm stream. "Just swipe up to clear that message."

"What's a Zibby?"

Chuckling, she pinned a corner of the picture onto the drying line. "My roommate. She's at a wedding with my other roommate, Fern. Wonder what she wants?" She clipped the opposite corner and reached for the battery-powered light. "Flick off the safe light, and we'll check out the print. I think about twelve seconds will be the optimum exposure time." She blinked against the glare and waited for her eyes to adjust.

He came up beside her and crossed his arms over his chest. "Not bad."

The focus was perfect and the image absolutely enchanting. Unsurprisingly, his eye was impeccable. She nudged an elbow into his ribs. "You jerk."

"Did I do something wrong?"

"Yes! You made what's likely the best photograph in the bunch. Why are you so good at everything?"

He sniffed and tilted his head, examining the print. "I can't ride a mechanical bull."

All manner of images she had no business entertaining scrolled through her brain. She took a slow step back. "How would you know?"

For a hot second, the devil took up residence in his eyes.

"I'm not even going to ask." She shot out a hand. "Let me see those negatives. I need to find one of mine that's half as good as yours."

They'd entered the darkroom as dusk fell. With no ambient light, time went squishy, and she had no idea how long they worked. Soon, dangling scenes of

273

mushrooms and mountain laurel created a magical landscape fit for a fairytale. Surveying them, she rubbed her fingers into tight muscles at the base of her skull and lingered over her best shot. She'd caught a single open blossom amid a cluster of buds. Before a misty charcoal background, the little flower showed a brave face, as if it alone dared to gaze into the unknown. "Now, I really do feel like a bumblebee in a blossom." She yawned, and her throat creaked. "And I could fall asleep right here."

From behind, he threaded his arms around her waist and buried his face in her hair. "I could use a nap. How about you?"

Blood shot through her veins like a cab gunning for the next green light. A nap could be both fun and messy, but, hey, he suggested it. She laid her arms atop his, snuggling back against him. "I got nothing against napping."

And then her phone went berserk.

A barrage of messages detonated on screen. The ringtone pealed, and she swiped. "What's going on?"

On the other end, Zibby burst into tears.

So much for a nap.

****

Darcy's alarm chimed at seven the next morning, and bleary-eyed, she packed an overnight bag with a few changes of clothing and her toiletries. How many nights would she be in New York? Two? Maybe three? The arts festival was Saturday. She had to return by Thursday to help the women prepare. She slid her computer, phone, and chargers into her backpack, then suddenly remembered the special roll of film with the family photos. She could drop it at the photo shop

274

around the corner from her apartment and have prints for Rebecca the same day.

Her suitcase zipper stuck, and she yanked it back and forth before the teeth parted, revealing the hidden roll snuggled next to Pammy's borrowed romance. She tucked the film into a backpack pocket and whirled. The sooner she left, the less traffic she'd face. What she'd find when she arrived was another question entirely.

Zibby had finally calmed down enough to share what happened. According to their super, the three-year-old in the apartment upstairs decided to give his toy dinosaurs a bath right before the family left for the weekend. Apparently, he was summoned before bath time ended, and he neglected to turn off the tap. Thanks to a cat sitter, the flood was discovered fairly soon, minimizing damage but not preventing a partial collapse of their bathroom ceiling and significant water damage to Zibby's and Fern's bedrooms on either side. The wedding was in Nashville, and her roommates were scheduled to fly back Tuesday. Darcy assured them she could handle it.

Samuel had made her tea and offered to go, too. She bit back the *yes* that clamored at her throat. She longed to take him to New York, and having someone with her who understood construction would be invaluable. But the damage sounded extensive, and she would certainly have to stay with her parents. No way would she subject him to Park Avenue, no matter how tempting. Maybe she really did love the guy.

She tidied the quilt and slung her backpack over one shoulder, checking to make sure she remembered everything. Even on a cloudy day, the room filled her with lightness, and she hated to swap it for her parents' stuffy apartment. The homey scent of bacon wafted from downstairs. Verna had already made breakfast, and the family would soon depart for church. She'd hoped to accompany them. Another time, maybe. But, if she wanted to catch Samuel, she needed to scoot.

Over a hurried breakfast, she explained the situation to Verna. With Dave's camera slung over one shoulder, she packed the car and dashed through the fruit trees, past the garden, and over the creek. Developing photos with Samuel had been…. She filled her lungs, the scents of the farm and the creek saturating the air until she could almost taste them. Their evening was simply wonderful—both simple and full of wonder. Had a preschooler in Brooklyn not flooded a brownstone, where would the night have led? Melty mushiness blossomed in her core. Then again, maybe she knew. Samuel was a man of honor. He'd already declared his desire keep whatever was between them mess-free and fun. She'd have a lot of hours on the interstate to relive that fun.

She scampered over the bridge and down the lane toward the woods. His workshop came into view. Its clean lines were so pleasing she couldn't resist. She pulled the phone from her pocket, opened the camera app, and shot. Just for her. Just so she'd remember. *As if she'd ever forget.*

After saying a quick good-bye, she'd leave him with the camera. She'd loaded a fresh roll of film, and if he liked, he could shoot and develop it while she was gone. The whole process seemed to delight him. Though she doubted he could acquire his own camera, the gift of a few days' loan was easy and nowhere near enough to thank him for his help.

To her left, bushes rustled, and a rabbit streaked out, cottony tail like a bobbing snowball. He'd do well to avoid the kitchen garden. Nora and Verna would take none too kindly to an interloper in the pea patch.

A figured moved inside the workshop, and she sidled to the window.

He wasn't dressed yet for church but had pulled work pants over a textured, long johns top, unbuttoned at the neck. Barefoot and tousle-haired, he let his suspenders hang loose at his hips and sipped from a mug, regarding a small sculpture on the workbench. What was it?

She took out Dave's camera and with nimble fingers, reversed the lens, restoring its telephoto properties. With two stealthy steps, she crouched in front of the glass and peeked over the sill. The shutter depressed halfway, and the lens autofocused.

Stationed at the workbench, he lifted the doodad to eye-level and spun it slowly. Through wide windows, the morning sun kissed the burnished wood and his ruddy skin with equal affection. But that affection paled to his expression as he studied the bumblebee made from tiny spoons and springs, nestling among the splayed petals of a flower.

Her. He sculpted her.

Her heart hammered. She framed the photo and shot.

One neural impulse. One tiny flick of the finger. One click, and the deed was done. She lowered the camera. Adrenaline seeped from her body, giving way to regret that burned her insides like toxic slime. Never had she violated someone's privacy as grossly as she did just then. And she did it to Samuel, the man she supposedly loved. How right he was to distrust her. Oh, the picture was exquisite. Rebecca would cherish it. But Darcy never felt uglier. Had she shot on digital, she would have deleted the photo instantly, but his likeness was seared onto film. In a way, it didn't yet exist. In another, it was as permanent as a tattoo.

As if he smelled her betrayal, he glanced sharply toward the window.

Like a thief, she slunk into shadows and skulked back to the farm, taking the camera with her.

****

True to form, Darcy's father had a contractor on call. By the time she collapsed onto a chair in his study that evening—having driven into town, dropped off the film, inspected the apartment with her super, triaged her roommates' possessions, cleaned and laundered what she could, and hopped the train for the Upper East Side—she could barely see straight. In a stroke of luck, her mother was at a committee meeting. On a good day, Darcy needed every faculty to negotiate the minefield that was a conversation with Isabelle King. Exhausted, who knew what she might have let slip?

The leather chair was shiny and smooth, the color of merlot, and she mindlessly stroked it while sipping seltzer from a crystal goblet that seemed to weigh fourteen pounds. The fizz tickled her nose, and she sneezed.

Keeping one eye on the ballgame, Lloyd nursed a bourbon. "I'll have my secretary call Carlos in the morning. He runs a top-notch operation."

"The super wants his guy."

Dad snorted. "I'm sure he does, but all contractors

278

are not created equal."

Nor all carpenters. Every moment in her apartment, she imagined Samuel there, too. What would he think of Fern's botanical collages and Zibby's collection of sci-fi bobble heads, all of which were blessedly unharmed by the deluge? Sprawled on her loveseat and updating her roomies about the damage, she could almost see him at her bedroom window, gazing out over Brooklyn.

He'd love every brownstone, tenement building, and skyscraper. He would appreciate it all. He'd take the time to look.

She heard the crack of a well-hit ball and the roar of the televised crowd.

Dad lunged from his chair, ice cubes clinking. "Attaway, boys!"

With a carefully controlled step that made her wonder how many bourbons he'd enjoyed, he went to the brass bar cart and refilled.

"Can I get you another seltzer, Peanut? Or something stronger?"

Peanut. The childhood nickname landed in her lap like a tiny present. He hadn't called her Peanut for years. She roamed her gaze over framed photos lining the wall-to-wall bookcases. He had more family pictures than she remembered. Most were snapshots of herself and her siblings when they were young. Who'd taken them? Try as she might, she couldn't recall either of her parents with a camera. "I'm good. I could use another slice of pizza, though." Upon entering the apartment, she'd been assaulted by the smell of pepperoni and was gobsmacked to find her father parked in front of the ballgame with an entire pie on his imposing mahogany desk.

"Help yourself." With a muffled "oof," he settled into his recliner. "All evidence of pizza must be in the refuse closet before your mother returns." He scowled. "She left me soup."

Darcy slid a generous slice onto her plate. "Never fear. I will bury the body."

"That's my girl." Pressing a fist to his chest, he stifled a patrician burp. "So, how's the old hometown treating you? The cousins haven't recruited you yet?"

She giggled. She liked this version of her father, slightly soused and free from Isabelle's influence. "From what I gather, they don't really want us."

He flicked a fleck of sauce from his sweater vest. "Who wouldn't want you, Peanut?"

With its brass lamps and oriental rugs, her father's study had always seemed stiff and unwelcoming. Tonight, garlic-scented and with the quiet sounds of the ballgame, it was more like a cozy pub than a room in some stately British mansion. She snuggled into the chair and blotted her pizza with a paper napkin. "Sarah greeted me like a long-lost sister." The surprise of Sarah's affectionate welcome still tickled her. "Most everyone else was leery until they found out *Mammi* Leora was my grandmother. Her name is like a secret password. It unlocks every door."

The bourbon glass clunked onto the table between them, teetering on the edge of a coaster. Her father straightened and studied her, squinch-eyed. "Really?"

"Absolutely!" Darcy chewed and chatted, blissfully unconcerned with manners. "So many of her students told me stories. She was beloved."

Lloyd's bushy brows furrowed. "I don't remember

that. I always felt as if something dreadful occurred well before I was born that set all my relatives against me. I was helpless." He sank back into the recliner, shaking his head. "Our family dwelt in a strange in-between. We weren't Amish, of course, and we rarely saw our Amish relations, but I wasn't like the kids at school, either. I dressed plainer, and I didn't have a car or a fine house. My friends' parents were professors and lawyers. My mother taught second grade, and my father sold tires. I'm ashamed to say it, Peanut, but they were rather…an embarrassment."

He gazed at the television without seeming to see it. While her mother's youth was immortalized in home movies, photos, and family stories, her father's was rarely mentioned. She balanced her plate on one knee, hardly daring to move for fear he would stop talking. "Is that why you left Green Ridge?"

With a sharp nod, he took up his drink. "Your grandmother was a clever woman. She had courage, but she lacked drive. To do what she did, to give up everyone and everything, and then to settle for teaching elementary school in Green Ridge?" He made a disgusted sound in the back of his throat. "Senseless. I wanted more for my life. And for yours—you and Maddy and Garrett. So much more."

By modern metrics, Lloyd King was a success. His status and Park Avenue address were evidence of how far he'd come from that humble house in the country. But at what cost? She tucked a knee and turned. "*Mammi* Leora mattered. She made a difference in peoples' lives. I'm proud to be her granddaughter."

He took a deep swig and exhaled forcefully, staring into his glass. "So you've said."

His hair had faded from salt-and-pepper to gray, and, though a former college athlete, his belly pooched, and his cheeks sagged. Years of hard work exacted a price, and as he said, breaking from one's family took a toll. He'd done it with nearly as much finality as his mother and for many of the same reasons. *Mammi* Leora wanted her children to have education and opportunity exactly as he did. Could he be blamed for having taken those opportunities and run? Could Darcy be blamed for rejecting them? Theoretically, of course.

Her family rarely touched. For most occasions, a European kiss on the cheek sufficed. Now, she reached across the table and took her father's hand. Though the knuckles protruded, and the bones seemed closer to the surface, his hand was as warm and solid as she remembered from when she was a girl, clinging tightly as he walked her to school. "*Mammi* would be proud of you, too."

His arm stiffened, but his gaze didn't leave the television. He frowned. "So, what shall we do about the property and the items in storage? Sell them, I suppose."

The thought of selling *Mammi's* things gave her a pang. No house remained, but only acres of rolling property and a charred skeleton. How much land had they owned? To her as a child, the yard seemed vast. In reality, it was likely just big enough for a tire swing, a vegetable garden, and creek full of tadpoles. She released him and took a clarifying sip of seltzer. "I suppose."

He frowned into the swirling amber liquid. "Take what you want and sell the rest. I'll split the proceeds with your aunt and uncle, and we'll donate our share to charity."

Tears she thought she left in Pennsylvania pooled on her lashes. Her father found excessive emotion distasteful, and she quickly brushed them away. "Sounds good."

"Well, that's settled." He heaved a long breath. "Where shall we give the money? It won't amount to much, but it should go somewhere that would please your grandmother." He lifted his glass her direction. "I'd like the decision to be yours and mine."

And not your mother's was strongly implied. That took some of the sting out of selling. She allowed her thoughts to roam over her time in Pennsylvania, all the people she'd met and the places she'd photographed, and instantly, she knew. "Not long ago, a doctor opened a non-profit medical clinic to serve the Amish and Mennonite communities. As you probably remember, the Amish don't have health insurance. They rely on support from the church. Dr. Richard Bruce is the man's name. I photographed a patient of his at the local hospital. A member of the family I'm staying with was badly injured when a truck hit their buggy. Because of Dr. Bruce, she had a full hip replacement."

"I like the sound of that." Lloyd finished the drink in one gulp, and his eyelids sagged.

"Good." She extended a hand for his empty glass.

"Leave the dishes for Martha. She'll get them in the morning." He reclined and put up his feet.

The matter of the property resolved, she sat with her father in silence. She'd have to find a realtor. And how in the world would she dispose of the storage unit? Maybe Pammy would have an idea. The New York catcher knocked in a run to take the lead, sending her back to the Lumberjacks game. Would Samuel enjoy a giant stadium with its sky-high bleachers and rowdy crowds? She rather thought he would. Her father's head lolled, and she was on the verge of grabbing the pizza box when he shifted, groggily knocking a newspaper to the floor.

"How's goes your photography? Those Amish allow you take their pictures?"

"Once I mention *Mammi*, yes. The work is going beautifully. I believe it's the best I've ever done."

His chin tucked against his chest, and he yawned. "That's a relief. Your mother won't have to rescind her donation to Kids Art...or Arts and Kids...or whatever the dickens Margo calls her organization." His head tipped back against the chair, and his eyes closed.

The hairs on the back of her neck stood on end.

Donation? What donation?

Desperate for more information but afraid to ask, she waited, her grip on the plate growing sweatier. Clearly, he meant as a devoted board member and regular donor to Art4Kidz, Isabelle wouldn't want Darcy to disappoint Margo.

A snore issued from the adjacent recliner.

Or worse yet, to see Darcy fired. After all, her mother introduced her to Margo. If Darcy were let go, then Isabelle's position on the board would become awkward. Surely, that was what he meant.

Another snore, louder than the first, seemed to startle him to consciousness. He mumbled incoherently and lapsed back into sleep.

All the better. She didn't really want to know the details...

Did she?

Chapter Twenty-Three

Darcy didn't own her Brooklyn apartment. She rented. The lease came due in June, as a matter of fact. But the next morning, her super surrendered his turf to her father's personal contractor with surprising alacrity.

Carlos won over the man with his quick smile, thorough assessment of the damage, and, perhaps most importantly, a firm guarantee that all repairs would be financed by Lloyd King. Having assured her the apartment would be habitable the following week, Carlos flashed a thumbs-up over one shoulder and followed the super downstairs, hotly debating Mike Piazza's best play at home, while fully agreeing never to step foot in a Bronx baseball stadium.

Over video chat that afternoon, Fern and Zibby were cagey. Darcy told herself the sidelong looks they shared as she walked them through the damage and construction plan were nothing. Her friends were busy with post-wedding activities and a last-minute visit to Graceland. Besides, the issue of Darcy's money was always thorny. Her friends really were starving artists, while she simply acted the role. She might not live off the trust fund, but it was always there. Having no one in Green Ridge aware of how much her parents were worth was so refreshing. Life was far easier as *Mammi* Leora's *kinnskind* than as Lloyd and Isabelle King's daughter. She could simply be herself.

She envied Fern and Zibby their time in Nashville. They were much closer with the grad-school classmate who got married than she'd been, just as they were closer to each other than to Darcy. But they were solid roommates. She missed them, but even more, she missed Green Ridge. After ending the call, she ran a few errands and caught up with friends over dinner, but the city felt loud, and the dirt and crowds she habitually tuned out clamored for notice. Why was everyone walking so fast? Did anyone else see the dandelion pushing through a crack in the sidewalk? What about the bunch of helium balloons soaring between skyscrapers?

Darcy did not want to throw her father under the bus, but as she rode the 6 Train uptown, she chewed over his revelation. Though half asleep at the time, he implied her mother's donation to Art4Kidz was significant and likely recent. What compelled Isabelle to write a check? She'd no doubt made a huge year-end donation, and the gala fundraiser took place in July. Darcy shoved aside speculation and hatched a plan to steal into the guest suite, chow down on sushi, and binge-watch TV.

Even at night, the guest room wasn't dark. The city glow seeped through her eyelids, nudging her to wakefulness. She tumbled out of bed and drew the blackout shades, but not before catching sight of her backpack on the desk chair. Rebecca's prints were inside. She'd retrieved them that morning and slid them carefully between her laptop and this month's issue of *Hudson Magazine*, rescued unread from her parents' recycling bin. The envelope remained sealed. She had no need to open it. The photos were exquisite. They would give a teenager comfort. She knew these things, but the pictures nagged at her. City traffic whooshed in the hissing voice of betrayal, and a fitful night of sleep ended at an hour as early as any she had on the farm.

As she leaned her elbows on a marble-topped kitchen island the size of Delaware and nursed a cup of strong black coffee, she was fairly certain the sun had risen. The sole kitchen window opened into a darkened interior courtyard. Cucumber and mint floated in a carafe like lily pads, awaiting Isabelle's post-workout arrival. Though the water dispenser was like something from a modern spa, the kitchen was a hardwood homage to traditional design. Ornate cherry cabinets and top-of-the-line appliances welcomed caterers. The room hadn't changed since Darcy fruitlessly begged her mother to just once let her tear open a brownie mix and bake. Though immaculate, the space needed updating, as did the entire stodgy home.

Given that Darcy couldn't wait to leave it behind, she'd do well to jot a quick note of thanks, pack her bag, and flee. Isabelle was Isabelle. Nothing Darcy said or did would change her into an affectionate mother who loved her daughter unconditionally. Why poke the hornet's nest?

"See you Tuesday, Trent!" Her face flushed, and her short bob swept back in a headband, Isabelle dismissed her trainer and bounced into the kitchen on pristine white sneakers. With a cupboard door opened and her fingers already straining for a glass, she paused and sniffed the air. "I fear a charcuterie board died in my kitchen."

"It's called pepperoni." She manufactured a smile over her coffee cup. "Good morning, Mother."

"No wonder I threw out a quart of soup." Isabelle dabbed her brow with a fluffy towel and filled a glass. "Martha will have to dry-clean the drapes." Sipping delicately, she gave Darcy a lingering appraisal. "You're up early. I thought you kept artists' hours."

"I'm on farm time now."

"How charming."

Ignoring the sarcasm, Darcy slid her coffee to one side. Beneath her clasped hands, the marble was cool and impenetrable. Still smiling, she let her gaze go equally as hard. "It is. I enjoy watching the sunrise over the ridge, and the fresh air on my morning runs is extremely restorative."

Isabelle propped a hip against the counter and narrowed her gaze. "They must feed you well. You're positively cherubic."

Leaning to one side, she ducked the thinly veiled insult and let her thick, blonde hair slide over one shoulder. "Thank you. Green Ridge suits me. In fact, I like it so much I've decided to stay." Spurred by some evil gremlin, the lie seemed simply to fall from her lips. Inwardly thrumming at her own daring, she marshalled a sincere expression. "Schools always need art teachers. I think I'll be very happy." Her intent was to get to the truth behind the mysterious donation, but the announcement gave her a thrill. What if she really did stay?

Cucumber water appeared to slide down the wrong tube, and Isabelle choked. "Don't be ridiculous," she spluttered through a tissue.

Darcy flipped open her palms. "What?"

"You can't."

"With the apartment flood and our lease ending,

now is the ideal time." *Was it?* She nearly had herself convinced.

Isabelle blanched. "You'd give up your job after all we've done for you? All *I've* done?"

"I'm grateful for my education. I'll put it to excellent use as a teacher."

"I'm not speaking of your education." Isabelle marched to the sink and dumped an entire glass of cucumber water.

"Then what are you talking about?" She crossed her arms with a stony stare. "Mother? What did you do?"

Isabelle's laugh rang from the cabinets. "Nothing!" She whirled and speed walked toward her bedroom. "I'm going to freshen up."

"Did you bribe Margo to send me to Green Ridge?" Even asking felt crazy. But she couldn't deny how the question froze her mother faster than a dermatologist with liquid nitrogen.

Revolving slowly, Isabelle gave a withering look. "Of course not."

She dropped from the chair, ambled toward the built-in desk that served as her mother's home office, and opened the top drawer. A leather-clad checkbook sat in its customary spot atop a matching address book. Darcy tapped it with one finger. "So, if I peeked in here, I wouldn't find a substantial donation to Art4Kidz made in the last, say, two months?"

Blood rushed to Isabelle's cheeks. "How dare you snoop through my personal things!"

She would have liked to slam the drawer, but the glides whooshed soundlessly. "I didn't. I'm simply asking."

Isabelle flung the towel onto the counter. "You were always an ungrateful child."

A microscopic dart seemed to pierce Darcy's throat. Isabelle aimed for the jugular, and more often than not, her aim was true.

"What's so wrong with a mother helping her daughter? Especially when that daughter is chronically single and dead set on a hobby only one in ten thousand will leverage into a proper living?" Isabelle's hands anchored on the slender waist she toiled so hard to maintain. "Thanks to me, you might actually be one of those few."

A hobby? She'd believed for years her parents didn't take photography seriously, but to hear her mother say it outright made the entire building sway. She shot a steadying hand against the refrigerator. "I don't need your help. I'm good at what I do."

"Everyone needs a nudge. Otherwise, what am I here for?"

"To love me?" Her voice sounded small, and immediately, she was a girl again, begging for her parents' attention. She leaned into stainless steel as unyielding as her mother's heart. "To love all of us—me, Maddy, and Gar." Her mother pulled a comically dramatic face, frowning like a sad mime moping along the River Seine.

"You think I don't love you?"

Darcy's heart plummeted. Isabelle King could make anything about herself, even Darcy's career. The conversation was pointless. Still, having lived among a healthy, functioning family, she couldn't stop herself from trying. "Of course, you do. But I wish you knew me well enough to realize that never in a million years would I want you to bribe anyone into giving me a job."

Isabelle held up a hand. "I only secured an interview. You earned the job. Margo is very impressed with you."

"And the photo essay?" Must she drag out the truth? "The three-week assignment in Pennsylvania?"

Isabelle huffed. "If I'd known she'd send you there, I'd have only given half as much."

The admission landed like a dead fish on the counter. Darcy slumped against the fridge. The truth gave no satisfaction. Her mother had known her longer than anyone. Through all the ups and downs of growing up, Isabelle was there. Turned out, she hadn't been paying attention. She didn't know Darcy at all. Given several decades of therapy, maybe she and her mother could forge an authentic connection—the kind she felt every single time she sat at the Rishels' dinner table. Did she even have the heart to try? Her conversation with her father was some progress. Knowing that made leaving easier.

She stared at her mother long enough that Isabelle coughed and twitched, but she didn't offer a word of remorse. Pity welled but not a single tear. "Good-bye, Mother." Darcy rinsed her coffee cup, racked it in the dishwasher, and packed her bag, by no means certain she'd ever come back again.

****

Three hours after leaving Manhattan, Darcy pulled up at the traffic light beside Green Ridge High School and ogled House of Pizza. A tuna sub wouldn't solve everything, but it might make her feel good. Especially if followed by one of Pammy's cupcakes. With a sigh, she shifted into the opposite turning lane. After the scene with her mother, she still had no appetite.

What now? Should she march into Margo's office and declare she wouldn't work for someone who could be bribed? Her boss could take the staff photographer position and shove it. That would show her.

But show Margo what exactly? Behind Darcy was a line of photographers a mile long, ready to snatch any crumbs *Hudson Magazine* tossed their direction. She flipped the blinker and turned toward a community who climbed ladders only to literal roofs. The window flew down, and sweet country air filled her lungs. Not completing this assignment hurt no one but herself. Her work was superb. The story it told deserved to be heard, and nobody could tell it quite like she. Darcy was a good photographer—better than good—she was excellent. Given time and a dash of luck, she would have earned this opportunity on her own. But Isabelle King made her own luck, shaping reality to her will with a simple signature on a check.

Darcy tromped the gas pedal. She'd driven well above the speed limit the entire way. Maybe if she traveled fast and far enough, she could outrun her mother's scheming. Had she accomplished anything on her own? What else had Isabelle manipulated? Even now, a family-financed contractor was hanging drywall in her apartment. The Kings were everywhere, greasing wheels and making backroom deals. Could she ever escape?

A farm market passed in a blur, offering a glimpse of a stooped Amish woman arranging flowers. The old woman's dress cut a vibrant slash of purple in a blurry green landscape. Sometimes photographs composed themselves. No, her mother didn't control everything.

Darcy's artistic eye was entirely her own. Even more, her Pennsylvania family and friends were hers, too. Pammy and Al. Sarah and Amity. Verna, Tucker, Nora, and the girls. Rebecca.

Samuel.

She lunged for the dregs of her iced coffee. Despite a longing so palpable she could feel his fingertips on her skin, she was also reluctant. When she saw him, she'd probably burst into tears and spill all about her mother and the bribe. On one hand, she wanted to tell everything, to lay it all out so he could share her outrage and help plot the next move.

On the other…she was mortified.

Her mother paid off her boss.

She couldn't imagine a less Amish transaction.

Coffee gurgled in the bottom of the cup, making up in cold what it lacked in strength. Her vision sharpened. She swung onto Old Cowan Road, entering a landscape all the greener for its contrast to concrete. Through polarized sunglasses, the sky was deep cerulean above a barn so ruddy it set the standard against which all other reds should be judged. That trees flowered at all, let alone in masses of bubblegum-pink, was a miracle. The city trees were no longer in bloom, and she'd jogged over vast petal carpets the previous morning. Here, though, they were glorious.

Freshly painted, Sarah's sign sprang from its planter of flowers.

Darcy yanked the wheel and skidded into the parking lot. She hit the brake and winced. Just once, she'd like to arrive at a relaxed pace. But suddenly, she was desperate to sit among women and sew. According to Rebecca, a round-the-clock frolic was underway in

Sarah's living room as the ladies finished quilts for the arts festival. Darcy would be welcomed with pie and set to work.

She jumped down from the rental SUV and rolled her shoulders, feeling her joints loosen. Entering that farmhouse, she would be accepted not because she was a photographer at a fancy magazine or Lloyd and Isabelle King's youngest child but because her heart was willing, and her stitches were neat. Even had she no skill as a seamstress, she would still be welcomed and put to work stirring a pot or minding children. The only prerequisite was presence.

Sarah opened the door, and her dark eyes rounded. "You survived the flood! Did you build an ark?"

A wee girl emerged from beneath Sarah's skirt, peering up with her lower lip pooched in a frown. "Did you save the giraffes? I would miss the giraffes if they floated away."

Darcy knelt, unsurprised that word of her misfortune traveled so quickly. "My flood wasn't quite as epic as Noah's, although from what I hear, several dinosaurs were rescued."

"The giraffes are fine." Sarah patted the child's bottom and beckoned. "Come see what we've done with your *Grossmammi's* quilt tops."

Darcy entered the living room, and her spirits soared. On the rack was one of *Mammi* Leora's quilts. It was a traditional log cabin pattern, pieced so the center formed an eight-pointed star set in two concentric diamonds. She recognized many of the women, but more had joined. They nodded hellos and quickly returned to work.

She sat beside Sarah's grandmother, Orpha, and

took up a needle. Much as when she visited the Troyers, she worked quietly while Pennsylvania Dutch eddied around her. The soothing sounds were punctuated by clatter from the kitchen and children's songs. A whiff of homemade bread made her stomach rumble. Lunch would come soon. Meanwhile, she was content to simply stitch.

From the corner of her eye, she saw Orpha slide a spoon beneath the quilt. Under pretext of tying her sneaker, Darcy peeked underneath and watched how the old woman used the spoon to protect her fingers and guide the needle up through the layers in a row of perfect, tiny stitches. Her gaze was as vacant as before, but Orpha hummed a tune Darcy recognized. The hymn was one *Mammi* Leora sang while she weeded her garden or mopped the floors. In a miracle of memory, the melody came back, and Darcy hummed along, catching Orpha's gaze and smiling. For the first time in three days, she felt truly at home.

Could she really buy *Mammi* Leora's house and stay? She'd never join the Amish of course, but these women were family. She could attend frolics and gatherings and maybe even a wedding someday. Rebecca's? Or Verna and the deacon's, if ever they realized they were in love?

"Leora broke our hearts when she left."

Startled, Darcy turned. Orpha's voice was thin and reedy, but the words were clear.

"When she told me her decision, we held onto each other and cried. Oh, she wanted to stay, but she couldn't. Her conscience wouldn't allow it." Orpha lighted a watery gaze on Darcy, then returned to her work. "You're so like her." Her needle rocked back and forth, and she pinched the tip and pulled. "Shunning Leora was the cruelest thing I ever did. I'll have to live with that the rest of my days. She died so quick I hadn't time to say good-bye. Or to tell her how sorry I was." Gnarled fingers stroked the quilt top. "Finishing her quilts feels like a second chance. *Denki*."

The tears weren't finished with Darcy. They surged, tracing salty paths down both cheeks. Her throat went thick, and she nodded, unable to speak.

Orpha had her good-bye. Tomorrow, Darcy would go to her grandparents' property and take her turn.

That evening, as the setting sun ribboned the sky with satiny bands of pink and orange, Darcy knocked at Samuel's workshop.

The door swung open, and he froze, still gripping the knob.

Equal parts shock and relief showed in his face. Did he think she wouldn't return? Suddenly shy, she buried her hands in the pockets of her hoodie. "I'm back. Carlos is fixing the flood."

Bareheaded and barefoot, he twitched his lips but didn't quite smile. "Glad to hear it." He wiped his hands on a dingy towel, leaving greasy streaks. "I'd hug you but…"

"No worries." She inched back, fully aware that if she touched him, the whole let's-keep-this-non-relationship-mess-free endeavor would crash and burn. So few days remained. She wanted to do it right. "Hey, will you come with me to *Mammi* Leora's house tomorrow? I need to say good-bye. I figure you might have work but…" The corners of her eyes prickled, and she screwed up her face. "I don't think I can do it alone."

He rested a forearm on the doorframe and let out a breath. "Of course."

Relief crashed over her like a wave on a coastline he'd never visited. His body angled toward her, and the urge to nestle into him waged an epic battle with her better angels. "Maybe it'll be fun?" As if the same war might be taking place in his chest, too, his gaze traveled from her face, down her body, and back up. She swallowed. "It won't be fun."

His teeth flashed white in the dusk. "I'm always fun." He cupped her cheek and dropped a gentle kiss on her lips. "Surely, you know by now." He straightened and let his head fall to one side. "Goodnight, Brooklyn."

She stood immobile, like a princess who, instead of being awakened by the prince's kiss, was turned to stone. Maybe if she waited, he'd do it again. What was wrong with messiness, anyway? Messiness was fun. Break out the finger paints, mud puddles, and hot fudge sundaes! If she could convince her limbs to move, she'd throw herself at him and worry about messiness tomorrow.

Inside, his studio was lit in pools of white light. From the shadows, the darkroom beckoned.

He took two slow steps away.

"Come find me when you're free." She spun and jogged down the lane before he could close the door.

Gravel crunched beneath her sneakers. Tucker's music floated on the wind.

Darcy wasn't one to chat with the departed. Her Presbyterian upbringing didn't leave much room for ghosts. But with the breeze restless in the moonlit treetops, she felt her grandmother near. The presence was comforting. She no more wanted to bid it farewell than Samuel.

And yet, in the next few days, she'd need to do both.

"Guide me, *Mammi*," she whispered to the night. "Teach me how to say good-bye."

Chapter Twenty-Four

Dry-eyed, Darcy stared at the black and rotting ruins of her grandmother's house. The morning had been rainy, but now, at almost noon, the sun threatened to break through clouds still spitting mist. In a largely fruitless attempt to keep Samuel dry, she shifted her umbrella and sniffed the air. After spring rains in New York, a tangy, earthy scent utterly foreign to a concrete world rose from the sidewalks. Imagining it made her homesick for a city that, twenty-four hours ago, she couldn't wait to escape. At the same time, deep melancholy over the loss of *Mammi's* home washed over her. She suspected much of adulthood was finally having agency to return to places she loved, only to discover they were gone, or if not, they no longer bore any resemblance to what she remembered.

Beside her, Samuel hunched against the weather, his work coat beaded with fine drops and damp hair curling from beneath his hat.

He didn't shuffle or sigh. He simply stood like he had nowhere he'd rather be than knee-deep in weeds by a charred shell of a house in the rain. She tried to think of anyone else who would show up for her like this. She failed. "When I was nine, my mother sent me to *Mammi's* for two months because she wanted to go to Paris more than she didn't want me to come here. Which is saying something because she really didn't want me to come here."

The mist changed its mind and reverted to rain. She shifted, lifting the umbrella higher over his head.

"Let me." Taking the handle, he slid an arm around her waist and held the umbrella over them both.

"Yesterday, I told my mother I was moving to Green Ridge." She felt a microtremor shake him, but he said nothing. Still, she felt compelled to clarify. "I was joking."

"Odd joke."

A moment passed. "Maybe I wasn't joking," she said almost to herself. The ruins looked like a scar wrapped in a chain-link fence. She struggled to superimpose the sweet white farmhouse upon the blackened skeleton choked by brush. Closing her eyes, she pressed her cheek into the rough wool of Samuel's coat. It smelled like a petting zoo. Raindrops pattered the umbrella, and for the first time in years, she let herself remember arriving at *Mammi's*.

The weather was foul that day, too. A heavy storm hammered her father's striped golf umbrella, and she didn't hear his good-bye. Standing on the front porch with *Mammi* and Pop, she waved as the town car vanished like a silent ghost.

Pop lumbered around the corner of the house, shaking his head.

Darcy felt her cheeks sag. She crossed her arms tight over her tummy like she could cage the sob that threatened to choke its way out ever since her mother announced Darcy would spend the summer alone in Pennsylvania. It felt like a punishment. Well, if hating Camp Kitcheeweewah was a crime, then she was guilty as charged. Maddy and Gar flat-out lied when they said it was the happiest place on earth. After only one night, she knew she'd never been somewhere so damp and smelly and horrid.

Mammi sighed and wiped her hands on a red-checked apron. "Your father and I have had our disagreements, but I certainly hope he never felt like a sack of potatoes dropped on a doorstep for safekeeping. No matter. Whatever he and your mother are thinking, I'm not sorry you're here. In fact, I can't imagine anything nicer."

Mammi's face brimmed with kindness. Her hair was pulled back into a bun, but frizzy strands in a color between blonde and white undulated like she floated underwater. Her eyes were deep and chocolatey, and she didn't wear even a trace of lipstick. Darcy frowned, certain her grandmother was fooling. Did *Mammi* not realize she wasn't Maddy or Garrett, but just plain old Darcy?

Mammi pulled up a stool and sat. "Maybe we aren't well acquainted, but I have a good feeling about us. What do you say we skip all that awkward get-to-know-you stuff and go right to the part where we're pals? Sound good?"

Darcy nodded. No adult had ever spoken to her like an equal. She almost couldn't believe *Mammi* was for real.

"You'll be living with us, and as such, you'll have certain responsibilities, as do we all. Once you finish your chores, you're free to do as you like, so long as you stay out of trouble and come home by dark. I hope you'll choose to spend a little time with me, but that's up to you." She'd returned the stool and opened the door, releasing the smell of fresh-baked bread. "Grab your bag and come inside. Your second cousin, Sarah, has a new baby brother, and we've got to bake a cake."

No season can be perfect, but Darcy knew now that just one or maybe even two gold-tipped, rainbow-striped summers attained perfection. The summer she quit Camp Kitcheeweewah and was summarily dumped in Green Ridge was one. Later that August—when the wall calendar in the kitchen showed three days until school started, and *Mammi* gently suggested Darcy pack her belongings Darcy refused.

"I'm not going home." Sitting on her bed, she pulled skinned knees to her chest, twined her arms around them, and stared at Aunt Mary's shiny 4-H ribbons, tacked to the shelf beside the window. After a whole summer, she felt ownership of her aunt's girlhood room, and she imagined adding her own ribbons to the collection. Maybe raising prize chickens ran in the family?

Mammi sat next to her, and the mattress sagged. "Who said you're going home? I've chartered a research vessel for an expedition around the world. You've seen bluebirds in the backyard, but have you ever spotted a purplebird? I hear tell they live on a remote island in the South Pacific. We leave the day after tomorrow, but only if you pack. Shake a leg. I'll help."

So, Darcy packed, and plans for the purplebird voyage buoyed her until the moment she stood on the front porch, seeing the town car idling in the lane and rain bouncing off her father's umbrella as it had the day she arrived. She'd flown at her grandmother, flinging her arms around her waist, and burying her face in her apron. "I'll go, but only if you promise I can come back next summer."

"I promise." *Mammi* stroked her hair and planted a kiss on each cheek. "No good-byes, you hear me? We'll just say, 'see ya round, pal.' "

"See ya round, pal," she'd whispered through tears, untangling the apron strings from her fingers, and wiping her nose on her shirt.

Samuel's soothing voice brought her back to a present in which she appeared to be weeping snottily. She jerked away, dragging her sleeve across her face and sniffing. "I told you it wouldn't be fun."

With a soft laugh, he pulled her close. "Your *Mammi* meant something to you. Cry all you like."

"She was the best," Darcy sobbed. "She called me *pal* and made meadow tea with mint and honey, and sometimes, we had ice cream sundaes for supper for no reason at all. She told me I could come back, but then she died, and I never did." He rocked her gently side to side, patting soothing circles between her shoulder blades like she was still that broken-hearted nine-year-old who didn't get another summer. Who never said good-bye, only *so long, pal*. "My father wouldn't talk about her. He pretended he never even heard of meadow tea. After a while, I started to think maybe I imagined everything—the house and Pop's workshop in the garage. Maybe no one ever did love me like that."

"It was real," he whispered. "You know it was. Look hard enough and you'll see. Go on, look."

He released her at the precise moment the clouds cracked open, and sunlight gushed through, flooding forests and fields. The air was still heavy with mist, and the tiny droplets sparkled like crystals. Every leaf, every petal, and every blade of grass glittered. *Mammi's* house was real. Darcy could see it. It was real and magic, past and present, dead and living all at once. She owed it to herself and to her family to capture it exactly as it was today.

With a quick squeeze of Samuel's hand, she dashed to the car and grabbed Dave's camera. The clouds shifted. The light swelled and dimmed and swelled again. She had to move fast. She framed...and shot. Daisies and chain link. A blackened beam covered in vines. A brick hearth sprouting a spindly sapling. A flagstone path and tiny blue flowers. What remained of the porch.

Breathing the scent of lilacs, she roamed.

Her grandmother had photo albums. Rows of them filled the sitting room bookcase beside the television. *Mammi* would turn the pages, pointing out faces in black and white. "That's your father when he was your age, and Pop's father in the chair. Oh, and that's the day we moved in. My goodness! How small the cherry trees are."

Photos mattered. They held the gift of history. She'd scour the storage unit for the albums and add today's. Maybe...just maybe...her father would want them.

All at once, clouds seemed to swallow the sun, and the day shifted from gold to gray. She lowered the camera. She'd said her good-bye. She could leave now, couldn't she?

With no memory of having knelt, she rose. Bits of clover clung to her knees, and when she brushed them, they stuck to her fingers.

"Did you get what you need?"

Deep and soft, the voice came from behind. She

glanced over one shoulder and nodded.

He was leaning against the tree from which her tire swing once hung. A frayed rope dangling from a thick bough was all that remained. Pushing off the trunk, he came toward her. He extended a hand, and one corner of his mouth quirked.

She tilted her head, unsure for a moment what he wanted, and then she knew. The worn and weathered strap slid over her head, and she handed him the camera. "There's only one photo left."

"I only need one." Stepping back, he pointed the lens directly at her.

"Samuel…" She lowered her gaze, letting her fair hair drape her face. Her sneakers were wet, and the toes were streaked with red farm dirt. She didn't dislike being photographed; she simply preferred to be the photographer. Besides, no one ever wanted to take her picture. Not when grandchildren were around.

"Please, Darcy?"

Something in his voice made her look. He'd lowered the camera, and desire and sadness mingled in his gaze.

"I might not be in the photo," he went on. "But I'll know you have it, and that I was the one who took it." He flicked his gaze to the burnt house behind her. "And you'll never have to wonder if I really did exist."

Love, loss, and the brutal inevitability of good-bye sliced through her with the smooth force of a chef's knife. With a strangled cry, she lunged for him, longing to reveal she photographed his family for exactly that reason…vowing to keep the house and never leave …promising to rescue him from this too-small life…wishing for a world where they made sense.

He shot out a hand. "*Nee*. Let me take your photo."

She stopped short, skidding over wet grass. "You can have it. You can have any pictures you want. I'll give them all to you. Everything." *Everything.* Fear flickered in his eyes, and he shook his head like she'd offered a deal with the devil. Like he was an alcoholic, and she came at him with a gallon of whiskey. Like if he didn't force a *no* right this second, he knew beyond doubt he would say *yes*.

Say yes. Let me give you everything. Let me take you away.

"Please." His spine caved, and his shoulders went slack. "If you have any love for me, don't tempt me. Not when you know I can't resist."

Her breath was a million butterflies in her chest. Her pulse zinged so bright and electric she was sure he could see it. "I do have love for you, Samuel," she breathed. "Just a bit."

"Then let me take your picture."

She met his gaze, and a smile that felt like sunrise broke over her face.

And he lifted the camera.

And the shutter went *click*.

And being photographed felt like the tenderest kiss.

She'd leave off talk of buying the house. She'd allow the afternoon to drift quietly back to normal and walk with him around the property one last time before getting in the car and leaving. She'd do it because he asked. But she wouldn't stop thinking.

****

Snug in her attic room that afternoon, she couldn't keep her thoughts from spiraling, returning again and again to the same simple question. *How?* Say she'd had enough of this particular brand of fun and wanted to take it to the next level. Say she wanted a ten-ton truckload of next-level fun. He was Amish, but he hadn't joined the church. Clearly, he yearned to experience the world beyond this valley. She could give him that life. She could...dare she even think it...rescue him.

She was a New Yorker, laser-focused on advancing her career and doing all she could to secure the promotion of her dreams. Everything short of what Margo asked, of course. But once Margo saw the work, she'd realize photos of Amish kids smoking cigarettes didn't get at the true intersection between the Amish and modernity. The story was more nuanced—as complicated and contradictory as the Amish people themselves. Could she do it? Could she live part time in the country, working remotely and traveling when her position as a staff photographer required? Her trust fund ensured she could afford it. But would Margo agree?

During family dinner and clean up, she chattered and joked as if she'd always been there and always would be, but she kept thinking. All the while, she felt Samuel's gaze and sensed he wasn't quite himself. If the family noticed, they didn't let on.

Throughout a golden evening by the creek, she thought, dipping her toes in icy water while Rebecca and the twins played with a brand-new litter of kittens.

As dusk crept down the valley, the women lounged in lawn chairs and chatted.

On hands and knees, Samuel gave pony rides to the giggling girls, tickling them and joining Tucker in silly songs.

Nora shifted uncomfortably and slipped a pillow

behind her lower back. "Tucker and Samuel head to Troyer's farm tomorrow. They'll be gone all day and most of the next. I'll be glad to have Rebecca stand market with us."

Verna surveyed her granddaughter, sitting on a rock by the creek with her nose in a book. "The *maedel* is a hard worker, for sure and certain. When the time is right, she'll make some man a good *fraa*."

Nora rubbed a hand over her growing belly. "Not too soon, I hope. I'll need her when the *boppli* comes."

Darcy knew Rebecca's mother and grandmother loved her, but she bristled at the way they took her labor and imminent marriage for granted. "I'm happy to help if you need another set of hands."

Nora turned up her nose as if she smelled something distasteful.

After two weeks in Green Ridge, Darcy felt a connection with every member of the Rishel family, except her.

"*Denki,* but we'll make do," Nora said. "From what I hear, you're needed at Sarah's. They plan to have dozens of quilts for the fair."

Verna caught Darcy's gaze over her crochet. "What you're doing for the school is wonderful *gut*."

"*Yah*." Lifting tight lips, Nora rose with effort and beckoned her daughters. "Wonderful *gut*."

That woman was a hard nut to crack.

Nora took the twins' hands and ducked beneath the fruit trees.

Carrying a cardboard box of kittens, Tucker joined her, long legs slowing to toddler pace.

Nora was so private as to be nearly unknowable, but Tucker was an open book. They seemed living proof that opposites attracted, but she knew their relationship was more complicated than the easygoing singer let on. Still, Darcy envied them. Their life might not be simple, but it was doubtless happy.

Rebecca sidled close. "I'll be sad to see you go."

Darcy's heart squeezed. "I have something for you. I'll give it to you later."

"Oh." The sound was barely more than a whisper. "*Denki*."

"*Gern gschehne*."

With a skip, Rebecca trotted behind her family, managing to read and walk at once.

On the far side of the yard, Verna stood at the garden fence, finishing the last of her coffee and surveying the spring plantings.

Not much got by that woman. No way could Darcy slip off unnoticed to the workshop. Where was Samuel, anyway? The last she saw him, he was toting away the chairs.

He emerged from a shed and ambled toward her, coming up behind and resting his hands on her hips.

She looked pointedly in Verna's direction, in case he wasn't aware they had company.

He brought his lips to her ear and kissed her. "I've been meaning to say…I have a little love for you, too, Brooklyn."

She did not see that coming. The permanent retainer on the back of her bottom teeth melted, and her heart took flight. Allowing her shoulder blades to brush his chest, she tilted her head, exposing the tender skin of her neck. He dropped another kiss where her pulse pounded a zillion beats a minute. "I'm not ready to say good-bye," she breathed.

"So, let's not." He caught her ponytail and gave it a playful tug. "Good night, Brooklyn." He slipped away and strode purposefully down the lane. "*Gude nacht*," he called to his mother.

Verna bent and yanked a leggy weed from the chicken wire.

Could she wait the woman out? Idle in the backyard until Verna retired and rendezvous with Samuel around the firepit? She wrinkled her nose. She was too old to sneak around. Besides, tonight she had to make her final photo selections and email them to the camera shop along with Verna's short-term rental flyer so the prints would be available before she left. Not to mention the fact Samuel hadn't invited her.

She meandered toward the house, admiring summery flowers in terra-cotta pots on either side of the steps. The air was still, and she heard Verna singing as she pulled weeds. Darcy opened the back door, and the quiet house welcomed her.

Tonight was good night, not good-bye. She paused on the second-floor landing, peeking in the open door to his room. Apparently, having determined Darcy wasn't a threat, he'd retreated to the workshop completely. Wise choice. What exquisite agony sleeping a floor apart would be. Less agonizing, however, than the good-bye that awaited in three short days.

The house was so quiet, not even the attic stairs creaked. Her room was stuffy, and she threw open the windows, inviting a breeze. She flopped onto the bed and, dangling over the edge, fished the computer from her backpack. Once she emailed the photo files and flyer, she'd take a stab at a rental listing for Verna. Drafting a speech in which she said good-bye and wished Samuel well, however, would be infinitely harder. If, in fact, she could bring herself to say good-bye...now that she revealed the little bit of love she felt...and he said the same words back.

Chapter Twenty-Five

Darcy took the gallery owner's business card with as much excitement as if she were brokering a million-dollar Wall Street deal. "Rebecca!" She stood on tiptoes and beckoned over the crowd of arts festival shoppers. "Someone here would like to meet you."

Rebecca folded one of *Mammi's* quilts carefully, tucked it in a bag, and gave it to a customer.

The day was picture-perfect. Darcy should know. She took pictures for a living. A crowd like she'd never seen thronged Main Street, mobbing pearly-white vendor tents that fronted the Victorian buildings from the high school all the way to the river. Lush flower baskets provided pops of vivid color, and live music from the post office steps added to the cheerful hubbub. At well after noon, the crowds showed no sign of waning, and the quilt stock was significantly depleted.

With each sale, Sarah's, Amity's, and Rebecca's smiles widened. The solar panels were well within reach.

The girl slipped between shoppers and bounced to Darcy's side.

The gallery owner thrust out a hand, displaying a chunky silver bracelet studded with turquoise. "Megan MacNeil. I own several children's boutiques on the Main Line in Philadelphia. Are you the artist behind these enchanting wall hangings?"

Cheeks flushed, Rebecca shook the woman's hand. "I am."

Megan MacNeil gestured toward the intricate bird blanket Rebecca finished the day before. "Are the designs original?"

"*Yah*." Rebecca straightened the quilt on the rack. "Each one is unique. I draw the patterns first and piece them from scraps I bring home from the fabric shop. I work there during the days and quilt nights after I finish chores."

The woman slid oversized tortoiseshell sunglasses into her dark hair and lifted a corner of the quilt, flipping it to examine the backing. "This is exactly the type of bespoke item my customers crave. Do you have more? I'd love to chat about stocking them in my stores."

From behind the woman's back, Darcy flashed two thumbs way up.

Rebecca clasped her hands beneath her chin. "I'd like that very much. I have lots more quilts—birds and animals and even one that's all cats."

The woman beamed. "Well, aren't you a delight. I'm so glad I made the drive. This is a charming town, and the quality of work is excellent across the board."

Darcy handed Rebecca the business card. "Rebecca will call Monday from the fabric store. I'm sure you can come to an arrangement."

Megan MacNeil glided from the tent, her flowy dress wafting the scent of sandalwood.

"What did I tell you?" Darcy squeezed Rebecca's shoulders. "Your quilts are a hit."

With a girlish cry, Rebecca seized Darcy in a fierce hug. "*Denki*. For everything."

She placed a hand between the girl's delicate shoulder blades. How would she ever say good-bye? "You're so welcome."

Rebecca tightened her hold. "I don't know why *Gott* keeps sending *Englischers* to our house. But I'm grateful."

"Me, too." When Darcy opened her eyes, she spotted Samuel outside the tent. Shadows hid his face, but the softness of his shoulders and angle of his head felt like an invitation.

"You should walk with my *Onkel*." Rebecca released her hold and straightened her *kapp*. "We'll mind the booth. I understand how that credit card thing works on your phone."

How was the kid so perceptive? "I could use a breather. *Denki.*" Giving Sarah a wave, she ducked under the awning and followed her heart to the man who waited. Over the last two days, they'd seen each other only in passing as work took him to the Troyers, and she sewed until her fingertips were raw. Yet somehow, everyone seemed aware they were…well, not courting in any traditional sense, but spending time together.

While perfectly cordial, the women were tight-lipped. They believed him a full church member, of course, and nothing about Darcy hinted she'd join the community. Giving grudging approval to her photos, they accepted her as Leora Mast's granddaughter, a passable seamstress, and an *Englischer* who, for whatever reason, was moved to help with the school. Where Samuel was concerned, however, they shook their heads, exchanging knowing glances. They thought they knew him.

They were wrong.

After three weeks living among his friends and family, she was increasingly convinced Samuel Rishel was trapped. Bareheaded in a room full of prayer caps, she'd stitched her grandmother's quilts and let her thoughts wander. He'd revealed himself to her. So much of what he said and even more of what he didn't pointed to an all-too-familiar sensation: failure to fulfill expectations, no matter how hard one tried. She'd been able to take her education and run, but Samuel was stuck. He had his workshop and his business, but he clearly wanted more. He craved a bigger life, and she could give it to him.

Once the idea took root, it twined around her heart like the weeds in Verna's garden fence. The snow-white fabric she stitched became the French Alps. After a day on the ski slopes, they'd wander Chamonix, snapping selfies with a backdrop of Mont Blanc. They'd visit Christmas markets in Prague and get lost in Venice before the ancient city sank into the sea. She'd always wanted to see the Pyramids. What better traveling companion than a man who was interested in literally everything. A man who wanted to devour life.

She looped an arm through his, and they plunged into arts festival madness like it was a market in Marrakesh. Among jewelry, furniture, and ceramics were several stalls of photography. As she perused landscapes and wildlife photos, pictures of pickups and gas stations, shots of flowers and even the odd Amish farm, Darcy felt Samuel's gaze.

He tilted his head toward a moody image of a fog-shrouded waterfall. "Have you thought of selling your photos like this?"

The vision of her macro shots artfully displayed in a stall gave her a thrill. "You've got to move a lot of five-by-sevens to pay the rent."

"Well, aren't you a dishy duo!" Hand-in-hand with Al, Pammy bustled into the booth. "The Amish ladies are making a killing!"

A twinge of discomfort tightened her belly. Was Samuel cool with being a duo? Smiling at Pammy, he appeared as wooed by her as the starry-eyed mailman. Garbed in another vintage concert tee, Al was tidier groomed than Darcy had seen him and beaming like he couldn't believe his good fortune. Darcy kissed Pammy's pink cheeks. "The quilts are flying off the shelves. Thank you both for helping bring them over this morning."

Al hitched up his shorts. "Only folks up before mail carriers are farmers." He hooked a thumb at Samuel. "Am I right, or am I right?"

"You are right." Samuel chuckled. "And I echo Darcy's thanks. We couldn't have done it without you."

The sound of accordion music rose to a crescendo, finishing with hoots and applause. A man's voice came over the loudspeaker at the outdoor stage. "Let's hear it for Earl Zabek, the Polka King of Carbondale!"

The crowd cheered again, and the amplifier squealed.

"For any who don't know, I'm your emcee and mayor, Gene Stackhouse, and I have the tremendous honor to introduce a group that's near and dear to my heart. Ladies and Gentlemen, the TipTop Tappers!"

Pammy zhuzhed her hair and tugged Al's hand. "Let's go! I don't want to miss Marion and Joan, and you know Edna will outdance them all. Maybe we should join the group. What do you say?"

Al's moustache flattened atop a toothy grin. "Sounds like a fine idea. So long, you two."

With a chuckle, Samuel watched them go. "That woman could ask him to jump into a pit of snakes, and he'd say it was a fine idea."

She gave a satisfied look just short of gloating. "I told you he loved her. I can spot it every time."

He hooked an arm around her waist and pulled her close. "What do you see now?"

The man I love. The man I want to kidnap and throw in the trunk of my rental. A man I'd take to ballgames in the Bronx and rooftops in Gowanus and then get him a passport and sail around the world. I'd kiss him until kissing got old, which would be never, and then I'd figure out what comes after fun. I'd swim in his aquamarine eyes and sleep in his arms and never ever let him go. And then...I'd rescue him.

"I see a little bit of love." She ran her tongue over her lips, watching as his gaze anchored on her mouth. "Just a teensy-weensy bit."

"You need glasses," he murmured into her cheek.

And he kissed her long enough to show he meant it, but not so long that she worried the photographer sitting three feet away would pull out his camera. Because if he did, Samuel might chuck it into the river. Then again, he might grab it and take her picture.

Finally, she recovered strength enough to speak. "Let's go see the tap dancers."

He gave a mischievous smile. "Do I have a story about them."

The expression was so classically him she wanted to bottle it and tuck it away for long nights alone in

Brooklyn. Assuming, of course, she didn't go through with the whole kidnapping plot.

Alone in the attic, late that night, she rubbed lotion into her tender fingertips. Handmade quilts cost a pretty penny, and rightly so. But the Green Ridge Spring Arts Festival attracted a clientele to pay for them, just as she'd hoped. The women raised the required funds and then some. A festive potluck supper at Sarah's had followed the sale. All the Rishels attended, and as the meal wound down, and Darcy joined the women in the kitchen, she marveled at how comfortable she felt. She, Darcy King, hand-washed dishes with no concern for her manicure and ate a delicious chicken and stuffing dish she was pretty sure they called *roasht* with no care of the carbohydrate count. She drove home Nora and the babies, parting from Samuel with only a look and the promise to come the next morning and develop the final roll of film from *Mammi* Leora's before leaving for New York.

A look.

A look she filled with more than a little bit of love.

A look that was an invitation. An invitation that, once put into words, she prayed he'd accept.

****

If Sunday had been as sunny and beautiful as the day before, Darcy couldn't have considered leaving. The sound of rain woke her fairly late, by farm standards. She gazed out the window to discover the sky gently crying. At least she wasn't. For now. Properly mourning her grandmother would likely take years, but the tears had lost their sting. She didn't fear them, and that felt good.

The night before, she'd folded back Rebecca's

quilt and laid beneath the open window in a tank and sleep shorts, letting the breeze soothe her flushed and sweaty body. A late shower brought scant relief, and as she passed Samuel's empty bedroom, she relived that first encounter, three weeks ago. The memory sent blood rushing to every square inch of skin where it apparently took up residence for the night. The breeze didn't have a chance. For hours, she'd wiggled and twitched, unable to cool down and quiet her mind.

How could she rest when she didn't know what the morning would bring? They'd develop the roll of film including the picture he took of her—a picture he swore he couldn't keep. When she looked in her own eyes, what would she see? Even now, as she shoved dirty laundry into her bag and nibbled one of Verna's biscuits, she debated what to say.

Let me take you away from all this.

I won't go without you.

I want to show you the world.

All true. All clichéd. She sipped lukewarm coffee and popped a final buttery bite.

I'm Darcy, and I'm here to rescue you.

He'd hate it.

The zipper strained, and she sat atop her suitcase.

When you said you wanted to leave, did you mean it? Because I have room in my car.

Yes. Better a question and a conversation. She had so much to say, but listening was essential, too. As for practical matters like where he'd sleep in New York and who would take over the solar business—those details could be ironed out. Odds were, he wouldn't drop everything and leave. He had a life. Besides, she'd be back to handle the sale of *Mammi's* property. They'd have time. Today, she had only one task: to throw him a lifeline. She was his ticket to freedom, should he accept it, and she'd be his companion on the road.

How could he possibly say no?

Her phone leaned against a vase of fading flowers, and she reversed the camera to act as a mirror. With tinted sunscreen, a swipe of lip gloss, and her hair in a messy bun, she looked presentable. In snug jeans and a flowy top, she wasn't the New Yorker who arrived two weeks ago, but she was far from plain. The camera showed a nervous version of herself. So nervous in fact, that when she greeted Samuel at the workshop door, she fell into the old do-we-hug-or-kiss-or-what trap, resulting in him patting her back while she went in for a kiss and nearly impaled her eyeball on his nose. *Super smooth.*

As she followed him to the darkroom, she drank in the rumpled sheets and half-full coffee cup, hard evidence of a morning she would have given anything to share. How did he take his coffee? She searched her memory but couldn't remember. Could she really proposition a guy when she didn't know if he liked cream and sugar? But as she relaxed into the easy working rhythm of the darkroom, she felt middle-school awkwardness melt into a far more delicious kind of tension, in which every touch was loaded, every word carried ten different meanings, and every look smoldered.

Still, they were careful. In a very narrow room, they gave each other space.

Be patient. Wait for the right moment…

She pinned the final strip of negatives to the line and spun, nearly colliding with his chest.

He jumped backward, crashing into the counter. "*Ach.* Sorry."

She shot a hand around him and caught the bottle of developer. A giggle burbled out, and she felt strong arms slide around her waist.

His answering chuckle rumbled from his chest. "Come here, Brooklyn. Today has me all *ferhoodled.* I'm afraid if I hold you, I'll never let go."

"Same." She pressed her cheek into cool cotton and drank in soap and sky. "I have something I want to ask, but I don't know how."

He tightened his grip. "Go on."

Was this the moment? Here in his arms in the darkroom he made? She inhaled courage and opened her mouth to speak. Or would outside be better? Up on the mountain where they watched the sunset? *No. Now.* She caught another quick breath. "What will you do with the darkroom when I leave?" The words came out in a rush, and she screwed up her face and smushed it against his shoulder. *Chicken.*

"I'll keep it."

She pulled back and searched his eyes. "Why?"

His shoulders twitched. "You never know when someone will want to use it."

"Welcome to the darkroom, Deacon Elmer and Bishop…?" She gave him a questioning look.

"Mordechai," he supplied.

"Bishop Mordechai. Would you care to develop some photos?" A thought slammed into her, and she gripped his forearms. "The bishop! I need to pick up the prints for the bishop, and the camera shop closes at two." She yanked open the door and dashed into the hall.

Following, he pointed at the wall clock which showed minutes after one. "You'll make it."

A loose strand of hair slipped from her bun and flopped in front of her eyes. She blew it with a puffing sigh. "Your mother's flyers are ready, too. I almost forgot."

He tucked the lock behind one ear and ran a thumb over her cheekbone. "You have time."

Just how little time sent a pang through her chest. She yanked the phone from her back pocket as if it might have a different opinion regarding the hour. It didn't. The day was slipping away. "I'll drive to the camera shop and then the bishop's, and I promised Pammy I'd say good-bye. Then, I need to run by the storage locker and grab *Mammi's* photo albums. I want to give them to my father along with the pictures we took. Selling the property might be easier if he has them."

He snagged his hat from the peg. "Do you want me to come?"

"So much, but I need you to develop the pictures once the negatives dry. Do you mind?"

"I'd be happy to." He tossed the hat back onto the hook. "As I recall, there's a special photo I'm eager to see."

"Thank you." She scurried to go, stopping in the doorway to peek over one shoulder. "And when I come back, we'll talk?"

"We'll do whatever you like, Brooklyn."

The wall clock clicked to one-eleven, and she closed her eyes, slinging a quick wish into hyper-space. *Please, oh, please let that be true.*

Chapter Twenty-Six

Shrouded in mist, Green Ridge was every ounce the Victorian town. Driving to the camera shop, Darcy could almost see carriages trundling down Main Street. How different the Amish experience must have been when their way of life wasn't so backward. At one point, horse-drawn buggies were the pinnacle of modernity.

The night before, having surrendered the notion of sleep, she'd pulled out her phone and done a deep dive into Amish culture. A good journalist does her research. This research just also happened to be personal. The fact that Samuel never joined the church, she discovered, was everything. His leaving wouldn't be encouraged, but he'd escape shunning like his older brother, Jonas, or *Mammi* Leora. He could still visit family, share meals, and watch his nieces grow. His life didn't have to be either-or. In a more progressive church district like theirs, it might be both.

Maybe he'd known all along someone would come and take him away. Perhaps that's why he never was baptized. Maybe he was waiting for her.

Rain spattered the windshield, and the wipers squeaked and thunked a tuneless song. She shook her shoulders, trying to dispel the gloom, and pulled into a spot by the camera shop. This good-bye was temporary. She grabbed her umbrella and dashed into the rain.

She'd be back in a week or two.

The errands took longer than she predicted, and afternoon became suppertime before the farm appeared through her windshield. Her stomach grumbled. She should have grabbed a tuna sub from House of Pizza. Next time, for sure.

Crossing her fingers the photos would be dry enough to pack, she hunkered her bags into the SUV and hurried to Samuel's, laying a trembling hand on her stomach. Apparently, nerves and hunger weren't mutually exclusive. Maybe he'd have something she could nibble before she left.

Maybe once they talked, they'd be too happy to eat.

The rain had stopped, but mist still shrouded the ridges. No matter. Sunsets galore awaited. Quickening her step, she hopped a puddle and skittered, fleet-footed, over the slick wooden bridge. Where they spoke wasn't important. Only that they did speak. The studio came into view, nestled among trees like part of the forest.

The air stilled, and the creek burbled, swollen from the day's rain.

She saw him then, sitting on the front step with his hands clasped between his knees.

His broad shoulders slumped, and his head hung low.

Her belly clenched. Did something happen in the short time she was gone? Today was an off Sunday, and Verna, Nora, and the kids all went to visit Deacon Elmer. She could have sworn she saw the buggy in the shed. Surely, they traveled safely in the rain. If tragedy struck again, he wouldn't be alone on the porch.

Someone would have come.

The simplest answer, of course, was the hardest to believe. Her insides unwound, and her heart soared. It was also the most wonderful. He loved her. He loved her, and he thought she was leaving. But she wasn't—not without him. She was close, but he still didn't stir. Did he not hear her footsteps? She stopped beside the firepit. "Samuel?" Her voice sounded thin but hopeful, and she let herself smile. "Sorry I'm late."

He raised his head like he was compelled to, and the doing cost something. Hollow, haunted eyes bored into her, and cold fear shackled itself to her spine. Something was deeply wrong. "What happened? Is it your mother? Are the twins all right?" His snort was an acid-laced slap, and she winced.

"You don't know?" He rocked back on his hands, head cocked, and eyes narrowed. "You really don't know?"

Her neck flamed. "I just got back. I have no idea."

Muttering in Pennsylvania Dutch, he jerked around, groped behind him, and thrust out a partly crumpled mass. It was a piece of thick paper, eight-by-ten, with printing on one side. Knuckles going white, he crushed it and tossed it at her mud-caked sneakers.

Before she saw it hit the ground, she knew.

The memory exploded, bleaching her vision, and ringing in her ears until she heard nothing but her own strangled breath and the echo of the shutter button like a cannon shot. Samuel, gazing at a little metal sculpture of a bumblebee. One exposure. One shot. One stolen image.

How could she have been so careless? How could she have been so dumb?

Unseeing, she fell to her knees and groped for the photo.

The roll of film she gave him to develop—twenty-three pictures of *Mammi* Leora's house and one precious photo of her, right?

Wrong.

She always knew math would be her undoing. Twenty-*two* pictures of *Mammi* Leora's, one very precious photo of her, and one portrait of Samuel Rishel taken through a window on the morning she left for New York.

He raked his fingers through his hair and yanked the ends hard. "Did you want me to find it?"

Sharp stones dug into her kneecaps, and she sat back on her heels. Her vision was still too blurred to make out the photo, but she knew what she'd see: the man she loved gazing at a tiny sculpture like it was the most precious thing on earth. She blinked, and a single drop fell on the photo paper, blossoming in a gray stain. Was it raining again?

"Did you?"

His voice was insistent, yanking her back to a reality she'd far prefer to escape. A reality in which, no matter the reason, she had majorly mucked up. She blinked, swiping at burning eyes and forcing her mind to sharpen. A searing breath cleared her lungs, popping her ears like she descended from thirty-five thousand feet.

A crow cawed, harsh and astringent.

She met his gaze. "Of course not."

His jaw tightened, and he stared at her hands. "I made it for you." He waved at the half-crumped photo. "The bee in the flower. I planned to give it to you, so you'd have something to remember me by. But that morning, I decided not to. That sculpture is the closest thing I'll ever have to your picture. I wasn't strong enough to let it go. Not when I knew I was losing you, too."

Like a runaway subway car, the moment careened out of control, racing toward disaster. This day was not supposed to end with betrayal. She couldn't let it. Breathing hard, she scrabbled to her feet. "You won't lose me. Not ever." She thrust out the mangled photo. "It's just one picture—one picture I never should have taken. I knew it then, but I did it because—" She swallowed the thought as her predicament landed like a boulder in her belly. She was trapped. For Rebecca's sake, no way could she tell him the truth. No matter how much she longed to.

"Just one?" He sat up, scowling. "Or did you take more that evening in the yard when you said you were working on the flyer. I didn't believe you then, and I don't believe you now."

Helpless, she let her head fall back, searching for an explanation in a sky as impenetrable as cement. Rebecca's request violated the one Amish rule Samuel cared most about, and throwing a teenager under the bus was out of the question. Besides, Darcy took the photos of her own free will. No one forced her. She lowered her gaze and told the closest thing to the truth. "I thought you might want the pictures someday. Don't you wish you had a photo of your father? Just one? How will you remember your mother's face when she dies? I can give that to you, and no one ever needs to know."

Grabbing a porch post, he lurched to his feet,

towering over her. "My father lives here. And here." He rapped his skull and pounded over his heart. "I need no *Englischer* to give me what I already have."

Everything she longed to give welled up inside. "But I can offer so much." She clutched at her chest as if she could crack open her ribcage and reveal the secret dreams of her heart. "This has all gone sideways, but I can't leave without telling you. Just set aside the photos for a second—and I know how much of a betrayal that is. I'll make it up to you, I promise." She planted her feet and drew courage from as deep and true a part of herself as she could. "But if you're serious about leaving…I'll take you. I love you, Samuel. I want to give you everything."

"Love me?"

His laugh could have stripped paint. Standing beneath him, she felt like a supplicant. As if for the first time, Darcy King was not Park Avenue royalty but the granddaughter of a simple tire salesman. She had no one but herself for support. "I have it all planned out."

His step off the porch was heavy and deliberate. "Did you ever think to ask what *I* wanted?"

What did he think she was doing right now? "You told me. You said you want to see New York—to travel the world."

He scrubbed a hand over his face and gripped the back of his neck. "I say a lot of things—"

"But I know you." She lunged toward him, longing to touch him but afraid to get too close. "You didn't join the church. You were never baptized, so you won't lose your family."

"You don't know me." Anger flared in his gaze. "You have no idea what you're talking about."

"I do!" She grabbed the phone from her back pocket and thrust it out like evidence. "I read all about it last night."

His mouth contorted into a mocking grimace. "Did you search on the Internet and study our backward ways?" He stalked to her and loomed, sweat beading his upper lip. "So, you'll take the quaint Amish man to see the world. How many magazine assignments will that earn you?"

Her neck burst into flame, fanning hurt and outrage until her skin nearly blistered. "Unless my mother pays off my boss again, likely none." Her voice was so steely it shocked even her. "Turns out this photo assignment was bought by my family. Surprise! So yeah, you don't know me, either."

He reeled and took a slow step back. "That's the first truth you've spoken today." His face went slack, and his chest caved in on itself. "Good-bye, Darcy." The door closed quietly behind him, and he was gone.

Tears burned but never fell. Maybe she loved him too much for regular crying. Samuel deserved tears of vinegar…tears of turpentine…tears of blood.

She was behind the wheel of the rental car without knowing how she arrived. Maybe she time traveled. She'd certainly entered a nightmarish alternate reality. The crumpled photo lay on the passenger's seat, but creases couldn't dull its beauty. He was miraculous. She had a brief, crazy impulse to buckle it in.

She should say good-bye to Verna and Rebecca…to her cousin and the women at the shop. After they extended themselves on her behalf, to do anything less was rude. But knowing they'd likely hear about the portraits turned her empty stomach, and she had no strength to pretend. Betrayal changed people. The hurt shrouding Samuel was thick, and once she left, rumors would fly. Word traveled fast on the Amish grapevine. One way or another, the likelihood of the bishop approving her photos was precisely nil.

She drove the farm lane without looking back. Like a horse with blinders, she saw nothing but road. She wouldn't even say good-bye to town. Good-byes were painful, and she resolved to shove this ache down deep. She'd done it when *Mammi* Leora died. She'd do it again. Suppressing emotions was practically her birthright. When she got home, she'd write everyone thank-you notes on thick, creamy paper and mail Verna the rental flyers. She'd apologize to Rebecca. She was her mother's daughter, after all.

Alone in her apartment, she'd wait for the call from Sarah that was sure to put her in an impossible position. What would she tell Margo when the bishop inevitably said no?

Chapter Twenty-Seven

Darcy chased gingery Palak paneer with a shot of seltzer, gazing goggle-eyed at her roommates over the glass. The empty void she'd felt since Samuel closed the door that morning now housed a queasy mix of curry and shock. "You don't want to renew the lease?"

Fern and Zibby had ordered Indian food while she returned the rental car, and her bags were still in a jumbled pile in the entryway. She bounced her gaze from Fern, bent over a sketchbook, her round blue glasses sliding down her nose, to Zibby, sprawled on her yoga mat in flowy pants and a crop top, dark hair splayed like a frizzy halo.

"I always thought New York or nowhere." Fern tilted her head and tucked her short, red hair behind one ear. "But I want to live somewhere I can afford, and Nashville is dope."

"No, I get it." Darcy speared a chunk of tofu but couldn't bring herself to eat it.

Flat on her back, Zibby put the soles of her feet together and let her knees flop open. "And Max and I decided it was time. I'm so glad we took a year to discover each other, instead of moving in immediately."

Darcy worried the velvety, corded edge of the sofa cushion with the tip of one finger. The living room furniture was communal. She honestly couldn't remember who thrifted, inherited, and salvaged which pieces. She nudged Zibby with a toe. "You guys are the fairy tale—my belief that love at first sight is possible. Don't tell me I was wrong."

Zibby waved a toned arm at Darcy. "Not wrong." She toggled her index finger to her chest. "Not stupid."

"Not that your contractor didn't do an amazing job. Thank you again, by the way," Fern said. "I just feel like the flood was a sign."

"Totally." All trace of the deluge was gone, but the scents of fresh paint and sawdust lingered in the air. The familiar odor hit her with a pang. Her attic room at the farm had smelled much the same when she moved in. Sighing, she scanned the mishmash of end tables, throw pillows, and shelves. The space was comfy and inviting, proof positive a zillion-dollar budget was not required to create a cozy home.

Zibby plopped a hand on Darcy's knee. "Sorry to spring it on you when you just got back, but we wanted to give you time to find other roommates or a new place."

"Thanks." She downed the cold tofu. The last twelve hours had been a freak fly ball to the throat with no cosmic hand snagging it just in time. "I'll figure something out."

Thanks to the manhole cover lodged in the pit of her stomach and blocking all her feelings, she floated through the next few days curiously numb. If *Mammi's* death had taught her anything, it was how to bury grief. Annoyingly, this manhole cover was apparently cracked, and dribbles of emotion occasionally leaked out. As she rode the elevator to work or carried groceries upstairs, she was struck again and again by the feeling she'd forgotten something—as if she left her phone on the train or the oven on.

Firmly entrenched in the real world, she realized her plan would never have worked, even had Samuel agreed. A high-powered position at *Hudson Magazine* and the freedom to travel the world with the man of her dreams? Impossible! Having it all was a myth; everyone had to choose. Maybe she was lucky the choice was made for her, with help from the three-year-old upstairs, fate, and her own idiocy.

She'd asked herself a million times how she could have forgotten about his portrait. Forgetting was sloppy and completely unlike her. During long lonely nights, she also wondered whether a teensy-weensy part of her knew the photo was on that roll. Because she never found the courage to tell him about Rebecca's request, did her subconscious take matters into its own devious hands?

Lying on the yoga mat for *savasana* the next night, surrounded by sweaty and toned New Yorkers, she relaxed tired muscles, and tears welled like she turned on a tap. As her classmates coiled their straps and put away blocks, she sniffled but didn't move. What had Verna said? She let a prayer dwell in her heart, and if she didn't get an answer, she likely asked the wrong question. Bare feet padded inches from Darcy's face, and still, she lay. What was the right prayer? She'd made such a mess of her life she honestly had no idea. The job, the apartment, her family, Samuel...what should she pray for when everything was wrong?

She sent up a thought.

I'm home, but I'm lost, and I'm so very sad. Show me the way.

Figuring God helps those who help themselves, she

was half-heartedly browsing a real estate website after breakfast the next morning when her phone rang. She checked it, expecting Rolff. Her photos were two days late. When she saw Sarah's shop number, she almost broke a finger swiping to answer. Had the bishop come to a decision? "Hello?"

"Rebecca says you left without saying good-bye."

Sarah's tone was curt. Had she heard about the pictures? Darcy nestled into her loveseat and cuddled a bed pillow. "Please tell her I'm sorry and that I'll write." In the background, she heard voices chattering in Pennsylvania Dutch and a baby's cry. How she longed to be cozied up to the table with Sarah and Amity, gossiping over pie. "I'm sorry I didn't say good-bye to you, too."

"Darcy," Sarah said in a gentler tone. "Did aught go wrong between you and Samuel?"

Cramming the pillow into the corner of the sofa, she stood. "Why do you ask?"

"You know I don't shy from speaking my mind. Samuel would honor his family by choosing a good Amish woman and marrying her. I can name half a dozen *maedels* who'd wed him tomorrow."

The line went silent. She had the sensation Sarah was waiting, but Darcy had nothing to say. She almost felt Sarah's impatient huff on her cheek.

"The problem is he loves you, and I've a sneaking suspicion you broke his heart, and not the other way around."

Like a tree hacked at the base and shoved, Darcy toppled onto her bed. "I did."

"Plenty of folks will think that for the best, but I've known Samuel since we were *kinner*. Right now, he's a dried-out husk. Another woman might make him a good *fraa*, but he'll never be the *mann Gott* intended without you."

A thrill shimmered through her. Was what Sarah said true? "I…" She stared at a spidery crack in the ceiling and searched for the end of the thought. Sarah might believe Samuel loved her, but she didn't have all the facts. Some betrayals were too deep for love to heal. "I don't know what to say."

"Have faith, Darcy, and pray on it. Meanwhile, the bishop approved your photos. You may print them if you like." Her voice went muffled as if she smushed the phone to her cheek. "Text me your address, and I'll write. Now that I've found you, I won't lose you again."

Darcy ended the call, and as she quickly texted, emotions flooded through the breaks in the manhole cover. Tossing aside the phone she was instantly addicted to again, she grabbed another pillow, clutching it like a floatation device. Faith, huh? What did Sarah know, anyway? Other than Samuel for his entire life.

Sprawled on her back, she shifted her gaze out the window where the brownstone roofs kissed hazy blue sky. The world was exquisitely beautiful, and Samuel didn't expose her to the bishop, and none of it mattered, because he never wanted to see her again. She sat, and Brooklyn flipped right-side up. Sarah said it perfectly: Samuel should marry an Amish woman and settle down. Of course, he'd need to join church first. An act even she understood was more easily said than done.

She hopped up, grabbed her laptop, and plopped onto the loveseat. His church status was one hundred percent not her problem.

Just a few quick keystrokes and her photos were ready. One flick of the finger had been enough to forever change her relationship with Samuel. One twitch and the shutter went click. One wrong choice.

She took a deep breath, typed in Margo's email address, and with another click, she submitted the work that could change her life forever. She simply had to have faith.

****

Darcy must have jogged fifty miles that week. From Prospect Park to the High Line, she ran and ran and ran. With every step, she let go a little more. She stopped listening to podcasts and clocking her pace. She let her gaze soften and her heart open, and mile by mile, running became more like prayer. She'd always loved the adrenaline high and sense of accomplishment, but now, she needed running like she needed oxygen. Between editorial meetings, apartment hunting, and surreal dinners with friends, she laced on her shoes, pulled back her hair, and ran, certain if she stopped, missing Samuel would render her unable to move.

Moving was a necessity in New York, her actual, real-life home. Oh yes, the city was home. Whether she stayed in her apartment or found somewhere else, she lived and worked here. Her family was here. Her friends were here. Those three weeks in Pennsylvania weren't real life. New York City was.

So, she kept moving.

Rolff emailed that her photos were approved. Her essay would run in the Modernity issue.

She read it and ran.

Another email from Rolff: Margo wanted to meet ASAP to discuss Darcy's future with the magazine.

This is it, girl, Rolff added in a postscript. *Welcome to the funhouse. I knew you were fierce.*

The staff job was hers. She read it and ran.

Sarah texted:

—School solar panel install starts next month. Verna has several bookings for the room rental. All very grateful. Will write a proper letter soon.—

She read the text early Saturday morning and ran across the Brooklyn Bridge, up the Hudson River Greenway, across Fifty-Ninth Street, and into Central Park, joining thousands of joggers on the Park Drive. The scent of carriage horses sparked another fear she'd forgotten something, and she instinctively patted her jogging belt, tracing the shapes of keys and phone. She couldn't mesh the pungent scent of horses with the funk of city garbage, and the combination unsettled her stomach. Outrunning the odors, she yanked down her visor and veered north.

The East Side was an uphill slog made tolerable by lush greenery in early summer glory and views of the Boathouse, The Metropolitan Museum of Art, and the North Meadow fields. Today, she only half perceived those familiar landmarks. Nine miles in, she was nothing but breath and sinew and bone.

A new question for God settled in the humming cavity of her chest.

Should I take this job?

To her right, majestic Fifth Avenue apartment buildings towered. Her birthright. The black iron gates of the Conservatory Garden emerged, and without thinking, she darted across the drive and down the narrow path, dashing lamppost to lamppost toward the entrance. As a girl, she'd loved to curl up on benches beneath the massive arbor of fragrant purple flowers and feel the cool spray from the fountain, but she hadn't visited the garden in years. Inside the gate she stopped, heart pounding and breath coming fast. Like a sailor come ashore, she swayed, gradually readjusting to stillness. And then, she entered the secret garden in the heart of the city.

Through a tree-lined allée, she wandered. Her pulse slowly quieting, she climbed a few stairs into a garden within a garden, its winding paths teeming with flowers in full bloom. In the center lay a hidden pool beneath a graceful statue of a gossamer-draped girl and a recumbent boy playing a flute. Fat green lily pads studded with flowers occupied every square inch of water. How easily a frog could hop from end to end. She sat on a bench while visitors strolled, snapping photos as if they were perfectly safe—little knowing a single picture had shattered her life. Mothers pushed strollers, lovers held hands, and across from her, a white-haired man propped on a cane and stared at the sky.

She wanted to share this place with Samuel and see his eyes brighten at the unexpected beauty. The garden was almost as surprising as a stairway to nowhere in the middle of the woods. She wanted to hold his hand and kiss him beneath the arbor. She wanted to give him the world. He was right, though. She should have asked. She should have had the courage to tell him everything. He deserved the chance to say *no*.

From behind came a buzz, and she peeked around to see a fat bumblebee land on the mouth of a purple, bell-like flower and crawl inside. The stalk waggled, but it didn't break, and the bee's head reemerged, powdered with yellow. With another buzz, it blooped to the blossom below and entered like the flower was home.

They were equal, flower and bee. Uniquely complementary, they each had something the other required. As living creatures went, they couldn't be more different, and yet, they were a perfectly matched set.

She watched the bee until it flew out of view, dopey on pollen and sunshine. And then she studied the flower, gazing into its petaled depths until she almost believed it was her home, too. Like the tiny, beautiful sculpture Samuel made.

She sat silently, one person in a city of millions on a planet of billions. The prayers of the last week lay upon her heart, and all at once, she had her answer. She knew what she forgot.

The running pouch unzipped with a swish, and she pulled out her phone.

First, she dashed a text to Sarah.

—*Magazine job a no go. Career up in the air. Will write more soon.*—

Then she pulled up a text chat with her mother. She took a deep breath, and let her thumbs fly over the miniature keyboard.

—*I'm sorry I was so angry. I've thought about it a lot, and I know you were only trying to help because you love me. I've learned the hard way that when you love someone, you'll do anything to give them what you believe they want. The mistake is forgetting to consult them first. I won't make that mistake again. I'd ask that you don't, either. I'll see you tomorrow night for dinner.*—

She clicked Send. And then, with a rush that might have been adrenaline but was mostly nature-drunk joy, she added one more thing.

—*Tell Dad I'm buying Mammi Leora's house.*—

Chapter Twenty-Eight

The sharp corner of the photo enlarger dug into the crook of Samuel's elbow. He shifted, scraping his knuckles against the doorframe. Rebecca's sewing machine whined, and he swallowed a curse. In the week since Darcy left, he subjected his family to a plague of foul moods. Better not teach Rebecca to swear, too.

He jostled around the corner and headed for the door. Deconstructing Darcy's darkroom wasn't his idea of a restful Sunday evening, but he wouldn't sleep until it was done. Exactly what he'd do with the stuff until he contacted Al, he didn't know. Maybe leave it in the barn, assuming he could get it there without breaking either the equipment or his back. He'd need a wheelbarrow...or a mule. Mostly, he needed it out of his sight.

He balanced the enlarger on one knee and strained for the doorknob, wondering, for the thousandth time why? Why had she taken their photos? She'd stammered an excuse about doing it for him, but he knew she was lying. Her face was like glass. He'd known she was lying about the pictures from the moment he stopped her in the yard that night. He just didn't want to believe.

She said he shouldn't trust her. She was right.

Rebecca's chair screeched across cement, and she stood, scattering bits of fabric. "What are you doing with Darcy's things?"

The enlarger wobbled, and he righted it, straining again for the door. "Sending them back where they belong."

"Did you ask her permission?"

"No." Jagged and sharp, his voice sliced from his throat, and he bit his tongue. Lately, Rebecca moped morning to night, pausing only to glare like he'd ruined her life. For his part, he avoided the girl—something he did not enjoy. These days, Rebecca was the company he most desired, even if she didn't want him. "Will you help me with the door?"

Rebecca shoved in front of him, blocking the way. "I will not."

Anger flared, but he choked it back. "If I drop this contraption, I'll break it and my toes. Now, please open it."

She crossed her arms and glowered.

Turning, he heaved the enlarger onto the workbench with more force than he intended. It rattled ominously. Not seeing obvious damage, he returned to the problem of his niece. Best deal with her before either of their mothers got involved. He straightened and met her icy stare. "If you have something to say, out with it."

"Is Darcy coming back?"

The question landed like a horse kick to the gut, and he braced a palm on the workbench. "*Nee*." His voice sounded ragged. He needed sleep.

Rebecca gave a strangled cry. "But, Samuel, why?"

Why? Because of his cowardice. Cowardice and stubbornness and tradition that bound him to this farm like irons. Because he wasn't strong enough to listen.

He closed his ears to everything but pain and pride, refusing to see Darcy for who she was—the only woman he'd ever met who gave him courage to live the life he wanted. And that scared him half to death.

This mess wasn't Rebecca's fault. She cared for Darcy. Darcy believed in her, and because of him, she was gone. He let his body relax, gentling Rebecca like a skittery foal. "Her family is in New York."

She flung her arms wide. "Her family's here!"

He pulled up a stool and one for her. "Her *Mamm, Daed, Schweschder,* and *Bruder* all live in New York. She has an apartment in a place called Brooklyn—"

"I know where Brooklyn is," Rebecca huffed. "I read. Besides, she doesn't like those people. She likes us."

Unable to disagree, he sat and patted the stool at his side. "Well, and she's got her magazine work. After the story she did, she'll likely get an even bigger, fancier job."

Rebecca frowned and dropped a knee onto the stool, jutting a hip. "No, she won't."

Impatience simmered in his chest. Did he have to say the words? To revisit all the reasons Darcy couldn't possibly have stayed? "Just as soon as those pictures are published—"

"She didn't get the promotion." Rebecca's pointed chin lifted. "I heard Sarah read Amity the text message. Something about Darcy losing her job and needing to find something else. The magazine wanted photos of Amish youth getting into trouble. I don't think Darcy took them."

He jammed his fists against his thighs. Darcy's photos were perfect. He couldn't imagine her sullying

343

that work with ridiculous pictures of Amish boys acting stupid at a ballgame. Still, that job meant everything. She must be devastated. His gut clenched. He should have helped. He should have done more.

"If she didn't leave us for family or a new job, then why…" Rebecca's voice faltered, and her eyes went round as dinner bowls. "The photos," she whispered. "You saw the photos of our family, didn't you?"

He drew back sharply. How did Rebecca know what Darcy had done? A sickening suspicion lodged like a fishhook in the back of his throat. "Darcy and I had a deal. I'd help with her pictures so long as she didn't take photos of faces. She broke her word, Rebecca. She broke my trust." His niece was so rosy fair that he could often see the blood pulse just beneath her skin. In that moment, however, she went a sickly shade of gray.

"Me." Her fine-boned hand spread across her chest. "She took the photos for me. I asked her to."

"What?" He shook his head, feeling his brain rattle like loose hardware in a coffee can. "Why?"

Tears pooled on her lashes, and she balled her apron in tight fists. "I don't remember *Daed*'s face. I close my eyes, but I can't see him. What if you die? Or *Mammi* Verna? I don't want to forget you, too."

"Oh, child." The heartbreaking truth hit him square in the chest. A girl shouldn't know such sorrow. He stood and gathered her in his arms.

Trembling, she pressed her face against his shoulder. "I thought maybe *Gott* sent Darcy so I wouldn't have to forget anyone else."

He ran a hand up and down her back like she was the tiny girl he remembered, sitting quietly while the grown-ups went to pieces. "You haven't forgotten. You might not see his face, but you can still feel his love. He'll always be with you."

"It's my fault Darcy left." She clung to him and sobbed. "I didn't know she made a promise. She never told me."

"Don't cry. I understand." He closed his eyes and lowered his cheek to her gauzy *kapp*. "I forgive you. Please forgive me, too."

"I'll always forgive you, Samuel." She relaxed but didn't let go. "*Ich lieba dich.*"

"I love you, too." He held her, marveling at how the top of her head was even with his collarbones. Darcy took the photos for Rebecca? But she never mentioned... His heart squeezed. Of course, she didn't. Darcy would never betray a child.

Finally, Rebecca pulled away. She wiped her cheeks with her sleeve and frowned at the enlarger. "Now, put that back where it belongs and go find Darcy."

He huffed a laugh. The girl had learned a thing or two from her mother and grandmother. She was hard to disobey. The bulky enlarger suddenly seemed no heavier than a sack of flour. His thoughts in a whirl, he returned it to the darkroom Darcy loved so much. She was somewhere out in the world beyond this valley. He had no idea where or how he'd find her, but he wouldn't rest until he did.

****

On Memorial Day, Darcy helped Fern and Zibby move out. Once the decision was made, they were eager to go. Though her chest tightened with every moving box, Darcy was excited for them. Thanks in no minor part to Carlos' excellent work, her super agreed to let her stay until June fifteenth, which was enough time to free up funds to purchase *Mammi* Leora's property, haul anything she didn't want to the stoop, and buy a car. And to quit her job.

The next day, with dry eyes and an unblushing neck, she met Margo Ricconi-Gladstone in her sunny corner office overlooking the Hudson. "Thank you very much for the promotion, but I'm afraid my answer is no." She let her gaze drift across the river to New Jersey and beyond. "I appreciate the confidence you placed in me, but my future lies elsewhere."

Margo waggled a finger with breezy aplomb. "I told you not to fall in love."

Darcy hadn't spoken a word about Samuel, of course. She twitched one shoulder and sighed. "I never intended to." Leaving *Hudson Magazine* was the bravest thing she'd ever done and was likely to stay at the top of the list...until she found courage to meet Samuel face-to-face, apologize, and ask for a second chance.

A week later, her apartment was nearly empty. On the afternoon of her move, she swept her gaze over the exposed brick bedroom walls, bare except for one item: a wrinkled and tear-stained black-and-white print taped right next to where she slept. She released the cap on the air mattress she'd used since selling her bed. Stale air whooshed, and she knelt on the plush surface until the mattress lay flat enough to roll and stuff into the bag. She'd sleep on it at Pammy's tonight.

Faced with the puzzle of where to stay until she rebuilt, she'd called Pammy. In a stroke of luck, the third-floor apartment above the bakery was vacant.

Darcy could rent it as long as she liked, and she planned to stay a while. A whirlwind romance was fun, but true love took time. Whether Samuel was willing to grant it was an open question. Either way, she was all-in with starting over in Green Ridge, no matter what he decided.

She heaved the bulky bag over one shoulder and traipsed through the living room, her footsteps echoing. Stripped of her roommates' artwork and posters, those walls had been bare, too, until she made an impromptu gallery wall of photos. She'd take them down last. The landscapes were hers, made on a farm in the golden hour of a late spring evening. The portraits were on loan from Rebecca Beiler and would be delivered later this week. A promise was a promise. Rebecca could do with them as she pleased.

Leaving the door on the latch, she made her second-to-last trip down the long winding staircase. She was getting a later start than she'd hoped. At the eleventh hour, she'd found a friend to take the loveseat, but the trains were messed up, and his car service app crashed. The whole process took way longer than she planned. Still, she'd be eating a House of Pizza tuna sub in her new digs by nightfall. A shiver of anticipation danced up her spine, despite the effort of lugging a bulky air mattress down three flights of stairs.

By some miracle, she found a parking spot for her new, used hybrid SUV close to her building. The car was jam-packed with suitcases, kitchen sundries, a tub of keepsakes, and her camera equipment. Of course, she had a whole storage unit in Pennsylvania, but paring down to bare essentials had been liberating. She didn't own much to begin with. She'd left behind a lot when she moved from Park Avenue, and she had no idea what Isabelle did with her remaining childhood possessions—likely sent them to the same place as the missing letters from Sarah. Since Darcy was going back to *Mammi's*, though, she really didn't care.

The air mattress refused to leave New York without a fight. First, she popped the rear door and, shoving aside a tote bag of shoes, did her best to force it inside. When the door wouldn't latch, she yanked out the bag and tried the back seat. Only when she inched the passenger's seat almost to the dashboard, did she finally wedge in the mattress, ensuring a comfy rest that night.

Sweaty and mussed, she slammed the door with satisfaction and gazed up at the brownstone she'd called home for the last few years. Children's happy shrieks floated from a nearby playground, and her remaining possessions sat on the curb like an outdoor theater set. Brooklyn was famous for stoop finds. Her pretty things would be gone by nightfall.

With a deep breath, she jogged up the outside stairs, shouldered the propped-open door, and let it latch behind her. From upstairs came the creak of a door opening. She'd said good-bye to the neighbors. Bumping into someone again after bidding farewell was always awkward. In the dark, cool entry, she paused to retie her sneakers, hoping to avoid it. Her legs were tired, and breathless, she stopped again at the top of the stairs, leaning heavily on the chunky banister. Though she was trading one walkup for another, she guessed the climb at Pammy's would feel less like summitting Mt. Everest.

The sound of movement grabbed her attention,

even over her hammering heart. She jerked up her head. Her door stood slightly ajar. Another shuffle was followed by footsteps. Adrenaline surged through her body, and she battled an impulse to run. Someone was inside her apartment.

Which was totally empty.

Except for her purse.

She shrank back on the landing. Charging in was reckless, but she was fast, and her bag was right inside the door. With the element of surprise, she could grab it and flee before the intruder knew what happened.

Fingers shaking, she took hold of the knob. The hinge creaked, and she jettisoned the idea of sneaking. She flung open the door, burst into the living room, and froze like a cartoon character knocked over the head with a frying pan.

He stood with his back to her, gazing at the gallery wall. Black suspenders over a sky-blue shirt. Long dark pants. Straw hat. He carried a faded canvas duffle over one shoulder and a folded-up map in his hand. Hearing her gasp, he turned, smiling. "*Guder daag*, Brooklyn."

She fought for breath, but whether from the stairs or the shock of finding Samuel Rishel in her living room, she couldn't say. "You broke into my apartment."

He shrugged. "The door was open. Shouldn't you keep it locked? This is New York City."

"I do. Usually," she spluttered, flinging an arm around the room. "In case you haven't noticed, there's not much left to steal."

"Except for that." He pointed at her gaping leather bag and then returned to the photos. "And these. They're beautiful."

He'd been so angry about the pictures, but he regarded them now with something like reverence. A weight she carried since their parting lifted. "Thank you."

He slid a sidelong glance. "One is missing."

A neck blush threatened. She didn't fight it. Her whole body was flushed from packing and moving and the part where he was standing in her apartment, rumpled and handsome and smelling of sky. "It's in my room next to my bed—or where my bed used to be. Do you want to see?"

"Later." Dropping the duffle, he strode to the center of the room, opened his arms, and lifted his chin. "First, I want you to take my picture."

He presented himself like a sacrificial lamb, albeit one who was strangely eager to go to slaughter. She blinked and considered the distinct possibility she was hallucinating. Had she remembered to eat lunch? "I'm sorry, what?"

He gave the map a shake. "I figure the bus station might be good. Or the subway? I've seen dirt in my time, but those tunnels are something else."

"Is that a paper subway map?"

"*Yah.* It's not easy to read, but Juanita at the Port Authority Bus Terminal was very helpful."

Laughter started in her belly and bubbled toward her throat. She choked it back, afraid it might come out as tears.

"If not the subway," he continued, "maybe a motorcycle bar? One with plenty of smoke?"

"I'm not sure we have those in Cobble Hill." She yanked a water bottle from her bag. Clearly, proper hydration was required to survive this day. "But

Samuel…why?"

He met her gaze over the map. "Why what?"

The water was cool and sweet. She'd miss New York City water. She swallowed slowly, calming her racing thoughts. "Why should I take your picture in a biker bar?"

His expression clouded. "I know you didn't get your job promotion, and one way or another, I'm likely the cause."

"Wait, what—?"

He snapped the map and began folding. "I can't imagine why that magazine wouldn't accept your work, but if those people want photos of Amish breaking rules, I'll do it." The unwieldy paper smushed into an awkward bundle in his hands. Frowning, he shook it out and began again. "I went to buy a pack of cigarettes, but they're incredibly expensive. Anyway, I only smoked one once, and I almost coughed up my liver. I can drink beer, though." He paused and studied the misshapen map, still not properly folded.

He was nervous. The Samuel she knew could fold a subway map with his eyes closed. "I did get the job." Her voice was breathy, but it bounced off the empty walls, seeming finally to penetrate his racing thoughts.

Blank-faced, he stared. "But Rebecca said Sarah got a message."

"Yes. I sent it." She hated to laugh, but his blatant confusion and the ridiculous map and the unbelievable fact he was really truly here were simply too much. "She must have misunderstood. They offered me a staff photographer position. I turned it down."

The map crumpled in his fist. "Why? And where is all your furniture? Where are…?" He flapped a hand toward the empty bedrooms.

"Zibby and Fern?"

"Right."

"Sunnyside and Nashville. Our lease is up. I'm moving out." No wonder he was baffled. Time and again, she expressed how desperately she wanted the promotion. Her actions barely made sense to herself. She drained the water bottle and refilled it in the kitchen sink. This conversation was not supposed to happen like this. She planned it for several days hence and on her own terms. Foiled again. But by some miracle he was here, and she owed him an explanation. She waved a weak hand at the empty space. "I'd offer you somewhere to sit…but. Care to pull up a windowsill? I'll give you the full tour." Bashfulness and longing accompanied her into the room where she'd spent lonely nights dreaming of him. Sunlight slanted in the window, painting the floor with a giant golden diamond that glowed like a magical door. If they stepped inside, would it transport them to another dimension? One where they could actually be together?

He followed, swinging his gaze from the brick walls to the ornate painted fireplace before landing it on the photo. The tension in his face eased.

A teensy flame of hope kindled in her chest. In the awkward shock of meeting, they hadn't touched. Now, he was very near. She patted the sill and extended the bottle.

Sitting, he closed his eyes and took a long drink.

By what sorcery had he gotten even hotter? Heart galloping, she wanted to kiss every inch from his collarbone to his chin. How did he get here? And how in the world did he figure out where she lived?

He finished and handed her the bottle.

Her fingers brushed his, and she met his gaze. She had a trillion questions, but first, he deserved answers. She pushed up her sleeves and began. "Margo loved my photo essay. It earned me the promotion."

"Congratulations." He studied her face, and the lines on his forehead deepened. "Isn't that what you wanted?"

"I did want it, yes. I don't anymore."

Sea-blue eyes rounded. "Why?"

She spun toward him, tilting her head until her temple tapped sun-warmed glass. "I love this city. I'm the person I am because of it, but now, I need to go. I want to make my own way somewhere far from my family." She cast her gaze over the leafy green street where a young mom pushed a baby in a deluxe stroller while a toddler skipped behind. "My parents love me. They'd do anything to give me what they think I want." She caught his gaze and tucked her chin. "I guess I inherited a smidge of that tendency."

"Maybe some."

His expression brimmed with humor and possibly even…with love? Feelings that went far beyond desire for fun surged from the soles of her well-worn running shoes before catching on the guilt at the back of her throat. "I'm sorry. I made you a promise, and I broke it—"

"Because Rebecca asked you to."

"Yes—but I was still wrong." She jerked back, digging her spine into hardwood molding. "Hold on. You know?"

He nodded. "Rebecca told me. When she doesn't blame herself, she's furious with me for sending you away."

Rebecca feeling guilty was the last thing she wanted. She had half a mind to call the quilt shop immediately and set the kid straight. "No one sent me anywhere! I left."

He sputtered a laugh. "Tell that to Rebecca."

"I will. At least, I hope to soon." She blew out a breath. *Too late to stop now.* She fisted her hands and summoned courage to look at him. "I'm moving to Green Ridge. Tonight, as a matter of fact."

His face went white, and he stood, backing away. "Darcy—"

"Let me say this." He was as watchful as a hawk on a skyscraper ledge. At any moment, he might dive. She planted her feet, bracing her hands on her knees, even as nerves rattled her bones. "Since I came back, I've had the nagging feeling I forgot something. I kept checking for my sunglasses and keys." She inhaled, filling her lungs with New York City moxie and Pennsylvania faith, and rose. "It was you. I drove away, and I left you behind. I tried to bottle my feelings like I did when *Mammi* died, but I can't do that anymore." She snagged one corner of her bottom lip between her teeth and peeked up at him. "I wasn't prepared to have this conversation today. Not gonna lie, I'm kind of mad at you for out-grand-gesturing me. How the heck did you even get here?" She waved away the question like a pesky fly. "Never mind, you can tell me later."

He lifted one cheek in a wry smile. "Surprise."

Reaching out, she caught his hand, and though she feared he might, he didn't pull away. *Time to put faith to the test.* "I bought *Mammi* Leora's property, and I'm rebuilding."

The color rushed to his cheeks. For a long moment, he didn't appear to breathe.

Was he happy? Horrified? Or simply stunned? She shook his arm gently. "Can you recommend a good carpenter?"

He staggered back a few steps, pulling her along, until his backside hit brick, and he wrapped her in his arms.

"Surprise to you, too," she murmured into his collar.

"You are absolutely *narrisch*."

His voice was rough, and the chuckle that followed nearly undid her. But he hadn't run. Quite the opposite in fact. She slid her arms around his waist and snuggled against his chest, relishing the rightness of his embrace. "If that means crazy, I'm not. I have all kinds of ideas. I want to teach like *Mammi* and have my own booth at arts festivals on the weekends. I want to get to know my father's side of the family and learn how to bake." She lifted her chin and gazed into eyes as bottomless as Mexican cenotes—also on the list of things she wanted to experience with him. "I want to get to know you, too. For real."

He bent and pressed his lips to hers.

And kissing him felt like coming home. Relief filled her like helium until she thought her toes would leave the ground. "I'm sorry I took your picture," she whispered.

His arms tightened. "I forgive you. And I understand why."

She nestled in a hollow beneath his chin that smelled like ozone and oatmeal soap and fit her body like it was made for her. "I should have told you what

Rebecca asked. I should have trusted you."

"I should have trusted you. I'm sorry, too."

Though letting him go was the last thing she wanted, she forced herself to untangle from his arms. To finish what she started, she needed to stand on her own two feet. "I realize moving to your town without asking is kinda pushy. Nothing's been done I can't undo." She straightened her spine, and sending up a wordless thought of a prayer, she jumped. "Would you like to give us a chance? To take it slow and really get to know each other?"

Laughter filled his eyes. He tipped his head against the wall and gazed down from beneath thick lashes. "I do, Brooklyn. Very much. But we've got one little problem that might mess up your timeline."

Her stomach twisted and she pressed her arms into her sides, willing herself to stay strong. "Okay?"

"I'm leaving Green Ridge."

Outside, a siren blared. The sound pierced her brain, and she gawked, dumbfounded. His family...his business? He planned to leave it all behind? For how long? To go where? "You're leaving home, too? But what about Verna?"

"As someone wise once said, a more capable woman than my mother I have never met. She supports my choice and very much hopes I'll come home again." He laid a gentle hand on her face and traced a thumb across her cheekbone. "You're not the only one who needs a fresh start. Seeing as you're already packed, maybe you want to come along?"

She leaned into the touch, letting her eyelids close and surrendering all the guilt and fear and loneliness of the past weeks. Anywhere...she'd follow this man anywhere. A slow, delicious breath unwound all she'd held so tightly. Joy rushed in like apple blossom petals on the wind. She peeked up at the dear face that still hung on her wall in the one-and-only photo of a lifetime, feeling passion and playfulness brim in place of tears. "I suppose. Besides, wherever you're going, you'll need someone to drive."

Epilogue

Point Reyes National Seashore, California
Fifteen months later

Darcy never tired of the smell of the sea. Slung wide, the van door welcomed a cool salty breeze, and she snagged a hoodie from the narrow closet at her back. Breathing deeply, she ran her gaze over the sleek wood interior, vintage upholstery, and faded calico curtains. A smile touched her lips. The van smelled like home.

The way Samuel transformed the old pop-top camper into a tiny house still amazed her. She'd known he was an engineer. He could make anything run, even an almost fifty-year old camper. She wasn't surprised when he rigged it with solar and installed a water filtration system, but the design was still such a delight. She'd photographed it from every angle, and yet, he kept tinkering, squeezing another closet, another cup holder, or another cubby into the bones of the grand old machine.

She gazed over the parking lot to where he stood, ankle-deep in surf. In the misty morning light, he shimmered like a mirage. Sometimes, she still couldn't believe he was real. A year ago, he'd never seen the ocean, and now he'd swum in the Atlantic, the Gulf of Mexico, the Great Lakes, and finally, the Pacific. A backward baseball cap replaced his straw hat, and a faded denim shirt and cargo shorts stood in for sky-blue cotton and work pants. But he was still her husband. And his Amish clothes were folded neatly in a drawer, just in case.

Their lives were works in progress. She opened her laptop and, using her phone as a hotspot, navigated to her blog, smiling at the pretty autumn header she created when the calendar turned to September. Thanks to her website, she was a work in progress for thousands to see. The site was gorgeous and genuine. She edited and curated, yes, but she prided herself on keeping it real. Rewarding as it was, van life presented challenges. While maintaining privacy, she endeavored to share all the benefits and drawbacks of putting ninety-eight percent of your stuff in storage and living on a shoestring budget on the open road.

She pulled a bottle from the mini fridge and unscrewed the cap. The cold brew was creamy and strong. Licking oat milk foam from her upper lip, she clicked the button to create a new post. For the last two days, while he drove and she leaned out the window, snapping photo after photo of the spectacular Pacific Coast Highway, she couldn't stop her thoughts from racing. How would she tell her followers? And once she did, would they leave in droves or hang around for the next chapter? Either way, they wouldn't hesitate to say.

After a good night's sleep and an early run on the beach, she felt calm. The Internet was fickle and fame even more so, but she had to live her life. She hovered her fingers over the keyboard and opened her heart, as she'd done every single day since she began.

Dear VanGirls,

One year ago today, at Brooklyn City Hall, I stood

beside S with the hotdog vendor he befriended as witness and said, "I do." Then, as most of you know, we hopped in the vintage camper S's brother and sister-in-law gave us as a wedding present and began the epic journey of a lifetime. We'd met just over four months earlier. Not a long time, but enough. You've heard the saying a million times: when you know, you know.

What I never could have imagined is how thousands of you would come, too. And you stuck around! From Hurricane Benita on the Outer Banks to double flat tires in Moab, you lifted us up and kept us laughing every mile. You recommended your favorite restaurants and campgrounds, referred us to barbers and doctors—remember S's insane spider bite in Big Bend? I'm so grateful to every one of you who commented, emailed, and liked my posts here and on social media. This adventure quite literally could not have happened without you.

For my husband to leave the Amish wasn't easy. Watching him use his skills to make this camper into a stunning home—and come on, didn't he kill it?—all the while relishing every new experience with humor and stone-cold hotness was the greatest joy of my life. I know you have to trust me on that since I still haven't shown his face—sorry not sorry. I've loved every minute...except maybe the stomach flu in Jackson Hole. A van is not equipped to handle that magnitude of misery in so many ways.

I'm writing now from Drakes Beach in Marin County, California, a location so spectacular no photographer can do it justice. Least of all me. Having spent all morning repairing the air conditioning again, S is on the beach with his feet in an ocean he only imagined before last week. Seeing this country with him has been a gift. His spirit is light. Mine is, too. It's true what's written: God reveals Himself in nature. Whether you go to the woods to lose your mind and find your soul, or to live deliberately, or because it's excellent for your skin, just go. Driving through New Jersey that first week, I started to fear America was one endless strip mall with the same six stores repeating infinitely. I was wrong. The full spectrum of this country is staggering. It's varied, diverse, and colorful, full of generous people and unimaginable beauty. I've done my best to share it.

My heart is full.

And it's time to go home.

This will be the last post of VanGirl in its current incarnation. I'm not sure what the next phase of my life will be or what this shared space will become. I promise you'll be the first to know. And no, I'm not pregnant...yet. I'll keep you posted on that too. Remember, you can always find me on my socials.

But because this is the end of this particular chapter, I feel I owe you, my readers and friends, a thank you. So today, with his permission, I give you a photo of my husband's beautiful face. He is my north star, my sounding board, and my home. He is my love. I'm so happy for you all to meet him.

Be kind to one another, VanGirls.

As always...

With a little bit of love and a gallon of faith,

Darcy

She tapped her short, neat nails on the table, rereading. Blogging their life had come remarkably easily, and the modest income it granted made a year on the road possible. Camping was cheap, and careful budgeting suited her. He did the van; she did the blog. She couldn't ask for a better partnership.

When they got home, she and Samuel owed Jonas and Tessa a five-star dinner. Now that her brother and sister-in-law had moved back to Green Ridge, she was excited to get to know them in real life.

When Samuel left town, Jonas took over his job, and from all reports, the solar business was booming. Samuel would return to more work than he left. Jonas also oversaw the crack team of Amish carpenters rebuilding *Mammi's* house. Every phone conversation and email exchange seemed to ease the strain between her husband and his older brother. Though she couldn't understand much of the overheard conversations, Samuel's tone grew ever lighter, and he laughed a whole lot more.

She picked up her phone and scrolled to the house pics that came in this morning. Her sunny-faced sister-in-law posed on the shady front porch, holding two cups of iced coffee. The accompanying text said simply:

—Ready when you are. Can't wait to hear about Cali.—

After texting for a year, Tessa already felt like a friend.

Patterned after photos from *Mammi's* albums, Samuel's design was perfect. Simple and pleasingly proportioned, the house wasn't an exact replica but a modern update on the original design. The exterior was complete, and the interior well on its way. She'd get home just in time for the fun stuff: choosing tile, wall colors, and finishings. Who knew? Maybe the VanGirls would become FarmGirls? Could she be a lifestyle blogger while applying for teaching jobs? The prospect made her tummy fizz with excitement. Darcy was no interior decorator, but she had a good eye. Besides, she had a secret design weapon in her husband.

Forget the dinner, when they got home, she and Samuel should take the kids so Tessa and Jonas could have a real vacation. They owed the couple hugely. Then again, maybe that's how this family worked. People gave and took and helped and accepted help, and no one kept track or held grudges. That sort of generosity was family. That…was love.

When they got home.

A longing for rolling ridges, cool pastures, and a cozy white farmhouse among the lilacs twinged in her heart. It was a good twinge. A twinge that told her they'd made the right choice.

She slipped into flip-flops, grabbed her phone, and dropped onto sand-dusted asphalt. The van door closed with a wham, startling a flock of gulls into a squawking tornado. The sea breeze whistled, but she'd braided her hair in a long, thick plait, and only a few wisps escaped to dance around her face. A person could get drunk on salt air. But, oh, how she loved the sweet grassy scent of home.

Sand gritted between her toes. She quickened her pace, half skipping, half jogging, and finally ditching the shoes to run up behind him in the surf, slide her arms around his waist, and press her cheek between his shoulder blades.

"Hi, Brooklyn." His forearms covered hers, and his shoulders softened.

"Hi." Keeping hold of his waist, she ducked under

his arm and snugged against his side. Tightening his grip, he lifted her onto tiptoes, and for a moment, she flew. Then, she settled down to sandy-bottomed sea and withdrew her phone. She checked in with him first, squinting into sunshine. "Are you ready?"

He cleared his throat and ran a hand over the close-cropped, tawny beard he kept meticulously trimmed. "How do I look?"

He was joking, but she clocked a glimmer of nerves. She squinched her face and gave him a teasing once-over. His hair was shorter but no less irascible. His face was tanned and rugged. His slow, tender smile still unstitched her insides. "You'll do." She came up on her toes and gave him a feathery kiss. Lightning quick, he wrapped his arms around her, kissing her until every nerve in her body glowed like the northern lights…which they had also seen on this once-in-a-lifetime adventure. Dizzy and gasping, she opened her eyes to find him grinning.

"Now, I'm ready." Releasing her, he drove his hands into his pockets and shrugged. "What do I do?"

She slipped into the space beneath his chin and held the camera up high. "Smile."

Before towering white sand cliffs and beneath skies a million miles wide, she matched his toothy grin with her own.

Frame. Shoot.

She tapped on the photo and stared, momentarily stunned it was real. Impossibly, she was with Samuel on the shores of the Pacific. His warm hand clasped hers, strong and steady. She gazed into bottomless eyes, brimming with joy and love, and bumped his shoulder with hers. "Thanks."

"I love you, Brooklyn." He lifted her hand and brushed a kiss over her knuckles.

His soft beard tickled, and she giggled. "I love you, too." She scooped up her flip-flops and spun, her toes tracing a perfect circle on the sand. "Now, let's go home."

A word about the author…

A city girl with a hometown heart, Wendy Rich Stetson grew up road-tripping in a 1979 VW camper van, and she keeps a running list of favorite roadside attractions from Carhenge to Wall Drug. Now an award-winning, sweet romance author, Wendy is no stranger to storytelling. She's a Broadway and television actress, an audiobook narrator, and a mom who loves collaborating on children's stories with her teenage daughter. Wendy lives in Upper Manhattan with her family of three and a rambunctious Maine Coon kitty.

http://wendyrichstetson.com
Other Titles by this Author
Hometown
Heartsong Hills

Printed in the USA
CPSIA information can be obtained
at www.ICGtesting.com
JSHW011047170824
68171JS00002B/7